About the Author

I was born in Hong Kong in 1950 to a wealthy Indian family. I went to study at Pepperdine University in Los Angeles, California and, after graduating, returned to Hong Kong to work initially in the family business. After five years with the family, left to start my own businesses from retail to manufacturing. Opened offices all around the world to sell products which were electronic based. Moved headquarters to Tokyo, Japan in 1998 and was there till 2004. Although having lived a lot of my life away from Hong Kong, still consider it home. Currently retired and living in the U.K. with my partner of sixteen years. This is my first book and recent events in Hong Kong and the Covid-19 pandemic has inspired me to write this book.

Warriors of the Sun

M. J. Harilela

Warriors of the Sun

Olympia Publishers
London

www.olympiapublishers.com
OLYMPIA PAPERBACK EDITION

A CIP catalogue record for this title is
available from the British Library.

ISBN: 978-1-80074-315-1

This is a work of fiction.
Names, characters, places and incidents originate from the writer's imagination.
Any resemblance to actual persons, living or dead, is purely coincidental.

First Published in 2022

Olympia Publishers
Tallis House
2 Tallis Street
London
EC4Y 0AB
Printed in Great Britain

Dedication

Book is dedicated to my dear partner Sara Best and the noble citizens of Hong Kong.

Part 1

"THE TIMES THEY ARE CHANGING"

"We shall not cease from exploration. And the end of all our exploring will be to arrive from where we started and know that place for the first time."

T.S. Eliot

FOREWORD

On June 30th, 2020 China passed the National Security Law. The law was aimed at stamping out opposition to the ruling communist party in the former British colony of Hong Kong. Without any consideration or consultations with the people of Hong Kong and its legislative council, the law was passed unanimously and without any objections by the communist Party in Beijing. It became law on July 1st, 2020. Many took to the streets of Hong Kong that day and many were arrested in accordance with the new law. The maximum sentence for protesting for Hong Kong's independence is life imprisonment.

The new law sets up a vast security apparatus in the territory and gives Beijing broad powers to crack down on a variety of "political crimes", including separatism and collusion. The law basically took away the rights of the people of Hong Kong to voice against the communist party. It encroached on Hong Kong's civil liberties.

It has concerned me over the last year of the plight of the people of Hong Kong. I was born in Hong Kong in 1950 and lived most of my life there. I spent my best times there during my primary and secondary school years. I was fortunate to come from a wealthy family who helped me set up my early business years there. I have travelled all over the world and spent time in many major cities around the world, but no city has been close to captivating my heart, more than Hong Kong. I now reside in Birmingham in the U.K. I have been here since 2004. I have revisited Hong Kong many times over the past fifteen years and have noticed changes in the colony. People seem less happy and more concerned of their future. I was certain with the protests and demonstrations of last year that the Chinese government would come down hard on the people of Hong Kong. Unfortunately, my fears have now been realised.

Hong Kongers are hardworking people who believe in equality and are united in their political views. Hong Kong residents have long cherished the city's independent judiciary, a legacy of British rule that stood in stark contrast to the secretive, party-controlled courts in China. The new law is a violation of Hong Kongers' freedom and a flagrant break from the Basic Law signed between Britain and China guaranteeing Hong Kong's democracy for fifty years from 1997 to 2047. The formula of one country two systems which was applied to Hong Kong since 1997 and was to last for fifty years is now over.

I am truly saddened by this. Hong Kong will never ever be the same place that I grew up in. China is keen to portray that the legislation is aimed at the anarchic and extreme minority. How is this the case when millions of pro-democracy protestors took to the streets of Hong Kong? What about the landslide victory by the people in last November's local elections? The people's wishes have been totally ignored. The U.K. is right to take the dramatic step of opening a pathway for citizenship for up to three million residents of the territory. I truly hope that many will take up this opportunity.

The Chinese have condemned the U.K. government for interfering in what they say are internal affairs of Hong Kong. Should they not be the ones condemned for breaking International Law?

This is the opening book of three, each with two parts. It starts from post-war Hong Kong and covers seven decades. It is fictional, but I must admit that I have taken some historical facts and added them to the stories, sometimes having to change dates and incidents to suit the plot. I apologise for the liberties taken. At the end of the book, I have acknowledgements citing where I have acquired some of the historical facts.

This is the first book I have written. I was going to write an autobiography initially as I had promised my partner but somehow, I ended up with this. I hope you enjoy reading this as much as I loved writing it. I dedicate this book to my darling Sara, and the noble people of Hong Kong.

INTRODUCTION

The first Opium War between Britain and China lasted from 1839 to 1841. Britain defeated China comprehensively and China was forced to cede Hong Kong in perpetuity to Britain in the Treaty of Nanking signed on August 29th, 1842. Hong Kong thus became a Crown Colony of the British Empire. Over the next fifty years Britain gained control of all the three main regions of Hong Kong: Hong Kong Island, the Kowloon Peninsula and finally the New Territories which was leased to Britain from China for ninety-nine years in 1898.

In 1949 the Chinese Civil War took place with the communists led by Chairman Mao Tse Tung defeating the nationalists led by General Chiang Kai Shek. The nationalists were driven out of mainland China and forced to flee to the island of Formosa, later renamed Taiwan. Many nationalists fled to Hong Kong including the more extreme of them which were known as triads.

Hong Kong in the 1960s was a vibrant city that was going through an economic boom. This era was considered the first turning point of Hong Kong's economy. The living standard was rising steadily but low wages continued. It had a population close to three million people with half of the population under the age of twenty-five and the group became Hong Kong's baby boom generation.

The Hong Kongese were hardworking, with a lot of them working in factories which grew from three thousand in the 1950s to over ten thousand in the 1960s. Most of the factories dealt in the manufacture of garments. An estimated six hundred and twenty-five thousand residents were supported directly or indirectly in the textile sector. Registered foreign companies in Hong Kong continued to increase with close to five hundred such companies by the early '60s established; a growth of almost 100% from the 1950s. There was demand for labour in almost every sector of the economy. It was around this point that the cheap low-grade products became high quality products and the "Made in

Hong Kong" label was respected worldwide. Hong Kong was soon categorised as one of the four Asian Tigers along with Singapore, South Korea and Taiwan.

The government took an ambitious role in education and from the mid '50s to the mid '60s created over thirty thousand primary schools. By the mid-1960s, 99.8% of school age children were attending primary school, though the primary schools were not free. The government also spent money in construction which continued to increase with the demand of highways, buildings, tunnels and reservoirs. Also, in this decade the government planned a low-cost public housing scheme to house over a million low-paid workers as the population was growing very rapidly due to the large number of refugees entering Hong Kong from China. The government had to define tighter regulations and guidelines on how to construct among the high-dense population.

Besides all the economic positivity of the mid 1950s up to the 1960s it also was a time of political unrest in the colony. The riots of 1956 were the beginning of such unrest in the colony which continued on to the 1960s peaking at the communist inspired riots of 1967. It all started on October 10th, 1956 when a nationalist flag was removed from a building by a Communist Party member. This caused a full-blown riot between the nationalists and the communists to break out causing many to be killed and thousands arrested.

The tensions between the nationalists and the communists grew rapidly during this period. Many refugees fled from China as they were persecuted by Mao's Red Guards, an army of elite young soldiers, designed by Mao to complete his revolution which, in his opinion, was petering out and losing momentum. It was a strange time: a Hong Kong which was economically booming and flourishing, enjoying the best of times, yet with periods of unrest followed by violent rioting between the political parties and the British government, making it the worst of times. Thus, it all begins...

Chapter 1
Leslie

888 Nathan Road, Kowloon, Hong Kong
Friday, 13th July, 1960

The winds outside were starting to pick up quickly now. It was apparent that the typhoon was approaching towards the colony. Typhoons were common this time of the year. The word typhoon was derived from the Chinese words "Tai Fung" which literally meant "Big Wind". Dr Leslie Sun sat on his desk looking out of the window whilst speaking on the phone and could see the branches of the trees bowing with the might of the wind. The rain was slashing down without relent and every now and then a lightning bolt would light up the room giving it an eerie feel. The window where he looked out from was in his private study. The back windows of the study ran from the top of the ceiling to the floor and were separated in the middle by a glass door that led to the Japanese garden. He thought he must remind Wan-Yu to board up the windows before the typhoon strikes.

Leslie finished talking and put the phone down. He looked around the room, this, his private study. It was his domain where he found peace and could concentrate on his work without disturbance. He recalled when he first told his wife Nancy how he desired this room for his study and wanted it done the way he fancied; she had frowned on that idea. It was the only room in the house where his wife did not take any part in decorating. He did the room, not pretentiously as Nancy would have, but rather quite uncomplicated and to his personal taste.

On one side of the wall there were large bookshelves made from mahogany, they were from the ground up to the ceiling and filled with books that Leslie had sensibly collected over the years. The shelves looked magnificent with their leather-bound books. Leslie was careful with every book he purchased, making sure that all of them were bonded in leather and most being first editions. He disliked the new books of today which he found rather scruffy with their soft covers.

The opposite wall was split into two main areas with shelves also made from mahogany. In the centre between two shelves sat a white marbled pedestal on which stood a stunning trophy shaped like a pyramid. It was made of solid silver with a large green gem on the top. In the centre of the trophy was engraved a rose gold plate: "World Kung Fu Champion 1939". Leslie, during his life, had won numerous trophies but this was one he revered most. He worked very hard to win this exclusive trophy and even though he had several failures he persevered and through pure determination, many hours of hard work and training, finally accomplished his goal on his fourth attempt at the age of twenty-nine.

On the left side of the wall the shelves were filled with certificates that he had received during his high school and university years plus other accomplishments and accolades he had gained over time. There were also pictures of his proudest moments captured and framed in special hand carved oak frames. One of his most cherished pictures was that of him receiving his O.B.E. from King George VI in the summer of 1950 for all the work he had done in helping rebuild post-war Hong Kong. He remembered that day with great pride. His parents were there along with Nancy when he received this prestigious award from the king at Buckingham Palace.

His most prized possession, however, was the certificate of his PhD in Law with honours from Oxford University. He received that in 1937 prior to World War II. It was one of the happiest times of his life. His parents had flown from Hong Kong to be with him. That was when he told them about Nancy and how much he loved her and his plans to marry her later that year. He remembered how he and Nancy first met. It was at a local pub off the university grounds when going out with friends to celebrate his final year at Oxford. Nancy was there that evening with her close friends, one who was dating Leslie's best mate Ajit. Leslie, when introduced to her, was immediately fascinated with her beauty. They started dating for about a year and fell deeply in love. Within the year Leslie proposed and she accepted.

The first time that Leslie's parents met Nancy Poon was when they visited London the year that Leslie got his doctorate. Leslie got Nancy to come to meet them at their holiday apartment in Harley Street, London. Nancy had just completed her Master's in Economics from Oxford. Leslie's parents knew Nancy's parents well. The Poons were a very prominent family in Hong Kong and owned a variety of businesses in manufacturing, real estate and retail. They were thrilled with the prospect of having a future daughter-in-law from such a prominent and well-respected family in Hong Kong.

On the right side of the wall there were shelves, again from the ground, up filled with trophies won by racehorses that Leslie owned. Leslie was a keen racegoer and loved that sport. He was the Chief Steward of the Royal Hong Kong Jockey Club. His position as Chief Steward entitled him to an exclusive private box every race day. The box was the best in the racecourse facing the finishing post on the third floor of the main building, where he would entertain overseas visitors, friends and family during race days.

The Royal Hong Kong Jockey Club was one of the oldest colonial institutions in Hong Kong. It was not just the only legal form of gambling in Hong Kong but a leading social centre where the very rich and influential mingled in discreet private rooms set high above the racecourse. The Happy Valley Racecourse was one of the most well-known racecourses in the world. It was situated in the heart of Hong Kong Island in the Happy Valley district and thus its name. Races were held from September till May yearly on Saturdays and occasionally on Sundays and public holidays. Leslie owned eight horses worldwide, five in Hong Kong, two in the U.K. and one in Australia. His favourite horse was "Winter Sun" who won the HK Gold Cup, the Queen Elizabeth II Cup and the Hong Kong Derby all in the same year. No other racehorse in HK had ever achieved such a feat before.

In the centre of the room rested his beautiful teak table, which he had purchased in Thailand. The tops of the legs of the table were hand carved with elephants. The table was semi-curved and was polished so well that one could almost see their reflection from it. On the left side of the table was a chest of three drawers with gilt-plated handles which were rather plain in design. On the bottom of the third drawer there was a hidden area where Leslie kept his special martial art weapon passed down to him from his father Sun Li Man.

To open the hidden area in the drawer, you had to twist the handle of that drawer to the right and then to the left swiftly which would spring open unlocking the panel that hid a storage space. In it was a nunchaku in a soft leather case with a drawstring. Etched on the leather case in gold were the initials S.L.M. Most nunchakus were made from two connected sticks joined usually by rope or a metal chain, however, this was not just any nunchaku but one that was unusual. Unlike most nunchakus which were usually made of wood, these were made of ivory and connected by a hardened gold chain. The tip of both ivory sticks, were encrusted with diamonds. This was one of Leslie's most beloved possessions. In the same drawer was a Feng Shui Wrist Amulet made of silver and engraved on the sides were little dragons whilst on the top centre lay a large, round, polished black crystal. Leslie would only wear it when he hosted the clandestine Warriors of the Sun meetings or in combat. It had brought luck and prosperity to the Sun family for years. Its mystical powers were said to help stave off black magic. This has been passed down from generation to generation to the eldest of the Sun family.

Leslie's father came from a wealthy family, he had a younger brother who he never got along with and who left the family's business to go on his own prior to the war. Leslie's father was the only one in the family that did not have a Christian name which was uncommon to anyone of his stature living in British Hong Kong. Even after he married an English woman, he would not add a Christian name. He was known in the community simply as Taipan Sun. Taipan in Chinese meant literally "top class". It was a name given to senior business executives or entrepreneurs operating in China or Hong Kong. He was kind and generous and contributed to charities in Hong Kong and was well loved by the community.

At the young age of ten Leslie's father Sun Li Man made him learn the proper use of the nunchakus from Shinken Taira, an Okinawan Karate master and the creator of Kobudo, a type of martial art that was popular in Japan. Among the students involved in Shinken Taira's classes was Bruce Lee who later became famous as a Kung Fu Hollywood movie actor. Leslie learned Kobudo quickly and was top of his class within three years. He also took lessons in Kung Fu from the world famous "See Foo", Wong Fei Hung. "See Foo" in Chinese meant "skilled person" or "teacher." His dream was to one day be the World Kung Fu Champion. On his twenty-first birthday, as part of family tradition, his father passed down to Leslie his personal nunchaku explaining to him its powers. He was told, however, not to use it openly in public. It was only to be used in times when he needed it to protect the family against the Dark Society. Little did Leslie realise that the time was now drawing closer to when he would be required to use that nunchaku.

The chair he sat on was from Beddington & Young of London and made of the finest leather available. It had cost him a small fortune as he shipped it in by air freight, but money was no matter as he loved it. The swivel chair was done in a glossy medium brown leather and was quite stunning. One would think that someone from royalty once owned it.

Even at forty-nine years Leslie looked a lot younger than his age. He was tall for an oriental but that was probably because of him being Eurasian, half Chinese and half English. He was fair in colour and one would think him more European than Eurasian. He had bright blue eyes just like his mother's. Unlike most Orientals he had a square jawline, was clean-shaved and had dark brown hair which he kept rather long and slicked back. Leslie kept himself in good shape by doing his Kung Fu routine religiously every morning for an hour and then followed by a five-mile run outside his Kowloon residence.

Leslie's house was in one of the most sought out locations in Kowloon, on the mainland side of Hong Kong. Kowloon was separated by Victoria Harbour and the only way to get from Hong Kong Island to Kowloon was by using the Star Ferry. The Star Ferry crossed the waters between Tsim Sha Tsui in Kowloon and the Central District in Hong Kong. The Star Ferry was the primary means of cross harbour transport. During the Japanese occupation of Hong Kong most of the ferries sank or got damaged during battles with the allied forces but were restored soon after the war. In 1957 the ferries were all updated from the old style which was only one level to two levels. The lower level was cheaper to ride in and used mainly by the masses whilst the upper level was a bit more comfortable with padded seats and for the more affluent. It was one of the cheapest forms of transport but also one of the most scenic rides in the world which would cost around HK$0.20 (around two U.K. pence) for the lower class and HK$0.50 for the upper class which was equivalent to about five U.K. pence! In the 1960s £1.00 was equivalent to approximately HK$10.00 and US$1.00 equalled HK$5.50.

The island side was where the government offices were located and where the governor resided at Government House. The Central District in the island was where most of the commercial businesses and headquarters of banks were located, the largest and most prominent being the Hong Kong Shanghai Banking Corporation (HSBC) or simply referred to by the locals as "The Bank. "Most of the expats and rich lived in the Mid-Levels of this hilly island and the super-rich would live in the Peak. To access both the Mid-Levels and the Peak one would have to drive through extremely winding narrow hilly roads. The only other access was by using the Peak Tram. The Peak Tram is a funicular railway in H.K. which carried both tourists and residents to the upper levels of Hong Kong Island. Running from Garden Road to Victoria Peak via the Mid-Levels, it provided the most direct route and offered breathtaking views of the harbour.

Leslie, however, chose to live on the Kowloon side. His family had resided in this part of Hong Kong for generations and he felt comfortable living on this side of the harbour. He went to a high school near his family home, the Diocesan Boys' School, probably the most respected Anglican Church school in the colony. His son, Herman, also attended the same school and recently completed his "A" Levels with exceptional grades and was preparing after the summer holidays to go to England to continue his studies there. Nancy's family, on the other hand, had always lived in the Peak where the super-rich lived. She tried to convince Leslie to move there after they got married but he refused and insisted on living in the family home with his parents. Leslie's family lived in the swanky residential side of Kowloon at 888, Nathan Road just before Boundary Street. According to Hong Kongers, 888 was a very auspicious address as the digit 8 in Chinese numerology symbolised luck and good fortune.

Nathan Road was largely residential with colonial style houses with arched verandas and covered archways. The road on both sides was lined with banyan trees. The road ran for four miles south to north. On the south side of Nathan Road towards the harbour were mainly small retail stores, open food markets and a few five-star hotels, the most famous being The Peninsula Hotel. Leslie lived on the north side of Nathan Road, which was mainly residential, just off Boundary Street and near the oldest and largest Anglican Church in the colony, St. Andrew's, which he attended with the family regularly every Sunday morning.

Leslie's house was two storeys high. He had spent hundreds of thousands in redecorating and modernising the house four years ago soon after his father passed away. Nancy did most of the interior and she did an amazing job, making it one of the most envied properties in Hong Kong. The side facing the main road was protected by a white brick wall about eight feet high. In the centre of the wall was a beautiful silver-plated metal gate with two shaped golden dragons in the middle that secured the house. It was one of the most high-status houses in Hong Kong, not only because of the enormity of the area it took up, but the way it was decorated.

As you entered the gates and moved forward you would face two heavy crimson lacquered doors. As you opened the door you came across, on either side of the wall, beautiful murals, one of "The Last Supper," a portrait depicted by Leonardo da Vinci and on the other side "Sir Galahad and the Holy Grail" by Edwin Austin Abbey. When you got to the centre of the house a large chandelier faced you which was hung from the top of the second-floor roof all the way to hang about ten feet from the ground. The chandelier was made out of Baccarat Crystal and made in France, it was eight feet wide and three feet high. It was one of a kind and priceless. On the ground floor at the back end of the room under the stairs were two statues, one of the Buddha standing with a walking stick hand made in Jade about five feet tall. The other statue was of Guanyin known as the Goddess of Mercy in Chinese folklore. This statue stood at almost six feet and was made of porcelain and hand-painted in vibrant colours. A circular staircase led to the upper floors where the family and guest bedrooms were located. Recently

Leslie installed a lift that was suitable for up to four people. He built this for his mother Elaine as he did not want her walking two flights up to her room at her age.

The entire ground floor of the house was done in white marble which made it look grand. As you walked in the house to the left you would pass through the back stairs which led below to the basement where the gym, sauna and massage rooms were located. Also, on the ground floor on the back was the laundry room and where the garage was located. The back stairs also continued to go upwards to the family and guests' bedrooms. Continuing ahead to the left on the ground floor, led to the family dining room, the bar area and the main family lounge room. On the outside just past the bar through a glass door was the swimming pool and barbeque area. Turning from the hall to the right side you would find Leslie's study. Walking on beyond you would pass the Men's and Ladies' guest restrooms and past that you would come across a huge room known as the "Pearl Room". The Pearl Room was only used when entertaining VIP guests.

The Pearl Room was quite magnificent with curved archways made of Calcutta marble with Mother of Pearl inlays in shapes of flowers that separated each area. The room was divided into four areas. All four areas were lit by chandeliers made of brass and with real South Sea pearls hanging downwards in a spiral. The main area was the dining area which had two large round glass tables with a cut-out in the centre where a small fountain with water flowed into a beautiful hand-carved black marble basin. There were two such tables which were divided by an archway and sat twenty people each. The Suns liked to keep their parties to smaller groups as they felt that was more intimate. There was another area which was where pre-dinner cocktails and hors d'oeuvres were served, this too was divided into two parts, each opposite to the dining area. Then there was a small private lounge area where aperitif was served. Beside this there was the bar area which sat eight people on bar stools and additional sofas seating another ten. In this area was a side door which led to the kitchen from which the servants would bring out the food.

On the back of the house was the kitchen area which could serve both the family and party areas in the house. The kitchen was big with three huge refrigerators, a large freezer, two enormous range cookers, several serving stations, two large dishwashers and lots of storage space. There was a dumb waiter which would send food up to the different levels in the house. The kitchen was run by chief cook Ah Wong who had been with the family for over thirty years. He had two other cooks who assisted him. Ah Wong was a talented cook and could cook all types of cuisine from Chinese, Indian and French to name a few. Every day he would make a menu for lunch and dinner and have it approved from Madam Sun the night before. He would then get up early the next morning and go to the market to buy the appropriate ingredients as fresh as possible. Usually there were around two to three parties a week which kept him relatively busy, however on the other days when things were quiet, he would only need to cook for the family members who were staying in. So, in those days he only had to make dinner for Leslie and Nancy, Leslie's mother Elaine, Leslie's sister Irene, her son Richard and daughter Yvonne, and Leslie's two children Herman and Lucy, that is if they were staying home that day.

Back of the kitchen were the servants' quarters. There were servant quarters on each floor at the back side of the house. On the ground floor they housed manservant Wan-Yu, the cooks, and the three maids whose jobs were to serve during party days and to ensure that the party and common areas of the house were kept clean. On the first-floor servants' quarters were Madam Sun's two private maids Ah Fung and Ah Ming. Also, two other maids whose jobs were to ensure the rooms were kept clean and to serve Leslie's children. On the second floor there were three other maids who served Leslie's mother Elaine and his sister Irene and her two children.

Climbing up the stairs to the very top there was a glass door that led to a roof garden with beautiful flowers such as Chrysanthemums, Lotus, Peony, Hibiscus and many other varieties. In the centre was a little handmade pond with different types of fishes like goldfish, catfish, rainbow trout and many other local varieties. In the centre of the pond was a rock structure like a small knoll with water pouring from it into the pond. There was a stone walkway going around the garden and lounge chairs set up at the end of the garden where you could lie to take in the sun on hot sunny days. This was Nancy's favourite spot. Every morning around six thirty a.m. providing the weather was kind, she would come up and walk around making sure the garden was kept groomed. She worked very hard with the gardener Ah Loong to ensure he kept it in good condition as he did the Japanese garden on the ground floor.

Nancy, before her son Herman was born, taught Economics at the Hong Kong University. She was brilliant in what she did. She wrote a book on how to improve your wealth called "Easy as 1-2-3" which became an international bestseller. She was invited to do seminars all around Asia and loved her job but as soon as Herman was born, she decided to dedicate her full time in being a mother and looking after the family. Now that the children were grown up, she started writing again, not on Economics but on gardening. Her first book was an instant success, and she was almost about to finish her second book.

Suddenly a bolt of lightning followed by loud thunder brought Leslie back from his thoughts to the room and his work. He looked at his watch, a solid gold Rolex Oyster, given to him by Nancy for Christmas last year. Leslie loved collecting watches; it was one of his passions. He had a collection of over twenty classic watches which he had collected over the last twenty-odd years and each one to him was irreplaceable. As he looked at his watch, he was surprised how quickly time had flown as it was almost six p.m. He had been working in the study now for five hours straight. He decided it was best to finish up and join Nancy in the family room for their usual pre-dinner drinks before she started worrying where he was.

The wind was now picking up and Leslie sensed that the White Dragon was angry. It has been some time that Hong Kong experienced a super typhoon. Typhoon Mary as it was named was heading directly for Hong Kong with maximum wind speeds exceeding one hundred and sixty m.p.h. Leslie had spoken earlier to Phil Hammond, Head of the Hong Kong Royal Observatory, about how bad the typhoon could be. According to him this would probably be the worst typhoon ever to hit the colony and would cause regrettably massive damage and loss of lives. He expected Typhoon signal 10 to be raised by ten p.m. that night and thought the eye of Typhoon Mary would pass directly over Hong Kong around four a.m. The signal 10 was the highest warning of an impending typhoon with wind strengths of over one hundred and sixty m.p.h.

Suddenly there was a knock on the door. Leslie knew it must be his head manservant Wan-Yu who had served the Sun family for over fifty years

Wan-Yu was now well over seventy years of age but still relatively fit for his age. For a Chinese man he was rather tall standing close to almost six feet. He always wore a silk Chinese black cap with his long neat singular pigtail falling to the back of his waist. He dressed the traditional Chinese way that most head servants did wearing his black pure silk suit with a Nehru type collar with white inner linings on both the neck and folded sleeves. He wore black silk type shoes which looked more like night slippers. Wan-Yu had served the family now for almost four generations and was totally loyal and attended to the family well. He knocked again.

"Enter," said Leslie in a rather subdued manner sensing the urgency of the knock. Wan-Yu entered the room, gestured a small bow at Leslie whist informing him that Madam Sun was asking for his master's presence in the family room immediately. Leslie replied he would be there shortly and asked Wan-Yu to board up the windows in the study when he left. "Yes sir," he replied, "I have already done the rest of the house and was just waiting for you to finish up your work in the study to do that. Would there be anything else you need Master?"

"No thanks," replied Leslie. "Please tell Madam I will be there shortly." He had been working on other matters, his speech for the governor's ball which was to be held on August 10th, at Government House. He and Nancy were two of the key guests and were to be seated at the head table. The governor, Sir Andrew Hancock, had personally called Leslie and asked him to make the opening speech. What an honour.

Leslie started reflecting on when he first met Nancy. It was the spring of 1936 whilst he was in his final year at Oxford. He was doing his PhD for Law and she was doing her final year of her Masters in Economics. They both came from similar backgrounds, both born in Hong Kong and from families with good standing in the community. The only difference was that Leslie was known as a half-breed by the wealthier Chinese social circles because his mother was English. Although his father was from a well-respected Chinese family in Hong Kong, he was half "Gwai Lo" which literally translated in English to White Ghost. Nancy on the other hand came from a wealthy Chinese family who ran numerous large businesses in Hong Kong. Her father was heavily involved in politics and had been awarded an Order of the British Empire (O.B.E.) for his charitable work in the community. Leslie's parents were thrilled when they announced their engagement, especially Leslie's mum who loved Nancy from the first time they met. However, when Nancy's family heard of the engagement, there was great uproar in her household as some members of the immediate family were unhappy because of Leslie's heritage, that of him being half "Gwai Lo". However, with Nancy's persistence and threat that she would marry Leslie with or without her parents' approval they finally caved in.

Leslie's mother, Elaine Rebecca Smith, was born in Gloucestershire in the heart of the English landscape. She was born to a farmer and loved the countryside. She missed the outdoor life in Hong Kong, but she sacrificed to move there because of the love for her husband. She was quietly spoken and was not one that enjoyed high society life. Leslie's father was completely the opposite and enjoyed being in the limelight. He was involved in many businesses and did a lot of work for the community. He was born from an affluent family from Shanghai. The family moved to Hong Kong in the early 1900s as Leslie's father chose Hong Kong as a place to settle. The colony was just starting to thrive, and he saw it as a safe place to raise his family and recognised that it presented many opportunities for business.

The wedding took place on December 20th, 1939 prior to the outbreak of World War II. The Poons threw one of the largest wedding parties ever witnessed in Hong Kong. Everybody who was of significance was invited. The high society from both the British community and the Chinese elite attended. The governor of Hong Kong at that time, Sir Mark Young, was the guest of honour. It was held at the ballroom of The Peninsula Hotel. The Peninsula was the first luxury colonial style hotel in Asia and known as the finest hotel east of the Suez. It was built in 1928 by the Kadoorie family who were very close friends of the Poons. The wedding was elaborate with no expense spared and was considered the wedding of the year.

Leslie continued to grow his father's business when his father retired in 1950 due to bad health. Besides running a huge successful business which involved real estate, shipping and utilities, he also was on the advisory board of the government to help advise them in dealing with the Dark Societies. The "Dark Societies" were various rival triad gangs who lived in their own specific areas around the colony. There were nine main triads operating in Hong Kong and they had divided the land according to their ethnic groups and geographical locations, with each triad in charge of a region. The nine triads were namely Ping On, Ah Kong, Wo Shing Wo, Wah Ching, Tung Ching, Ma On, Big Circle Sun Yee On, and the 14K. The largest and most prominent society was the 14K led by a person known as Ponytail. The 14K were located at what was known as the Walled City which was situated in the mainland side of Hong Kong in the district known as Kowloon City. They were a right-wing gang who got their income from illicit businesses and were partially financed by the Nationalist Chinese Government in Taiwan. The triads were involved with illegal activities like prostitution, drugs and gambling. The revenues they raised were spent in growing their numbers by recruiting new members and to create trouble for the HK Pro-Communist Party by discrediting them through chaos via protests and rioting.

China at this time was ruled by Chairman Mao Tse Tung who gained power in 1949 and was known as the founding father of the People's Republic of China (PRC). Chairman Mao was a communist revolutionary who adhered to the ideology theories of Marx and Lenin. He believed in military strategy and ran the country with a strong hand, anyone who got in his way was done away with by execution, imprisonment or forced famine. Chairman Mao was concerned that the democratic British Colony of Hong Kong would one day influence his philosophy and beliefs over the border to his beloved communist regime. He thus got his Red Guards to infiltrate into Hong Kong joining with the Pro-Communist Party there to instigate unrest and hopefully one day to overturn the British regime. Mao's philosophy of "Political power grows out of the barrel of the gun" scared the British government in Hong Kong. This, together with the protests and the deadly riots of 1956 and the fact that the Red Guards were building up their presence around the border town Lowu in the New Territories, reinforced the British to step up their military presence in the colony.

The armed force created was called the Hong Kong Garrison led by Major General Christopher Wolfe. The garrison consisted of the British Army, the Royal Navy and the Royal Air Force. There were several barracks scattered around both sides of the harbour housing the forces. The two larger ones were Stanley Barracks on the island and the other the Whitfield Barracks located in Kowloon. The harbour was patrolled by one of the largest British aircraft carriers, the HMS Victorious, which was supported by a couple of frigates. The Royal Air Force was stationed at Kai Tak Airport which also acted as the commercial airport on the Kowloon side. The Royal Auxiliary Hong Kong Air Force (RAF) as it was later to be renamed had the 28 Squadron RAF stationed there. The might of the British armed forces discouraged the People's Republic of China forces from starting a direct conflict with Hong Kong. The tension around the border, however, continued and was causing real concern to the people of Hong Kong who were worried about it reaching dangerous levels.

Leslie was commissioned by the British government to keep them updated on the situation between the various political groups and gangs and to try and ease growing tensions. Leslie and his family had always been well respected by all the parties thus making him the ideal choice for this position. His role was to mediate and discuss relations between the HK Pro-Communist Party and the various rival triads and see how he could come up with a plan that could make them exist together in harmony. A tough task as both parties were suspicious of each other and blamed each other for causing disturbances in the colony. The triads were particularly difficult as there were so many factions of them and they all had different ideologies and often were involved in gang wars amongst themselves.

Besides the triads and the Pro-Communists, a larger worry to the British was the Black Ninja gang. The Black Ninjas was borne out of the Japanese Army which occupied HK during the Second World War. When HK was recaptured by allied forces in 1945 a lot of the generals and top-ranking members of the Japanese army took refuge underground and formed this evil group. Unlike most other Japanese they refused to believe the war was lost and continued to undermine the British in HK by targeting killings of British expats and soldiers in HK. They were ruthless in the way they went about their work. Every victim had their heart cut out and carried away leaving the body to lie bleeding on the ground. They would then leave a sign showing that the killing was planned by them by tying a white scarf with a printed red sun to the victim's head. They were the Number 1 enemy to the British who were determined to find and arrest their leader Agana San who was known as the "Butcher of Osaka" named after the hometown where he was born. Many believed that one of the larger triad gangs supported the Black Ninjas by housing and financing them and equipping them with weapons so they could continue their deadly objectives. Many triad members left their clans to join the Black Ninjas as they felt they were making a bigger impact than the triads were against the establishment. It was also believed that the Yakuza was also involved in supporting the Black Ninjas. Yakuza are members of transnational organized crime syndicates originating in Japan.

Leslie quickly cleared his desk. Monday was going to be a busy day he thought, he did not realise then that what was about to transpire in the next couple of days would shake up the whole colony. He stood up, stretched and headed for the lounge room to catch up with Nancy and the rest of the family. The typhoon outside continued to roar…

Chapter 2
Ponytail

The Walled City
Friday, July 13th, 1960, six p.m.

Ponytail stood in front of the door of 14, Tuen Chun Road, the headquarters of the 14K triad. It was on the north side of the Walled City within Kowloon City. It was larger than most of the other apartment blocks in the area but from the outside it looked like any other. The Walled City was a 2.7-hectare enclave of opium parlours, whorehouses and gambling dens run by triads, it was a place where police, health inspectors and even tax collectors feared to tread. The locals called it the "City of Darkness".

Though it may have been a fetid slum, crawling with rats and dripping with sewage, it was stoutly defended to the last by those who lived there, the triads, as well as an unlikely ensemble of Chinese shopkeepers, faith healers and self-taught dentists. It was once thought to be the most densely populated place on earth, with 35,000 people crammed into a few tiny apartment blocks of more than three hundred interconnected high-rise buildings, all constructed without contributions from a single architect. In 1898, it became the only part of Hong Kong that China was unwilling to cede to Britain under the ninety-nine-year lease of Kowloon and the New Territories. In the '50s two rival triad gangs controlled the Walled City the Sun Yee On and the 14K. The British began to adopt a "hands off" policy in relation to the Walled City.

The 14K was formed by Kuomintang (Chinese Nationalist Party) soldier Lieutenant-General Kot Siu Wong in Canton, China in 1945 as an anti-communist action group. In the years that followed the communist takeover of the mainland in 1949, Hong Kong's main internal security threat came from the ousted nationalist regime, by then the majority of which were driven into exile to Formosa (nowadays known as Taiwan). Nationalist-affiliated criminal gangs known as triads flooded into Hong Kong when the communist victory became apparently inevitable, the most powerful and feared of them being the 14K. Originally there were fourteen members who were part of the Kuomintang, hence the name 14K. However, other sources say 14 stands for the road number of its headquarters and K stands for Kowloon.

The 14K was led by "Ponytail", who kept his identity secret except for few in the inner circle. Whenever he was seen in public his face was covered in a silk scarf. The 14K was the largest triad group in the world with around 30,000 members worldwide split into thirty subgroups. The 14K was responsible for large-scale drug trafficking around the world, most of it heroin and opium from China or Southeast Asia.

The primary business of the 14K in terms of generating income was drug trafficking, but they were also involved in illegal gambling, loan sharking, money laundering, murder, arms trafficking prostitution, human trafficking, extortion, counterfeiting and, to a lesser extent, home invasion robberies. They were allied with other gangs, the likes of Ping On, Luen and Wah Shing triads. Their biggest rivals were Sun Yee On who were allied with Ah Kong, Big Circle Gang, Wo On Lok, and Wo Shing Wo. The Sun Yee On headquarters was also within the Walled City but on the southside.

"Damn it," Ponytail cursed out loud as he entered the building. After all the months of planning the impending typhoon had ruined his well thought plan. He was warned by his Buddhist soothsayer Bo Ling that 1960, the year of the Rat, was not one that was lucky for the 14K. Maybe he should have heeded his advice and planned this for the next lunar year, however, the opportunity was there, and he had to take it but alas the typhoon had foiled his plan. He had planned his plot to be poetic justice for the death of his cousin and his ultimate vengeance against the establishment. "Damn it," he cursed aloud again; he had waited four years since the 1956 riots to have the right opportunity come up. He was in a foul mood.

Following the communist takeover in 1949, Hong Kong celebrated two national holidays. October 1st as the foundation date of the

People's Republic of China (PRC), observed by the communists in Hong Kong as National Day and October 10th, popularly known as Double Tenth, which was the anniversary of the 1911 Wuchang uprising, which led to the establishment of the Chinese republic in 1912 and celebrated by the nationalists. This event continues to be commemorated by nationalist supporters in both Hong Kong and in Taiwan to this day.

During the fifties, localised tensions steadily mounted as ongoing political problems spread into Hong Kong. In one dramatic incident, in April 1955, nationalist secret agents had blown up an Indian airliner, the Kashmir Princess, which was to transport Premier Zhou Enlai to the Afro-Asian conference in Indonesia. Premier Zhou Enlai was the first premier of the People's Republic of China. The Hong Kong protests and riots of 1956 were the results of these escalating provocations between the pro-nationalist and the pro-communists factions in Hong Kong, and took part during Double 10, or October 10th, 1956. This was the National Day of the Republic of China celebrated by the nationalists. The initial spark for the October 1956 flare-up was the removal of a nationalist flag from the veranda of a resettlement block, ordered by a junior government official. When the nationalist flag was removed all hell broke loose.

Protests broke out and turned into rioting and looting. Most of the violence took place in the town of Tsuen Wan, five miles from Central Kowloon. A mob stormed and ransacked a clinic and welfare centre, killing four people. The protests spread to other parts of Kowloon including along Nathan Road. By October 11th, some of the mob began targeting foreigners. Hong Kong's leftist press behaved with hysterical abandon, accusing the "white-skinned colonial pigs" of not doing enough to protect their "compatriots" and issuing veiled threats that Chinese troops would be sent in to do what the Hong Kong Police seemed unable or unwilling to do. This only inflamed the situation where protestors in Kowloon turned over a taxi carrying the Swiss Vice Council Fritz Ernst and his wife on Nathan Road. The protestors doused the cab in gasoline and set it on fire resulting in the death of the driver.

Mrs Ernst, who succumbed to her injuries, died two days later. It was believed the attack on the Gwai Lo Fritz Ernst was the doings of the Black Ninjas. There was an international outcry and the British government was condemned for not doing enough to bring back peace and order to the territory. The British decided to be more decisive and involved the army to aid the police force.

To quell the protesting, the Colonial Secretary at that time, Sir David B Edgeworth, ordered extra manpower from the British forces in Hong Kong, including armoured troops of the 7th Hussars, this to reinforce the Hong Kong police and disperse the rioters. At the end there were fifty-nine deaths and approximately five hundred injuries. Six thousand people were arrested and over 2,500 charged. Property damage was estimated at HK$16,000,000.

To make a statement to the rioters a committee was commissioned by the government with Leslie Sun heading it to make decisions on how to punish the rioters, especially their leaders. Leslie and the committee concluded that to make a strong statement they had to show a hand of strength to discourage unrests like this from ever happening again. Over five hundred were sentenced to long term prison sentences lasting from ten to twenty years. They also decided that from those arrested, four of them should hang. The four to be chosen were leaders from each faction that was involved in the riots, namely the 14K and Sun Yee On triads, the Black Ninjas and the Pro-Communist Party. In this way they felt that no rival faction would feel that they were being deliberately chosen. They chose the highest-ranking individuals they could find from those arrested and from each of the opposition groups and had them publicly hanged. Ponytail's cousin Liu Wei aka Snakehead was one of the four.

The Organised and Crime Triad Bureau (OCTB) was created after the riots of 1956. It became the division of the Hong Kong Police Force responsible for triad counter measures. The OCTB and the Criminal Intelligence Bureau worked in conjunction with the Narcotics and Commercial Crime Bureaus to process information to counter triad leaders. Other involved departments included Customs and Excise, and the Immigration Department. They all were to co-operate with the police to impede the expansion of triads and other organised gangs.

Ponytail was born in Canton in the summer of 1910. He was from an affluent family that was well respected. His father, Li Wei Ho, was a trading merchant who did business with the British Hongs; the name

Hong in Cantonese was given to the major foreign commercial establishments in Hong Kong. Li Wei did business with two of the largest British Hongs in the colony, namely Jardine Matheson & Co. and the Swire Group, supplying them with Chinese tea, silk and porcelain which they would sell on to the U.K. and other western countries.

Li Wei had two sons, the eldest being Wang Wei (Ponytail) and the younger Tang Wei (aka Dragonfly). Li Wei had high hopes for his eldest son. At the age of eighteen he sent him off to England to further his studies there. He wanted his son to improve his English and learn that country's heritage and its culture. He was hopeful that one day when he did retire Wang Wei would continue to grow his trading business with the British in Hong Kong. Unfortunately, Ponytail hated his time in England. He disliked almost everything about the country, the weather, the food and the British people whom he found racist and pompous. He only lasted a year there and happily returned home to the dismay of his father. From that point there were constant disagreements between father and son.

In 1945, when Civil war broke out in China, Ponytail joined the 14K triad, an anti-communist action group led by General Kot, against his father's wishes who wanted him to stay neutral and join the family business. However, as the war dragged on it became obvious to Li Wei that the communists were being ruthless with anyone with wealth, calling them "Capitalist Pigs". He decided to send his wife and children to Hong Kong where he had business friends and where he felt they could stay safe. He gave them all the gold and money he had so they could start a new life there. He asked Ponytail, being the eldest son, to ensure the family got to Hong Kong safe. He himself decided to stay behind hoping to convince the communists that he could be an asset to them by continuing to trade with the British Hongs in Hong Kong and share profits he made with them. This was not the case as when the communists got to Li Wei's house, they ransacked it and when they did not find any gold or money, they burned his house and warehouses down. They took him to the square of his hometown and burned him at the stake to make an example of him. Ponytail however was able to get his family safely to Hong Kong where he became leader of the 14K triad after General Kot Siu Wong died in 1953.

Ponytail's hate for the British grew in Hong Kong, he mistrusted them and felt that they should never have allowed the Pro-Communist Party to exist in the colony. He set up the headquarters of the 14K triad in the fortress of the Walled City in Kowloon and continued to recruit and grow the organisation. Under his leadership the organisation grew and expanded around the world. The triad gangs were feared even by the police who were scared to enter the Walled City. The British government wanted to demolish the whole area but soon realised how difficult that would be. The Walled City was like a fortress that was well defended and any attempt to get rid of it would have been resisted strongly by the triads as well as the residents living there. They decided to adapt a wait and see attitude, and allow it to exist; for the time being at least.

Ponytail safeguarded his identity by keeping it secret, for in this way he could interact with his enemies without them knowing him to be the head of the 14K. Ponytail was handsome, tall and well built. He had a Chinese red dragon tattoo from the back of his neck to his waist. When doing his duties as head of the 14K he always dressed in a black Kung Fu outfit. The outfit was made of pure silk with front handmade frog buttons, foldup white cuffs, with a white cotton lining. On the back was sewn the 14K logo of the red dragon. He wore a black scarf around his face to cover up his identity at all times. He was a merciless leader who did not take failure lightly and got rid of anyone challenging his decisions with gruesome punishments. He set up an organisation that was professional and well-structured and well skilled in combat. The monies he made from the criminal businesses were spent partially on building his own wealth and that of his generals but also to buy weaponry for the gang to ensure they could stand up to the communists, police, British forces, and rival gangs.

Ponytail was married but his first wife did not give him any children. He had her banished to Thailand as punishment for not giving him an heir. He then secured two concubines, Siu Ling, whom he officially dropped when she did not give him a male heir and Jenny Ma, his current and favourite, who finally gave him twin boys. Last year he sent both Jenny Ma and his twin sons to Taiwan for their own safety.

His mother has been living in Taiwan for a while now, and he sent Jenny to stay with her. He knew that the government was coming hard on the triads but more worrisome for him was that the Sun Yee On was becoming aggressive with the 14K as they continued to encroach on their controlled area of businesses. Over the last six months there have been over a dozen clashes between the two triads. He needed to concentrate on leading the 14K through these turbulent times so in a way he was happy that Jenny and his sons were not around to cause any distractions.

He met both of his concubines through Mama Wendy Liu who used to be his first mistress but who later left Ponytail to pursue her career. He had a very weak spot for Wendy and every now and then visited her in her clubs to spend some quality time with her, discussing issues that bothered him and to seek her advice. He trusted Mama Wendy more than any of his family or his generals. She made sense of things and was not afraid to tell Ponytail exactly what she thought without hiding the truth, which no one else would dare. Ever since she started her business their relationship had been purely platonic. She was a true friend and he was so happy that he had someone like her in his life, someone he could be open with and whom he could trust explicitly.

Mama Wendy was totally dedicated to Ponytail. He was very kind to her and without the money he provided her she could never have fulfilled her dream of opening the nightclubs she did. He told her never to reveal to anyone where she got the money from. That was to be their secret.

Her clubs were done up luxuriously and visited by top businessmen and government officials in Hong Kong. It was well recognised as the best place in town to entertain guests and VIPs. As a return of favour, she would feed Ponytail with information that concerned him that she gathered from guests who visited her clubs. She had her hostesses collect gossip from conversations that they heard from their customers concerning anything to do with the triads or government issues. She would, many a time through conversations, get insider information on stock listed corporations which she would intelligently invest in by buying shares in the stock market. She was very clever and invested wisely. She also made her hostesses who sat with government officials gather any information that they may overhear concerning the 14K whilst attending their clients, which she would then pass on to Ponytail.

Ponytail was looking forward to today's meeting. He would probably have to cut it short however, due to the impeding typhoon.

Ponytail opened the door and entered the building.

Chapter 3
The Initiation

The Basement,
14 Tuen Chun Road, The Walled City, Kowloon City.
Friday, July 13th, 1960, six thirty p.m.

Traditional Triad Organizational Structure as created by General Kot

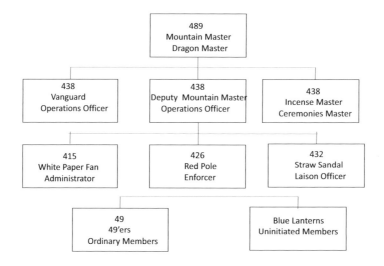

The triads used numeric codes based on I Ching, an ancient text read throughout the world, to distinguish between ranks and positions within the gang. The number "489" referred to the Mountain" or "Dragon" Master and in the case of the 14K, Ponytail. The number "438" was given for the "Deputy Mountain Master" second in command which was previously held by Snakehead, Ponytail's first cousin but later replaced by Wild Ox. Number "426" refers to the military commander also known as Red Pole whose role was overseeing defensive and offensive operations, while "49" denotes a soldier or a rank-and-file member. The White Paper Fan "415" provided financial and business advice, this was run by Ponytail's younger brother Dragonfly, and the Straw Sandal "432" functioned as a liaison between the different units.

As Ponytail entered the building, one would see that the inside of the building was dimly lit and had a rather overpoweringly foul smell. As you entered, on the right was a table with a book that one had to sign in to. This was manned by two guards. Each one who entered the building had to sign in with the date of his initiation and his specific triad number. This would be checked if correct with another guard who would scan through a massive library of books on a shelf behind the desk which were all in chronological order. Behind the guards hung a flag with the 14K logo where also on the back wall was a little black box with a red button switch. The button was pressed when there was a security breach. An alarm would set off and a solid huge metal gate six inches thick would fall from the ceiling ten feet from the entrance blocking anyone from entering the building any further. This would allow triad members in the building enough time to escape through the back where there was a secret door located under floorboards that led to a one-mile tunnel which guided them to Kowloon Bay, near the airport. The security at the 14K headquarters had been stepped up since the 1956 riots when the OCTB (Organised Crime and Triad Bureau) was set up specifically to infiltrate the triads and to close them down.

When Ponytail entered the guards immediately stood up and gave him the Dragon Master salute which was raising the right hand with the three middle fingers. The triads had several hand signals with which they greeted their fellow members and some that were used to warn or alert their fellow brothers of threats. This was learnt after a member had been initiated. Ponytail walked on, passing the food hall on the left and the combat training room on the right. The food hall was there for the members staying in the building, in this case the one hundred and twenty top generals by rank and their families. A buffet type Chinese breakfast was served every morning from five thirty a.m. till seven thirty a.m. and dinner from five p.m. till seven p.m. The meals were prepared by three cooks who lived in.

The training room was a large room with mirrors lining the walls.

They were built for special training sessions given by the generals to their relevant teams. Each general had a unit of around thirty to eighty members that they controlled. Kung Fu was taught here and the art of using the Jian and Dao swords. The Jian are double edged straight swords while the Dao are single edged and curved. All generals and their seconds in command were made to carry a butterfly sword which is a short Dao which was no longer than a human forearm allowing it to be easily concealed inside loose sleeves or boots. Because of the size and weight of the sword it allowed greater manoeuvrability when spinning and rotating during close quarter fighting.

Just beyond the training room were two rather dilapidated lifts that served the building which was fourteen storeys high. There were also stairs that led to the upper floors. The stairs were narrow, dark and unlit except on the landing of every floor. From the second to the twelfth floor were quarters for the inhouse generals and their families. They were specifically stationed here to provide training and to protect the building if needed. There were four apartment blocks, each fourteen storeys high, immediately next to the main HQ building on numbers 12, 13, 15 and 16 Tuen Chun Road which housed another hundred and fifty generals and twelve hundred 49ers (ordinary gang members).

As Ponytail walked to the end of the hall there were stairs in front of him that led to the basement where the secret council meetings were held weekly, usually on Friday evenings. It was a large room where at the very back was a raised platform on which sat a table where the seven council members presided. In the centre was Ponytail's chair which was plated in 14K Gold. The chair was magnificent and embossed in its frame all over was the insignia of the 14K. On the left side of the table in a corner was a large clear jar about five feet tall and a foot in circumference which were half filled with human eyeballs. This was known as the "Jar of Evil Eyes" and kept there to remind all as to what happens to anyone who betrays or breaks the thirty-six oaths of the 14K. Below the platform was a large space on the left of which there was a round altar and a statue of Guan Yu, the God of War, with candle holders around it which were lit during initiation days, as it was now. On the right there was the "Archway of Swords," so named as the curve of the archway was all lined with swords of 14K members who died serving the gang and this led to a small room with a table. Beyond that was the torture chamber.

There were three main types of torture that the triads used. The most fiendish of all was the rat torture. This involved placing a rat inside a half-cage and atop a restrained person's abdomen. The cage is slowly heated and the rat desperate to escape the heat begins to burrow through the only soft surface it can find: the victim's flesh. With sharp claws and teeth, the rat quickly gnaws its way into the victim's bowels, causing excruciating pain and terror. Then there was the Chinese torture chair which was made of wood with twelve steel blades in the arm, back and footrests and seat. It was common to have a victim strapped to the chair to watch another person get tortured whilst slowly bleeding to death. The chair was used in a psychological way to coerce confessions out of people watching other people suffer. Lastly, there was the Lingchi torture also known as "the death of a thousand cuts" which was usually practised on someone facing a death sentence and performed in front of the council and generals. In this form of execution, butterfly knives were used to methodically remove portions of the body eventually resulting in death. Lingchi was reserved for crimes viewed as heinous such as treason.

All the six committee members were already seated and below a group of around eighty generals were standing, all waiting for Ponytail to enter. As he arrived the thirty-six oaths were chanted, Ponytail continued walking down and got seated on his chair whilst the rest of the people in the room continued to stand. The oaths were created by General Kot and all 14K triad members followed the oaths to the letter. Anyone breaking any of the oath faced punishment of the most horrific kind, immediate and without recourse. The thirty-six oaths were:

1) After entering the triad gates, I must treat my parents and relatives of my sworn brothers, as my own kin. I shall suffer death by five thunderbolts if I do not keep this oath.

2) I shall assist my sworn brothers to bury their parents and brothers by offering financial or physical assistance. I shall suffer death by five thunderbolts if I do not keep this oath.

3) When brothers visit my house, I shall provide them with board and lodging. I shall suffer death by five thunderbolts if I do not keep

this oath.

4) I will always acknowledge my triad brothers when they identify themselves. If I ignore them, I shall be killed by a myriad of swords.

5) I shall not disclose the secrets of the triad family, not even to my parents, brothers or wife. I shall never disclose the secrets for money. I shall be killed by a myriad of swords if I do so.

6) I shall never betray my sworn brothers. If, through a misunderstanding, I have caused the arrest of one of my brothers, I must release him immediately. If I break this oath, I will be killed by five thunderbolts.

7) I will aid my sworn brothers who are in trouble, in order that they may pay their passage fee. If I break this oath, may I be killed by five thunderbolts.

8) I must not cause harm or bring trouble to my sworn brothers or Incense Master. If do so I will be killed by a myriad of swords.

9) I must never commit an indecent assault on the wives, sisters or daughters of my sworn brothers. I shall be killed by five thunderbolts if I break this oath.

10) I shall never embezzle cash or property from my sworn brothers. If I break this oath I will be killed by a myriad of swords.

11) I will take good care of the wives or children of sworn brothers entrusted to my keeping. If I do not do so I will be killed by five thunderbolts.

12) If I have supplied false information about myself for the purpose of joining the triad family, I shall be killed by five thunderbolts.

13) If I should change my mind and deny my membership of the triad family I shall be killed by a myriad of swords.

14) If I rob a sworn brother or assist an outsider to do so, I will be killed by five thunderbolts.

15) If I should take advantage over a sworn brother or force unfair deals upon him, I will be killed by a myriad of swords.

16) If I knowingly convert my sworn brother's cash or property for my own use, I shall be killed by five thunderbolts.

17) If I have wrongly taken a sworn brother's cash or property during a robbery, I must return them to him. If I do not, I will be killed

by five thunderbolts.

18) If I am arrested after committing an offence, I must accept my punishment and not try to place the blame on my sworn brothers. If I do, I will be killed by five thunderbolts.

19) If any of my sworn brothers are killed, arrested or have departed to some other place, I will assist their wives and children who may be in need. If I pretend to have no knowledge of their difficulties, I will be killed by five thunderbolts.

20) When any of my sworn brothers have been assaulted or blamed by others, I must come forward and help him if he is right or advise him to desist if he is wrong. If he has been repeatedly insulted by other brothers, I shall inform my other brothers to help him physically and financially. If I do not keep this oath, I will be killed by five thunderbolts.

21) If it comes to my knowledge that the government is seeking any of my sworn brothers who has come from overseas, I shall immediately inform him in order that he may make an escape. If I break this oath, I will be killed by five thunderbolts.

22) I must not conspire with others to cheat my sworn brothers at gambling. If I do so I will be killed by a myriad of swords.

23) I shall not cause discord amongst my sworn brothers by spreading false reports about any of them. If I do, I shall be killed by a myriad of swords.

24) I shall not appoint myself Incense Master without authority. Only the loyal and faithful may be promoted with the support of his own sworn brothers. I shall be killed by five thunderbolts if I make unauthorised promotions myself.

25) If my natural brothers are involved in a dispute or lawsuit with my sworn brothers, I must not help either party against the other, but must attempt to have the matter settled amicably. If I break this oath, I will be struck by five thunderbolts.

26) After entering the Heavenly Gates, I must forget any previous grudges I may have against my sworn brothers. If I do not, I will be killed by five thunderbolts.

27) I must not trespass upon territory occupied by my sworn brothers. I shall be killed by five thunderbolts if I pretend to have no

knowledge of my brother's rights in such matters.

28) I must not covet or seek to share in any property or cash obtained by my sworn brothers. If I have such ideas, I will be killed by five thunderbolts.

29) I must not disclose any address where my sworn brothers keep their wealth, nor must I conspire to make strong use of such knowledge. If I do so I will be killed by a myriad of swords.

30) I must not give support to outsiders if doing so is against the interests of my sworn brothers. If I do not keep this oath I will be killed by a myriad of swords.

31) I must not take advantage of the brotherhood in order to oppress or take violent or unreasonable advantage of others. I must be content and honest. If I break this oath, I will be killed by five thunderbolts.

32) I shall be killed by five thunderbolts if I behave indecently towards small children of my sworn brothers' families.

33) If any of my sworn brothers has committed a big offence, I must not inform upon them to the government for the purpose of obtaining a reward. I shall be killed by five thunderbolts if I break this oath.

34) I must not take to myself the wives and concubines of my sworn brothers, nor commit adultery with them. If I do so I will be killed by a myriad of swords.

35) I must never reveal triad secrets or signs when speaking to outsiders. If I do so I will be killed by a myriad of swords.

36) After entering the Heavenly Gates, I shall be faithful and loyal and shall endeavour to overthrow the Qing (communists) and restore the Ming (nationalist) by coordinating my efforts with those of my sworn brothers, even though my brothers may not be in the same profession. Our common aim is to avenge our Five Ancestors.

As the chanting ended Ponytail stood up from his chair and called for the meeting to start by raising his Jian sword and shouting out loud "Death to our enemies may they all die by the Sword of Freedom." Ponytail treasured his sword which was passed down by General Kot to him just before he died of cancer in Taiwan in 1953. The sword supposedly had special magical powers and was feared by all triad members, it was known as the Blaze. It was created from the strongest steel and had one of the sharpest blades ever made. The handle was made of ivory, hand carved with dragons surrounding it. Ponytail sat down and the meeting began. The meeting was to be conducted by 438 the Deputy Mountain Master who was known as Wild Ox.

"Let us start with 438 the Incense Master. What do you have to report to the committee?" Wild Ox asked.

The Incense Master stood up from his chair and walked down the platform to the main open space below and faced the committee. "My triad brothers, today we will have two level one initiations. Unfortunately, we have lost two generals since our last meeting and need to replace them. One of the generals, General Chiu was from our Macau division who was involved with supervising our gambling businesses there. Our brothers there were attacked by the Sun Yee On gang who were trying to infiltrate into our territory. In the fight that ensued our gang was forced to retreat as we were overwhelmed by the numbers of our enemies and unfortunately General Chiu was killed during the skirmish."

Macau was a small Portuguese colony just 44.5 square miles in size and about 66 kilometres from Hong Kong. To get there one would have to use a ferry which would take a little over an hour. The 14K had their own speedboats that they operated between Macau and Hong Kong. Gambling in Macau had been legal since the 1850s when the Portuguese government legalised the activity in the autonomous colony. Since then Macau has been known worldwide as the "Gambling Capital of Asia" or "Monte Carlo of the East." The gambling there was controlled by the triads who paid a small tax to the government for obtaining licenses to operate. Many, however, were unlicensed and where rival triads seek to gain control. The two main triads that controlled the licensed and unlicensed casinos were the 14K and the Sun Yee On.

"What?" shouted Ponytail banging his hand on the table. "That is totally unacceptable. We must take our revenge immediately." He pointed to "426" Red Pole. "Send at least two of our top generals and their squads immediately to Macau, strengthen our position there and act against the faction of the Sun Yee On that attacked General Chiu's team and wipe them out. I want a report within two weeks confirming that we have taken our revenge against them. We cannot show any weakness, we must show our enemies that we keep to our sacred oaths seriously and be merciless towards anyone who challenges the 14K."

"Yes, My Lord," replied Red Pole. "I will act immediately on your instruction and will report back directly to you when it is done. We will destroy that division of the Sun Yee On in Macau, and bring back the evil eyes of the general of the Sun Yee On who did this to our comrades and add them to our Jar of Evil Eyes." Ponytail nodded and looked at Wild Ox "Please continue."

"Very well," replied Wild Ox. "And what happened with the second General?" he asked the Incense Master.

The Incense Master replied, "Sadly General Lo, who looked after the hostesses Clubs and the prostitution business mainly in the Tsim Sha Tsui (TST) district, has become seriously ill. It seems he has caught pneumonia and is in ICU at the Baptist Hospital at this very moment. I have spoken to the doctors there and it seems highly unlikely that the general will recover."

"I know General Lo well," replied Ponytail. "He was very good in what he did and brought in the most revenue from all the other prostitution divisions in the colony. He was a loyal and trusted soldier." He looked towards "415", his younger brother Dragonfly. "Please ensure that all his family members are well compensated and that for the rest of their lives they will be financially looked after by the 14K."

"Yes, of course, My Lord, that will be done," replied Dragonfly. Ponytail continued "The Tsim Sha Tsui (TST) 14K prostitution division is very important and whoever takes over must be as good as General Lo was. Who do you have in mind, Incense Master, to replace him?"

"I have put up the second in command of General Lo's group, "49er" member Chan. He has been following General Lo for over five years and knows the territory well and has the respect of all the mamas and most of the hostesses working there. His name was brought forward by Mama Wendy Liu of the Sing Sing Club in TST. She has personally asked me to inform you that she has full faith in him and recommends him highly." Ponytail smiled. "Anyone Mama Wendy recommends must be good. Yes, Chan will do as long as he passes the initiation."

Ponytail had a sweet spot for Mama Wendy as she had been his mistress and was with him for three years. She recommended him to invest in a chain of exclusive high-end clubs for the very rich and for her to run. She saw it as the right timing as there existed at that time no place where the rich and elite could go secretly to seek companionship with women. There were many sleezy bars around like Suzy Wong in Wanchai, but the high-class society would never be caught going to any of those establishments. So, with a little persuasion the Sing Sing Club in Tsim Sha Tsui was opened, financed by the 14K via a rich businessman in Hong Kong, Raymond Ho, who worked secretly for the 14K. The club was huge with over sixty private rooms of various sizes and had over four hundred and fifty girls working. It did so well that a sister club was opened in the Central District in the Island side within two years which was called the Sing Song Club. Both were owned and run by Mama Wendy.

Wild Ox continued, "OK let's start with the initiations before we go through the rest of the agenda. Call out "49ers" Po and Chan!" The initiation in becoming a general was more complex than that to be an ordinary "49er" or member. It was designed to test the strength and loyalty as a "49er" goes up the ranks to becoming a general.

The Incense Master and the Vanguard presided over the ceremony. First it was the turn of Po who walked to the centre of the room and bowed to the board. He wears only a black robe with straw sandals on his feet. He moves to the front of the altar and recites the thirty-six oaths loudly for all to hear. Two metal cages are then carried into the altar by "49ers", one with a chicken and the other a monkey with its hands and legs tied firmly by rope so it could not move. Po disrobes and is totally naked. The Incense Master approaches and chants a few words which Po repeats. Po is then handed a butterfly sword. Po opens the cage, picks up the monkey and with a swift movement cuts the top of his head off exposing its brain. The monkey is still alive and screaming as the Vanguard passes Po a metal spoon. Po scoops the spoon down on the monkey's brain and eats the brain which drives the monkey into a frenzy, shaking and screaming louder than before. He then returns the monkey to the cage as it slowly dies inside. It was believed that the eating of the monkey's brain is to give the initiated strength and virality and therefore for him to be able to perform his duty adequately.

Next positioned on the altar was the cage with the chicken in it. Next to it the Incense Master placed a bottle of red wine and a deep ceramic bowl. Po unlocks the cage, takes out the chicken and cuts off its head with the butterfly sword. He then allows the blood dripping from it to fill the bowl placed there. When the bowl is half filled, he puts the half dead chicken back into its cage. He then fills the rest of the bowl with the red wine and drinks from it. The bowl then is thrown onto the floor and broken. This is to illustrate what will become of traitors and to show the "49ers'" loyalty to the brotherhood. Po then takes some incense sticks from the altar and lights them from the candle around the altar and says a prayer to Guan Yu.

Immediately after that, two "49ers" come forward and wash away the blood on Po's body. Once clean they bring a fresh white robe and dressed Po with it. This to signify that his past life has been washed away and he can now move on to his new life. He is then led to the Archway of Swords and does a ritual dance as he walks through the archway. The archway is made of crossed swords and on top of it is a sign stating, "On entering do not proceed any further if you are not loyal." On crossing over to the other side the Vanguard passes him a note which now records his number as general, replacing his old "49er" one. As general he now must take this to the tattoo artist appointed by the 14K to have the 14K insignia and his new number which will indicate also the date of the initiation and have it tattooed on his back just above the waist. He was not to share this information with anyone. He then walks back to the hall and faces the board members, swearing his allegiance to them. He lifts his hand, stretching open five fingers as a sign of total loyalty. That ends the initiation. Chan followed Po and went through the initiation smoothly and he too was inducted as a general.

"What do we have next on the agenda?" asked Ponytail to Wild Ox.

"Treachery my dear Lord," replied Wild Ox. "Treachery of the worst kind! General Tong of the TST drug triad division was infiltrated by a member of the Organised Crime & Triad Bureau (OCTB) and had been feeding him information of our meetings in return for money. He is a "25er" and needs to be punished in the worst possible way!" The number "25" was the one that the triads used to label a traitor. "He has broken the following oaths; 5, 6, 10, 14, 29, 30, 31, 33 and 35. Thank God that because of the typhoon we had to cancel the attack on the opening of the new offices of the Chinese Communist Party's People Daily, a newspaper publication, that was scheduled for five p.m. today. A lot of dignitaries were to be there as well as high ranking officers from the government including Leslie Sun. General Tong had informed the officer of the OCTB of our plot and the OCTB were ready to ambush us and thwart our plan."

"Oh my God," replied Ponytail. "Thanks to Guan Yu we have been saved and I was so angry about the typhoon foiling my plan. Guan Yu is truly looking after us and we must all say a prayer to him for calling upon the typhoon and thus stopping a possible massacre and arrests of many of our members. How was Generals Tong's treachery discovered?" he asked.

"Apparently General Tong was entertaining the person from the OCTB, a Mr John Milhouse, at the Sing Song Club in Central. One of the hostesses there, Samantha, was in the private room with them. As the spy, John, from the OCTB left General Ho stayed on and got very drunk, floundering the money he had received from the spy and showing it off to Samantha saying how he could have her for the night and for many nights to come as he still had another payment coming to him once the OCTB captured the gang whilst they planned the attack on the communist newspaper," replied Wild Ox. "Fortunately, Samantha reported this to Mama Wendy who immediately informed me, we sent a team to his house last night and brought him back here. We have been torturing him in the chamber for the last ten hours and he has finally admitted to the crime."

"Reward the hostess Samantha well for bringing this to the attention of Mama Wendy," replied Ponytail, talking directly to Dragonfly. "Now bring the traitor here to face us!" snarled Ponytail at Wild Ox. General Tong was dragged out to face the council. It was obvious he had gone through some horrific tortures. His face was totally scarred, bruised and swollen making him unrecognisable, he had cuts all over his body and was bleeding profusely. He fell to the ground as the two "49ers" led him in front of the council, and he begged for mercy.

"Finish him off, Wild Ox, with the Lingchi punishment," cried Ponytail. Five generals came forward and with their butterfly swords started slicing and cutting up parts of his body and as he started to slowly die, they dragged him away to the torture chamber to continue their slicing of his body till he succumbed to death.

It was finally the turn of White Paper Fan Dragonfly to give his report.

"My Lord I am very happy to announce that on the month of June our revenues went up by 8% which is a massive rise! This was mainly from revenues from our foreign brothers, especially in Singapore. Also doing well were our gambling divisions which showed a higher rise in income than expected. I have placed a copy of the full report with our cash balances in each of our safe houses in front of all the board members to have a look at and if any questions we can discuss this further in our next meeting."

Ah, some good news at last, thought Ponytail.

Ponytail looked at his watch. It was already ten p.m. and he wanted to clear the halls by the latest ten thirty p.m. being aware that Typhoon Mary was soon approaching, and they had to take shelter. He looked up at Wild Ox and said, "If there is nothing else let us close the meeting. I know that we might have more to go through, but I will feel a lot better if everybody leaves and takes shelter from the typhoon. We will pick up things again next Friday when we meet."

"Yes of course My Lord you are right!" Wild Ox stood up and announced to all there, "This meeting is now officially closed and we will continue on Friday the twentieth of July at seven p.m. Please move out quickly from here and keep safe and we will see you back Friday week."

As the members left Ponytail turned to his brother Dragonfly. "Will you be staying here tonight, or will you make the journey back home? I plan to stay here till Monday."

Dragonfly answered, "Dai Lo with your permission I will go back home." In Cantonese Dai Lo meant either head boss/gangster or someone who is respected. It also was used to greet an older brother.

Ponytail was happy that Dragonfly was heading back home as he would be safer there. He had arranged for Mama Wendy to send two of her newest hostesses to his apartment up on the fourteenth floor of the building. They had been escorted there and had been waiting for him since nine p.m. After all the events of the week he looked forward to an evening of pure lust. He had not had any sex all last month and wanted to release all the built-up pressure he had gone through. He had asked Mama Wendy to ensure the two were very young and willing to do whatever he requested from them. Mama Wendy had assured him that he would be happy with her choice. She knew Ponytail well and knew these girls would give him the pleasure he wanted and would not disappoint.

She had sent him a young Russian girl called Ivana who had just turned sixteen. She told Ponytail this girl would do whatever he asked of her and for her age knew how to make men happy. The other was quite the opposite, she was from mainland China and her name was Zhang Li, which translated meant "beautiful". She had just turned fifteen and was still a virgin but had been taught by Mama Wendy herself on how to make love and give men pleasure.

Ponytail headed to the lift and pressed the button for the fourteenth floor. Outside he could hear the wind howling and the rain falling heavily. He was so looking forward to the evening with the girls. As he waited for the lift his mind went back to General Ho and how he had snitched on the brotherhood. He was very alarmed that the OCTB had been able to infiltrate the 14K so easily. That worried him a lot and he thought they must consider more ways to be secured and deal out even harsher punishments to "25ers". and to all of their close families if they were caught betraying the oaths. This cannot happen again.

"Damn," cried Ponytail. Thinking all that made him get into a foul mood yet again.

Chapter 4
Lillian's Secret

Twelfth Floor,
8 Peking Road, Tsim Tsa Tsui (TST). Kowloon.
Friday, July 13th, 1960, ten p.m.

Lillian gazed into the full-length mirror, totally naked except for her holding a crystal flute topped with Dom Perignon in her hand. Since she met Leslie, who introduced her to French champagne, that was the only alcoholic drink she consumed. She turned from side to side admiring her figure which was close to being perfect. She stood at five feet five inches tall and had a bust-waist-hip of 36-23-36 inches. Her breasts were large and firm unlike most Chinese women. She had an "all-natural body" without any surgeries or alterations. Her skin was fair and smooth like velvet. She had a beautiful face, broad, with a high forehead, a small chin and nose with high cheekbones. Her eyes were especially haunting: they were dark brown, wide and deep set, unlike most Chinese women who had narrow eyes. She had long straight jet-black hair that reached down to her waist. She had wanted to cut it short for the summer, but Leslie was dead set against it.

Lillian was Leslie's concubine and she was proud of it. A concubine is basically a second wife. Concubines would not have the same rights of the first wife and were always considered inferior. Children of concubines had lower rights in account to inheritance which was regulated by the Dishu system. Dishu was an important moral system involving marriage in ancient China and still applied in Hong Kong in the '60s. Leslie, in 1957, took Lillian as his official second wife and concubine.

Having a concubine in Hong Kong in the '60s was legal although challenged by women councillors in the local parliament who wanted to force a law illegalising the rights to have a concubine. Traditionally the concubine's main function was to produce heirs but as time passed, the concubine became an integral part of a man's relationship and her role, besides bringing sexual pleasure and bearing children, was to keep her man happy by being attentive and listening to his problems. Nancy was aware of Lillian and had met her a few times, but she kept away from her as much as possible and never discussed her with her husband.

Lillian could hear the wind blowing outside which was becoming louder by the minute. She did not enjoy being alone especially with the typhoon approaching and wished Leslie was there with her. Usually Tuesdays and Friday nights were reserved for Lillian by Leslie unless he had to attend to some formal function or when he was hosting a party at home. He would spend the evenings with her those nights, making excuses to his wife that he was either having a poker night with the boys or some other lame excuse. It was understood and accepted by Nancy that Leslie was going to spend the night with Lillian. As long as Leslie treated Nancy with the utmost respect, which he did, she resigned to the fact that Lillian was his lover and number two.

Lillian had spoken to Leslie earlier that day and he had told her that due to the typhoon approaching he would not see her that evening. He had to remain in his home in case of any emergencies that may occur and be close to his immediate family. He told her to be sure to secure the apartment, especially making sure the iron railings by the windows and balcony were all locked and secured to avoid shattering glass getting into the apartment.

"I spoke to Phil earlier and he informed me that Typhoon Mary will probably be the strongest to directly hit Hong Kong for quite a while, so please take care," Leslie told her. "I wish I could be there with you, but you know I can't, anyway you should be safe but if anything occurs that causes you concern give the caretaker of the building, Ah Chuen, a call or if it is really serious just dial 999 for the emergency services. Do You understand?"

She loved the way Leslie fussed over her and the way he protected her. She was a very lucky woman. She thought, if Phil said the typhoon will be powerful and could cause damage, I must take care. Lillian knew Phil Hammond, who was head of the Hong Kong Royal Observatory, well. He used to come down to the Sing Sing Club when she worked there some years ago. He was a good customer who was always very kind and thoughtful and treated Lillian respectfully even though she was just a hostess in the club.

"When will I see you next my darling?" Lillian asked Leslie. "I miss you so much and had planned a surprise for you tonight."

"I will see you Tuesday. There is nothing in my calendar for that day and you can give me my surprise then." Leslie laughed and continued, "I really do have to go now; I will call you tomorrow to see how you are. Take care and I will definitely see you Tuesday. I should get to the apartment by six p.m. Goodnight my love and take care. I love you." Leslie hung up. She was sad but accepted the fact she would be alone this evening.

She had planned on giving him the best meal ever tonight for looking after her so well and for the very special present he brought for her on her birthday just over a month ago. Leslie got her a Jaguar E-type, for her passing her driving test, receiving her driver's license and for her special twenty-first birthday. She could not believe it. It was the best thing anyone had ever bought for her. She was more in love with Leslie than ever and thought God had been kind. Before she met Leslie, her life was dreadful and many a time, she had contemplated suicide. Meeting Leslie changed everything.

Earlier in the week she had gone to the ParknShop, the largest foreign supermarket chain, and bought two dozen French oysters and two Australian twelve-ounce fillet steaks which she planned to cook the way Leslie loved, rare. She went on to purchase four bottles of Dom Perignon. She continued her shopping and got six fragrant candles for the table setting and went to the music shop and bought a record of his favourite classical music to be played on her new gramophone, thus setting a romantic mood; dinner by candlelight and classical music. Perfect!

She had gone later that day to a boutique in Tsim Sha Tsui that imported the latest fashions from France. She found a black floral laced bodysuit with a low plunging neckline. When she tried it on, she knew she must have it, irrespective of the price. It was an original from Yves Saint Laurent's latest lingerie collection. This would arouse Leslie for sure, she thought and that is what she wanted to do. That is what I will wear for dinner on Friday, she thought. It had cost her around HK$10,0000.

Finally, as it was Leslie's fiftieth birthday on the twentieth of the month, which was the coming Friday, she bought him a Cartier Tank watch in eighteen carat white gold with diamonds around the case. She had it engraved on the back "From your One and Only. L.W. 30/07/1960." She purchased it from Ajit Lalwani's store, Lalwani Emporium in Nathan Road in Tsim Sha Tsui. The swanky Lalwani shop was the largest department store in Hong Kong and carried all the famous brands from Europe. Ajit was Leslie's best friend and they went to the same high school and university. Ajit and Lillian got on well, in fact better than Ajit did with Nancy, Leslie's wife. Even with a huge discount the watch cost a small fortune, but it was beautiful and well worth it for her darling. Leslie loved watches and this would be the perfect gift as he did not have a Cartier in his collection.

Leslie had told Lillian that Nancy was throwing him a huge party for his fiftieth birthday at the newly opened Mandarin Hotel on the island. The Mandarin Hotel was a five-star hotel, decent enough to rival the Peninsula hotel, which till then was the only true five-star hotel in Hong Kong. It had five hundred rooms with forty suites and eight bars and restaurants as well as a large ballroom that seated up to three hundred people. Nancy had invited the very elite in the colony for the occasion and it was to be the party of the year! Lillian was sad she could not attend but Leslie had promised her, that the day after his birthday on Saturday, he would celebrate his birthday with her by taking her to the Gaddi's restaurant in the Peninsula Hotel. The Gaddi's was considered to be the finest French cuisine restaurant in all of Asia and although Lillian heard about it, she had never dined there and was looking forward to the experience.

She was still disappointed that tonight had been cancelled but thought at least all was not wasted as she could transfer the big secret surprise that she had for him to Tuesday. She went to pour herself another glass of champagne which was being chilled in a silver ice bucket on her dining table. She had almost finished three quarters of the bottle and was feeling a bit tipsy. She went to her record cabinet and picked up the latest album by Elvis Presley titled "Elvis is back!" She had a great collection of popular music in vinyl which she prized. She loved Elvis and thought he looked like Leslie however, she would never play any contemporary music when Leslie was around as he disliked popular music and only enjoyed the classics. The track "Are you lonesome tonight?" came on, and she sang it out loud to herself as she listened to Elvis croon, "Yes I'm lonesome tonight and I miss you tonight and I'm sorry we are so apart." As she listened to the music, she started dancing around the room imagining she was dancing in Leslie's arms.

The apartment Lillian stayed in was owned by one of Leslie's companies, the Sun Corporation HK Limited. It was one of the more prestigious apartment blocks in Tsim Sha Tsui. Lillian's apartment was the penthouse suite on the top floor. In all other floors there were two apartments but on the twelfth floor, the penthouse, there was one large apartment of two thousand square feet with views of Hong Kong Harbour unobscured. To get to the twelfth floor of the apartment you needed a special key that you turned on entering the lift. It would then take you straight to the floor where the lift door would open on to the main lounge area of the apartment. The apartment came with a private underground car park space which was considered a luxury in Hong Kong.

The apartment was well decorated and done more to the taste of Leslie who, unlike his wife Nancy, liked things modest. It had high ceilings and full height glass doors towards the balcony which helped to create an open airy atmosphere. There were two large bedrooms with en suites and both with walk-in closets. There was a private roof terrace and a state-of-the-art kitchen which added to the luxury of the apartment. The parquet floor throughout the house was of Canadian maple wood. On the right side as you entered there was a white Steinway grand piano. Lillian had taken piano lessons from the age of six and was good at it. She loved playing the piano and it totally relaxed her. Lillian loved her apartment and felt blessed. She thought to herself, if I did not meet Leslie where would I be now?

Lillian Wang, whose real name was Wang Lei Chou, was born in Canton, nowadays known as Guangzhou, on June 21st, 1939, which was the same year that Leslie married Nancy. Her parents both worked at the U.S.A. Embassy in Canton. Her father, Wang Yee, was a cook and the mother, Wang Li, a housekeeper there. Although they were not very wealthy, they were considered lucky to have jobs working in the embassy as it paid well, and they were treated kindly by the consulate general and his wife. In December 1939, with the Japanese invading China and looking that they would soon invade Canton, the U.S. consulate had to shut down, forcing the Wangs to flee to Hong Kong as refugees. In 1941, just before Lillian turned two, her mother gave birth to another girl in Hong Kong.

Because Lillian's parents both spoke perfect English and had good working backgrounds, they soon found decent jobs in Hong Kong right after the war in 1945 working for Sir William Smith, head of Jardine Matheson & Co. the largest and most famous trading company in Hong Kong. Lillian's father was hired as a cook and her mother as the private maid to Sir William's wife Yvonne. The Smiths loved them and treated them as family rather than help. The Smiths themselves could not have children and loved their two little girls. They gave the Wang family all English names. Lillian's father was renamed Jimmy and her mother Grace. They renamed the girls as well, the eldest Lillian and the little one Bella. The Wangs all lived in the special servant quarters which was an outhouse at the Smiths' residence which was located in the very élite area of Hong Kong Island at Number 1 Peak Road.

Lillian's parents were both happy in Hong Kong. Lillian was sent to an exclusive international school, the Island School, on Hong Kong Island with the help of the Smiths. The International Island School was set up by the English School Foundation for expats and their colleagues living in Hong Kong. It was one of the top schools in the colony. Lillian loved school and enjoyed reading and was well versed with all the classical British novels. After school, as extra-curriculars, she took private lessons that included piano and ballet. It was a great time in her life.

Unfortunately, from then on, things got bad. In early 1951 Lillian's mother Grace developed breast cancer. It was a difficult time for all the family. The Smiths did whatever they could to help by sending her to the best doctors available and paying for all the medical fees but unfortunately on Christmas Eve of that year Grace passed away.

It was the saddest day of Lillian's life. It seemed her whole world had come shattering down. Lillian was especially close to her mother and took it harder than Bella did. Her father Jimmy did not take his wife's death at all well and soon took to drinking to drown his sorrows. The drinking got worse and the Smiths tried to help with his problem but to no avail. He became a hindrance in the household, and they had no choice but to let him go. They were obviously concerned about the little girls but their Uncle Billy, Jimmy's younger brother, came forward and told them not to worry and he would look after Jimmy and the kids and make them stay with him in his apartment in Kowloon. The Smiths were unsure but had no say in the matter and Jimmy and the girls moved out of the beautiful house in the Peak to a resettlement estate in Shek Kip Mei on the Kowloon side where Billy lived alone in a two-bed apartment of two hundred and fifty square feet (approximately twenty-three square metres).

A large fire in 1950 destroyed the slum area in the Shek Kip Mei district where immigrants from mainland China lived leaving fifty-three thousand people homeless. After the fire the governor Sir Alexander Grantham then launched a public housing programme to introduce the idea of "multistorey buildings". All the apartments were small, each unit could house a maximum of five people and each block had a capacity of two thousand five hundred people. The estate consisted of seventeen housing blocks containing nine thousand two hundred units of between one hundred and twenty square feet and three hundred square feet (11.1 and 28 square metres respectively). Foreigners who visited these resettlement estates referred them to as "prisons."

For Lillian, this change in her life was a disaster; it seemed that her whole world had crumbled. From living in the most esteemed area of Hong Kong to a confined space in this eighteen-floor high-rise building. The room where Uncle Billy put up Jimmy and the girls was no bigger than seventy square feet with a bunk bed for the girls and a roll-on bed under the bunk which was pulled out at night for Jimmy. The rest of the apartment was made up of Uncle Billy's room, which was about the same size as Jimmy's, and a small lounge/ kitchen with a small room with a toilet, a wash basin and a hand shower.

Both girls had to leave Island School and join a public school near where the estate was. Because of money issues Lillian had to stop both her piano and ballet lessons. Their father Jimmy was a total mess; he tried getting jobs but could not hold on to any of them. He was a total drunk. Uncle Billy did try to get him involved with Alcoholics Anonymous groups, but he never lasted longer than three sessions and when pushed to continue Jimmy became very aggressive. In the end Uncle Billy had to give up on him and allowed him to stay home controlling his drinking as best as he could. So basically, Uncle Billy had to finance the whole family.

Billy was an illegal bookmaker. Gambling in Hong Kong was illegal except with the Royal Hong Kong Jockey Club (RHKJC). Besides being able to bet on race days inside the racecourse the RHKJC had betting shops throughout the colony where punters could place their bets. However, a large portion of the population bet with the illegal bookies as they gave a 10% discount on losing bets and gave the punters up to thirty to sixty days to pay. Of course this was depending on agreements made beforehand between the bookie and the punter.

Billy took bets on international football games and on horse racing when the season was on. He had a reasonably large clientele, mostly from people living on the estate. Although he had lots of customers the bets were relatively small. The 14K, who controlled all the illegal activities in the estate from prostitution, drugs and gambling, allowed Billy to continue to be a bookie and he was made a "49er" for a fee of HK$2500 per month in which he had no choice. The fee, according to the 14K, was for them guaranteeing Billy no interference in the running of his business and protection from the police. They also helped him collect monies from punters who were late in payment, usually by force, and charged an additional fee for that service. Billy just made ends meet after paying the 14K. If Billy was late with the payment, he was charged interest at 5% per day.

On Christmas Eve 1953, two years after Lillian's mother died, a terrible occurrence was to change Lillian's life forever. Lillian and Bella had, for the last two years, accepted living in the estate although they both missed the lifestyle whilst living with the Smiths. They had adapted to living in tight quarters and attending public school. Uncle

Billy was kind to them both, and even though they had not much, they were grateful that their Uncle Billy was there for them like a father. Their real father Jimmy was getting worse daily with his alcoholism. Most days he would just stay in one corner of the apartment ignoring all and getting drunk. Lillian and her sister avoided him as much as possible as they did not want him shouting abuse at them, which was what happened every time they tried speaking to him.

Lillian was now fourteen years old and developing to be a young, beautiful woman. She had charcoal black long straight hair that fell to the top of her waist and had striking features. For a fourteen-year-old her body was almost fully developed. She was cheerful and outgoing and had made many friends in school and was by far the most popular student. She was top of her class and considered to be the prettiest girl in school. Bella too grew up to be a beautiful young girl but unlike Lillian she was shy and very quiet. She did not have much confidence in herself and relied deeply on Lillian for almost everything.

On that day, December 24th, 1953, Lillian, after finishing up with her last lesson in school, had gone to pick up Bella from her class and head home. It was the last day of school before the Christmas holidays. Lillian was looking forward to the holidays as she had planned to stay with her best friend May for Christmas and Boxing Day. She had asked Uncle Billy permission and he had said it was fine. May's family was relatively well off and lived in a three-bedroom apartment at Beacon Hill which was not far from the Shek Kip Mei estate where Lillian lived but was considered a much more affluent area. Lillian was thrilled with the idea of being away from the confined space at home for the next two days and being able to spend some quality time with her best friend. She had told May that she would take Bella home, get packed, spend a little time with her dad and Uncle Billy, before taking the number bus route seven to May's home and would be there by six p.m. just before dinner.

On entering her house Lillian yelled out for her Uncle Billy to let him know that they were home but there was no reply. She thought he was probably out doing the food shopping for Christmas as the next two days most of the supermarkets would be closed for the holidays. She entered her room which was where she and Bella slept with her dad

Jimmy. What Lillian saw when entering the room was terrifying and one that she relived for many years to come. She let out a chilling scream so loud that it could be heard throughout the whole of the seventh floor where they stayed. Staring straight back at her with open bulging eyes was her father hung from the top bunk bed with his trouser belt around his neck. Bella, who was just behind her, cried out asking what happened. Lillian quickly dragged her out of the room before she could see her dad hanging.

Her next-door neighbour came running to the apartment when she heard the screams and saw Lillian sobbing away by the doorway of her room. Entering it she saw Jimmy hung from atop the bunk bed and immediately went to call the police and ambulance. Before the police arrived, Billy had returned back and found that Jimmy had committed suicide. His main concern was for the girls and tried to comfort them as much as he could. He thought best for the girls not to stay in this apartment for the next few days. He called May's parents whom he met when attending parent meetings at the school and told them what happened and asked if Bella could join Lillian and stay in their house till things settled down. They were very sympathetic and told him that of course they could. Later that day when Billy was clearing up after the ambulance took away the body, he found a suicide note left by Jimmy. The note read, "To my dear girls Lillian and Bella — I am sorry. I needed to be with mom please understand. Dad." Billy never showed this note to the girls and destroyed it.

The next few months were sad times for the family. Billy was extra kind to the girls and did his best to ease the girls' sorrow. Lillian was more affected than Bella, she felt that her life was going from bad to worse and many a time she considered suicide. Life to her was not worth living, for just as things got better something bad would happen. Her school grades were dropping, unlike Bella who concentrated on her studies to forget all that happened and was top of her class. Lillian would go every day after school to a Buddhist temple near the estate to light incense and say a prayer for her parents and begged that life for her and Bella would improve. Unfortunately, things only got worse.

In the spring of 1954 Uncle Billy ran into some bad fortune. One of his gambling customers got lucky. The punter had a winning multiple all up bet on a race day which returned for a HK$10 bet a sum of HK$38,400. The bet was an all-up bet on four races with the horses coming in at 20–1, 6–1, 8–1 and 4–1. Billy could not believe his bad luck, for in all his years as a bookie he had never come across something like this. To keep his reputation and his business running he needed to pay off the punter. The weird part was this punter had been gambling with Billy for over six years and had never won, not once! His bet was a maximum $10 on multiple bets on race days and just chose three or four horses trained by either the same trainer or by the same owner without any knowledge of the horse's form. That day he decided to follow four of Leslie Sun's horses and all four won their respective race. That was the first time Lillian heard the name of Leslie Sun, as Billy swore out his name cursing it countlessly for the next few days.

Billy was short of cash to pay the punter and went to General Ming of the 14K who handled his account to explain to him what had happened and that he needed a temporary loan of around HK$25,000 to be able to pay this punter off and also to ask him to delay the HK$2,500 fees he needed to pay that month. He promised he would pay it all back within six months. The general was quite sympathetic to him and said he would loan him the money, not for six months but rather for three months. He also said instead of charging him interest of 5% per day he would only charge him 25% monthly. So, in three months he would need to return back to him HK$25,000 plus HK$2,500 for his back monthly pay plus interest charges of HK$20,625. So, a total of HK$48,125 had to be paid in three months. Billy bargained hard and finally got the general to agree to HK$45,000 on the condition that he could not delay further than the three months and had to pay it back in one lump sum.

General Ming and his team were known to be ruthless amongst the people living in the estate. It was said that previously two of the residents there who owed monies to the 14K had mysteriously disappeared and were never seen again. General Ming had thirty "49ers" in his team who controlled the estate with a strong hand and were feared by all there. The general himself was tall and muscular. He had a curled-up moustache and a deep scar on his left cheek. He walked with a slight limp which was rumoured to be caused by him being stabbed on his thigh during a clash with the Sun Yee On triads which had damaged the nerves.

Billy had no choice but to agree to the terms of the general and hoped that he could recover it back from his bookie business. He was hoping against hope, but he had no alternative otherwise he would lose his business which he had taken so many years to build and was his only source of income. Lillian noticed a huge change in Uncle Billy, he was more agitated with the girls and stayed out for long hours coming back home most days late at night. He spent less and less time with the girls and Lillian took over most of the household chores from making sure the house was cleaned daily, cooking dinner for the family and looking after Bella as well. Her grades continued to drop in school, and she became more reclusive and spent less time with her friends.

General Ming would visit Billy at the house every week on Fridays to ensure that Billy would not run away and to remind him of the loan and asked how he was getting along. In the first two months Billy had been able to make a revenue of HK$20,000, way short of the total of HK$45,000 that the general demanded. He tried negotiating with the general to delay for another three months but to no avail, the general would not budge and reminded Billy that if he did not come up with the full amount, he would face the fury of the 14K which probably meant his life. Lillian heard the conversations between the general and her uncle and was scared for him.

On the day that the money was due the general came to visit Billy with four "49ers". Two guards waited outside the door while the general entered the house. Lillian answered the door and said Billy had not yet returned home and it would be best if he came back a bit later. The general was upset as Billy knew that was the time they had arranged to meet. The general said he would wait, and Lillian offered to make him some tea, which he accepted. Lillian had noticed for a while that the general, whenever he was around her, looked her over with desire. She was scared of the man and felt very awkward being alone with him. Bella was in her room doing her homework whilst they were sitting in the lounge area of the apartment waiting for Billy to return. The general kept eyeing her over and she felt totally uncomfortable. It was crammed there and the general moved closer to her and whispered, "You are beautiful," and stroked her hair. Lillian did not know what to do and started shaking, just then Billy walked in and apologised for his lateness.

Lillian moved from the lounge to her own room and shut the door. She could hear Billy pleading with the general to accept what he had collected so far which was HK$34,000. He explained he tried his hardest and had also borrowed some of the money from loan sharks to reach this amount. He was just short of HK$11,000 but promised to get it to him by the end of the next month. The general looked at him and grunted, "You had your chance; you accepted my terms and you have not met them. Now you must face the circumstances. I am a fair man and I am willing, in lieu of what you owe me, to take your niece Lillian into my custody, as balance payment."

Billy was stunned and said that was not possible and asked the general to do whatever he wanted with him but to leave the two girls alone. The general ignored him and headed towards the girl's room and as he did Billy rushed to the kitchen, grabbed a Chinese chopper and struck the general on his back. The general, in pain, turned around, whipped out his butterfly sword from his sleeve and with one movement cut Billy's throat. Lillian meanwhile had heard all this and cried out for help. The general quickly entered the room, bleeding profusely from where he was cut by Billy, grabbed Lillian and covered her mouth with his hand. He yelled out for the "49ers" who were outside guarding the door to come and help. They entered the apartment and he told one of them to take the girls back to HQ and he would meet up with them later. He then, together with the other guard, took the money that Billy had brought for him, found some cooking kerosene in the apartment, splashed it all over the apartment and on Billy's body and set it on fire.

The fire department and the police were phoned by residents of the block about the fire and came rushing to the estate and were there within twenty minutes. They evacuated everyone from the fifth up to the eighth floor and within an hour put the fire out. They found Billy's body burned to a crisp but did not find anyone else. The two girls were not around and were missing. When the police questioned the neighbours none of them said they saw anything although that was not true as a few of them did see the general's guards take the two girls with them but was fearful of saying anything as they knew if they did the 14K would come after them. The police questioned anyone who knew the girls of their whereabouts, but no one seemed to know where they were. They searched all around the resettlement estate but could not find any trace of the girls. After two months of investigating, they gave up their search and just added that incident to the many missing people files they had and closed the case.

The general took the girls back to the 14K HQ where he lived. He asked one of his guards to look after Bella for a few hours while he interrogated Lillian privately. When they were safely locked away in his apartment he reached out for Lillian and started feeling up her body. Lillian resisted him and he got violent, tearing off her clothes. She screamed and fought as hard as she could to break away from him, but he was too strong. Lillian put on a good fight, but it was a losing battle and soon she was battered and bruised throughout her body. He kept on hitting her until she became unconscious and he then raped her. That was the day she lost her virginity. After that he tied her up and gagged her. He brought back Bella to his room and did the same to her. Bella, unlike Lillian, did not resist and just wanted him to finish quickly which he did. He then tied up Bella as he did Lillian.

General Ming knew he had to report the whole incident with Billy to the council the next day at the council's weekly meeting and explain to them why he had brought the two girls back to the HQ with him. He was a bit nervous for, according to the ethics of the 14K, children were sacred and not to be harmed. He wished now he left the girls in the apartment to burn with their uncle. He was stupid to have attacked Lillian and Bella for if they told the council what he had done he would himself be punished for breaking an oath. He thought, I must think of how I am going to report to the council. He met with his two guards who were there with him during the incident and came up with a story which he asked them to back him on. He threatened Lillian and told her that if she did not say exactly what he told her to say to the council he would not hesitate to kill Bella. Lillian was so scared of what General Ming would do to Bella and agreed to do whatever he asked.

The next day on Friday as the weekly council was being held General Ming was called upon to give his report on what took place at Billy Wang's apartment. General Ming explained that he had been there to collect monies owed to the 14K. He further went to say that Billy had not raised the money and when the general had asked him to come back with him to HQ, he attacked him with a chopper. The general went on to describe that a brawl broke out and as he tried to defend himself a kerosene lamp, which was on the floor, fell and that Billy caught on fire. He could not rescue Billy and worried for the safety of the girls so he and the two guards who were there accompanying him brought the girls back to the 14K HQ.

Wild Ox, who was conducting the questioning, then asked the general whether he received any monies at all from Billy to which General Ming replied no.

"So, you got nothing is that correct?" asked Wild Ox.

"Yes, My Lord, it all happened so fast that we had no time to look around the apartment to see if there was any money around. My only thought at that time was to save the girls as the fire was spreading fast," replied the general.

"I see," said Wild Ox. "And where are the two girls now?"

"They are safe and asleep in my room at this moment," replied the general.

Wild Ox looked at the general suspiciously and called out to two of the "49ers'" who were guarding the archway of swords. "Go up to the general's room and bring the two girls down right now to face the council so we can question them."

"Let me go instead," pleaded the General, not expecting Wild Ox to call for the girls. "They may be afraid of the '49ers.' I will go and fetch them and bring them back here." Wild Ox shook his head to say no and reiterated to the "49ers" to fetch the girls.

When the girls came to face the council, they were both sobbing profusely. Lillian was dressed in a white gown printed with little flowers. The gown covered her whole body. It was long sleeved and concealed her arms completely. Bella was dressed likewise and was clinging onto Lillian. Ponytail was taken aback with Lillian's beauty. In front of him stood a beautiful woman, he could not believe that she was barely fifteen years old. He looked at her and gently asked if she was OK and whether the general had looked after them well.

She was sobbing but answered, "Yes the general has been kind, please do not hurt us we will do whatever you say My Lord, and please do not injure my sister Bella if anything hurt me instead." Ponytail could feel the pain in her voice for, as she answered, her whole body was quivering with fear. Ponytail already knew what had happened, but he wanted to make a statement to all the generals and "49ers" there.

"Lillian please disrobe, now!" ordered Ponytail. Lillian looked back at him and then at General Ming who was staring at her in horror from the doorway of the arch of the swords while Ponytail was questioning her, fearing the worst. "Sorry My Lord but I cannot," replied Lillian. "Yes, you can, and you will," replied Ponytail. "Nobody will harm you or your sister I promise you, you will be safe from everyone."

She looked first at the general who was staring at her with enraged eyes. She then looked at Ponytail and saw him give her a reassuring smile. Ponytail repeated for her not to worry and do as he said and nothing bad would happen. She slowly disrobed from her gown, revealing nothing but a white bra and undies on. She was totally covered in bruises all the way down from her neck to her toes. It was apparent to all there that she had been beaten up badly. "What happened to you my dear girl? You have bruises all over your body."

"My Lord I slipped down the stairs and hurt myself that is all," she replied.

"No," cried Bella. "He did this to both of us!" She started to disrobe as well and pointing at General Ming. "He is evil, he killed Uncle Billy and then raped us both. He told Lillian if we were to tell you he would kill me! I hate him!"

Wild Ox stood up and informed the council that General Ming had been lying all along. He lied about how Billy died, he lied that there was no money when actually he took it for himself and he had raped the two girls. One of General Ming's guards had told Wild Ox everything that morning before the meeting, the guard was disgusted with what the general did and reported it to Wild Ox. Wild Ox told Ponytail the whole tale before the meeting started. They both decided to let General Ming tell his side of the story first as that would show to all there how evil and despicable he was, thus warranting his punishment. Wild Ox shouted to the two guards near the archway to immediately arrest the general and bring him to the torture chamber.

"He has broken our oaths nine, eleven, fourteen, thirty-one and thirty-two. He must suffer for his horrific deeds."

As the general was dragged out of the hall, protesting that he was innocent, Ponytail turned towards the girls and asked them if they had family they could go to. Lillian replied that both her parents were no longer alive and the last of her known relatives Uncle Billy had been killed by General Ming. She was scared and did not know what to do. She had no home to return to as it was burned down and no one to look after Bella or her. She started shaking and continued sobbing.

Ponytail called for General Lo to come forward. He asked the general to take the girls to Mama Wendy's, and to tell her that he sent them to her. She was to look after them as if they were her daughters and ensure that no harm befell them. He turned to Dragonfly and told him that he was to provide Mama Wendy with whatever funds or support she needed to look after the two girls. He asked Dragonfly to reward the guard who reported the general's crime and told Wild Ox to arrest the other guard who kept quiet and send him to the torture chamber. He then turned back to Lillian and told her not to worry, Mama Wendy was a very kind lady and would look after Bella and her like her daughters. Lillian looked confused and did not know what to say. She fell to her knees and thanked him on behalf of Bella and herself. Ponytail replied saying they need not thank him and said he was sorry that one of his generals had been so cruel to the girls. Lillian stood up, bowed again at Ponytail and, still sobbing, followed General Lo to Mama Wendy's.

Mama Wendy received the girls and told General Lo to let Ponytail know that she would look after them as her own and not to worry. When she first saw the two girls she was taken aback, surprised how beautiful both girls were, especially Lillian. Mama Wendy lived above the Sing Sing Club in Tsim Sha Tsui in the penthouse. The building was fifteen storeys high with the club taking up the basement, ground, first and second floors. From the third floor to the fourteenth floor were apartments which were rented by Mama Wendy to the hostesses working for the club at very reasonable prices. She was clever to do this as this way the girls would stay loyal to the club. Each floor had six apartments, two of which had two bedrooms and four one-bedroom apartments. Most hostesses shared the apartments with up to three or four other colleagues so as to save on rent.

Mama Wendy set Lillian and Bella up in her penthouse. She wanted to be sure that she was nearby if they needed anything. The penthouse was huge with five large bedrooms and a large lounge area with beautiful views of the harbour. Mama Wendy would throw many wild parties here for her VIP guests who sometimes would end up in one of the bedrooms with a hostess. When Lillian and Bella moved in, she thought, I have to be careful now and not to throw any more parties. Lillian and Bella loved living there. Mama Wendy was super nice to them and looked after them well. She bought a whole new wardrobe for both of them, new clothes, shoes, handbags etc, all branded of course. She never had any children of her own and she loved looking after them as her own and was actually grateful that Ponytail sent the girls to her.

Mama Wendy sent the two girls to an all-girl Roman Catholic boarding school, Maryknoll Convent School, which actually was in Kowloon Tong near where Leslie lived. It was founded by Maryknoll sisters in Hong Kong in 1925 and was well known for its distinguished academic results and school traditions. The school was run wholly by nuns. Lillian, who was in her GCE year, did not board, but Bella wanted to be a boarder. Bella was quick to make friends and loved school life. She did well and was top of her class. Lillian, on the other hand, did not enjoy school at all and was dying to finish her GCEs and end school life. She, unlike Bella, had no desire to continue with her education or going to university, she was more interested in mixing with the hostesses who worked in the club whom she was fascinated with and the stories they told. Deep down inside she desired one day to be a hostess and be as glamorous as they were. She was loved by all the hostesses who found her beautiful and friendly.

Lillian would on weekends follow Mama Wendy to the club; she loved all the glitz surrounding the club. She would sit with the hostesses in their waiting room chatting with them and wanting one day to be a high-class hostess. She told Mama Wendy of her wishes, but Mama told her it was not as glamorous as she thought and there were sometimes difficult situations that occurred with customers and one must know how to handle that. She also said that sometimes customers expected sex from them in return for payment. Still Lillian pushed Mama on allowing her to be a hostess and said that she could learn from Mama how to handle customers and study from Mama Wendy how to please them sexually if need be.

The Sing Sing Club was in its peak in the late 1950s. Customers at the club would be driven from the entrance of the club to their private booth or VIP rooms in golf carts kitted out as gold Rolls-Royces. They could spend up to HK$10,000 a night just buying hostesses drinks, paying for using the private rooms, and for the hostesses' time spent sitting with them. They would pay extra for taking them out of the club for sexual activities. The hostess would negotiate a price with them for sex depending on what the customer wanted her to do; the fees which she kept could range from HK$1,500.00 to HK$5,000.00. This was nouveau riche conspicuous consumption where sometimes shady business deals were done under the cover of whirling lights and lavish floor shows.

The main area of the club had one hundred and fifty tables and sat six hundred people. It had a stage with a seven piece band playing the latest music and where strip shows were held every hour on the hour. The dance floor could hold four hundred people. The décor ranged from ersatz Versailles to Japanese, always with a generous portion of glitz. The money spent there had no limits. One of the girls that was close to Lillian was a girl nicknamed Betty Boop, she was the number one hostess in the club. She told Lillian that money was like sand. One day she took out a wad of bills of HK$1,000 notes and showed it to Lillian. Lillian was impressed and thought to herself, one day I will be the number one hostess and be respected by all and be able to afford to move out from Mama Wendy and have my own apartment.

Lillian graduated from school just after she turned seventeen on June 30th 1956. She was happy to complete her GCSE and was dying to leave school life behind and become a hostess. She finally convinced Mama Wendy for her to be a hostess. Mama gave in as Lillian was stubborn and determined and felt if she tried holding her back, she would just join other clubs. So, Mama Wendy gave in and took time to teach Lillian on how to be a formidable hostess. She showed her ways to make customers yearn for her and want to keep coming back. How to not give in to their sexual requests easily but rather tease them along. If she was to have sex, she must always be sure that she was protected and paid well for it. Lillian was given lessons in the art of making love and how to give men ultimate pleasures. She learned quickly.

On her first day as a hostess, she had three tables that she was invited to and was requested into two VIP rooms. She was an instant success with the customers, for whoever she sat with came back as repeat customers and her reputation grew. She soon was the number one hostess in the Sing Sing Club. She knew how to play her customers well and make them spend money in the club whilst not having sex with many. She only chose to have sex with customers she truly liked. The very first customer she slept with was Raymond Ho whom she found kind and attractive. He was rumoured to be part owner of the club although some believed he was just the front man for the 14K who owned it together with Mama Wendy.

Raymond entertained his customers at the Sing Sing often. Whenever he came, he got the best VIP room in the club and Mama Wendy would always be in the room to supervise and ensure that he and his customers were kept happy. He was a big spender and a flirt. He hardly stayed with the same hostess more than twice. When he was first introduced to Lillian by Wendy, he was stunned by her beauty and she became his favourite hostess. Many a time he would bring his VIP guests and introduce Lillian to them expecting her to look after them. Lillian was not jealous when Raymond would push his customers to her, whilst he was with other hostesses. She knew that Raymond did that because he was sure that Lillian would entertain his special clients well which would help in closing his business deals. He had only slept with Lillian once and he really liked her but was scared to become too attached to her. He would always tip Lillian well, even if she was not his hostess for that night.

It was in mid-September of 1956 that Lillian first met Leslie Sun. She had been working in the club full time then for over four months and had never seen him in the club before. Mama Wendy had come to her earlier that evening telling her that Raymond had booked the VIP room and that he had specifically asked for Lillian to join him. Lillian explained she had already booked two clients for that night, but Mama Wendy said to cancel them, and she would arrange for other hostesses to look after them. She told Lillian that the guest of Raymond's was Leslie Sun and he was important and to look after him and to do whatever pleased him. She had heard Leslie's name mentioned before by Uncle Billy and knew that he was rich and owned horses but that was all.

When Raymond and Leslie entered the VIP room that evening both Mama Wendy and Lillian were there with two other hostesses, one being Betty Boop, waiting for them. Lillian was wearing a cheongsam. The cheongsam is a close-fitting dress that originated in the 1920s in Shanghai and was worn on formal occasions and by the wealthy. The cheongsam Lillian wore that night was a classic wine red and gold sheath cheongsam made with a beautiful brocade patterned fabric. It had two slits on both sides running from the hip down the bottom of the dress. She had her hair up and looked stunning! Leslie could not take his eyes of her and was stunned by her beauty.

Leslie had arranged this meeting with Raymond as he knew that he had a good relationship with the 14K, and he needed some inside information as it was rumoured that the triads were planning some form of protests on Double 10th Day which was but a few days away. Raymond and Leslie were good friends and had known each other for a while. Many a time Raymond was the go-between the 14K and the government via Leslie. Even though the 14K were involved in illegal businesses it was important that they kept the balance with the government and thus they were tolerated. Raymond accepted to meet Leslie for dinner and discuss the situation but had Leslie promise that after dinner he joined him at the Sing Sing Club.

Leslie had been asked many a time by Raymond to visit his club but had always refused. He did not like the club scene at all and looked down at the hostesses who worked there as high-class prostitutes. This day he accepted as he needed Raymond's help and information on what he knew. So, when he walked in that VIP room with Raymond after dinner, he intended to stay there for a half an hour to give face but instead he ended up there till the early hours of the morning, all because of Lillian. He just loved being with her and was surprised how knowledgeable she was on current affairs. They spoke for hours on things they both enjoyed like classical music, love of poetry and famous English authors like Dickens, Austen, Bronte etc. Leslie did not know it then, but he was slowly falling in love with Lillian. She too was attracted to him and although he was much older than her, she found him handsome and interesting. He treated her differently from most of her clients who were always trying to grope her whilst he on the other hand was extremely polite and kind and treated her like a lady.

From that day on Leslie used to come to the club at least twice a week to see Lillian. After a while he would just take her out for dinner and book her out for the night with the club. On his fifth date with Lillian, he invited her to his penthouse suite in Peking Road in TST which he kept for his important overseas clients and friends when they came to visit. That was the first time they had sex together. Lillian was looking beautiful that night, she was wearing a white mini dress made of pure silk with a low neckline that accentuated her breasts. She loved the apartment and as she entered and saw the grand Steinway piano, she gave out a small yelp. She had not played for a while and asked Leslie if she could play something for him. He, of course, was shocked that she played the piano and when she performed, "Symphony No. 41 Jupiter" the most difficult symphony of Mozart's to play, he was impressed. He walked up behind her whilst she was playing and put his hand around her waist slowly lifting it up to her breasts. He was sexually aroused, and Lillian could feel his manhood pressing on her back. She turned around, slowly unzipping his trousers and kissed his penis lightly at first before putting it in her mouth and making him come. He then led her to the bedroom where he undressed her slowly and then made love to her not once but three times that night.

They both fell madly in love. Lillian knew he was married but she did not care she was just happy to be with him. After dating for a few months Leslie asked her to quit her job and be there only for him and that he would look after her. He could not bear the thought of her working in the club and entertaining other men, although after she first made love to Leslie, she did not sleep with any of her other clients. She could not believe he asked her to be exclusive and accepted without any qualms.

He moved her into the penthouse apartment and looked after her every need. Lillian was happier than she had ever been. She set up a small temple in the apartment with a jade statue of Buddha whom she believed in and every morning when she awoke, she would light up incense and thank Buddha for bringing Leslie into her life.

Lillian asked Bella to move in with her, but Bella refused and continued to stay with Mama Wendy. She explained to Lillian that she did not want to be around when Leslie visited her as she felt uncomfortable with that. In reality she did not trust Leslie or any men for that matter. She was more attracted to women but kept that a secret from her sister although Mama Wendy knew. She was currently dating one of the hostesses working at Mama Wendy's club and that was another reason she did not want to move in with her sister. She told Lillian that after the summer she planned to go to the U.K. to continue her studies. She would, however, stay with Lillian some weekends before she left for her studies, when Leslie was busy and keep her company. Lillian, although not happy with Bella not being near her, accepted her sister's wishes.

The winds outside were at gale force now as the typhoon approached. Lillian looked at the champagne flute she was holding, it was empty. She walked to the table where the ice bucket was and poured the last of the champagne into her glass. It was getting a bit cold in the room, so she went to the air condition control on the wall and switched it from high to low. She walked into the bedroom to get a gown to wear and went back to the lounge listening to Elvis singing "Fever".

She was feeling quite sloshed now, she realised that she had drunk a full bottle all by herself. She gulped up the last of the champagne, switched off the gramophone, turned out the lights and walked back to her bedroom. She laid down on her bed and looked at Leslie's framed picture on her bedside table. She was feeling very horny and missed him so. She opened the top cupboard of the bedside table and pulled out a small red vibrator. She took off her gown and went under the blanket thinking of Leslie as she used the vibrator to make herself come. She had a quick fulfilling orgasm and was content that everything was turning out the way she had hoped for.

She rubbed her tummy and thought how Leslie would react when she told him she was pregnant. She had only found that out the day before when she visited her gynaecologist. That was the big surprise she had planned on telling Leslie that night. Oh well, she thought, at least it won't be long till Tuesday when I can tell him face to face and see his reaction.

She smiled and went to sleep.

Chapter 5
Troubled Times

Police Headquarters
1 Arsenal Street, Wan Chai, Hong Kong.
Monday July 15th, 1960, seven thirty a.m.

His chauffeur stopped in front of the station and John stepped out and headed towards the door. It's going to be a crazy day, he thought. The weekend had seen the typhoon passing through the colony, causing much damage and disruption and the call he received from Inspector Lee late last night added to his anxieties and totally disturbed him. He had a lot to do this morning and was not looking forward to the day. On top of that he had Maggie, his wife, nagging about getting someone to fix the pump for the swimming pool as he was rushing to leave for the office. She really is a lazy cow, he thought to himself, why the hell can't she do that herself knowing how busy he was?

As he walked through the door, he passed reception. The police constable at the reception desk stood up and saluted, behind him was an insignia on the wall with the police motto "We Serve with Pride and Care".

"Has Inspector Lee come in yet?" asked John.

"No sir, but he did call and said he would be late as he was still waiting for the coroner's report which would be ready shortly after which he would come directly here."

"OK as soon as he walks in send him straight to my office."

He walked towards his office and was greeted by his personal secretary Angela Ho.

"Good morning, sir, I got out all the reports you asked for when you called this morning and have put them on your desk. Is there anything else I can do for you? Would you like some coffee?"

"Yes, coffee would be excellent! Also, could you contact someone who could fix the pump for my swimming pool at home. It seems it is not working and please let my wife know once you have organised it. Thanks!"

He liked Angela, she was efficient and hard working. He felt grateful for Raymond Ho for introducing her to him. She was Raymond's niece and initially he was hesitant to hire her because of that but he was so glad that he did. He could not have found anyone better as a secretary. Everyone who knew her or had contact with her praised her highly for her diligence and efficiency.

As he approached to enter his office on the glass door was printed in gold letters:

John Woods C.B.E.

Commissioner of Police

Hong Kong

He went in sat on his chair and looked at the pile of papers in front of him. Yes, it was going to be a long day.

Firstly, he had to deal with the aftermath of the typhoon. It had caused a lot of damage around the colony causing eight deaths so far. There were numerous trees blown by the wind causing roadblocks in several roads. These all needed to be cleared as quickly as possible. The rain had caused a lot of flooding to many areas around the colony especially on Hong Kong Island where there had been numerous landslides. All these needed looking at, as some of the high-rise apartment blocks were in danger of collapsing due to the severity of the landslides. People living in those areas and nearby needed to be evacuated. During this period the police had to look after such calamities. There were no special emergency units who handled this, and all operations had to go via the police. He buzzed Angela on the intercom and asked her to get Inspector Hill to come to his office immediately.

Inspector Hill was in charge of the clean-up and to ensure all was secure and safe. He reported back that they had already started the clearing up process and his team was now examining where the major landslides took place and were checking if they were safe. The major concern was apartment blocks that were built on hills that could collapse with the loose soil. He would continue to keep the commissioner in touch with all the progress and give him an updated report twice a day, one in the morning and one in the evening, so that he would be fully well-informed of all that was happening and could report back to the governor if need be. John nodded and thanked him. Now back to the bigger problem.

John was born in Berkshire in the town of Windsor in the U.K. on Valentine's Day 1919. He was the first child of Major Samuel Woods C.B.E., a war hero, decorated with the Victoria Cross for his bravery and valour, by King George V in 1919.

Major Samuel Woods earned his Victoria Cross during the Great War of 1914-1918, when the Coldstream Guards, with whom he was stationed, had employed the First, Second and Third Battalions to France to fight the Germans. In the Battle of the Somme, where the Coldstream Guards were deployed the British sustained over four hundred and twenty thousand casualties with over eighty thousand deaths. It was during one of the skirmishes with the German army there that four soldiers from his battalion were surrounded by fourteen German soldiers. Samuel rushed in not worrying for his life, broke through, and led the soldiers back to safety and in the process shot six Germans and dispersed the rest.

When he returned home, he was promoted from Staff Sergeant to Major and awarded the Victoria Cross. At thirty-four years old he was one of the youngest in the British army to hold such a high position. Major Samuel Woods was made in charge of the First Coldstream Guards regiment which was based in Windsor.

Major Samuel Woods married his childhood sweetheart, Sylvia, in 1918. A year later they had a son whom they named John. They went on to have two more sons, Alan, who was born a year after John, and William, who was born in 1922. John was very tall and scrawny with sandy hair and blue eyes. He grew to be six-foot one inch tall, had a slightly crooked nose and had a stutter in his voice when he got nervous, he was also asthmatic. Among his brothers John was the weakest of the three. His father tried toughening him up but gave up as he would turn to his mother crying when pushed to do things that he found difficult. His mother, Sylvia, favoured John the most from her three sons and totally spoilt him. John's two younger brothers on the other hand were well built and loved to rough it with their dad, spending many a time outdoors with their father playing rugby or football whilst John watched them.

All three boys were sent to Eton College when they turned thirteen like their father before them. Eton College is a secondary all male boarding school in Windsor and was considered to be the most elite in the U.K. It was the most expensive school in the country and cost up to £34,000 a year to study there. John did not enjoy school life, unlike his two younger brothers. He was not as athletic as them and did not partake in football or rugby as his brothers did who were both in the school team. He was also weak in most subjects and the only things he enjoyed were the arts, specifically painting.

Major Samuel Woods came from a wealthy family and his father, like him, was a major in the army. He lived in the family house, a beautiful eight bedroom listed eighteenth century manor home in Church Road in Windsor which he inherited from his parents. Both his parents passed away during the war in a freak car accident. He was well respected in the community and did a lot of charity work and was a Freemason. He was very religious and attended church every Sunday with his whole family. He was strict and brought up the boys in an orderly way and ensured they were well-mannered. Of all the three boys he was most disappointed with John and found him a sissy. His favourite was Alan who was very much like him, tough and committed to all that he did. He also was impressed with how well Alan did at Eton, getting top grades, great at sports, and regularly being praised by his housemaster, unlike John who was constantly getting bad grades and did not take part in any sport activities, often using asthma as an excuse.

On September 19th, 1939, Germany invaded Poland. Both Great Britain and France responded by declaring war on Germany. Both Alan and William enlisted in the armed forces. Alan joined the RAF, where he learned to be a pilot, whilst William joined the Royal Navy. John could not join any of the armed forces due to him being asthmatic, although he did apply, wanting to impress his father, but failed the medical tests required. Major Samuel, at fifty-five years old, had just before the start of the Second World War retired from the army. He was proud of his two boys enlisting and thus continuing the family tradition. John wanted to do something to help the war effort but due to his asthmatic condition had to instead settle with joining the local police force.

It was during this time, while in the police force, that John met Margaret Mollers. One day in the summer of 1942 he was sent to a munitions factory in Windsor where Vera Lynn and her quartet were performing as part of their effort to boost morale. He and his team were there to ensure that the venue was protected and to keep things orderly. Vera Lynn was an English singer best known for her popular songs like "We'll Meet Again" and "The White Cliffs of Dover". She was known as the forces sweetheart and did concerts all over U.K. to help in the war effort by building confidence. Margaret was standing up in front of the stage and when Vera started singing there was a rush from the crowd from the back all wishing to catch a glimpse of her. This caused Margaret to stumble and fall on the concrete ground hurting herself. John came to the rescue and carried her out of the factory away from the gathering. She was not hurt badly and just sustained cuts to her legs and knees.

He brought her to the local hospital where, while waiting for the doctor to examine her, started chatting to her, enjoying her company. When she learned that he was the eldest son of Major Samuel Woods she was impressed. Margaret came from a very poor family. She never attended secondary school and started working from the age of fourteen. She had been working in the same factory now for over three years and hated her work. Her mother had died when she was just nine years old and she had been living with her father since in a single room apartment in the centre of Windsor town. Her father was a railway worker and spent most of the money he earned on alcohol. He adored Margaret but just did not have the drive to make life better for the both of them. Margaret had to fend for herself from a very young age. She dreamed of one day meeting her Prince Charming who would sweep her away from the hellhole she lived in and bring her to his castle where they would live happily ever after. She was a beautiful girl. Her most distinct features were her breasts which were huge for her age, a size 38D. She was blonde with bright blue eyes and stood at five feet seven inches. John immediately was attracted to her and she was fascinated by him, not romantically but more so because of his heritage. She was younger than John who was twenty-four and she just seventeen, but she was certainly more street smart then he was and was very astute. So, when John asked her to go to the cinema on a date that weekend, she immediately accepted and could not believe her luck, meeting someone so cultured who actually took interest in her.

They dated for over a year. He had brought her to meet his family after their third date and when Margaret saw where he lived, she was determined to make him fall in love with her and hoped with any luck, one day he would propose to her. She was sexually aggressive with him and gave him pleasure by doing outrageous acts to stimulate him. John's parents, especially the father, did not like Margaret from the beginning, finding her totally unsuitable for John. She dressed different to how a lady should, with part of her breasts showing flagrantly, wearing low-cut dresses. Her use of language especially bothered him which he found foul with a cuss word in almost every other sentence. However, John was blindly in love with her and Margaret got her way for in September of 1943 he proposed to her against his parents' wishes and got married to her on Christmas Day that year.

The wedding was a small affair as the war was still on and held at the Woods residence followed by dinner. The Woods invited only their immediate relatives and closest friends. On Margaret's side she invited three of her friends who worked in the munitions factory with her, and of course her father. Margaret made sure her father was sobered up for the wedding and made him dress in a formal tuxedo. She warned him if he did anything stupid during the wedding ceremony to spoil her special day, she would disown him completely. He was good, he walked her down the aisle and behaved the whole day. He did not even have an alcoholic drink at the after party held at the Woods residence in fear of letting his daughter down.

Samuel did not want the newlyweds to live in the house and told Sylvia he was thinking of getting them an apartment in town, but Sylvia was dead set against it. Finally, Samuel had to give in, and Margaret moved into the family house. Sylvia, simply because of her love for John, accepted Margaret faster than Samuel did. She was happy that her favourite son was living with them. Margaret however cared not what John's father thought of her for as far as she was concerned, she got what she had always dreamed of: a prince and a castle.

Two months after the wedding as the war was winding down and it seemed the Allies were gaining advantage over the Germans. News came that Alan was shot down by anti-aircraft guns while flying his Spitfire over Berlin. He was in the act of protecting an Allied bomber when shot and was reported missing in action. Pilots in a Spitfire flying alongside Alan that day that got back safe said that they saw Alan parachute out before the plane crashed, so he may have survived and probably was taken prisoner by the Germans. Samuel and Sylvia were devastated with the news and prayed that their son was still alive and was just held prisoner by the Germans.

That same year on Christmas Day, the same day that John and Margaret got married, John and Margaret gave birth to a son, Ben Samuel. Margaret appropriately named him after his grandad, which was purely political as she wanted to win points with her father-in-law. The Woods were thrilled that they were grandparents. The baby was so cute and had his father's features, he was blond and had brown eyes just like his dad. Margaret was happy for at least both of John's parents were now nicer to her with the birth of Ben. Her baby was the centre of attention in the household but that was until William returned home from his service in the navy in April of 1945. The attention turned to William, who unfortunately had had his left leg amputated due to an injury during a sea battle. William took his injury bravely and never complained.

On May 8th, 1945 the Germans surrendered to the Allied forces. Major Samuel Woods immediately got in touch with the State for Foreign and Commonwealth Affairs to see if they had any information on Alan's whereabouts. They received good news in early June that they had located Alan in Berlin in a prison camp, he was well and would soon be returning home. They were elated, it was a great year even though their son William had lost a leg. Both their sons came home safe from the war, and they were grandparents. They soon found out also that Margaret was pregnant once again and was expecting in December.

A month after Alan returned the Woods planned a party for Alan and William for their return from the war. They invited their immediate relations and everyone of high status from the community. They did not invite any of Margaret's friends, nor did they invite her father. She was infuriated and nagged John, demanding he asked his parents to invite them. However, even though John requested it, Samuel was unwilling to do so. He had invited special VIP guests like the Mayor of the City and his wife and children, and the Duke of Berkshire and his wife and two of his daughters and did not want any commotion during the party. He remembered how Margaret's friends acted during John's wedding and how they got drunk and were boisterous and vulgar. He did not want them or her father to attend as he found them all crude.

Alan and William equally did not get along with Margaret from the moment they met her as they both found her loud and unsophisticated. They were surprised that their older brother had married someone so unrefined when he could have chosen almost anyone that he wanted. They were embarrassed by the way she acted especially when she had a little too much to drink which was frequent. She did not like the royals and would put down the monarchy and voice her belief that Britain should became a republic. Samuel had many times reprimanded her and told her to keep her beliefs to herself, especially when in public. Margaret started to isolate from the rest of the family and did not get involved in any decisions they made.

The party took place in late June at the Woods residence. They had invited over a hundred and twenty guests for cocktails followed by a sit-down dinner. They also invited single available women of refinement to attend with their parents hoping that Alan and William could get to meet someone refined and get romantically involved. They set up a marquee in their garden and had a seven-piece band playing and a dance floor. The marquee was done with such class with a navy-blue linen roof lit by hundreds of small tea lights making the ceiling look like the night sky with bright stars. The table setting was beautiful with each table seating eight people. All the glasses were of crystal and the cutlery of silver. The table centrepiece was a crystal vase with oversized hydrangeas, pink roses and peonies.

The table seatings were arranged by Samuel and Sylvia. On the head table were seated Samuel and his wife, together with the Duke of Berkshire and his wife, the Mayor of Windsor and his wife and the Commander of the Coldstream Guards and his wife. Alan and William sat in the second head table which was located near the dance floor by where the band was. On their table were the Duke of Berkshire's two teenage daughters, the Mayor of Windsor's son and daughter, and two of their classmates from Eton. John and Margaret sat quite apart, away from the rest of the family, together with John's colleagues from the police station including the commander of police for Windsor. Margaret was fuming to be treated like this especially as John was the eldest son and she felt that he should have been better respected and sat on one of the head tables. She drowned her sorrow in wine even though she was four months' pregnant then. She flirted with one of John's colleagues who came to the party without a partner during cocktails and was clearly drunk before dinner. John felt embarrassed by the way she was acting but knew when she was in this state it was best to leave her alone and not cause a fuss.

John, before sitting down at his table for dinner, went to the head table to welcome all of the guests there and to have a toast with them. Unfortunately for him, when Margaret saw him heading there, she followed him and as he was making a toast she shouted, "Let us drink to the coming up of the real people of Britain and to the new republic!" Everyone sitting was shocked at her outburst, Alan, who was sitting in the next table got up, took her by the arm and dragged her out of the marquee. John just stood there flabbergasted at what just happened. Margaret could hardly stand by then. John gathered his thoughts, ran outside and carried her away to their bedroom where he changed her into her night clothes and went back to the party. He apologised to the guests at the head table and headed back to host his table.

The next morning all hell broke out during breakfast. The family always ate breakfast together as it was family tradition. Samuel blasted Margaret for what she did the night before saying she had embarrassed the whole family. He further went to say that she was never again to attend any party he held. He told both John and Margaret to find a place of their own soon and move out of his manor. Sylvia was really upset and calmed Samuel down saying Margaret was pregnant and to wait till the baby came before making such a rash decision. As usual Samuel backed down. Margaret was upset, not so much at Samuel but more at her husband for not defending her. It was then that she lost total respect for him and never again made love to him whilst they lived in that house.

Living with the family after that day was a strain for all. John wished he could change the way the family treated Margaret and wished Margaret would at least try to be civil with them. Margaret became solitary and stayed most times alone in her section of the house. She did not join the family for breakfast, did not attend Sunday church, and never attended any of the parties that the family held. On December 24th, Margaret gave birth to a girl. They named her Mabel Jane Woods. Margaret loved the baby so much and spent most of her time fussing over her. She was very possessive with the baby and intentionally did not let her see her grandparents. She only finally consented to send her to her grandparents when John stood his ground and said she must do so. Even then she would only send the baby once a week to the grandparents and then only for a few hours. Ben was allowed to see his grandparents any time, though.

In the Spring of 1947 Alan gave the family a pleasant surprise. He had been dating Irene who was the daughter of the Duke of Berkshire for over a year and had now asked her to marry him. The family was ecstatic, all except for Margaret. She felt even more threatened and knew that Irene would rule the roost and would get anything that she wanted from the family. She really did not want to live in the house any more and nagged John almost every night to please find them a house to stay in as far away from the Woods residence as possible. He asked her to be patient and wait till Alan got married as it was not the right time for them to make such a drastic move. He promised he would, after Alan's wedding, look for a place for them to stay. He did not want to upset the family now, especially when they were in such a joyous mood.

The wedding was planned for the summer and to be held in the Duke of Windsor's manor. Almost anyone of importance was invited, including members of the Royal Family. It was to be the wedding of the year and was well covered both by the British and international press.

Margaret dreaded that day. She attended but was standoffish throughout the ceremony and at the party that followed, she kept to herself and did not socialise with anyone. John was saddened by her attitude and wished she fell out of this ugly mood and was back to the old girl he fell in love with who was outgoing and full of life. He knew then if he did not do something soon to fix this the marriage it would be over; which was the last thing that he wanted.

In July of 1951, John, who had been working now in the police for almost eight years and promoted to deputy chief constable of Thames Valley Police in Windsor, was asked by his superior the chief constable to see him at his office to discuss something that could be exciting for him. He asked if John would be interested in relocating to Hong Kong. Apparently, there was a position for a British officer with experience, to become assistant commissioner of police and eventually become commissioner when the current one retired in two years. The pay was better than what he currently earned and came with many benefits, including lodging for him and the family in a four-bedroom house, two servants and a chauffeur to look after them, fully paid education for the children in the best English primary school in Hong Kong, free medical care for the whole family and a fully paid one-month annual holiday. John could not believe this was being offered to him but acted nonchalantly and said he would need to pass it through his wife and family as it was a big commitment to make. He would come back to him within the week.

When John told Margaret that evening when he got home, she squealed with joy. This was the miracle she was looking for. A chance for her to go somewhere exotic where she could be somebody of importance and where she could express herself freely and best of all start a new life with her family. She hugged John and thanked him for bringing such wonderful news to her. She was prepared to go any time. When John told his parents, his father was elated as finally he could get rid of Margaret. His mother, however, was unhappy as her favourite son and her grandchildren would be leaving. John cheered her up by saying they would come back every summer during the children's holidays to visit them.

John, the next day, went back to the chief constable and said he had spoken to the wife and his family and he was ready to make the commitment and move to Hong Kong. The chief constable told John he would let the foreign secretary know and get back to him once he got the approval. The approval came two weeks later. He was to fly to Hong Kong and be there no later than September 6th. He would be met in the airport by Inspector Tong who would show him around the house and introduce the staff to him. The next day he would go to police headquarters and meet with the Hong Kong Commissioner of Police Sir James Black who would let him know of his duties and where he would be stationed.

The flight to Hong Kong was long. The plane journey, however, was comfortable, as they were in first class courtesy of John's father who paid for their upgrade. It was the first time that Margaret had ever flown in her life, and she loved the experience. The air stewardesses were sweet and fussed over the kids, ensuring they got what they wanted. They kept filling Margaret's glass with champagne throughout the flight, and she was loving it. Margaret was excited and dying to get to Hong Kong, but firstly they had to make a refuelling stop in Bombay. They had to get out of the plane whilst that was being done. Bombay Airport was horrendous. It was very hot and there was no air conditioning. Most of the electric fans in the waiting area did not work and Margaret had to deal with the kids who were uncomfortable and tearful. The layover time was three hours before they could reboard. She was glad when they got back on the plane and by this time the kids were tired and went straight to sleep. John and Margaret soon followed the kids and slept all the way till they arrived in Hong Kong.

They arrived in Hong Kong airport at six thirty a.m. local time. They both were surprised at how clean and well-kept the airport was compared to Bombay Airport. In fact, it was even more organised and appealing than London Heathrow Airport, which they flew out from. They went through immigration and customs without any hiccups and were met by Inspector Tong who was holding up a card with their names as they exited customs. The children were now fully awake and very excited, especially Ben.

Inspector Tong was there together with the chauffeur who had parked the car in the basement car park. They got two large trolleys and carried the luggage to the car. The chauffeur introduced himself as Ah Ma. He was a small man who was no taller than five feet and was totally bald. He spoke in broken English and had a smile on his face and kept nodding when asked questions by the Woods. The drive to the house was relatively short, taking about fifteen minutes. The scenery outside was beautiful, they did not realise how mountainous and scenic Hong Kong was and were especially impressed by how clean the city was.

John and Margaret were impressed with the house which, according to Inspector Tong, was in the best residential area of Kowloon in the Kowloon Tong district. The house was large and luxurious. You had to enter it through a large metal gate, and it looked very secure with high walls. It was two storeys high with the lounge, study, dining area and kitchen on the ground floor. On the second floor were four bedrooms, two with en suites and a family bathroom. All the rooms had air conditioning as did the rest of the house. At the back of the house were located the servants' quarters. In the rear of the house, they had a back garden with a decent sized swimming pool and a play area with swings and a slide for the kids. Ben, who was seven now, and Mabel, six, both adored their new home.

They were introduced to the two helpers who both spoke perfect English. One of them was a trained cook called Ah Miu (who Margaret renamed Minnie), who would make the meals for the family and also helped in cleaning. The other named Ah Fei (who Margaret renamed Fanny), who was to look after Margaret and the kids. Margaret fell in love with the house immediately, it was much better than she had expected.

Inspector Tong, after they had settled in, went through all the things they needed to know. Tomorrow he had organised Ah Ma (who Margaret renamed Mike) to drive Margaret and the kids to visit the school where the kids were to go to and meet the teachers who would explain to her what to expect. After that Ah Miu (Minnie) would take her around the surrounding area where they lived and show them where the local supermarket was, and other places of interest that were around the area. Inspector Tong gave them the telephone numbers for the doctors and dentists and emergency help numbers. He left them his home and office numbers as well. He also explained he would be John's personal private chauffeur and drive him as he needed to business meetings and to social events. Mike was to chauffeur Margaret anywhere she needed to go and bring the kids to school and pick them up after. John would be booked all day tomorrow to meet the commissioner of police at the Kowloon city police station where John was to be stationed. The commissioner would fill John in of what was expected of him and of his duties.

John met Commissioner Sir James Black at the Kowloon city police station at nine a.m. the next day. Sir James was actually stationed in Hong Kong Island at police headquarters but specifically made the trip to Kowloon so he could show John himself where he would be working and to introduce him to the staff there and give insight to what was expected from him. They both got along brilliantly from the beginning. Sir James explained that John was to head the Kowloon City District police station which was the central station for Kowloon. His title would be Division Commander of Kowloon City District Police and Assistant Commissioner. He explained that this was probably the most challenging station in the colony as it was located close to the Walled City where the triads were. He gave John a quick history lesson about the triads, who they were, what they did and the illegal activities they were involved with. He said as long as the triads did not do anything that created disorder to the public to handle them with kid gloves. He also warned him that he should be careful of whom he sent from his station into the Walled City as they could easily disappear for good if they did not know how to handle the triads. He told John that if he had any problems with the triads to please get directly in touch with him and he would advise him how to handle them.

He was introduced to his personal assistant Mimi Lo who had been with the Kowloon District police station for seven years and had previously served two other division commanders. She was very knowledgeable with all that happened in the station and would help John adjust to his new surroundings and tasks over the next couple of weeks or till he got settled. Sir James said he planned a welcome party for him and Margaret at his home in the Peak the coming Saturday where he would have VIP guests from all walks of life attending. He wanted John to mix with people that he would be in contact with frequently and get to know them quickly. He also said that it would be a good opportunity for his wife to mingle with the other wives and make friends. He said it was most likely that the new incoming governor of Hong Kong Sir Andrew Hancock would also attend. He told John that the dress code would be formal. John felt comfortable with the meeting and was excited to start with his new career.

When John returned home, he found that dinner had been prepared by Minnie for the family. She had made them roast rack of lamb served with mint, mashed potatoes, carrots and peas. It had a lovely gravy with it and tasted fantastic. For dessert she had made apple crumble with custard the old English way and both John and Margaret were well impressed. The kids seemed happy, Ben and Mabel absolutely loved the house and the two maids Minnie and Fanny. They had had a full day and right after dinner both the children were tired. They were taken by Fanny to their room, initially they both shared one room which had two double beds, to get ready for bed. They went to sleep as soon as their heads hit the pillows.

That night in their bedroom John and Margaret compared notes on what happened that day. The room was all clean and the king-size bed turned down. All their clothes were washed and ironed and hung in the closet. Even the underwear and socks were carefully folded and placed in drawers. They were super impressed. John had not seen Margaret as happy as this for a very long time. She explained that she had spent some time in the school that morning and met with the teachers there and was pleased as most were from England. They had loads of extra activities for the kids to do after school. She had signed up Mabel to ballet and Ben to judo classes. She said the maids were brilliant and efficient and they did all the tidying up, cooking, washing and ironing. She felt like a princess once again.

John told her of his day with Sir James and told her that he had planned a welcome party for them on Saturday. John was so happy that he had made the right decision to come to Hong Kong as Margaret seemed her old self, cheerful and lively. That night Margaret, for the first time in years, dressed up in a sexy lingerie. She walked up to John as he stood in front of the bed, removed her lingerie showing off her voluptuous body and started to undress John. He grabbed her breasts hard and started kissing her nipples. As he did, she noticed he had a hard erection and went down on him after which he threw her onto the bed and entered her from behind. It was the first time in over two years that they had sex. From that day on John lost his stutter and his asthma was almost non-existent.

Inspector Tong picked them up from the house at five fifteen p.m. They had to be at Sir James's House by six fifteen for the party. As Sir James lived on Hong Kong side in the Peak they had to leave early as they would need to take the vehicular ferry from Kowloon to Hong Kong which took thirty minutes. From there they had to drive up to the Peak which would take another twenty minutes. The drive up to the Peak was spectacular. They had to go through winding narrow roads that kept going higher and higher. Inspector Tong stopped at a viewing point three quarters of the way up where they could see all of Hong Kong and Kowloon by night. The lights in the city and the harbour with the boats were some of the most beautiful views they had ever seen.

As they arrived at the commissioner's house, they had to pass a gate where two guards were stationed. They took down their details before allowing them to continue on the driveway. They drove up a slope that led to this stunning house. The house was old colonial from the Georgian era. As they entered, they were greeted by the butler who was English and introduced himself as Paul. The entrance hall was grand with a large, beautiful crystal chandelier which hung down from the high ceiling. The floors were of polished wood; the hallway had beautiful paintings of Hong Kong during the early 1900s adorning the walls. John whispered to Margaret that this was where they would be living when Sir James retired in two years and he became commissioner. She looked at him with amazement and smiled.

They were led to the main lounge area where there were already a few guests who had arrived. Sir James and his wife Niko came to meet them. They were taken aback as they did not expect Sir James's wife to be oriental. They later found out that she was Japanese but studied in Hong Kong and that she spoke perfect English. She was stunning to look at and was much younger than Sir James. They were offered champagne and James and Niko went about introducing them to guests who were already there. The first two they met were Leslie Sun and his wife Nancy. By the time dinner started they had met the governor of Hong Kong, Sir Andrew Hancock and his wife Julie, Major General Chris Wolfe of the British garrison and wife Anne, Sir William Smith of Jardine's Matheson and wife Yvonne, Sir Robert Kelps Chairman of the Royal Hong Kong Jockey Club and his wife Mary, Ajit Lalwani and his wife Maya and Raymond Ho. There were many more but those were the ones that made the greatest impressions on them.

Margaret was fascinated by how the women were all dressed. She felt intimidated as they were all obviously wearing contemporary designer gowns and were adorned with expensive jewellery, diamond earrings, watches, necklaces and bracelets. She was in contrast, dressed quite simply and felt out of place. She had a long sleeveless red gown on that was ordinary but was low cut that accentuated her breasts. The jewellery she wore was all imitation, a crystal Swarovski choker and imitation crystal earrings with her arms bare of any jewellery. If she had to live in these social circles, she would need John to buy her a whole new wardrobe and some fine jewellery, she thought.

They sat at the head table together with the hosts, along with the governor and his wife, Sir William Smith and his wife Yvonne, and Leslie and Nancy Sun. After the main course was served Sir James stood up and made a toast welcoming both John and Margaret to Hong Kong and asked the guests there to assist the newcomers to the colony with whatever they needed. After he spoke John stood up to respond, saying that both he and Margaret were excited to be in Hong Kong. That so far, they have been very impressed with the beauty of the city and the people and they hoped to be part of the Hong Kong scene for a long time to come.

After dinner they were led to the lounge for aperitif and coffee. Margaret and John sat next to Leslie and Nancy and the four immediately got along fine. Nancy asked Margret where the children were going to school and how they were getting on. When Margaret said they were attending Elvees private school in Kowloon Tong, Nancy let out a cry saying both her children, Herman and Lucy, were also in the same school as was Leslie's sister's children. Leslie stepped in and asked both of them what they were doing on their first Sunday in Hong Kong. John replied that they had nothing planned. Leslie invited them and their children to join his family for a dim sum lunch at one of the restaurants he owned, the Pearl Garden in Tsim Sha Tsui. Dim Sum, he explained to John, was a style of Chinese cuisine prepared as small bite portions of food mostly dumplings in a small steamer basket or on a small plate and was a very popular form of brunch in the colony. He said they could meet there around noon. After that they could all spend time outside his swimming pool with his family and later that day have a barbeque for dinner. He said it would be great for their kids to meet each other and bond especially since they all attended the same primary school. They both happily accepted.

From that day on John and Margaret and Leslie and Nancy became the best of friends. They would spend a lot of time together. Leslie would invite Margaret and John to his private VIP box almost every race day. They both enjoyed going to the races and mixing it up with all the top socialites of Hong Kong and meeting VIPs from all around the world. Margaret loved the atmosphere and the food and the fact there was a never-ending flow of French champagne being served. John loved watching the horses race, and having a wager which most times he would win due to Leslie giving him tips. Leslie helped John in obtaining a full membership to the Jockey Club which was the most prestigious club in Hong Kong. He invited John to his private boys' club where some of Leslie's best friends like Raymond Ho, Ajit Lalwani, and Phil Hammond, to name just a few, were in. They would meet monthly, each taking turns inviting the other members to dinner to wherever they chose but always ended up enjoying the best Cuban cigars with cognac in the best bar in Hong Kong The Havana Paradise.

Nancy and Margaret got on extremely well and became the closest of friends. They both were quite opposite in looks and character but somehow, they both connected. Nancy loved Margaret's love for life and her confidence. Margaret could get away with almost anything, her dress code, her cheeky remarks, her flirting, it did not matter as everybody loved her for being herself. She was always the belle of a party. Margaret at this time discovered Marilyn Monroe and watched every film of hers. She styled exactly like her keeping her blonde hair short up to her neck with light curls, wore only bright red lipsticks, and usually wore tight tops and short dresses. She only used Channel No.5 as her chosen perfume for that was what Marilyn wore. She pointed out to Nancy, that she actually had the same initials as Marilyn, as her maiden name was Margaret Mollers. She made everyone from then on stop calling her Margaret as she hated that name as to her it sounded old but rather to call her Maggie. Nancy on the other hand was pure class and sophistication and Maggie often said she reminded her of Audrey Hepburn.

They spent lots of time together as both were looked after housewives. Nancy brought her to all the stores she shopped in and introduced her to their owners. She took her to the jewellery stores where she purchased her cherished pieces of necklaces, earrings, bracelets and tiaras. Maggie tried keeping up with Nancy's spending habits initially but could not, as she was nowhere as wealthy as Nancy. Nancy would send her gardener Ah Loong every week to Maggie's house to ensure that her garden was well kept and to help her grow flowers. They shared all their inner secrets. Nancy told her about Lillian, when Leslie started seeing her, and how hurt she was but had to keep discreet about it. Maggie felt sorry for her but could not understand this custom of having concubines.

They confided in everything and one day Maggie admitted to Nancy that she actually had a short affair with Raymond Ho but soon broke it off. Maggie said she still had feelings for Raymond whom she found super attractive and charming unlike her husband who was boring and unattractive. From the first time Maggie met Raymond, she found him good looking, charismatic and sexy. She soon found out that he had been separated with his wife for years and was not seeing anyone seriously. She would flirt with him at the parties they attended. John, who was also very close to Raymond, was oblivious to it. Maggie told Nancy how the affair all started. It was at the governor's ball with Raymond being seated next to her. During dinner she would flirt and make sexual gestures which seemingly interested Raymond. When the speeches started the lights were dimmed and the spotlight focussed on the governor giving his speech. Maggie took this opportunity to put her hand under the table caressing Raymond's penis feeling his hardness.

He obviously was aroused and whispered to her to follow him discreetly to the men's room. He left the table and she followed a minute later. Everybody was basically engrossed in the speech the governor was giving. In the bathroom Raymond pushed her into one of the cubicles, locked the door, pulled up her dress and entered her. He was rough and grabbed her hair tightly whilst pushing himself hard and deep into her; she loved it. They were only at it for five minutes and they then left the men's room with Maggie heading to the women's restroom where she freshened up before re-entering the party. From that day on Raymond would call her and they met many times in various hotel rooms that Raymond would organise. However, after a while she thought it was better they stopped seeing each other, before they were found out which could cause a scandal. Nancy had suspected something was happening between Maggie and Raymond for a while, but she was shocked that they actually slept together.

John did keep up with what was happening with his parents and brothers back home, calling religiously every two weeks and speaking to them and finding out the latest news. He made sure his children spoke to their grandparents. Maggie was a bit standoffish still with them and that bugged John, but he let it be. The parents would always ask when they would visit them in the U.K. He did miss his parents and brothers and wanted to visit, but Maggie was happy in Hong Kong and had no desire whatsoever to visit the U.K, not even to meet up with her aging dad.

John and Maggie, in their first five years of living in Hong Kong, did not go back to the U.K. In fact, the family went on holidays around Asia. They visited the Philippines, Thailand, Malaysia, Singapore and on one of their holidays took a cruise to Japan joining Leslie and Nancy and their children. To them that was the best trip ever and in later years would plan many summer holidays away together. They finally visited the U.K. in the summer of 1956. They had to go as John was awarded a C.B.E. (Commander of the British Empire) and went to receive it from the Queen at Buckingham Palace, after which they spent two weeks with his parents. Ben was then twelve and Mabel eleven and both did not feel any attachment with their grandparents. John's parents had aged so much that John himself hardly recognised them. In 1959 John's father passed away after a long sickness. They both attended the funeral without their children as they were in the middle of their school term.

At this time Hong Kong was in a state of rapid growth and change. There were needs by the growing population that the government just could not handle. This provided an environment for the unscrupulous. Many people had to take the "back door" route simply to earn a living, and secure other basic services. "Tea Money", a bribe used to facilitate any business dealings became familiar and accepted by most in Hong Kong as an essential way of life. Corruption was particularly serious in the police force. Corrupt police officers offered protection to vice, gambling and drug activities. The government seemed at this time powerless to deal with it.

John, unfortunately, got involved in this corrupt circle, which was rampant from the policeman in the block to the higher-level rank officers. The only difference was the pay-outs' sizes with most of the "Tea Money" going to officers of higher ranking. It all happened so quickly and unexpectedly with John and after the first bribe it all became easy and frequent.

He was into the sixth month as deputy commander of the Kowloon City police station that he got his first bribe. It was customary for him, as part of his remit, to visit the Walled City to do a "check" with the inspector who was in charge of policing that district. The inspector in charge was Chief Inspector Lee who had been with the station for over ten years and who was well respected by all around the area. He took John inside the Walled City for the very first time. You could not drive around the city and the only way to go around was to walk as the roads were narrow and crammed. They were more like alleyways with all sorts of stalls and shops lining both sides. The Walled City was part of Hong Kong and therefore supposedly British, but the Chinese nationalists claimed it as belonging to them.

Inside the Walled City dwelled thirty-five thousand people living in a tiny land space of 2.7 hectares of which there were over two thousand squatters. After a failed attempt to drive them out in 1949 the British adapted a hands-off policy in most matters concerning the Walled City. To keep crime curtailed there they had to discuss with the "Mayor of the Walled City" through negotiations.

As John walked along the tight paths, he noticed prostitutes lining up on one area of a street which later he found out was the red-light area. The city was truly intimidating with drug addicts squatted under stairs getting high, there were strip show venues with neon lights flashing. It was a complex place, frightening but things inexplicably seemed to work. He was baffled that all this existed so close to where he operated, and nothing was done about it. When he asked Inspector Lee about it, he was told that this was "the balance" and as long as the triads did not cause any major problems outside the city, it was policy which came from the very top to let things remain. John was surprised and confused on how the British government would just allow this to transpire in their colony.

As they were about to depart Inspector Lee said they had to visit the "Mayor of the Walled City" out of respect before leaving as that was traditional. Inspector Lee took him to a shanty looking building where on the second floor they met up with Mayor Jing who made tea and offered them some Chinese snacks. He made John sit opposite him at his dining table and asked how he was getting along with his job and whether his family were settled in. He seemed like a very honest and humble man. He was small in stature but quite well built. John guessed him to be around fifty years old. John put it to him bluntly, that he was surprised just walking around, to see so many illicit things happening all around the city, and should not the mayor do something about it being its leader? Mayor Jing looked at him and started laughing. "You are new, and you will understand soon. As you can see since you have been here the last six months there have not been any serious crimes reported. This is the way it works, please understand."

As John was about to leave the mayor pulled out a black combination leather briefcase with the initials J.W. embossed in gold which he took from under the table and handed over to him. "This is a small gift from all of us at the Walled City as a welcome gift to you on your first visit." John tried to refuse but Inspector Lee stopped him and pulled him aside saying doing so was to be disrespectful to the mayor as he would lose face. "The combination is 148 148 which, for us Chinese, is a very lucky number," said the mayor as he handed him the case. John hesitantly took it and thanked him for it. The mayor bowed and led them to the door.

When John got back to the office, he unlocked the case the mayor provided him and was shocked to find HK$200,000 in cash inside. He did not know what to do and decided, just to be safe to call Sir James and tell him about what had transpired with his meeting with Mayor Jing and the money. He was even more shocked when Sir James said to him that as it was a gift from someone important to the police in keeping the peace and for him to just accept it and keep quiet about it. It would be the first of many such bribes that John would receive. That night when he got home, he told Maggie about what happened. He thought she would be worried but quite the opposite: she was delighted. She told him she had been eyeing a diamond necklace for the last two weeks which cost HK$57,500 and was saving up to buy it one day but with this windfall she could buy it immediately.

She gave him a deep kiss and said, "I am loving both you and Hong Kong more day by day!"

Just then there was a knock on the door which brought John back to where he was. "Enter," said John. Angela opened the door. "Inspector Lee is outside waiting to see you. Shall I send him in now?" asked Angela. "Also, do you need a refill on your coffee?"

"No to the coffee and yes please send Inspector Lee straight in and please hold all calls. I do not want to be disturbed at all whilst I am with Inspector Lee," he replied. She nodded and left the room.

"Good morning, Sir," said Inspector Lee as he walked into the room, "I apologise for being so late for the meeting, but the coroner took much longer than I anticipated."

"Well, what were the results?" asked John.

John had been worrying all night from the moment that Inspector Lee called him. It seemed that two U.S. naval officers were found dead in an alleyway in Wanchai near the Suzy Wong bar. These officers were on an R&R (Rest & Recreation) stopover in Hong Kong. All U.S. military personnel serving in Vietnam or Korea during hostilities there were eligible for one R&R during their tour of duty. The duration of the R&R was five days leave to R&R destinations, like Bangkok, Hong Kong, Kuala Lumpur, Penang, Manila, Seoul, Singapore, Taipei and Tokyo. The "official policy" of the United States Department of

Defence was to suppress prostitution. Prostitution, however, was relied upon by the U.S. military to combat the battlefield trauma many faced. Hong Kong was one of the most popular destinations as you could buy all kinds of things in Hong Kong, like expensive cameras, top-of-the-line Akai tape decks, Rolex and Seiko watches, all for one-third of the stateside price. Female companionship was available, but not per contract. You paid the girl, not the bar, although the owners of the bars were paid a small commission.

It was one of the hostesses working at the Suzy Wong bar who found the bodies and called the police. When Inspector Lee got to the crime site at around two a.m. the hostess who reported the crime was not to be found. He discovered the two officers with their throats cut and their hearts removed from their bodies. It was a gruesome sight: the bodies lying on the concrete floor bleeding copiously. There were white scarves on both the victims' heads with a red sun printed on it. It was obviously the work of the Black Ninjas.

"Here is the coroner's report," said Inspector Lee. "It seems they both had their throats cut with a sharp knife and then had their hearts removed. The hearts were obviously taken away as they were nowhere near the crime scene as we searched the area thoroughly. The time of death was an hour before the hostess called in around one a.m. It was a quiet night being Sunday and I questioned everybody who were still in the club, but nobody seemed to have witnessed the incident. They were U.S. Navy officers for sure as they had their I.D. bracelets on, we found their driver licenses in their wallets although all cash and other valuables were taken. From all accounts it must be the Black Ninjas, but we haven't had any incident since 1956 when we captured their leader Agana San and had him hung thus ending the Black Ninja threat. It all seems very strange."

He then went on to add, "Before I went to the coroner, I went to see Major Jing at the Walled City as I do monthly and asked if he knew anything about the crime. He emphasised that it was nothing to do with the triads. He then handed me your briefcase and asked me to pass it to you. Here it is."

"Yes, it seems very strange," answered John as he received the briefcase from Inspector Lee. "It may be a copycat type incident, or it may be one of the triads stirring up trouble and trying to upset the balance." John was extremely worried as this incident could cause an international political situation, especially if the United States government started putting pressure on the British forcing them to come down hard on the triads. This would instigate a war between the triads and law enforcement that nobody really wanted. More worrying for him personally was that this could initiate a whole look into the police force and corruption which could lead to him being discovered. He had to move fast and find the perpetrators and close this case down really quick.

"OK Inspector Lee this is what I need you to do. Find the hostess who reported the crime as she may have seen more that she reported and bring her back here for questioning. Also speak to all the bars around where the incident took place and question the staff there. See if they had seen these two officers that evening and if they saw anything unusual, if so bring them down here for questioning. Start with the Suzy Wong bar as that was the most popular bar where most of the R&R spent their time in. Also get in touch with Mama Wendy as she may have heard something as she knows everything that happens in the bars. Whilst you make your queries please try and keep it as quiet as possible as we do not want the media to report on this just yet, anyway not until I have spoken to the governor and the U.S. ambassador first. Understand?"

"Yes sir, I understand fully," replied Inspector Lee. "I will keep you in touch if I learn anything." Seeing the anxiety on John's face, Inspector Lee left.

John opened up the briefcase that Inspector Lee handed him and, as usual at this time of the month, it was filled with cash to the tune of HK$200,000. He had a large safe under his table to which only he knew the combination. He opened it up and put the cash together with the rest of the money that was there. In the safe were also U.S. government bonds that he had bought to the value of one million HK$ and cash of two million. Over the last four years he had received bribes of over HK$8,000,000. Some of it he had given to Maggie to spend which she did mostly on jewellery and clothes, and most which he had put into a Swiss bank account which Raymond Ho helped him to set up. He figured he'd better move the two million in cash which was in the safe to the Swiss account as soon as possible. He locked the safe and then buzzed Angela to come to his office.

"Angela, I need you, after I speak to my wife, to put in a call to the governor. Also locate both Leslie Sun and Raymond Ho and arrange for them to meet me at the Havana Paradise Club at five p.m. sharp and not to be late. Call the Havana Paradise and book a VIP room from five p.m. onwards."

Angela nodded and left the office. He then called Maggie and informed her not to wait for dinner as he had to deal with urgent matters. She was concerned and asked what the problem was, he explained it was too long to go through it now as he was expecting to speak to the governor soon, but that he would let her in all that happened when he returned home later that evening.

John dreaded what he had to do next: speak to both the governor and the U.S. ambassador.

Angela buzzed the intercom. "I have the Governor on the phone, can I pass him on to you now?"

John picked up his phone.

Chapter 6
Boom

Havana Paradise Cigar Bar
Mandarin Hotel Second Floor, 5 Connaught Road, Hong Kong
Monday, July 15th, 1960, five p.m.

It was raining heavily as John entered the hotel. The concierge greeted him and took his raincoat and umbrella and handed him back a reclaim ticket.

"Good evening, Sir John," greeted the concierge, "Mr Ho has already arrived and is in the bar on the second floor."

John looked at his watch; it was exactly five p.m. "Has Doctor Leslie Sun arrived?" he asked.

"No, not yet. I will let him know as soon as he comes that both of you are at the Havana Paradise Bar," he replied.

The Havana Paradise Cigar Bar was an exclusive all men's private club for the very rich and famous who could go there and enjoy a cigar and cognac while catching up with business deals. Fitted with a top-notch ventilation system and fantastically comfortable leather furnishings, one would have a great cigar smoking experience here. It had a common area in front with seating up to eighty guests for dinner or drinks and with a stage where a five-piece jazz band would play nightly from six p.m. till ten p.m. In the back of the bar were six private rooms, varying in size, holding from four to twelve people. The club employed a strict dress code which required one to wear a suit and a tie in order to enter. Membership was by invitation only and selected by the owners of the club who were two brothers from Portugal, Christiano and Silvio Rodrigues. It was believed that they were financed by the tycoon Raymond Ho who also had a small share in the business. The Havana Paradise was a picture of elegance and class located at the heart of the Central District.

The manager, a Mr Sonny Chaves, greeted John and led him to the private room where Raymond was waiting. As he entered, he noticed that Raymond was on the phone having a conversation in Chinese. He waved John to sit down whilst continuing his conversation. Sonny asked John what he would like to drink and if he had a special request for what cigar he would like. John smiled and replied that he would have the same as what Raymond was having, both drink and cigar.

"Very well," replied Sonny. "Raymond is smoking a Cohiba Robustos and having a Hennessey X.O. cognac. Is that OK with you?" John nodded and smiled and thought to himself, what else, as Raymond would always choose the best available. John had a great relationship with Raymond and relied on him for information especially with what was happening with the triads. He also trusted him to launder the bribe money he had. Raymond had special connections with Swiss banks where the money would be safe from investigations as the banks there were sworn to secrecy and would not reveal information on their customers. The Swiss law protected the banks and thus many monies that were laundered worldwide were hidden in Swiss bank accounts.

Raymond hung up the phone, putting it back on its cradle, and looked up at John with a smile. "Good evening. It must have been one hell of a day with all that's been happening. You must give us the full details as soon as Leslie gets in. I have just been in a call with a few of my friends who have been snooping around to see what they could come up with regarding the incident with the two U.S. naval officers. I think we may have some sort of a lead on who were involved. Anyway, let's wait till Les arrives and then we can all discuss this together. Meanwhile, cheers mate, it has been a while since we last met. Hope all's well with the family."

John lifted his crystal cut glass and clinked it with Raymond's, "Cheers Ray, the family is all good, however I do need a favour, I need to send some more money to the Swiss account that you set up for me. Obviously, it has to go through you as I can't show this income has come from me. I have about HK$2,000,000 that needs to go there, is that OK?" asked John.

It was a good time for John to ask Ray as they were alone, and Leslie had not yet arrived. Leslie had no idea that John was taking bribes and that Raymond was helping him to launder the money. They kept all their illicit deals away from Leslie as he was so close to the government.

"But of course, absolutely no problem, get it over any time this week before Friday and I will have it done immediately. Once done you can check that it has been completed by faxing the account that I gave you with the authentication code or by calling Credit Suisse Bank in Zurich directly with that information. The money will take about three working days to clear. I think it is smart to get the money out of here especially now with what is happening," replied Ray and continued, "I too need a favour back from you in return. I need to have this bill of lading signed off for a ship that has just arrived into port showing that the cargo has been inspected and is free to be released. It is a special favour to the 14K, and you will get HK$500,000 for that which I will transfer to the Swiss account together with the HK$2,000,000. Is that fine?"

John had done "favours" like this a few times now and could not refuse especially as Ray had helped him with the laundering of his cash over the years. There was now about eight million in his Swiss Bank account, not accounting for what Ray would be putting in this week. Quite a sum. None of John's other friends knew about this and John was very careful not to show off his newfound wealth in public. He had told Maggie to be careful when spending the extra money that he gave her and not to flagrantly show off. She understood and was quite good but of course occasionally went on a shopping binge with Nancy buying the latest fashion and jewellery. Ray had been Godsent as John had no way of how to hide away the money, until one day in the races when John had won a bit of money, he jokingly asked Ray if he should put it away into a Swiss bank for him for a rainy day. Ray replied, that if he ever needed any money to be hidden away, let him know. He was taken aback with that but soon found that Ray had helped many people in laundering "black money", charging a small commission for this.

He and Maggie had discussed the money and what to do with it. They had been to Australia for holidays and loved the country. They both especially loved Melbourne and discussed that when it was the time for John to retire and when the kids were settled to maybe buy a house there. Neither wanted to move back to England as Maggie's father had already passed away and John's mother had Alzheimer's. Both John and Maggie did not get along with either of John's brothers and their wives and did not want to return to the U.K. They both no longer had any friends there either and had more in Asia. They both loved their lifestyle out of the U.K. and cherished living in this part of the world.

Leslie walked into the room, apologising for being late. He explained he had an international call that took longer than he expected and thus the delay. Raymond looked at his watch, it was now five thirty p.m. He pressed the call button on the table and Sonny walked in and asked, "Good evening, Doctor Sun, can I get you something to drink? I will bring in the humidor so you can choose the cigar you want."

"I will have a Yamazaki eighteen-year-old single malt whisky please," replied Leslie. "And I will have a Cohiba Robustos like the boys. Thank you." Leslie had started with experimenting with the Japanese whiskies and found them surprisingly very good although very expensive. He loved the rich texture, palpable complexity and its unmistakable character. He preferred whisky to cognacs and found that the Yamazaki went well with the Cohiba that he smoked. "Cheers guys, it's nice to meet up after such a long while, although may I say not under such good circumstances. John, you must tell us in detail the latest and the reaction from the governor and the U.S. ambassador. All hell must have broken loose."

John replied, "Yes, it is bad but so far we have been lucky that the media are still not aware of the incident. I spoke to the governor and not the ambassador directly. The governor was stunned, as he believed that we stopped the threat from the Black Ninjas in 1956 when we executed their leader Agana. For more than four years now we have had no killings of any expat or anyone in military and now all of a sudden from nowhere, this? The signs are all there of what the Black Ninjas do to a victim. We were assured by Central Intelligence in 1956 that the Black Ninjas, after the death of Agana, had all dispersed and the gang no longer existed. It's all a bit strange. The governor asked if I could find out within forty-eight hours who were involved before he went to the press as he could not hold this news longer than that and had to go public with it. Of course, firstly he would need to convince the U.S. ambassador to do the same and keep it quiet for forty-eight hours before making it public. The governor said it was the right protocol that he called the U.S. ambassador instead of me. I agreed and left him to do that. He called me back within an hour after he had spoken to the ambassador, saying after long negotiations, he finally convinced him to go along with his decision. The ambassador suggested, however, after the forty-eight hours passed that they should have a joint news conference to make the announcement. Think I really do need you guys to help again like in 1956. We really need to nip this in the bud and act fast to find the culprits and bring them to justice otherwise it will affect every one of us."

Leslie and Ray concurred with John. Raymond was concerned that if the British government was pressured by the U.S. government to take decisive actions this would force the British government to call out the army to deal with the triads. The government knew that they could not depend solely on the police because they lacked the muscle to deal with the triads and secondly many were corrupt, taking bribes from the triads. This was common knowledge. If the army was sent into the Walled City to get rid of the triads it could expose Raymond's dealings with the 14K, and he could potentially lose everything he had built up. For Leslie he was more worried that it would bring chaos once again to the colony and would cause protests and rioting like in 1956 and affect the economic growth of Hong Kong which would make China's claim on the colony more valid.

Leslie's mind went back to 1956. The riots and the disorders of '56 caused so much pain and deaths to so many. That was the year his father passed away due to a massive heart attack soon after the rioting had broken out. Those were bad times and that was the time the Warriors of the Sun came together again after a long time under Leslie to help the government deal with the problem. Leslie's dad, who was known as Taipan Sun, went on to create a very successful business in Hong Kong.

The company he set up, The Sun Corp HK Ltd., started investing in properties, mainly acquiring land in the New Territories which the government was offering to developers at ridiculously low prices prior to the war. In time, with the influx of refugees after the war, and the population growing rapidly, the lands that Taipan Sun bought made him a huge fortune. He invested wisely in electricity and won the government's bid for privatising the electric companies, one for Hong Kong Island and the second for Kowloon and the New Territories. He won the bid for the Kowloon and New Territories as sole electric supplier and formed the China Light and Power Co. The only other electric company in the colony was the HK Electric Co. owned by the Poons which supplied electricity to Hong Kong Island. As exports started to grow in the colony he invested in shipping and owned one of the largest commercial shipping fleets in Asia. He also continued acting as adviser to the British government which was passed down from his forefathers. He gave counsel and helped the British to keep peace with China advising them on how to handle affairs in Hong Kong.

Leslie's father never got along with his brother and they both went their own ways when they moved to Hong Kong from Canton in the early 1900s. His brother Sun Yee On however went in a different direction from his brother, to the dark side and set up the Sun Yee On triad. At that time Sun Yee On was second in power to the 14K which was the more famous known gang. Sun Yee On himself was getting old and in 1957 passed the reins of the Sun Yee On triad to his only surviving son Herbert Sun. He had lost two of his other sons in the 1956 riots. One who was killed in a bombing and the other who was arrested by the authorities and sentenced to hang. The person who passed down the sentencing was Dr Leslie Sun. Ever since that day Herbert Sun the eldest living son of Sun Yee On had vowed to one day take revenge for his brother's death and destroy his cousin Leslie. Herbert was more aggressive than his father was and grew the Sun Yee On gang rapidly by aligning it with other smaller triads and moving into areas once controlled by the 14K. The Sun Yee On grew rapidly under Herbert and these days was considered the stronger of the two gangs with more members.

The 1956 riots were a dilemma to the British. They knew they had to quell the riots quickly but had to be careful not to antagonise China. The worse thing was that if China used the riots as an excuse that innocent people were dying and thus make it the excuse to invade Hong

Kong. They also could not side with the communists as that would enrage the nationalists and the triads who would rebel against the British. There were also the Black Ninjas to deal with who were also in the mix of causing the rioting.

The government called in Leslie to see if he could come up with a plan that could help solve the problem as quickly as possible. They asked John Woods who was assistant commissioner of police at that time to work with Leslie but to not make it publicly known that Leslie was involved. The governor did not trust to let the police handle this delicate part of the operation in fear that this could be leaked out to the perpetrators. Leslie realised they would, however, need the help of the 14K to succeed.

He turned to Raymond Ho for this. Raymond was their connection to Ponytail as he was the only one who knew him personally. It was a plan that had to be kept secret and to ensure that not any one party was treated unfairly. It was decided to form a group of people skilled in combat under Leslie to do the fight, but they needed to stay anonymous. Thus, the Warriors of the Sun was recreated. It consisted of eighteen members of Leslie's Kung Fu group. Leslie's colleagues from his Kung Fu group included his best friend Ajit and his brother Mohan. They were all sworn to secrecy. The Warriors of the Sun met at Leslie's house every Monday and Fridays during the rioting to plan on how to infiltrate and get to the gang leaders. They believed if the gang leaders were captured and punished that would put a stop to the rioting.

Ponytail finally agreed to help the Warriors of the Sun, knowing that if he did not, and the rioting continued, he risked the British coming down hard and destroying the Walled City by sending in the military to get rid of all the triads operating there. After the third week of rioting the breakthrough came. Ponytail told Raymond that through his spy network he learned that the Sun Yee On and the Black Ninjas were having a meeting to discuss what their next steps were to further exacerbate the rioting the coming Friday. The meeting was to be held at the Black Ninjas' headquarters which were located in Sai Wan on the Kowloon side. That was the best time to hit them and capture their leaders.

That evening Leslie went to his study where he kept his nunchakus and his Feng Shui bracelet that his father had given him. He carried the nunchakus in a waist holder bag, put on his bracelet and together with the Warriors of the Sun raided the meeting being held at the Black Ninjas' headquarters. Although it was heavily fortified, they were able to break through relatively easily as they were well equipped and had the element of surprise with them. They rushed in with grenades which they threw at the gathering causing a large number of members to disperse. However, most of the gang leaders were captured. Leslie was superb with his nunchakus, killing over twenty people by himself. The Warriors of the Sun suffered no loss. Amongst those captured were Agana, "the Butcher of Osaka" leader of the Black Ninjas and the youngest son of Sun Yee On, Wilbert.

John and his police station took all the credit for the arrests and John was celebrated as the person who had planned the raid that captured Agana, "the Butcher of Osaka", and Wilbert Sun. He became a national hero. Later that year he was awarded the prestigious title of C.B.E. from Queen Elizabeth for his effort in putting down the riots. There was no mention of the Warriors of the Sun ever being involved, this was kept secret to just the few who were involved.

The police had already captured Snakehead who was the deputy Mountain Master of the 14K and the first cousin of Ponytail earlier that week whilst he was caught rioting. Raymond had appealed to Leslie to release him as he was pushed by Ponytail to do so, but Leslie refused, saying he needed to be fair, that Snakehead had broken the law and there was no justification of him rioting while the city was in curfew. Ponytail had thought that by exposing the meeting to Leslie of the Black Ninjas and the Sun Yee On he could convince him to release his cousin Snakehead but that was not the case.

They now had enough of the leaders to make a show to other perpetrators. Many of the gang were tried and given long term jail sentences. Snakehead, Wilbert Sun, and Agana, together with a high-level pro-communist supporter, were sentenced to death by hanging. The group of judges that handed out the sentencings were led by Leslie Sun. Soon after the arrests and trials, all rioting stopped, and Hong Kong went back to being "normal". The Warriors of the Sun continued to exist after the riots. They would meet every Monday evening at

Leslie's house to discuss problems arising in the colony and work together to quash out any of the smaller gangs who caused crimes especially in and around the Walled City as the police avoided that area.

Raymond brought Leslie back from his thoughts to the meeting at the bar. "I heard from the grapevine that the people who did this crime is a small group from the original Black Ninjas run by Ken Hashimoto. Apparently when Agana was executed the leadership was in turmoil but a new group was formed led by a Yakuza member, Ken Hashimoto and they went under the name of the New Black Ninjas. They moved into a small location in the Shum Shui Po district. Apparently, their main illicit dealings now were the selling of arms which they got from Japan from the paramilitaries after the war and selling it off to the Vietcong and the North Korean communists to fight against the Americans who were defending South Vietnam and South Korea. They made huge profits as there was no competition in this form of illegal activity from the other triads. They were different from the old Black Ninjas that they stayed away from attacking Gwai Los. According to Raymond's sources a small breakaway faction of them however were responsible for the attack on the US naval officers.

"We would need to verify this before taking action," replied Leslie. "The worst thing is if we hit the wrong party and if later, another incident occurred, like the one with the naval officers, things could get worse."

"I got it from a reliable source," replied Raymond. "A member from the 14K had infiltrated the New Black Ninjas to spy on what they were up to and reported this directly to Ponytail. Ponytail told me this himself and I have no reason to doubt his source. In fact, if you want, we can meet this person later tonight as he has agreed to meet up with us tonight. His name is Wilson Ma and I have asked him to meet us at the Sing Song Club at around nine thirty p.m. Can you guys make it?"

John said it was essential they did, and he would call home and let Maggie know he would be late coming home that night. Leslie had already told Nancy he would stay up late. He was actually planning to surprise Lillian that night after meeting with John and Ray, but this was more important at the moment. He could always go to Lillian's after the meeting.

Ray looked at his watch, it was seven fifteen p.m. "We still have time before the meeting, shall we get something to eat?" They all nodded, and he buzzed the button and Sonny walked in. "Get us the menus," said Ray. "We will be eating here tonight."

"Yes," replied Sonny and left the room. Leslie asked Ray where the owners Christiano and Silvio were tonight as they were usually there, especially when Ray was around.

"They are both in Macau working on the new branch of the Havana Bar which will be one of the bars in my new hotel, the Hotel Faroe," replied Raymond. He was proud of this project which he had been working on for over four years. This would be the crowning part of his career and a landmark in Asia. He was building a five-star eighteen hundred room hotel whereby every room was a suite. It was going to be total pizzazz with the top acts in the world performing in a theatre that could seat over fifteen hundred people. It would have fifty thousand square feet where one could gamble, making it the largest and most modern casino in the world rivalling even the Sands Hotel and Casino in Las Vegas. It would have sixteen restaurants serving all types of cuisine and eight bars with two nightclubs. There would be over two hundred luxury shops within the hotel as well. It would rival most hotels in Las Vegas and to ensure that he had the top management team possible he hired as managing director, Joseph Moore, the person who ran the Golden Nugget in Vegas, making it a worldwide success. He was hoping to have Hotel Faroe opened by Christmas 1960 and so far, it was ahead of schedule.

He had booked Paul Anka to perform in the opening week from December 30th, 1960 to January 6th, 1961 followed up by Marilyn Monroe for two weeks after. Raymond had been a huge fan of Paul Anka and loved all his songs like "Diana", "Put your head on my shoulder" and "Puppy Love". He had to pay a high price for Marilyn Monroe to perform, plus she had stipulations in her contract. Firstly, he had to put a 20% deposit non-refundable in advance for the booking. Another clause was that if John F. Kennedy the democratic candidate running for president of the U.S.A. in the elections that November, was elected she would only do a week stint in Macau instead of two as she had promised John Kennedy that she would perform in his inauguration which would be around the third week of January 1961 if he won. Even despite this he booked Monroe because Maggie pushed him to do so saying she would come to Macau for the full time Marilyn was performing there and would stay in the hotel by herself without John or the kids and maybe she and Ray could pick things up then.

Ray liked Maggie a lot. It had been a while since any woman had attracted him like she did. He found her so different from the oriental women he had dated. She was frivolous, flirty and outrageous but that was what attracted him the most. He knew nothing could come out of it, but he kept yearning for her. They had an affair that lasted for a few months but recently Maggie ended it worrying that people may find out. He knew she still had feelings for him and hoped one day it may all still work out and that they could be together. He would call her every weekday in the mornings around ten a.m. knowing that her husband would be at work and the kids at school. They would not talk about anything serious, just silly little things; they were like two little kids who had found love for the very first time. John was totally unaware of the situation. Ray found this strange as Maggie was always by his side at parties flirting and chatting away with him.

Maggie had told Ray that she had told Nancy Sun about their affair but for him not to worry as Nancy would tell no one, not even Leslie. He liked Nancy and found her very classy. He was surprised that Leslie had fallen in love with Lillian. He knew Lillian well as she worked at his nightclub, the Sing Sing Bar. He actually was the first man to have sex with Lillian since she was raped by General Ming. He felt sorry for her going through what she did. Yes, she was beautiful and very sexy but for him Nancy was far more attractive and refined. It was common knowledge in the social circles about Leslie's affair with Lillian, as Leslie was quite open about it and made it official by making her his concubine. Although feeling sorry for Nancy he knew Leslie truly loved Lillian and looked after her. He appreciated that she too sincerely loved Leslie. Mama Wendy told him that Lillian had fallen head over heels with him and she was the happiest she had ever been. In a way Raymond was happy for Lillian as she had suffered so much in the past and deserved something good in her life.

Sonny returned with the menus. "I have reserved a table for you outside in the main area at the back of the room so it's away from the stage and band so the music will not be disturbing. As soon as you are ready to order buzz me and I will take the orders. Once the meal is ready to be served, I will come in and get you. I have also brought you the wine list if you are ready to order that?"

Raymond looked at him and said, "Just wait here, Sonny, we are in a hurry and need to order right away. For the wine we will have the Chateau Margaux '55. Boys do you know what you want? I will have the Oysters Kilpatrick to start followed by a 12-oz Rib-Eye steak as the main. Please have my steak done rare."

John said he would have the same as Ray except he wanted his steak well done whilst Les ordered escargots as a starter followed by Lobster Thermidor as the main.

The meal came quickly, and they were finished by eight fifteen p.m. It was a ten-minute walk to the Sing Song from the Havana, and they all decided it was better to walk as it had stopped raining. When they arrived at the Sing Song Club it was eight thirty p.m. and the club had just opened. They were greeted by the general manager there Frankie Chu. "Good evening, Boss," said Frankie, talking directly to Raymond. "I have your VIP room ready; you are a bit early as the club has just opened but not to worry. Your friend Mr Wilson Ma that you were expecting has not yet arrived. I will let Mama Mimi that know you are here, and she will join you in the room shortly." Frankie led them to the VIP room and left.

The Sing Song Club was the sister club to the larger Sing Sing Club in Kowloon which was also run by Mama Wendy. It was also supposedly equally owned by Raymond Ho and Mama Wendy and managed by Mama Mimi. The club, although much smaller that the Sing Sing, was decorated in a very similar way. It had all the glitz that its sister club had but the main area was much smaller with seventy tables that sat up to two hundred and fifty people and had a stage with a five-piece band playing the latest pop music. The dance floor could hold two hundred people, the décor, like the Sing Sing, ranged from an imitation of Versailles with a generous portion of glitz. The club was on two floors, the main entertainment area and VIP rooms being on the ground floor whilst the second floor was where the strip shows were performed. Also, on the second floor was a private area where customers could ask for a lap dance.

Mama Mimi knocked on the door of the VIP room and entered. She smiled and greeted them and sat down next to Ray. On the table in front of them were laid out four crystal glasses, an ice bucket, a bottle of Hennessy X.O cognac and a bottle of Yamazaki Malt Whisky. There was also a large plate of tropical fruits with plates and cocktail knives. "Is there anything else you need as far as the drinks already laid out?" asked Mama Mimi.

"No, I think we are good. How are things with you Mimi? It has been some time since I have been to the Sing Song. I usually entertain down at the Sing Sing in Kowloon as you know. How is business going and is everything OK?"

"Yes, boss all is good although the last couple of weeks have been a little slow but that is understandable this time of the year. Most of our customers are away on their summer holidays with their families. We are still, however, up from last year's numbers by 6%. Do you want me to bring in some hostesses to sit with you or will you wait until your friend Mr Ma shows up?"

"It is the first time we are meeting Wilson Ma as none of us really know him however he has been introduced by an important friend and can be useful to us so please ensure you give him the special VIP treatment. I think we are OK so far but if Liza Wong is around, I do not mind her joining us for a while anyway till Mr Ma shows up," replied Ray.

"Yes of course. I think I saw her around earlier I will send her in right away. Is there anything else I can do in the meantime?"

"No," replied Raymond. "That's all. Thank you." Raymond knew that John had been seeing a lot of Liza Wong since he first introduced him to her two years ago just before he got promoted to commissioner of police. In fact, she was John's secret mistress. Ray was happy with their affair as it served his purpose well. Through Mama Mimi he asked that Liza treat John special. He was cunning with this as it served him two purposes. One that he could find out what was happening with the police through her and secondly, he would have something over John that he could use if needed by letting Maggie know of the affair.

Raymond was surprised that John was attracted to Liza as she was nowhere as stunning as Maggie, she was flat chested and was short with long black silky hair. She was much younger than John and had just turned nineteen. Her personality, unlike Maggie's, was dull and she could not carry on a decent conversation. John, after being promoted to commissioner, never visited the club to see Liza, he would arrange to meet her privately at the Astor Hotel, one of Raymond's smaller hotels. He arranged that John use a special entrance to the hotel only accessible by a special key that only Raymond, John and Liza had. This led directly to a suite whereby he would bypass any of the staff and guests staying at the hotel. As demanded by Raymond, Liza would always refuse money from John when he offered to pay her and told him that she was doing this for love and not for money. That was furthest from the truth as Raymond paid her handsomely, every time she spent an evening with John. Neither knew that the room where they met was bugged, and everything said was recorded and kept by Raymond.

Liza entered the VIP room together with Mimi. Liza greeted them all and headed straight to John sitting down beside him. Mimi meanwhile went and sat next to Raymond. She whispered to him, "Shall I get a hostess for Doctor Sun?"

"No", replied Ray as he knew Les would be upset with that as he was not interested in anyone else except Lillian. Ray had tried many a time before to set him up with a hostess but got reprimanded for that. Leslie looked at his watch, it was nine thirty p.m. and Wilson Ma had not yet shown up. Unlike Raymond he was unsure that he would show and was suspicious of the fact that Mr Ma was willing to meet them so readily and help them to capture the culprits, all this seemed a little strange. He thought he would wait with the boys till ten p.m. at the latest and if Mr Ma did not show he would make an excuse to leave, at least then he could spend a few hours with Lillian, whom he was missing, before heading home.

9.50 p.m. and Wilson Ma had not shown up. The boys decided to give it half an hour more and if he did not show they would leave and go their own ways. Leslie looked around the room and saw Ray in a heavy conversation with Mama Mimi whilst John had a couple of cushions over his lap and he could see Liza's hand underneath and probably fondling his penis. They were kissing and getting very turned on. Les stood up and said he was going to the men's room which was located around ten feet from the VIP room towards the entrance. He said he would also call Lillian to check on her and would be back after he had spoken to her. He went to call Lillian first but there was no answer. He tried a couple of times and still no one picked up the phone. He thought that very strange as he had spoken to her earlier that day and she said she was staying home tonight and would wait for his call. He knew Lillian never went to bed till at least after midnight. He felt concerned and thought, after this I will go and check on Lillian.

As he finished with the phone, he headed towards the lavatory passing a man dressed in a black suit carrying a large briefcase heading toward the VIP rooms. That's weird, thought Les, why someone would carry a briefcase whilst in the club when he could have it checked in with the concierge instead of lugging it around. He thought little more of it as he was more concerned about Lillian not answering her phone. As he was heading back to the VIP room after the lavatory, he noticed that the black briefcase the man he saw earlier carrying was just outside the VIP room where his friends were. Ray was walking towards him heading for the men's room when he shouted at Ray to run and head for the entrance. He acted quickly.

He ran to the VIP room opened the door and cried out, "All of you get out of here now! Run as fast as you can and head to the main entrance now do not waste a second." They all got up and ran towards the entrance following Leslie. As they reached the doorway there was a huge explosion that rocked the club. Glass shattered all around and part of the ceiling in the main area collapsed. There were small fires around the club and many people were crying for help. They, however, came out unscathed thanks to Leslie and his quick reaction. If they had stayed just another two minutes more, they would probably all be killed by the explosion.

Frankie, who was at the entrance greeting customers when the explosion took place, was shocked and went up to them. "I have called the police, the ambulance and fire brigade, was that a bomb that exploded? I was worried for all of you. Where is Mr Ma? Is he all right? I thought he was with you."

116

Frankie informed them that Mr Wilson Ma showed up in the club around nine forty-five p.m. where Frankie met him at the entrance. He was carrying a large briefcase. Usually, the security guards stationed at the entrance would check the case as that was the prerequisite but when Frankie told them that Mr Ma was a special VIP guest of Raymond they let it go. Frankie was leading Wilson Ma to the VIP room when Wilson said he needed to go to the bathroom first and for Frankie to point out which room they were in and he would go surprise them after he finished with the men's room. Frankie carelessly did that and thought nothing of it and headed back to the front of the club to welcome customers. If it had not been for Leslie's instinct and him reacting fast, they all would have been dead. They all thanked him repeatedly.

Raymond advised Liza and Mimi to leave the club and to go back home. They were both in tears and obviously shaken up. John hugged Liza and told her not to worry everything would be fine but for now she must leave the club with Mimi and go directly home. John and Ray stayed on till help arrived looking around for survivors and seeing what they could do to assist them. Many of the staff who were not hurt were doing the same. There were bodies scattered all over the club with cries for help. The whole place was in chaos. People around the neighbourhood came by to see what all the commotion was causing more disruption when the police and ambulances arrived. The fire brigade managed to put out all the fires pretty quickly. As they started to clean up many bodies were discovered burned to a crisp and unrecognisable.

It was later learned that thirteen people died, eight of whom were hostesses and staff of the club, the rest guests. Fifty people were badly injured and in poor condition with five in ICU in critical condition. This was one of the worst crimes in the history of Hong Kong. This would cause a huge uproar publicly and there were demands for the police to find out who did this and to ensure that they were captured and punished quickly.

Leslie, in his mind, at first thought that maybe Ponytail set them up but that made no sense as why would he try and kill his friend Raymond who was there with them. Maybe it was all a plan of the Black Ninjas after all or a faction of them as Raymond had suggested.

He did not delve in it too long as he was anxious to go and see if Lillian was all right.

Leslie tried calling Lillian again a number of times but still could not get hold of her. Leslie told both John and Ray that he had to leave as he was very concerned about Lillian, as she did not answer any of his calls. They told him to leave and check out Lillian and that they would handle the situation there.

Leslie walked to the Star Ferry which was a ten-minute walk from the club and took it to the Kowloon side. From there he walked to Lillian's apartment which was another five-minute walk. As he reached the apartment building, he found it strange that the night caretaker Ah Chuen was nowhere to be seen. He looked around and noticed that the entrance lock to the main building had been tampered with and was broken which caused him to panic. He quickly pressed the button to the lift and when it opened, he put in his special key for the penthouse and pressed the twelfth-floor button.

When he reached the penthouse suite, he shouted out for Lillian but there was no answer, what he saw next was something he would never forget for the rest of his life. Sprawled on the white Steinway grand piano laid Lillian. Her throat was slit, and her chest had been cut open, there was blood all over the place. Her dress had been ripped off and laid on the blood that covered the floor. She was totally naked except for a white scarf tied on her forehead. Painted on the centre of the scarf was a red sun.

On the white Canadian maple parquet wood just under the piano, in Lillian's blood was written "Deuteronomy (19-21)".

Les knew immediately that it was a verse from the Old Testament Bible and knew exactly what that stated.

The quote was, "Thine eye shall not pity, but life for life, eye for eye, tooth for tooth, hand for hand, foot for foot."

The ultimate revenge. "An eye for an eye. "

Leslie fell down on his knees and cried out on top of his voice, "No God, no!"

He went to the bedroom, grabbed a blanket and covered her body up with it. He then sat on the floor staring at her body for at least half an hour not saying a word, sobbing away. He was thinking of who could have committed this heinous crime. In his mind he was already planning on how to punish the evil people who did this.

He swore to Lillian as she lay dead in front of him bleeding profusely that he would not rest till the people who did this were all dead or in prison.

He then got up, called the police and waited for them to arrive.

Chapter 7
Death of a Yakuza

Black Ninja Den
172 Lai Chi Kok Road, New Territories.
Tuesday, July 17th, 1960, five p.m.

Hashimoto Kentaro, also known as Ken or Ken San, could not believe what happened. "San" in Japanese was an honourable title that the Japanese gave to both men and women. Ken San read in the papers that morning of the two U.S. naval officers that were killed and about the bombing of the Sing Song Club plus the murder of Lillian Wang, all this happening within forty-eight hours. The worst part was that the papers assumed it was the work of the Black Ninjas who they claimed had returned and were back to their old ways. Obviously, this was all untrue as he had never directed any of his gang members to commit any of the crimes. It was a set-up but by who and why? This was the worst thing that could happen as he had been totally discreet during the last four years and never got involved with violent crime. His business was mostly international and nothing to do with Hong Kong. Over the four years he had amassed a fortune for himself and his followers. He covered up his main business of arms trafficking by importing brand name electronics and watches from Japan which were very popular at that time.

Ken was born in Tokyo in Japan; he was born to a well-known family who had businesses in Japan and around the world. His father owned the largest vehicle parts factory in Japan. Ken had a sister who moved to Hong Kong prior to the war to continue her studies in English. Before Ken graduated from university, his mother died of cancer, and so there were only the three left in the family. He joined his father's business when he graduated from Tokyo University and helped to expand the business worldwide. When the war broke and Japan started their conquest of Asia the Japanese government took over the factory and converted it to a tank manufacturing plant. There was nothing Ken San's father could do. He was forced to work in the factory and paid very little for it. Ken left the factory when the Japanese government took it over and got involved with one of the larger gangs in Tokyo. These gangs were known as "Yakuza". They were similar to the triads of Hong Kong but more respected in society. They were more organised and worked well with other Yakuza gangs unlike the Hong Kong triads who were constantly fighting one another. He did not enjoy his time working for the Yakuza and just before World War II started, left Japan and went to Hong Kong to be with his sister who was studying English there.

In mid-September 1945 the Japanese surrendered in Hong Kong. Most of the Japanese soldiers were rounded up and made to appear before the courts for atrocities they caused during the war. Some of the Japanese forces who were not captured went underground and took refuge amongst the triads in the Walled City in Kowloon City. They felt safe there as the British government left that part of Hong Kong alone. There Ken San met up with Agana San who formed the Black Ninja gang and was its leader. The Black Ninja gang consisted mostly of Japanese soldiers that were not captured by the British and who took refuge in the Walled City. They later grew in size as members from other triads joined. They could not accept the fact that the Japanese had lost the war. They hated the Allies and promised to take revenge on them. Their mission was to get rid of the "gaijin" from Hong Kong. Gaijin was the term used by the Japanese to denote a foreigner or a non-Japanese national. They were more against the white race whom they felt were responsible for thousands of innocent Japanese lives with the atomic bombs that were dropped in Nagasaki and Hiroshima which ended the war.

Ken hooked up Agana San with connections to the Yakuza gang bosses that he used to work for in Tokyo and they started doing business together. The Yakuza would sell arms of all types to the Black Ninjas who would sell it on to the highest bidders. The Black Ninjas controlled the illicit arms trafficking in Hong Kong

Agana San was a general in the Japanese army and was in charge of the Japanese occupation army stationed in Hong Kong during its capture. He felt his country lost face when they surrendered to the Allies and took his revenge by attacking the military stationed there via his Black Ninja gang. His form of execution was horrendous as he got his gang members to cut the throat of the victim and then cut the heart out and remove it from the body. He would then have his gang member tie a white scarf that had the red sun printed on it around the victim's head. He would pay any member of his gang HK$10,000 for bringing the enemy's heart to him. He was brutal and was the number one public enemy of the British government. When he was captured and hanged in 1956 most all of his gang dispersed and the British thought that was the last that they had heard of the Black Ninjas. For the next four years after that there were no reported killings until what happened with the two U.S. naval officers over the weekend.

Ken San was concerned about the events of the weekend, especially so if his sister read about it in the papers. When he restarted the New Black Ninja gang after Agana San's hanging he reached out to his sister to finance his illicit business as he needed capital to buy arms from the Yakuza in Japan. His sister said she would give him the money not as a loan but if he made her a partner and that he shared the profits he made equally with her. They were to be 50/50 partners. He was not to reveal to anyone who she was or anything about her. He had no choice but to agree. She also made him promise that the gang would no longer continue Agana San's killing of foreigners, and that they had to be peaceful and just concentrate on the business of arms trafficking.

His sister that morning freaked out when she read about the events of the weekend. She called him and started screaming, he swore to her that his gang had nothing to do with any of what she read. Either it was a set up or some member had broken the rules and did the attacks without Ken's blessing. He had a suspect in mind and would get back to her when he found out more. He was having a meeting of all his members and high-ranking staff that night and would try to get to the bottom of this and report back to her. She reminded him that she was a secret partner, and nobody was to know her identity, no matter what. She said he needed to sort this out immediately because the British would eventually find him out and destroy his gang and she could be arrested for financing the New Black Ninjas.

Niko San was nervous about the situation for if anyone found out that she was involved with the Black Ninjas, or that Ken San was her brother, she would lose everything she had built up. She was well respected in the colony. Her husband was the ex-commissioner of police of Hong Kong, Sir James Black. When he retired in 1957, because of health reasons, they decided to remain in Hong Kong. Sir James and Niko decided not to go back to the U.K. where Sir James was originally from but rather spend his retirement days in Hong Kong. They bought a five-bedroom house in Repulse Bay in the Island. This was one of the poshest places to live in Hong Kong. Their house faced the sea and the beach was only sixty yards away. They were very wealthy from all the bribes Sir James acquired during the time he spent in the Hong Kong police force. She had no reason to have gotten involved with her brother Ken and wished now that she never had. It was the money that tempted her to do this, she always wanted more. Her husband knew nothing of her business with Ken, in fact he had never even met him. Niko had been careful not to let anyone know of her brother. She wondered if now was the right time to open up to John Woods, the current commissioner of police and tell him the truth. She was very close to John and trusted him explicitly. She knew, like her husband, he was corrupt and took bribes from the triads. She thought it probably better to tell him everything about her brother, swearing that he had nothing at all to do with the crimes of the weekend. She was truly frightened for her brother's life as she was certain that the British would soon find out the whereabouts of the Black Ninjas and come down hard on them.

Sir James and Niko had no children. They both met at a social party in Hong Kong during the late forties. Sir James had been married before, but the marriage did not work out. Right after the war he was asked to be stationed in Hong Kong as commissioner of police. He previously was the chief inspector of police in London. He could not refuse the position and was looking forward to his new role. His first wife, however, hated Hong Kong from the start and constantly fought with James to return back to the U.K. This caused a lot of conflict between the two and finally they divorced, and she returned home to

England. When James met Niko, she had just turned nineteen whilst he was forty-nine. Despite the age difference they got along brilliantly. He was amazed by her beauty and found her very intelligent. They dated for three years and got married in 1951. Niko was the perfect hostess. As the wife of the commissioner of police she had to host numerous parties and attend many social events. She carried herself well and was well loved by all who met her. During his time as commissioner James had to entertain many dignitaries from all over the world and Niko loved meeting and entertaining the famous celebrities. Sir James and Niko got on very well with the Woods and they became very close friends. She loved Maggie and her quirky ways and spent many afternoons with Nancy at the lobby of the Peninsula Hotel having afternoon tea and gossiping about anything and everything.

Niko had only her brother left as family; her father died soon after the war. She never told anyone about him as she was ashamed of him being involved with the Yakuza. She loved him dearly though and many a time tried to dissuade him from working with the gangs, especially with Agana San whom she found evil. He never heeded her advice, and when in 1956 Agana San was executed, he started his own gang. He came to her asking for help to finance his illicit business. When he told her how much money he would be making and that it was all safe she got greedy and wanted a part of the action. She also got involved so she could keep an eye on him. She became a partner in the business but made him swear that he would not involve in any serious crimes or kill anyone. Now with all that was happening she wished to God she never had gotten involved. She was stupid.

Ken suspected one of the generals in his gang to possibly be involved with the murders and bombings. This was Kohei Inowaki. Kohei San was second in command under Agana San whilst he was leader of the Black Ninjas. When Agana was captured and executed, he joined up with Ken San's new gang. He was hoping that Ken would, like Agana San, continue to fight the British. He was disappointed when he realised that all Ken was interested in doing was making money. Many of the older soldiers, who had been at war with the Allies, in the gang were also dismayed with Ken as he was not carrying on the legacy of its original founder Agana San. Kohei San would always complain to

Ken San that they must continue to carry on the revenge on the British armed forces. Ken ignored his advice and reminded Kohei of the money he was making by not taking risks. This was more than three times what he earned whilst working for Agana San.

To Kohei San it was not all about the money but of pride and honour; to seek revenge on behalf of his motherland, Japan. He got some of the members of the gang to form a division apart from the New Black Ninjas. They still remained as members of the new Black Ninja as that provided them with money, but they wished to also fulfil their destiny and if need be, die as heroes. Kohei's offshoot gang was kept secret from the other gang members and especially Ken San. There were twenty members in total involved in this new offshoot which Kohei called the "Samurais". Most of them were skilled soldiers and had great knowledge of the use of swords. They would meet secretly and plan killings of British or Allied military personnel. The two U.S. naval murders were of their doing but they had nothing to do with the bombing or killing of Lillian Wang. Lillian Wang was either a copycat murder or of somebody wishing to put the blame on the Black Ninjas causing them problems. Kohei was going to bring it up in the meeting that evening. He felt he needed to tell Ken that it was his group that killed the Americans, but that they had nothing whatsoever to do with the bombing or the death of Lillian Wang.

As he was about to head off to the meeting Kohei got a call. The party on the line said, "Save yourself and your group. Do not attend the meeting tonight or you will die. Do not let anyone know of this call. Let the meeting that Ken San has arranged to go ahead but please you and your "Samurais" do not show up if you want to live. Are you clear?"

Kohei immediately recognised the voice and replied he was clear and would follow the instructions given. He started to shake violently and thought, what will happen at the meeting? He trusted the caller explicitly and started tracking down his group telling them not to attend the meeting that evening but rather meet up with him at a secret location. They were all a bit confused, but he commanded them to follow his order and that he would explain all when he met up with them later that evening.

Ken had called for the meeting to start at seven p.m. that evening.

It was to be held at the headquarters of the New Black Ninjas which was located in Shum Shui Po in the New Territories. It was a three-storey building which used to be an old warehouse but was now converted into an office, with storage facilities for imported goods on the ground floor. The offices and a meeting hall were located on the second floor. Ken had his personal apartment on the upper floor. Ken never did marry although he dated a lot of women but somehow none of them stayed with him longer than six months. Ken, however, currently was living with a girl whom he met in Tokyo during one of his visits to meet with the Kazuo Goto, the Yakuza boss he did business with. The Yakuza gang he was involved with was from the Shinjuku district of Tokyo. Kazuo Goto, was known to be a ruthless leader. He was heavy handed and laid down heavy punishments to members who did not adhere to his rules.

Kazuo San, after one of the business meetings, invited Ken for dinner. After having a lavish meal Kazuo brought him to his favourite Geisha Bar in the Ginza district of Tokyo. It was there that he met Himari Otsuka. She was young but well trained as a Geisha. During that evening she pampered to his every wish and kept filling up his cup with Sake. She kept bringing snacks for him and listened attentively about his life. He felt very comfortable with her and visited the club again three times by himself before he left back for Hong Kong. He invited her to visit Hong Kong saying he would pay for her flight and all her expenses if she decided to come. She thanked him and said she would think about that and let him know. Two weeks after he returned to Hong Kong, he got a call from Himari San saying she would like to visit him in Hong Kong. He was exhilarated and sent her first-class air tickets immediately. She arrived a week later and six months on was still with him.

It was now six thirty p.m. and Ken was pacing up and down in his apartment on the second floor. He had sent off Himari to stay with a friend of hers who was living in the Tsim Sha Tsui district. She at first refused but he said she must do so for at least the weekend as he had to make alternative plans to where to move to. The meeting tonight was to inform the members of his gang that he was closing down the Black Ninja Den as it was known, and tonight's meeting will be the last one to be held there. He would get in touch with them once a new location had been found and inform them. Totally there were approximately one hundred members who handled different parts of the organisation. Some in logistics, some in sales and marketing, others in administration and finance.

He had a good team and they moved over HK$2,500,000 worth of arms monthly making a gross profit of HK$1,500,000. After salaries and running costs, he netted close to HK$850,000 monthly. He lived a very high lifestyle. He had over the four years personally bought two expensive cars, owned two holiday villas in Thailand, a house in Tokyo and one in Australia. He personally also owned two racehorses and was a member of the Royal Hong Kong Jockey Club. The property in Shum Shui Po was also owned by his registered company Hashimoto Import and Export Ltd. Most people who knew him did not know about his illicit business dealings but thought he was a successful importer and exporter of electronic goods.

Ken decided he'd better head down and wait for his team to gather. He walked down the stairs past the office where people were tidying up and closing for the day and went to the meeting hall. Inside the hall there were already about forty people, they were from the warehouse team, the rest would be there soon, especially the sales staff who worked most times out of the building. At around seven p.m. most of them had arrived, only those who were missing were Kohei San and some of the people under him. This made him even more suspicious of Kohei San and he thought he must be involved somewhat with the incidents of the weekend, why else was he not be there? He thought he would wait till seven thirty and if they still had not arrived by then he would get the shutters of the warehouse pulled down and locked and start the meeting.

By seven thirty p.m. Kohei and his group had still not shown up and Ken asked for the gates to be shut and locked and for the meeting to start. He was expecting Kohei to show and was a bit surprised. He wanted to ask him straight whether his group was involved in the killing of the naval soldiers, the bombings and the horrific murder of Lillian Wang. Ken was totally confused as he could not understand why Kohei would do the crimes. It was possible that the naval soldiers had been killed by Kohei and his gang but why would he want to bomb the Sing Song Club which had no link with the British and was owned by a prominent Chinese businessman. More so, why the killing of the ex-hostess and lover of Leslie, Lillian Wang, who was Chinese; it made absolutely no logical sense.

Ken addressed the gathering, most of whom had already read about the killings and bombing of the weekend. They read with apprehension that the media was blaming probably a new faction of the Black Ninjas for the incidents. He said firmly and with conviction that he had asked nobody to carry out these atrocities and he doubted if anyone under his control would have done so. He felt this was a copycat style murder especially the killings of the officers and Lillian Wang. He believed that someone had done this purposely and thus caused a public outcry which would get the police snooping and possibly discover their workplace and raid it.

He went on to explain because of this he had booked a temporary storage place about a mile from where their operations were to store all the arms and merchandise that they had. The staff was to have a two-week break informing anyone who asked why they were off to give the reason that they were redecorating and updating the current warehouse by adding two more floors as the business was growing. He said that during these two weeks even though some of them would do nothing that they would get paid in full. Once things had cooled down, he would let them know of where their new operations would be but till then they all had to lie low and say nothing to the law.

As he was closing the meeting, they heard a huge bang like a bomb coming from the entrance. The gates were blown open and in rushed twenty people dressed in black wielding swords and other weapons. Many managed to rush out but were faced with John and his officers who rounded them up.

Leslie headed straight towards Ken. Ken took out his sword to defend himself, but Leslie was too quick for him and within a few seconds had his nunchakus around Ken's neck. Ken could not breathe and asked for mercy. Leslie released the grip and stared at him.

"It was you, you and your gang who killed Lillian. You asshole! Why for the revenge of Agana San?" Ken looked back at Les and started shaking his head to say no.

"Do not lie I know everything; it was your new Black Ninjas that killed the two naval officers and Lillian Wang. You left your tell-tale signs all over. It was pure luck that someone who worked with you read the newspaper this morning and fearing getting caught told us where the new Black Ninjas' den was located. I could not believe that you were the boss of the New Black Ninjas and that you ran an illicit business. I have known you for many years and you have been in my guest box at the racecourse a number of times." Leslie clicked the diamonds on the edge of the nunchaku, and it burst into flames. "Say goodbye this is what you get for killing my Lillian."

As he pushed the burning sticks into his eyes, he heard Ken San yell back, "It was not me it was Kohei Inowaki," and after saying that he fell to the floor dead.

Leslie stood there for a while whilst his team gathered up the rest of the gang. He had never heard of a Kohei Inowaki before this. Who was he and was it he and not Ken San who did the killing and the bombing? How was that possible, as everything pointed to Ken Hashimoto and his gang. It was confirmed by Ponytail to Raymond Ho that it was members of the new Black Ninjas that killed the two naval soldiers and probably also involved in the bombing and the murder of Lillian Wang.

John, who had spoken to Niko earlier that day, confirmed that Ken San was the leader of the Black Ninjas to Leslie. She, however, claimed he had nothing to do with any of the killings or bombing of the Sing Song Club, but John was sceptical of that fact as she had told him that Ken was her brother and thought she said that to protect him. He had repeated all that to Leslie. With those two facts it was quite clear to Leslie then that it was Kentaro Hashimoto and his gang who were responsible for Lillian's death and possibly the bombing.

Leslie questioned some of those captured and asked them about Kohei Inowaki. They told him that he was second in command after Ken San. He was an ex-Japanese general who hated the British like Agana San whom he worshipped and was his hero. He did not agree with the policies of Ken which was not to commit any crimes of hate against the British. When questioned where Kohei San was now he was told that he and his cronies did not show up for the meeting and they did not know of his whereabouts.

One of the members came forward. He identified himself as Ming Ho. He said that he had gone drinking with one of Kohei San followers the night before and during a conversation he was boasting to him that Kohei and his men, including himself, were responsible of the deaths of the two naval officers. Leslie asked whether he knew where this individual lived and what was his name.

"He was known as Hiro San, an ex-Japanese war hero. I do not know of where he resides, but he was trying to recruit me to join Kohei San saying that one day Kohei would take over the Black Ninjas as its leader."

Is this not the end of this saga, Leslie thought, have I killed the wrong person? Was it Kohei Inowaki who was responsible for the murder of Lillian and not Ken San?

He had to find the truth. He had made a promise to Buddha that he would take revenge on those who had caused Lillian to die. Leslie, after Lillian's death, never again stepped into a Christian church. He would go every week to the Buddhist temple that Lillian attended to say a prayer for her. Her ashes laid there in a golden vase that Leslie had purchased. He promised not to rest until he took revenge on the person or persons that committed the murder. This was a promise he would keep.

Part 2

"TO EVERYTHING THERE IS A SEASON"

"What we call the beginning is often the end. And to make an end is to make a beginning. The end is where we start from."

T.S. Eliot

Chapter 8
Summer of '64

The Lalwani Residence
Number 5 Durham Road, Kowloon Tong
June 6th, 1964, nine forty-five a.m.

Ajit looked at his watch: it was almost ten a.m. Although it was Saturday and the offices were closed, he did want to visit his retail shops which were open seven days a week. It was a routine he did every week together with his brother Mohan. Today, however, he was requested by his wife Maya to stay home a bit longer as Nancy Sun was coming to discuss the final preparations for Herman Sun's twenty-first surprise birthday party which was to be hosted at the Lalwani residence. Nancy, with the help of Maya, had been planning this for over a month now.

Herman Sun graduated in April from Oxford with honours. His parents both flew to England and attended his graduation. Herman took after his father's looks: he was both tall and handsome. He was very outgoing and was well liked at school. He was good with his studies and was a straight "A" student. He took his studies seriously and his ambition was one day getting into Oxford just like his father had done. He was appointed Head Prefect when in the Sixth Form. He was athletic and was in the school team for swimming, fencing and cricket. To Leslie and Nancy, he was the perfect son.

They thought he would fly back to Hong Kong with them together after the graduation, but Herman told his parents that he and a few of his friends wished to tour Europe for a couple of months before he returned to Hong Kong in June after which he would then start his training for the Tokyo Olympics which was from October 10th – 24th, that year. Herman was selected by the Hong Kong Olympic Committee to be in the Olympics for fencing. He was the number one in Asia in this discipline and the only person from Hong Kong to ever be selected for this event. He told them that he did not want to further his masters degree but instead wanted to come home and join the family businesses after he took part in the Tokyo Olympic games in October that year.

Leslie was proud of his son as he had lived up to everything that he had expected unlike his daughter Lucy who was more reserved. Lucy went to study in Diocesan Girls' School and was studious but did not excel in school and was an average student. She had a few friends in school and was bullied a lot during her school days which did not help in building up her confidence. She was not as attractive as her mother, in fact, she was slightly on the plump side and quite plain looking. Her best friend was Mabel Woods who she treated like her sister. Lucy looked up to Mabel who, unlike her, was extremely beautiful with blonde hair and blue eyes and had a gorgeous body. Mabel was very popular and was very mature for her age. Leslie wished that Lucy could be as sociable and confident as Mabel.

Leslie was thrilled that Herman had decided to join the business after the Olympics as he needed someone to help him with the management of his businesses and who eventually could run the family empire when he retired. Herman flew back from England on Monday, June 1st. His parents had told him that they would take him out for dinner on Saturday for his twenty-first birthday together with the Woods and Lalwani family to the Pearl Garden Restaurant, which Herman enjoyed. He did not imagine that a surprise party awaited him.

Ajit, his wife Maya and Nancy Sun with Ajit's butler Badu, who was taking notes, were seated in the main family room of the house. Nancy was explaining to Ajit what she had planned. They were catering from the Pearl Garden, a restaurant owned by Leslie Sun. The caterers would be all set by six p.m., and dinner would be a sit down ten course Chinese dinner. The plan was they would tell Herman they had to go first to the Lalwani's for a drink before heading to the Pearl Garden for dinner. What actually would happen is that when they arrived at the Lalwani's by six thirty p.m. they would be greeted by the guests with a huge cry of surprise as they entered the house. Nancy had told everyone coming that they all must be at the Lalwani house not later than six p.m. Champagne would be popped followed by cocktails and canapés for an hour, enough time for the guests to mingle before dinner. There would be eight tables set up, each seating eight guests. The main table would be where Herman and his best friends would sit. Right after dinner Leslie would say a few words welcoming the guests followed by Herman giving his speech. A toast would be made by Leslie, followed by the cake cutting ceremony and photograph taking. After that the adults would say their goodbyes and leave for the Suns' house to their "after party". Nancy had planned for all adults to come over to their house to continue on the party after dinner.

The after party for the rest of them was to be handled and planned by both Anita Lalwani and Maggie's daughter Mabel. As soon as the adults left, the tables were to be removed by the staff and a dance floor set up. Anita had hired a D.J. for the party as well as a live band. The band that they had hired for the night was the top band in Hong Kong. The girls had dressed up the room beautifully with loads of balloons printed with "Happy 21st" and "Welcome Home" signs. Badu would be in charge of lighting and sound and to ensure the electrician was on standby in case of any problems. The after party would be over by two a.m. as the staff would need to do the clean-up before retiring. Ajit asked to see the party list and seating arrangements for dinner. He wanted to be sure that there was enough staff there positioned to look after the guests' requests.

Nancy pulled out the party list. First on the list was Leslie's mother Elaine and her daughter Lucy. Ajit and his three brothers and their wives and children were next. Ajit had three brothers, together they built up the Lalwani business empire, one of the more successful companies in the colony. His three brothers, their wives and children all lived in the house together. Ajit was the eldest and had two children Dilip, who was twenty years old, and Anita, nineteen, both who now worked for the business, Mohan was the second with his wife Leela and he had two boys Ishaan, nineteen, who also was involved in the business and Aryan, seventeen, then came Anand (Andy) and his wife Sunita and their two daughters Prity, seventeen and Sheila, fourteen. The youngest brother was Laxman (Lucky) and his wife Mohini who had only one child named Ashwin who was fourteen.

Nancy continued reading her list. "I have also invited of course, Sir

John and Maggie and their children Ben and Mabel, Leslie's sister Irene and her children Richard and Yvonne, and Sir Anthony Brown the Chairman of Hong Kong & Shanghai Bank and his wife Elizabeth and their twin boys Danny and Harold. My brother David Poon will be attending with his wife Mia and their three children, Naomi, Robert and Michelle. We have also invited the Dadlani family, they will be a party of six. Some of Herman's old classmates will also be attending, about eighteen in total I believe. I also did invite Bella as requested by Leslie. She will be bringing a friend with her, a girl named Eileen Siu." Nancy felt uncomfortable inviting Leslie's ex-mistress's sister to the party but could not object as Leslie insisted as he felt responsible for Bella.

"I did inform all the adults that they could stay till ten p.m. but once the tables were cleared and the dance floor set up they should head over to our place where I have organised champagne, caviar, after dinner drinks, coffee and cigars for the boys," she smiled. "I did ask Raymond Ho to join, but he said he could not make dinner as he had other commitments he could not get out of, but promised he would join us at my place for drinks later."

"Oh, speaking of Ray," said Ajit, "he passed me this at my office yesterday when he came to discuss some business with me and said to pass it to you when we met this morning. He says it's his present to Herman and to give it to him after the cutting of the cake."

He handed her a red folder which printed on the bottom right corner was "Compliments from Raymond Ho Productions Limited". Nancy knew of Raymond Ho's entertainment company. One of Raymond's businesses was to bring famous artists to perform in Hong Kong. She and Les had been invited many times by Ray when he brought in various famous artists from around the world to HK. She opened to take a look and inside were six tickets all front row seats to see The Beatles perform live at the Princess Theatre on June 9th. The Princess Theatre was the most exquisite and up-to-date cinema in the colony. The theatre was built and run by the Hong Kong and Kowloon Entertainment Company, a company run by the family of Sir Hotung who was a famous businessman who recently retired. The theatre building had shops, offices and a restaurant in the front part, while the well-designed auditorium had perfect sight lines in the rear.

Also included in the folder were six VIP backstage passes to meet The Beatles. On top of that there was a lifetime membership card for the Havana Paradise Club and a VIP card for Hotel Faroe in Macau offering 30% discount on all rooms and restaurants. Ajit looked at them and said to Nancy, "Wow what a gift. Do you know how much these seats are worth? They are priceless."

"They're coming: 'YEAH! YEAH! YEAH!'" read the headlines of the South China Morning Post newspaper that Ajit read that morning. "Beatlemania", now at fever pitch worldwide, was sweeping into Hong Kong. The fab four would arrive on Monday, June 8th, en route to Australia, staying at the President Hotel and performing the following evening, doing two concerts at the Princess Theatre in Tsim Sha Tsui before departing on June 10th. "Beatles suits" and "moptop" wigs were selling like hotcakes at the shops. Ajit did not know till then that Raymond's company was bringing them to perform in Hong Kong for if he had known he would have bought tickets from him. His children and his nephews and nieces had been bugging him to get tickets for weeks. He did try but the problem was all the tickets were sold out within half an hour of them going on sale. He never thought to ask Raymond. Nancy was taken aback; what a great gift!! She knew Leslie and Raymond were close friends and they did a lot of business together but for Herman to get such a gift was a bit over the top.

Ajit stood up to leave. "Is there anything else you need me to do for tonight?" asked Ajit. "If not, I will be heading to the shops with Mohan. I will be home early tonight before five p.m. anyway." He walked out of the meeting. Ajit's chauffeur was waiting for him at the entrance of the house to take him to the store. He informed Ajit that his brother Mohan had already taken his own driver and gone ahead first. He had left a message that he would wait for him at the main store in Tsim Tsa Shui. What a waste of money, thought Ajit, he could not even wait thirty minutes for me as they could have left together in one car.

Ajit missed his father Haresh who passed away just after he graduated with his Masters in Economics from Oxford University in 1937. His father was born in Hyderabad Sind in 1875. He moved to Shanghai as did a lot of "Hindu Sindhis" in the early 1900s. He was married to Indra and they had four sons, Ajit, the oldest, who was born in Shanghai in 1914 just when World War I broke out. Mohan followed in 1916 and Anand in 1918 just after the war. His youngest, Laxman, whom he nicknamed "Lucky", was born in 1922. He wanted all his sons to study in England but could not afford for all of them to go. So, he first sent off Ajit to university in England when he turned seventeen in 1931. The other three boys stayed with their father helping him out in the business. Whilst Ajit was still in university Haresh moved his family from Shanghai to Hong Kong in 1935 as he was worried about the Japanese and their threats to conquer China. Ajit meanwhile completed his bachelor's and went on to do his Master's. When he returned home his father fell sick and within four months of him coming back home to Hong Kong his father passed away leaving Ajit to fend for the family. His father was very young, just sixty-two, when he died. His mother, after his father passed away, became very solitary and she died not too long after her husband, of, what Ajit believed, from a broken heart. At that time, the family owned two very small tailoring shops in Kowloon. The shops did relatively well and made enough to keep the family comfortable. In 1940 Ajit's uncle introduced him to a match maker for it was time he took in a wife he was told. This was very common among Indian marriages those days. There was no such thing as love marriages; all marriages were arranged. It was also imperative that you had to marry someone from the same race and caste as yourself. He was introduced to Maya. Maya came from a prominent Hindu Sindhi family in Hong Kong. Her father was Gulu Samtani who owned a number of businesses in Hong Kong from retail to import and export. They both went on dates three times, chaperoned each time by the match maker. It was after the third date Ajit decided to take Maya as his wife and told his brothers about his decision. They were all happy for him and looking forward to a woman entering the household.

Soon after Ajit's wedding the Japanese invaded Hong Kong and things went downhill for the family. The Japanese army took over the Lalwani shops and used them for their own soldiers to repair uniforms and as a place they could go to and top up on provisions. The Lalwani was paid a pittance for this and did not even have enough money for food to feed the family. They moved from their four-bedroom apartment to a two bedroom as that was all they could afford. Ajit and

Maya stayed in one bedroom whilst the three brothers slept in the other. The four brothers searched very hard to acquire any jobs that they could. Ajit and Mohan landed a job carrying rice from the train station to one of the Japanese warehouses about two miles away from the station and then returning back to collect more. They would carry two sacks of rice to and from the station to the warehouse. They were paid HK$0.30 per rice sack so they had to work fast and do many turns a day as they could just to earn a liveable amount of money. The other two brothers got whatever jobs that were available from clearing trash to sweeping roads.

In December of 1944 an incident was to occur that would change the fortune of the Lalwani family forever. That morning as the family sat down together for breakfast at six a.m. at their small apartment in Old Peking Road in Tsim Sha Shui near the Star Ferry, they were discussing as usual what each was up to that day. Ajit and Mohan were doing their rice routine whilst Anand had secured a job for the week sweeping roads from Mongkok (a district two miles from TST) down to Tsim Tsa Tsui. Maya had to do all the washing for the whole family, clean up all the rooms and have dinner ready for them by the time they got home. Laxman had not much to do so he was asked to go to the food market which was about three hundred yards from where they lived and do the shopping, following the list that Maya gave him. By the time Laxman got to the food market it was almost ten a.m. It was most crowded this time of the day and he had to plough through crowds to get from stall to stall. It was a cold morning and Laxman had his overcoat on to keep him warm. As he approached the fruit stall, he heard what he thought was gunshots. Everybody in the market were either ducking to the floor or running as far away from the gunshots. It was pure chaos. Suddenly a white man wearing a torn white jacket and wearing scruffy jeans bumped into him and held him by his arm.

"Please help me the Japanese military police are after me, they found where I have been hiding and raided that place this morning. I was lucky to escape but they are right on my trail. I am an officer of the British armed forces." Laxman could see in the near distance three Japanese military police holding guns rushing toward him and the officer. Fortunate for him the crowds were running amok making it difficult for the soldiers reaching them fast. He reacted quickly, took off his overcoat and told the officer to put it on. He then grabbed a towel from a stall and gave it to the officer telling him to cover his head with it. Next, he asked the officer to follow him to his house which was nearby, and he could hide away there for the time being. As he started running towards his home, he heard a couple of gunshots and felt a piercing pain on his left soldier. He had been shot! He did not stop running till he reached his home with the British officer following him. They seemed to have lost the soldiers behind them. Laxman tried to fumble for his keys but was in too much pain to find them. He banged on the door as hard as he could. Maya opened the door and saw that Laxman was bleeding badly and yelled out in utter horror.

She let them both in and started cleaning Laxman's wound and bandaging it up. They could not take him to the hospital as the hospital staff would have reported it to the Japanese army. He was lucky that the bullet went straight through his arm otherwise he could have died. Laxman was in terrible pain, so she brought him some painkillers to try and ease his pain. The British officer looked on while Maya nursed him. He kept thanking Laxman for his kind act which he believed saved his life. He explained to both of them that he was a high-ranking officer of the British forces stationed in Hong Kong and that he had avoided capture from the Japanese army. His title was that of a colonel: Colonel Patrick Williams. Colonel Williams had been hiding out in a friend's home for the last three years. She had managed to hide him away from the authorities till just today. He had no idea how they discovered he was staying there. This morning, after his friend had gone to work, there was a knock on her door. Colonel Williams peeped out the curtain from his room which was two doors from the entrance and could see that there were six Japanese military holding what he knew was a battering ram and armed with guns. Apparently, they had discovered his whereabouts. He put on his shoes quickly and headed towards the back door. He rushed out but the Japanese soldiers had one of their men watching the back. Williams without thinking ran straight at him before he could aim at him and had a punchout. Williams was able to knock him down and managed to escape. The other guards, who heard the commotion, went back around and spotted him and started chasing him.

He ran as fast as he could towards the market hoping to lose them and that was when he bumped into Laxman.

That evening when Ajit and his brothers returned home Maya revealed the whole incident to them. Laxman was fast asleep in his room and Patrick Williams was in the lounge talking to Ajit telling him who he was and how he avoided the Japanese the last three years. The Japanese were ruthless with prisoners of war and many of them got executed without a trial. He said it was dangerous for the family to harbour him as if they were caught doing so that the Japanese would punish the whole family possibly by execution. He felt sure that the Japanese Military Police would go around all the households in the vicinity searching for him. He also feared for the woman who had sheltered him for the last three years as she would surely be arrested and possibly executed. Ajit said he would not put Patrick back out into the streets for that would be suicidal for him. He said Patrick could hide in their home. There was a secret space under the flooring of the house in the kitchen area. Ajit had it done when they first moved to create a storage space for emergencies. It was large enough for Patrick to hide in if the Japanese military did decide to check their house. Patrick was really touched with the kindness of the Lalwani family and never forgot it.

After the war ended in September 1945 Patrick returned to his barracks. Of the five thousand, four hundred and seven prisoners of war that were captured by the Japanese only eighteen hundred and seventy survived. The Japanese had cause horrific war crimes by executing the prisoners of war without trial and breaking the Geneva Convention on how soldiers captured should be treated. The Lalwanis recovered their shops and started up their business once again. In December that year Patrick appeared in the Lalwani's main store which was located in Tsim Tsa Tsui in Hanoi Road which was just off Nathan Road. He told Ajit that Britain was sending out more army personnel to bolster the garrisons already there. He needed a good reliable supplier that could make uniforms for those coming there and a place he could recommend the soldiers to shop safely and to be treated fairly. He decided that the Lalwani should be awarded the uniform contract. Ajit let out a cry: he could not believe his luck as this meant his business would flourish. He disclosed to Patrick that he did not think his stores could cater to his request as they were too small. Patrick said not to worry he already thought of that and that the army owned a plot in the centre of Tsim Sha Tsui right on Nathan Road that was available and willing to lease it to the Lalwanis at a ridiculously low price. He also said he would introduce him to a construction company that worked for the army to help build the store and would do it to Ajit's specifications. There would be no costs to the Lalwanis as the building would still be owned by the British and that the land it stood on was leased to them by the British.

Ajit could not believe his luck, an act of kindness had given him the opportunity of building a great business. He remembered what his father told him, always be kind and love your fellow men. If you look after the world the world will look after you. The store was built, and the business blossomed. Patrick became a close friend to Ajit and would invite him to many of the parties he hosted. During one such party he met General Dwight E. Eisenhower who was Chief of Staff of the army for the United States of America and who later went on to become the thirty-fourth president of the U.S.A. General Dwight had a few custom-made suits from Ajit and loved them. General Eisenhower helped Ajit further to promote his business by letting the generals under him recommend that all U.S. soldiers visiting Hong Kong on R&R to shop at the Lalwani shop. He also introduced him to other generals of the U.S. army stationed in Asia Pacific and when the Korean war broke out and followed soon by the Vietnam war the Lalwanis were chosen to have stores inside the PX of U.S. bases around Asia at that time. PX stood for Post Exchange and was a system created by the U.S. army whereby soldiers stationed in the bases could go to the PX and purchase almost anything they wanted at a large discount from what was offered outside the bases. The Lalwanis soon had shops in PX bases in Japan, South Korea, the Philippines and Vietnam.

The Lalwanis' business grew rapidly. They had over thirty-two stores around Asia by 1954 and had over four hundred and twenty staff working for them. Most of the staff and managers that Ajit hired were from Hyderabad Sind. Ajit would interview every one of them. He bought a nine-storey building near the flagship store in Tsim Tsa Tsui to house the staff. He set up a food hall in the apartment where the staff could go have a proper cooked Indian meal by the Indian cooks he hired. The staff were served breakfast, lunch on their lunch break hours, and dinner. They would be trained in Hong Kong and after their training if Ajit felt they were good enough they would be sent to work in one of their PX shops in the U.S. bases. Most of the staff wanted that position as it paid almost double than what they got paid living and working in Hong Kong. The Lalwanis were kind to the staff and treated them like family. They were rewarded for working hard and received bonuses during Diwali and the beginning of every new year.

The business grew and the Lalwanis were making millions every month. Ajit decided to give each brother a division to handle. He would handle the finance as he had the most knowledge in that area and started a new division called Lalwanis Properties Ltd. He firstly invested in factory buildings and offices but then diverted to the hotel industry as he saw how much income it brought to his friends like Leslie Sun and Raymond Ho who both owned luxury hotels. At the time, the Lalwanis owned six hotels worldwide. They were not deluxe hotels and only classed as three to four stars. His desire was to build a five-star hotel in the heart of Tsim Tsa Tsui with eight hundred rooms. He formed a syndicate with some of the wealthier Sindhi community to purchase the land where the hotel was to be built. He was now only waiting for the Hilton Group to confirm that they would be partners and for the final plans submitted to the lands offices to be approved. He had numerous negotiations with the Hilton Hotel Group for leasing their name and for them to manage the hotel when built. They were in the final stages of finishing the contracts. He was hoping that if there were no hitches it could be approved within the next six months.

Mohan was in charge of the retail business. He was quite forward thinking and realised that once the wars in the Pacific were over the army business would slow down considerably. He converted a number of his stores from mainly just making suits and selling small gift items to larger department type stores carrying the latest gadgets from Japan, housewares from Europe and carrying luxury fashion brands. The main store which was twelve storeys high was on 46 Nathan Road, right in the heart of what was known as the Golden Mile, the most expensive area in Kowloon. They had three other stores, one more in Mong Kok, and two on the island, one in Central and the fourth in Wanchai. He ran the retail companies under the name of "Lalwani's Emporium Ltd."

The third brother, Anand, went into looking after their import and export and mail order division. It started from a small base but grew quickly. Many of the soldiers who went back home after the war would write to order suits or other items from the company. The Lalwanis kept all the details of all these people who had visited and kept their measurements so that they could reorder suits they had purchased previously. They had mail order catalogues made and sent them to all the addresses they had. The orders grew and the business skyrocketed. The reason they received so many orders was their prices were so much more competitive than that in the U.K. or the U.S.A. even after accounting for postage. From mail order the business took a turn and soon they were exporting goods to all over the world in bulk. This division was known as "Lalwani's Import & Export Ltd."

Laxman, who was only called Lucky now because of the fortune he brought to the family, was always fascinated by the stock market which was starting to flourish in Hong Kong. The family bought a seat in the stock exchange and formed an investment company and made Lucky in charge of that. The family, every month, would invest a certain amount of money into stocks mostly blue-chip companies like the Hong Kong and Shanghai Bank. Lucky did build up a large number of customers quickly through relationships of the family and had many Indian and expat clients. All of the four brothers were Rotarians and Lucky held a high position in the Masons. He invested the family's money wisely and it grew. His main aim was one day to convince Ajit for the Lalwani group to go public and list in the Hong Kong Stock Exchange. He felt that would give the family more prominence in the community. His company was named after his first son and called Aswin's Investment Corporation H.K. Ltd.

Ajit, after the war, looked into building a house large enough for the entire family and for their future children. He himself had two children, Dilip being the eldest who was born in 1944 and Anita, who was born a year later. All three of his brothers got married inside of five years after the war ended and all had children. The family was growing rapidly and Ajit wanted them all to stay together which was one of the wishes of his father before he passed away. He bought a site in Kowloon Tong not too far away from his best friend Leslie Sun. He envied Leslie's home and thought it to be the best decorated in the colony. He wanted to build a house as large as Leslie's if not larger and grander. He and his wife Maya travelled the world looking for pieces for the house. They wanted to keep an Indian flavour to the decoration but at the same time have it modern, which in itself was a contradiction and did not really work.

The house was finally completed in 1955 and the whole family moved in that year. There were eight apartments within the one house. Each apartment consisted of three bedrooms, one master room with an en suite and two double bedrooms with a Jack and Jill bathroom. There was a large garden on the ground floor with a large swimming pool and a lovely courtyard and barbeque area. Inside on the ground floor was the family room which was huge and could sit over ninety people if need be. This is where they celebrated their Diwali, Chinese New Year and Christmas parties when they would invite relatives and close friends for dinner and where the kids of the house would put on a show. On the other side was the formal party room which they named the mogul room which was decorated in an Arabian style décor. The apartments were on the second and third floors. On the second floor there was also a Hindu temple built where the family would go to pray before starting the day or on special holy days. They had a total of twenty-four live in staff members looking after the house. Most of them were from Hyderabad Sind in India. The house had a lot of glitz, although a bit ostentatious, and even though it was bigger in size it was nowhere as classy as the Suns' home.

The chauffeur arrived at the shop and asked Ajit whether to wait for him or should he take an early lunch. Ajit told him to take an early lunch as he would probably be busy for at least two hours. He and Mohan, after visiting the shop, would then cross the road and have lunch at Hugo's which was a popular restaurant at the Hyatt Hotel. He would only then need the car to visit the Central shops before heading home so the driver could pick him up then. As he entered the shop the staff there all bowed and greeted him. He felt very proud of what the family had accomplished in such a short time. The party tonight should be fun, he thought it has been a long time since he had spent time with Leslie out of work. Ever since the murder of Lillian, Leslie never went to parties. He even cancelled his fiftieth birthday four years ago and did not attend the governor's ball that year. He became a bit of a recluse and stopped throwing social parties and attended very few. Everyone was worried for him; this was the first time that Leslie had agreed to go to a party, and he was excited to spend some quality time with his best friend out of work.

Meanwhile back at the Lalwanis' house Mabel finally showed up late as usual. It was almost noon and she was supposed to be there by eleven a.m. Anita greeted her and together with Badu they went to the family room did a full recheck starting with the decorations and then the seating arrangements followed by testing the lighting and sound system with the engineers. Mabel loved the way the room was decorated but said they needed some more spotlights around the dance area. Badu nodded and said he would get the electrician to take care of that immediately. As Mabel went through the table seating with Anita, she noted she was on the same table with Herman and her brother Ben. Also, on that table was Dilip, Lucy, Naomi and Robert Poon, and Herman's previous girlfriend Ella Sousa. Mabel hated Ella, she found her too much of a goody-goody, but the truth was she was jealous of her as she was stunning looking, and very intelligent. She was half Portuguese, and half English and had an exquisite figure. She was twenty and was doing her last year at the Hong Kong University.

Herman met Ella at a school party five years ago when he was studying at Diocesan Boys School, and she at that time was studying at the sister school the Diocesan Girls School. Every year the two schools would throw a dance party for their fifth, and sixth form students wanting them to mingle with the opposite sex and that was where he first met Ella. He was performing with his band "The Mockers" in the party and during his break Ella walked up to him and boldly asked him for a dance. He was surprised with her boldness. He had been eyeing her the whole night and thought she was the most beautiful girl there by far. After that day they started dating for the next few years but just when he left to study in Oxford, they both decided that a long-term relationship would be difficult and decided that they should go their own ways. Nancy had invited Ella as she thought very highly of her and made sure that she sat on the same table as Herman. In reality she wanted Ella to one day be the future Mrs Herman Sun. Ella ticked all the boxes for Nancy, she came from a well-respected family, who owned the largest bookstore chain in Hong Kong, she was beautiful, intelligent and kind. She did a lot of work for charities and was a volunteer for one of Nancy's charities.

Ben, Mabel, Herman and Lucy all grew up together and were best friends since primary school days. The four of them went to the same primary school but when Mabel's dad John Woods was promoted to commissioner of police both Mabel and Ben had to move from Kowloon to Hong Kong Island. Herman went to study at Diocesan Boys' School, the same school his father went to. Both Ben and Mabel attended Island School which was styled for expats. They met up most weekends and used to go on holidays together with their parents. Herman's closest friend was, however, Dilip Lalwani and not Ben. Ben to him was a bit of a geek but was very clever with schoolwork and excelled in both mathematics and science. Out of school all he wanted to do was play Dungeons and Dragons or play a game of chess, both of which he was good at. He, unlike his sister Mabel, was not outgoing at all.

Dilip Lalwani also attended Diocesan Boys School like Herman and the both of them were best friends. They had both taken guitar lessons together since the age of twelve and were good at it. When they were in their fifth form, they formed a band called "The Mockers". Herman played bass guitar and was the main vocalist and Dilip played lead guitar. The two other members were Ajit's younger brother Mohan who played the drums and the final member and the youngest was Herman's cousin Robert Poon who played rhythm guitar and did backing vocals. They were really good and got many gigs to perform at tea dances and private parties. They unfortunately had to disband when Herman left to further his studies.

Mabel was very popular in school unlike her brother Ben. Ben was a bit of a nerd. He was not good at any kind of sports but was good at schoolwork. He was thin and tall like his father, had sandy hair and blue eyes. He wore enormous rimmed black eyeglasses that seemed too big for him: almost covering the top half of his face. He too, like Lucy, was bullied often and many a time Mabel had to get involved and stop him from getting hurt. Mabel, like her mother, was outgoing and very friendly. She was confident and as she got older realised how easy it was for her to manipulate boys who were constantly chasing after her. She was a flirt and dated many boys without getting serious with anyone. Although she teased her boyfriends, she never went all the way with any one of them and at eighteen she was still a virgin. She always had a warm spot for Herman ever since they were little. Herman however thought of her as his baby sister and never returned the same type of affection. When Herman had to leave to further his studies her heart broke as she realised then how much she really loved him and wished that she had told him that before he left. The only one who knew about Mabel's love for Herman was Anita Lalwani.

Anita Lalwani was a year older than Mabel but was way more matured. When she finished school, she joined the family business and worked under her Uncle Mohan in their flagship store. She was constantly bugged by her mother to mix more with the Sindhi community and try to get to know a few Indian boys. According to Maya, her mom, she would soon pass her marriageable age and if she did not get married within the next two years, she feared Anita would be an old maid. Anita knew that was absolute rubbish as any Sindhi boy would die to marry a Lalwani girl. Besides that, she was beautiful, intelligent and a lovely person, a fitting catch for any man. Her mother, though, was determined for Anita to marry the eldest son of the Dadlanis' named Kishore. The Dadlanis were the wealthiest Sindhi family in Hong Kong and the most respected. Vishnu Dadlani was the eldest in the family and was married to Chitra. He had one younger brother who was also involved in the business. Vishnu and Chitra had three sons and a daughter. The eldest son was Kishore followed by two boys Manu, Aron and the youngest their daughter Sheila. The Dadlanis were big in import and export and had offices in Singapore, Kuala Lumpur, London and New York. They owned five large manufacturing garment factories in Hong Kong and two in Malaysia. They supplied garments to shops like Walmart and Target in the U.S.A. and Marks and

Spencer in the U.K. Maya, Anita's mother, purposely invited them to the party and had Anita seated next to Kishore. Anita was dreading that as she absolutely hated him.

Mabel said to Anita, "Can we not rearrange the place cards on Herman's table. I am sure no one will notice or care. I can't bear the fact that Ella will be sitting next to Herman. Let's just move my card so I sit on the right of Herman and move Ella's card to the opposite side of the table, so she ends up sitting next to Ben and Dilip. I can't understand why Ella is even sitting at the same table as Herman as they have broken up almost three years now and I heard she is dating someone else. I noticed you are not sitting with us, how come?"

"Aunty Nancy did all the table seating together with my mom. I am not sure if we did change the place cards that they would be upset, but you know what you are probably right let's just exchange them around everyone will be so busy that they will probably not notice. My mom put me on another table with the Dadlanis' boys and I will be sitting beside Kishore on one side and Manu on the other. Believe me I would rather be sitting on your table. They are both so boring," replied Anita.

Mabel moved the cards around so that she would be seated next to Herman. Mabel at eighteen was very attractive. She had a beautiful body and was five feet six inches tall. She was busty like her mother and liked to show her boobs off by wearing low-cut dresses and tight sweaters. Like her mother she was blonde with curly hair and bright blue eyes. She decided that evening to wear the sexiest dress she had and make Herman aware of her.

"You know what Anita, by the end of tonight I will tell Herman how I truly feel about him and see what happens. It could be awkward if he rejects my honesty, but I think it is time he knows. I just feel we are so right for one another. Ben and I will be spending the night at the Sun's house after the party and if things work out the way I hope…" She crossed her fingers.

The last two summers when Herman came back for the summer from university both Mabel and Herman got really close. He did meet with Ella once in those two times for coffee. He told Mabel that although he still had feelings for Ella as far as he was concerned that relationship was over. The day he was leaving back for university after the summer holidays he told Mabel how he cared for her and that she was the best friend a person could have. She was at that time about to tell him that she loved him but thought twice as she was scared that it would freak him out and hurt their friendship.

Anita replied, "You know what, girl, you go for it at least then you know if he has the same sort of feelings for you and if not, you can move on. I seriously believe with Ella it is over as I heard that Ella was dating one of Sir Anthony's twin sons, Harold. It seems they have been dating now for around three months. She, anyway, I think, would feel awkward sitting next to Herman while her current boyfriend is sitting at another table. So, I do not believe she will be a threat. By the way does Lucy know how you feel about Herman?"

"Wow, I didn't know that. My dad is pretty close to Sir Anthony and I never heard anything about it. Your dad, Anita, is, however, so much closer to Sir Anthony. Is that how you heard about it? Hope you are right, and that Ella is over Herman, but somehow, I am not sure as when they were dating, they seemed very much in love. No, believe it or not, I have not told Lucy about my feelings for her brother, and I don't think she even suspects. I think it is the fact that all four of us have known each other for such a long time that she couldn't envisage me being romantically involved with her brother."

"I actually heard about Ella and Harold from my mom. She had mentioned it to Aunty Nancy and mom wanted to seat Harold next to Ella, but Aunty Nancy surprisingly ignored that and did the seating as she wanted. My mother found that strange that she put Ella next to Herman even after she told her that Ella was dating Harold, but she kept quiet. I think your main worry will be Aunty Nancy as she always speaks so highly of Ella and was upset when Herman and she broke up. Think she may be eyeing her as a future daughter-in-law. Although she probably has no knowledge whatsoever of your true feelings with Herman. I too, like you, dislike Ella as I find her very false."

"Well, I am going to make sure that does not happen. I will do whatever I can to win Herman over and I will. No way is that bitch going to marry the love of my life. Even if I do not get him, I will make sure she doesn't either."

Anita thought to herself, Mabel was pretty spiteful of Ella, but knew Mabel almost always got her way. Tonight, is going to be one interesting night. Anita was not far wrong and although initially it went smoothly it ended in drama.

Herman was totally surprised when he entered the Lalwani house that evening to be greeted by so many people. It was nice for him to catch up with old school friends and the family. During the cocktail hour he was startled to see Ella there as he did not expect her to be invited. He noticed her gluing very close to Harold and wondered if they were dating.

When Harold went to get Ella a drink, he made his move to speak to her. Deep inside he still had very strong feelings for her. She was the only girl who could make his heart flutter just by looking at her. Tonight, more so than ever, she looked exceptionally beautiful. She was dressed in a maxi evening black silk dress with sultry splits in the front and a daring open back. She carried an evening clutch with floral diamante and wore high heels that matched. Her hair was put up and she was slightly tanned. She wore a pearl necklace with earrings to match. He downed his drink to draw enough courage, stood up and walked towards her.

"Hi Ella, it's been a while. How are you doing? I have been thinking about you. Are the family all good?" asked Herman. "I notice that you were hanging around with Harold are you guys dating?" he asked inquisitively.

"Hi Herman, thanks for asking. The family is all well. I am doing good and am in my final year at Hong Kong University. I heard that you graduated with honours from Oxford and that you have come back for good to join the family's business. I thought you may have gone for your Master's, but it is nice to see that you decided to come back home. I was kind of surprised to get a call from your mother inviting me for tonight's party as I felt a bit awkward, but I am glad she did and am happy that I did come. It's been a while since we last spoke. Harold did escort me to the party, and we have been seeing each other but we are not exclusive. How about you have you been dating anyone special?"

"No", replied Herman, "not since being with you that I had a serious relationship with anyone. I have been concentrating on my studies and am glad I did as I got my Bachelor of Economics with honours. I am home for good now and will be joining my dad's business in October after the Olympics. I have been thinking a lot about you since I returned and was actually going to give you a call this weekend to see if we could meet and have a coffee together?"

Ella looked at him and smiled, "Well I just had a look at the seating list there on the board and I believe that we will be sitting on the same table while not next to each other. Yes, it would be nice to have a coffee and catch up. You still have my number, don't you? Just call me any time and we can arrange a time and place to meet."

Just then Harold reappeared holding drinks for Ella and himself. Herman greeted him and they exchanged a few words after which Herman walked off to mingle with the other guests there. He felt jealous of Harold, but knew that was stupid of him, as it was he who actually pushed forward the idea that Ella and him separate when he left for university and that each of them should have no obligations with one another. Yet he could not help it: he still had feelings for Ella and did want to see her again and hopefully rebuild the relationship they once had.

Meanwhile Mabel all this time had been watching Herman talking with Ella and got livid. Ella really looked good tonight which angered her more, but she thought, I look better. Mabel did look beautiful. She was wearing a white French laced dress that was just above her knee. It was from Chanel and she had bought this specially for this party. The neckline of the dress was low and helped accentuate her breasts. She had borrowed her mom's jewellery and was wearing a full diamond choker on her neck and her earrings were two diamond carat studs. She was wearing a petite platinum gold Cartier diamond watch.

She felt Ella was dishonest and evil, why the hell did she come with Harold but then flirt with Herman. Herman needed to know how two-faced she was and what a horrible person she really was. She began scheming and thought, I must do something to make Herman aware how false Ella really is.

The dinner went smoothly, and Leslie made his welcome speech, he told the guests how proud he was of his son and that he was so glad that he would be joining the Sun Corporation from the first of September. Herman replied saying how surprised he was with the party and thanked all that had planned it. He also thanked all for coming and the wonderful gifts that he had received. During dinner Mabel was especially sweet with Herman buttering up his ego by telling him how smart he was and how proud she was of him. The cake was brought out and a toast was made by Leslie followed by champagne being popped and served to all. The "adults" then said their goodbyes and left to carry on their party at the Suns' residence.

Halfway during the ten-course dinner Mabel had walked around to where Harold was sitting and started a conversation with him.

"Hi Harold, have not seen you in ages how are you doing? Is Danny here as well as I have not spotted him around?" she asked.

Mabel had known Harold and his brother Danny a long time. In fact, she had dated both. She found them very attractive, but their personalities were matching, both totally boring. She had dated Harold first for around six months and when they broke up, she was surprised that his brother Danny asked her for a date. She dated him for about a month. They all went to the same school and although the boys were in a higher class, they spent a lot of time together. Their parents, Sir Anthony Brown and his wife Elizabeth were very close to the Sun and Lalwani families. Sir Anthony was the chairman of the Hong Kong and Shanghai Bank and financed many of Leslie's and Ajit's businesses. They were two of the most important customers to the bank and Sir Anthony personally handled their accounts. The Hong Kong and Shanghai Bank was the largest bank in the colony and was the only bank at that time that had the license to print the Hong Kong currency. It was respected, not only in Hong Kong, but worldwide with offices in London, New York, Paris, Dubai and Tokyo. Sir Anthony as Chairman of the Group was well respected and helped with the growth of the bank from it being a local one to one of the top international banks in the world. To all Hong Kongites the Hong Kong and Shanghai Bank was simply known as "The Bank".

"Hi Sexy, you look stunning tonight," replied Harold. "Danny has not been feeling well for a few days and we think he has caught some sort of bug so unfortunately he will be missing all of this. This is one fantastic party is it not? I heard that you and Anita arranged for The Continentals to perform tonight. They are the best band in town; it must have cost quite a bit to get them to perform live at a private party. I heard their new single on the radio yesterday and it's fantastic! Can't wait to see them play. How is life with you? Are you dating anyone in particular?"

"Herman and I have been sort of seeing each other recently and that is why I came to talk to you. I noticed that Ella was flirting with him and he was flirting back. I thought you and Ella were going steady and that she was more than just a date to you, so I was a bit surprised. I think for both our sakes that you hold on close to her tonight and make some sort of a statement that she is your girl in front of Herman, that is of course if you have feelings for Ella."

Harold was taken aback. He truly adored Ella she was the most brilliant lady he has ever been with. She was elegant and full of class and they both looked so good together. Both of their parents were so happy that they were dating. No way, he thought, am I going to let Leslie spoil what I have.

"I am confident that the two were only catching up, I am sure that Ella is true to me. Anyway, thanks for your advice and looking after my back which I truly appreciate but don't worry I can handle this," replied Harold. Mabel smiled and walked away.

As soon as all the parents left the D.J. started playing his first set. The D.J. began by playing "My Guy" by Mary Wells followed by the song "Oh Pretty Woman" by Roy Orbison. All along Herman was building up confidence to approach Ella and ask her for a dance and when "Pretty Woman" started playing he thought to himself, this is the perfect song and most appropriate. He looked across the table at her and she looked right back, he stood up and walked towards her. Just before he reached her Harold was already there by her side asking Ella for a dance. Ella stood up and took Harold's hand as they walked up to the dance floor. He felt really awkward standing there alone when Mabel walked up to him.

"Shall we dance my handsome man? Your pretty woman awaits." Mabel led him to the dance floor, and they were only a few feet from where Harold and Ella were dancing. The song finished and the D.J. put on a classic ballad "Put Your Head on My Shoulder" by Paul Anka. The four continued to dance. Herman noticed Ella's head on Harold's shoulder while Harold was slowly stroking her back. Ella looked up at Harold and they went into a deep kiss. Mabel, who was dancing with Herman, noticed his disillusionment and reached out and turned his face towards her. She pushed down on his neck putting their faces close to one another. She closed her eyes and kissed Herman. The response from Herman was slow initially but then suddenly he started kissing her back deeply for what seemed a very long time.

Anita, who was on the dance floor as well with Kishore, could not believe what she just witnessed. She felt happy for Mabel and hoped it all worked out well for the two of them. After the song they all went back to their seats. Anita approached the head table and went to Mabel and asked if she would like to go to the ladies' room. Mabel nodded, stood up and followed Anita to the ladies.

"What the hell happened? Everyone was looking at the two of you kiss and were shocked. Think because they never saw you two as a couple. That was one long kiss and looked very passionate! It looked like Herman was enjoying it as much as you were!"

Mabel looked at Anita with the biggest smile ever, "My heart is pumping away like crazy and I am shaking. I have never ever been kissed like that before. I actually saw stars when he kissed me. I can't believe it all happened. I took the risk of kissing him, but I did not ever expect him to kiss me back the way he did. I am in love Anita, truly in love. I just do not know what to say to him when we go back out. I am so glad you asked me to go to the ladies with you at least it gives me a chance to calm down and stop shaking before going back outside."

Anita replied, "I really am so pleased for you; I think when you get back out and see Herman just act naturally as if nothing had occurred. I am sure that he will reach out to you and discuss what happened. Just act cool and let things materialise."

Anita was truly happy for Mabel as everything seemed to be working out well for her tonight. She was hoping it would lead to a long-term relationship for both of them and hopefully one day end in marriage. As they both walked out of the ladies heading towards the main table, they witnessed Ella standing up behind where Herman was sitting and chatting to him. Ella had her back turned towards the girls and could not see them. Mabel stopped Anita from advancing further to the table as she wanted to see what Ella was up to. She saw Ella laughing and obviously flirting with Herman. She saw Ella lean down and kiss him on the cheeks. Mabel was burning in anger. As they were watching a waiter passed by holding a tray of drinks and offered it to the girls. Mabel picked up a glass of red wine and walked towards Ella as she did, she pretended to slip and poured the whole glass of wine on Ella.

Ella let out a huge scream and shouted, "What the fuck! You clumsy bitch, you have ruined my beautiful dress!"

Mabel looked back at Ella and said, "I am truly sorry the floor here was wet and I just slipped are you OK? Come let's go upstairs to Anita's room and you can freshen up there, I will help you clean up and you can borrow one of Anita's dresses. I believe she is almost the same size as you so hopefully we can find something that will look good on you." Herman stood up from where he was sitting and offered to help but they said there was not much he could do, and they would be back shortly after they cleaned up Ella and got her a change of clothing.

"Come on then let's go and clean you up. I think The Continentals will be on soon so let's hurry," said Mabel as she grabbed two glasses of wine from a waiter nearby and offered one to Ella who refused so she passed it on to Anita. The girls went up to Anita's room and Ella went to the bathroom to clean up. She came back out and looked at some of the outfits that Anita had laid out on her bed for Ella to choose. Ella loathed most of them but found one that was more her style and headed back to the bathroom with it to change. She walked out wearing a white dress that was similar to what Mabel was wearing to purposely upset her.

"You know Ella I am really sorry for having slipped and getting the wine all over your beautiful outfit. I will pay for the dry cleaning and if any of the stains cannot be removed, I will pay for you to get a new one. I feel really bad about all this."

Ella turned and looked straight into Mabel's eyes and said, "You did that on purpose you bitch, and you know it. I am not stupid; you did not slip on the floor it was all planned. I know you have always been jealous of me and Herman. I have noticed that since I first started dating Herman. I saw how you dragged him to the dance floor tonight and forced that kiss on him. I can tell you one thing while I am around you are not going to get him!"

Anita defended Mabel and said, "Ella that was a genuine slip no way Mabel would have done that purposely. She has apologised and let's just put this behind us. She even offered to replace the dress."

Ella replied, "Stop protecting the bitch and let her fight her own battle. You know I am right Anita so stop defending her. She uses everyone, and I am surprised how you could be friends with that cunt. She will use you for her own purpose and when she gets what she wants will drop you as a friend. Harold and Danny, both of whom dated her, have told me how full of bullshit she is so you should take care girl!"

Anita started to defend Mabel, but Mabel stopped her from saying any more and looked directly at Ella, "Listen shithead you are the bitch and not me. You come here with Harold who is supposedly your boyfriend. You then flirt with Herman and later on the dance floor you kiss Harold in front of Herman obviously trying to make him jealous. I do not know what fucking game you are playing but do not mess with me. You had your chance with him but it's over. You go fuck yourself and if you ever try and get between Herman and me again you will regret it for the rest of your life. You know me and you know what I am capable of so stay out of my way!"

Ella replied, "Firstly I am not exclusive with Harold. Herman and I have history and you know that. You may think he does not care for me any more but believe me you are mistaken. He was mine before and I can get him back any time. I know he still has feelings for me for earlier tonight he even invited me for a date. He told me also that he was not dating anyone currently and since we split, he has not been interested in any other woman. So, what you say is full of shit. I am not scared of you and your inconsequential threats so do whatever you want, and I will carry on the way I want with Herman and let's see who finally wins out. You are too crude for him; you are a whore who shows off her tits to attract men. Even Aunty Nancy prefers me for Herman than you, so with his parents adoring me you have no chance with him. No man will marry you, but all would love to put their dicks between your colossal breasts and fuck you!"

That was the final straw. Mabel was not going to have Ella have the last say. She was clutching the glass of red wine which she replaced with the one she had spilt earlier.

"Well, my darling here we go again then," she walked up to Ella stared directly at her and poured the red wine down her head slowly.

Before Ella could react, she said, "Have a wonderful evening my love. Sorry I cannot stay longer and keep you amused, but I am going down to enjoy the rest of the party. I believe The Continentals will be on shortly, so if you want to watch them perform, I suggest you better get changed again and hurry, my love," she smiled and walked out of the room, slamming the door behind her. Anita stood there not saying a word. She was totally shocked. She could not believe that Mabel just did that. She finally pulled herself out of the trance and asked Ella if she was all right. Ella stood in the middle of the room, the red wine dripping down her beautiful white dress; she was in a state of shock. Anita rushed into her bathroom and got a towel and helped Ella to wipe the wine which was now all over her body.

"Do not worry, Ella, I will find you something to wear and clean you up so you can go back down."

"No," said Ella, "I am not going back to that party, not now after what just happened. Just lend me an old pair of jeans and a top and I will change into that. While I am changing, please go down to the party and find Harold and tell him to meet me at the entrance of the house as he needs to take me back home immediately. You need not tell him what happened, I will let him know."

Anita replied, "I am so sorry this happened I do not know why Mabel did that it was so unlike her. Maybe she had a bit too much to drink. You do not need to leave the party I can lend you a nice dress and we can work on your make-up together and you can return back to the party."

"No, Anita, I will not be around that bitch any longer. You can do me a favour though. Tell that little fucking shithead of a friend of yours that this is not over. She better watch her back for I am coming after her and I promise you she will suffer a lot more than what she did to me tonight."

Ella got quickly dressed and went to the front door to await Harold. Harold came to meet her and was surprised to see Ella dressed that way. He asked what happened, but she broke down and said she would tell him, but not now as all she wanted was to leave the party and go home.

Meanwhile Mabel returned to the table and was greeted by Herman. "Is Ella all right?" he asked.

"She is still upstairs with Anita choosing something to wear. She is just being a bit dramatic about it all. I accidently spilled the wine on her as you witnessed, but she insists I did that on purpose. I apologised, but she just kept on, so I decided to leave her to it and came down to be with you." The Continentals were playing and both Herman and Mabel turned their chairs towards the stage to watch them perform. Herman reached down and held Mabel's hand. As soon as The Continentals finished performing and the D.J. returned Herman asked Mabel if she would like to get some fresh air. She said yes and he took her out to the garden where he was alone with her.

"I don't know what happened earlier, but that kiss felt so good and right. I have never thought of you romantically, but I guess the feeling had been there for a while and that the kiss brought it all out." He looked at Mabel caringly and put his lips to hers and kissed her tenderly.

Mabel was the happiest she had ever been for the longest of times and looked back lovingly at Herman, smiled and said, "I have loved you for a very long, time Mr Herman Sun."

Chapter 9
She loves you, yeah, yeah, yeah.

The Suns' Home
888 Nathan Road, Kowloon, Hong Kong
June 9th, 1964, five thirty a.m.

Leslie's watch alarm started vibrating, waking him up. He looked down at his Casio watch and saw that it was five thirty a.m. He was wearing the digital watch that was given to him by his son Herman when he returned from England. It was made in Japan and had the latest technology built into it. You could programme up to four time zones. It had many other features but the most important to Leslie was it was able to record your activities and calculate how many calories you burnt. It was great for his running as it recorded the miles he ran and at what pace. He got up and went to the bathroom quietly making sure not to awaken Nancy. He put on his tracksuit and headed down to the basement of the house to the gym room.

The gym was divided into three main areas. There was the sauna room where one could go for a sauna and after have a massage in an adjacent room that had a proper massage bed. Whoever would want a massage would need to book it the day before from a masseur the family used and who would come to the house and give that person a full body massage. The main room was the one with all the gym equipment plus a special area for weights. This was used surprisingly most by Nancy and his son Herman. The weights area was equipped with heavy duty dumbbells, fixed weight barbells, Olympic plates, bars and collars as well as lifting platforms and jerk boxes. The third room was Leslie's special room where he would do his Kung Fu. This was fitted with mirrors all along the four walls so he could see what he was doing from all angles. He would go there religiously every morning for an hour to do his Kung Fu training.

After his Kung Fu workout, he would go for his run which started from his home up to Beacon Hill and back, which was a five-mile journey. It usually took him less than half an hour to complete. That morning as he was running, he thought of the events of four years ago. The death of his beloved Lillian affected him much more than he thought. It took him a long time to recover and what made it worse was discovering after the coroner did his examination that she was three months' pregnant. He remembered that day vividly, how he was shocked to find her naked lying on top of the piano. He could almost feel the pain she must have gone through with having her throat slit and body cut open. He remembered John Woods showing up with the rest of the forensic team to the apartment and how he was led out while they did their going-over. He refused to move from the apartment till the body was removed.

As the body was brought out on a stretcher with a white cloth covering it entirely Leslie removed the top part of the cloth revealing Lillian's face and kissed her lovingly on the lips. John brought out this beautiful gift-wrapped box with a birthday card stuck on it that he had found in the apartment and handed it to Leslie. Leslie opened the card. In it written in her handwriting was this: "I wish I could get you something more than this small gift, but I know you will love it and think of me every time you wear it. The last few years with you have been the most wonderful time in my life. You are the kindest soul I have ever met, and I thank God every day that he brought you to me. Have a lovely birthday my darling, I will always love you." He unwrapped the gift and opened the box. In it was a Cartier watch which on the back was engraved, "From your One and Only. L.W. 30/07/1960."

He swore to himself from that day on that his life would be dedicated to finding out who killed her and would bring on justice for Lillian. When he killed Kentaro Hashimoto, he thought that was the end of it but what Kentaro said to him on his dying breath made him think that maybe he had killed the wrong person. He had mentioned a person called Kohei Inowaki saying he was the real culprit who killed Lillian. Over the last four years he had been trying to find the whereabouts of Kohei but with no success.

His whole life changed after the death of Lillian. He became reclusive. He cancelled his birthday party which was to have happened the same week Lillian died and did not attend the governor's ball the following month where he was to be the main speaker. He did not attend any parties for the next three years and buried himself in his work and searching for Kohei. The meetings that the Warriors of the Sun held weekly at the Suns' residence became bimonthly meetings instead of weekly. In some ways that was appropriate as Hong Kong was going through a crimeless period.

Nancy was worried about him as was the rest of his family, but they thought better to give him time to get over it. This year, however, things changed for him and he grew more positive with his life. His son's graduation and the fact that Herman was selected to be a member of the Hong Kong Olympic team lifted him. He realised that it was time to break away from his melancholia and return back to his old self. He needed to be there for his family whom he had ignored for way too long. He decided to be more outgoing and get back to the social scene. He, for the first time in years, asked Nancy for dinner that evening, just the two of them. He decided that whilst the kids attended The Beatles concert, he would take Nancy to her favourite restaurant, Jimmy's Kitchen. He told her at the same time that it would be OK for her to plan his fifty-fourth birthday next month. She had been begging him to allow this as she thought it would bring him out of his grief. Nancy was shocked but ecstatic and gave him a big hug telling him she had waited a long time for him to get over what had happened and was so happy to have her old Leslie back.

He finished his run and looked at his watch, it was almost seven thirty a.m. He thought, I better have a quick shower, before the water restriction came on at eight a.m. Hong Kong at this time was going through a drought and the government was forced to have water restrictions in the colony. The water was turned on only from six a.m. to eight a.m. and from six p.m. to nine p.m. every day during the restrictions.

Leslie had a quick shower and moved into his study with a cup of coffee. There was a large blue file with the Hong Kong insignia on it. It was marked:

Confidential

"Information concerning the People's Republic of China (PRC) Current Influence and Potential of Political unrests in the Colony."

The governor himself had forwarded it to Leslie to read and to give his thoughts on the matter.

Hong Kong was suffering its second straight summer of drought. During the 1960s the Hong Kong government was concerned by the political gains China would reap from trade in water with Hong Kong and wanted to achieve a water self-sufficiency for the colony. This colonial water policy was made during the current crisis, a severe drought that risked economic ruination and social unrest.

The population was growing rapidly, and the reservoirs were not sufficient enough to fulfil the needs of the population of the colony. Hong Kong relied heavily on importing food and fuel from China and now also had to purchase water too making the colony even more reliant on China. The main fear was what if China turned off the taps?

The direct financial gains reaped by China from this trade were minimal, but they had more complex motivations for collaborating with Hong Kong. There were clear political advantages for the PRC. Firstly, the PRC enjoyed a propaganda victory by assisting their "compatriots" in Hong Kong to alleviate drought. More importantly, China strengthened its capacity to damage the Hong Kong economy and to threaten the social order by making the colony even more reliant on key commodities from the mainland. It was turning into a dangerous situation. The communist party was growing in Hong Kong and pushing more for Hong Kong unifying with China. Tensions with the communists grew during this period and the border between Hong Kong and China was on full alert. China, however, did not ever cut off the water supply although many a times they suggested that they would.

Leslie read the file comprehensively which was researched by a special commission to look into the water supply situation in Hong Kong that was set up by the governor himself. He started making notes and recommendations on what he thought was needed. Leslie was concerned. He felt one day things would flare up as he did not trust the Chinese government at all. The Communist Party in Hong Kong was becoming a headache for the British. The communist press was constantly writing propaganda about the British and stirring up the population. The only way Leslie thought to keep the balance was for the British to show strength and be committed to the colony and stand up to China's bullying.

On the water situation he was upset with the government for not heeding the report which he made three years prior. He had advised them then that if they did not look forward and prepare for the future by building more larger reservoirs that shortages of water could be a reality and a major problem for the population. Now the government was in a situation and at the mercy of China and needed to work carefully with them to ensure they kept the water coming from the mainland. He opened up his diary and pencilled in the end of the month to have a meeting with the Commissioner for Water Services, Lionel Nelson to discuss this situation in depth and to put a plan into action.

Leslie looked at his watch, it was almost 10.40 p.m. He had a luncheon meeting that afternoon at one p.m. with both Ajit and Ray. Apparently the two wanted to build a theme park in the New Territories and were thinking of approaching Walt Disney to ask him for a license to build "Disneyland, Hong Kong". It was the mastermind of Ajit who had visited Disneyland in Anaheim, California with his wife and children two years before and thought what a great concept it was and how it could work in Hong Kong. The project would be huge, and they wanted Leslie to invest together with them to lessen the risk. Apparently Ajit had found a perfect plot of one hundred and twenty acres in the New Territories which would be perfect for the park. Besides building the park they also had to build the infrastructure around it to make it viable. Leslie had visited Disneyland together with his family and the Woods five years ago and they had a wonderful time there. He thought Hong Kong was ready for this and it could be very profitable. He had asked his son Herman to join him for the lunch meeting as this could be a great first project for Herman to get involved in and he would be there to guide him through it.

After the lunch meeting, he had planned to meet up with Bella. After Lillian passed away Leslie got close to Bella. She was beautiful, just like her sister was, and every time he looked at her, he would see a younger Lillian. He felt so sorry for her for after Lillian's death she had no immediate family left. He treated her like his own daughter and was there for her whenever she needed anything. She wanted to purchase an apartment in Tsim Tsa Tsui in Mody Road and wanted Leslie to view it with her and have his opinion on it. She was headstrong and never asked Leslie for anything. She did get closer to Leslie after Lillian's death and came to him from time to time when she wanted his advice. Bella was an independent person who was very driven. She went on to university and finished her Master's in Business Management with honours. Leslie had offered her a job in his business when she returned back from university, but she turned it down and was now working for Raymond Ho in his entertainment company.

To end the day Leslie had a dinner date with his wife. Leslie thought it was going to be a busy sort of day although not much as far as business but more with being with friends and family. He stood up and headed for the family room to see what Nancy was up to. He was greeted by Wan-Yu who informed him that Nancy was up on the roof top looking after her garden and asked whether he should fetch her. Leslie told him not to worry and to let her be but asked Wan-Yu to let Herman know to be ready by twelve thirty p.m. and to also get the chauffeur ready by that time as he had a lunch appointment which Herman would be joining. He then went up to his room to change.

Wan-Yu knocked on the door of Herman's room. Herman, who was on the phone with Dilip, put the phone down, asking Dilip not to hang up and wait for him to return.

"Sir, your father has asked me to tell you to be ready by twelve thirty p.m. sharp and meet him at the entrance of the house. I have already arranged for the chauffeur to be there then."

Herman looked at his watch, it was eleven forty-five p.m. He did not realise it was that late and told Wan-Yu not to worry and that he would be ready to leave by twelve thirty p.m. He returned to the phone call and told Dilip he had to go and get ready but for him to remember that they were all meeting at his house at five p.m. sharp before heading out to see The Beatles that evening and for Anita and him not to be late.

Herman was looking forward to the evening. He could not believe that Uncle Ray had gotten him the tickets and especially the passes for backstage. He was bringing along with him to the concert his sister

Lucy, and invited Ben, Mabel, Dilip and Anita to join him. There were to be two shows that evening, the early one, which was to start at four p.m. and end at six p.m. and the second show, which was to start at seven p.m. and finish by nine p.m. Herman had tickets for the second show. Bella, who was managing the show that evening for the organisers she worked for, had asked that they be at the theatre no later than five fifteen p.m. She would meet them at the VIP room which was on the first floor of the theatre and take them to meet The Beatles before the show started. He thought to himself, what a great job Bella had working for Uncle Ray's entertainment company having the chance to meet famous celebrities who would perform in Hong Kong or at the Hotel Faroe in Macau.

He had gotten up early that morning and had gone down to the gym to do his weights. He did this almost every morning around six thirty for an hour, building up his upper muscle strength. He had to, from the next Monday, start a vigorous training routine with his coach Francois Bernaut at the Hong Kong Olympic training centre which was located near the Happy Valley on the island for five days a week. He was kind of dreading that as it meant he had to get up extra early to get there by seven thirty a.m. to begin training. He would then have to train on and off for six hours a day. He thought it would all be worth it though if he did do well at the Olympics. Realistically he had little chance of winning a medal as he was ranked around eightieth worldwide. His coach Francois Bernaut was an ex French Olympian medal winner in all three disciplines of fencing. The three forms of Olympic fencing were:

Foil, a light thrusting weapon where the valid target is restricted to the torso and double touches are not allowed. Epee, a heavy thrusting weapon; the valid target area covers the entire body; double touches are allowed light cutting and thrusting weapon; the valid target area includes almost everything above the waist (excluding the back of the head and the hands); double touches are not allowed.

Francois was hired by the Hong Kong Olympic committee to specially train Herman, however most of the cost of acquiring him was mainly borne by Herman's father. Herman was entered in all three disciplines. Herman was concerned that his training regime would mean that he would have less time to spend with Mabel just when he had realised how much he cared for her. He would also have to leave for Tokyo three weeks prior to his event to train there and would totally be away for five weeks starting from the first week of September. He could not believe how he unexpectedly felt these strong feelings for Mabel. He had never thought of her romantically before. They grew up with each other, their parents being the best of friends and the families went on many holidays together. They went to the same primary school and would spend many weekends with one another. They had always been close, like brother and sister. It was all so strange that just one kiss on the dance floor seemed to awaken his senses and suddenly opened up his feelings for her.

He had always found Mabel attractive and extremely sexy and loved her bubbly personality. Growing up they were very close and shared each other's secrets. What happened at the party had totally confused Herman, who before that was only attracted physically to Ella. That night, after the party, both Mabel and her brother Ben came for a sleepover to his house as it was too late for them to go home back to the island as all ferry services were closed. Herman's parents knew of this, and they had Wan-Yu prepare two guest rooms on the first floor for Ben and Mabel.

Mabel lost her virginity that night. She, in the middle of the night, sneaked out of her room and opened the door to where Herman was sleeping. She was wearing a red laced lingerie which was low-cut and very revealing. She crept silently to his bed, lifted the sheet and laid down beside him. Herman woke up and was surprised to see Mabel lying next to him. He was flummoxed and started to say something when she put her finger on his lips to silence him. She silently got up, turned on the lights and started removing her lingerie. She looked absolutely beautiful standing in front of him totally naked. She had a stunning hourglass body; her breasts were large but firm, she had a slim waist and a well-proportioned bottom. She walked up to the bed, pulled off the sheet and threw it on to the floor. She walked over to him, started by kissing him on his forehead moving her lips slowly down to his, kissing him deeply, and then moving her lips to his chest, kissing and sucking his nipples lightly. She continued moving down till she reached his penis which was rock hard. She cupped her mouth around it going deeper and gently moving her head up and down. Herman got really aroused and could not hold on much longer, he turned her around throwing her onto her back and started to enter her. She looked at him lovingly and said, "Darling please be gentle with me, you are my first." They made love for half an hour before Herman turned around and went silently back to sleep, snoring softly. Mabel stayed awake staring at him for what seemed like hours before she got up, put her lingerie back on and went back to her room. As she entered her room, she could see the sunlight coming through brightly from the crack in the curtain. She felt content and cheerful. She did not bother to go to sleep but instead walked into the bathroom to have a quick shower.

Herman got dressed quickly and rushed down to the entrance of the house where he was met by his father.

"We will be going to Hugo's at the Hyatt hotel for lunch. I suggested the restaurant to Ajit and Ray as I know you love the food there especially the Sydney rock oysters which are flown fresh from Australia daily. By the way how did your party go after we left? I have had no time to chat with you the last few days. I asked Wan-Yu to come and fetch you on Sunday as I wanted to take the family out to the new Thai Restaurant in town for lunch as I know how much you love Thai food. I also wanted to check with you on how the party went, but Wan-Yu said you were still fast asleep, so we left you alone. Your party must have ended up real late I guess, and you must have gone to bed in the early morning. I did take the rest of the family for lunch and left you to sleep as you must have been exhausted. We asked both Ben and Mabel to join us when we saw them at breakfast that morning, but they said that their parents had arranged for them to go to Repulse Bay and have lunch at the hotel there and spend the rest of the day at the beach."

In reality he had already heard from Nancy who got all the gossip from Lucy that there had been a huge commotion after they left the party between Mabel and Ella. Apparently, according to Lucy, Mabel had inadvertently spilled some wine on Ella who claimed she did it on purpose. Ella started swearing at Mabel loud enough for everyone in the party to hear. She kept cursing and using foul language even though Mabel kept apologising. Mabel tried profusely to calm her down, but

Ella was so upset and left the party with Harold even before The Continentals started playing. Both Leslie and Nancy thought it so unlikely of Ella. They both liked Ella very much and hoped one day she and Herman would end up together. Leslie was worried about Herman as for the last few days he seemed to be in a world of his own and wondered if the incident had something to do with that.

"The party was fantastic," replied Herman. "I really need to thank you and Mom for organising it I really had a great time. Everybody there enjoyed themselves I think, the food was fantastic and the entertainment amazing."

"I heard that Ella and Mabel got into some sort of argument from Lucy. What happened there?" asked Leslie inquisitively.

"Well Mabel slipped and accidentally spilled her drink on Ella. I was standing there and obviously it was not deliberately done, but Ella totally freaked out swearing and cursing at Mabel for absolutely no reason claiming Mabel did it on purpose. Mabel apologised and helped her to clean up but apparently, she was so upset and decided to leave the party with Harold. Ella was totally in the wrong. I feel she had no right getting so upset in what was obviously an accident. I will speak to Ella tonight and see if she is all right, she will be coming to the concert together with Harold and Danny. I believe her father got tickets directly from Uncle Ray and they will be seated two rows behind us according to Bella who organised it for them. I believe they too have VIP passes for the backstage. I heard also that Uncle Ray managed to get tickets for the rest of the Lalwani children but for the earlier show. I called Uncle Ray this morning and thanked him for getting me front row seats and the backstage passes to see The Beatles."

Leslie smiled, "Yes that was very kind of Raymond. Both Mom and I were surprised that he gave you such a lovely present. What will you do after the show? Will you be eating out or coming home for dinner? If you are coming home after the concert will Ben, Mabel, Dilip and Anita come as well? If so, I will call Wan-Yu later to inform the kitchen that you will all be home for dinner so they can prepare your meals. Mom and I will be out, I am taking her to Jimmy's Kitchen."

"No that's not necessary as we all plan to eat at the American Steak house after the show, which is near the theatre, after which we plan to head on to the Bayside Nightclub for a few drinks and watch the band play there. We also want to go and visit the Scene Nightclub at the Peninsula Hotel which I have heard is the newest and trendiest club in town. I heard that the action really starts there only after midnight. We may be home late so do not worry please. We have asked Ben and Mabel to stay over tonight as it will be too late for them to head back to Hong Kong. Do not worry, I have it all arranged with Wan-Yu to have the guest rooms arranged. You need not get the chauffeur to wait for us as we will just taxi back. I am really happy you are taking Mom out as it has been ages since you two have spent an evening together alone."

"The Scene Discotheque" was recently opened by Michael Kadoorie the owner of the Peninsula Hotel. It was located in the basement of the hotel and run under the swinging management of D.J./Dancer/Model, Sue Smith under her married name Sue Patel. Michael Kadoorie was inspired by the nightlife in London in the early sixties and wanted to reflect that scene in Hong Kong. He was impressed on how popular clubs like Annabel's and The Tramp were in London and how it catered to an exclusive younger, richer crowd. The Scene Discotheque was expensive, and you needed to pay an entrance fee just to get in. The cocktails they served there were about 50% higher than any other club in Hong Kong but every night there would be people lining up just to get in.

"I know Sue the manager at The Scene very well," replied Leslie. "I was introduced to her by Ajit a few years ago and have met her at many parties. She is married to an Indian businessman who has business dealings with Ajit. She is the currently the general manager of The Scene. I believe she also is considered the first lady D.J. in Hong Kong. I have not been to The Scene myself but heard that the young and trendy party there. It is usually very hard to get in and they do not take bookings I hear. If you have trouble getting in or finding a table, please ask for her and tell her you are my son. I am sure she will be able to sort you out."

Leslie was quite familiar with the nightclub scene and was tempted to invest in one together with Raymond who planned to open one at the Mandarin Hotel where he also owned the Havana Bar. The whole nightclub scene in Hong Kong was growing fast and was very profitable. His wife Nancy, however, talked him out of investing in it as she said he had already too much on his plate. In actuality, after what happened with Lillian and Leslie, she did not want him involved in the club scene at all. The Scene was one of many nightclubs that were popping up in Hong Kong during this era. Most of the swankier ones were in the top hotels, basically because of the security there and thus being a safe place for the rich and young to go to. The other popular clubs in Kowloon were "The Polaris", which was located at the top floor of the Hyatt Regency Hotel and the other in the basement of the Sheraton Hotel called "The Good Earth". The two most popular ones in Hong Kong Island were "The Den" at the Hilton hotel and "The Taipan Club" at the Furama Hotel.

The luncheon meeting went well. Ajit had heard back from Walt Disney on his proposal and he had shown some interest in the project but cited that if he got involved, he would want a majority stake in the business. Leslie was a bit concerned with that as from past experience with his other businesses where he was a minority shareholder it almost never worked well for him. Another of Walt Disney's requirements was that he would choose the companies to build the park and especially the rides. He explained that it took him many years to get the rides to a safety level that he felt comfortable with. He was worried that even though he gave all the blueprints to a local contractor they would not get it right and he would feel uncomfortable with that. Raymond questioned why they needed to have a Disney Park. Doing it together with Walt Disney would bring up the costs considerably. Obviously, Hong Kong was ready for some sort of an amusement park, but did they need the Disney brand? Raymond said he was presented a plan by a developer a year ago on building an Ocean Park on the island. He, at that time, shelved the whole idea but felt now was possibly the right time to take another look at it together with Ajit and Leslie. Herman agreed with Uncle Ray and said since it was going to be a huge project, whichever way they decided to go with, and suggested they looked deeper into Raymond's alternative plans before making any decisions. They ended the meeting by Raymond saying he would pass copies of the project he had to both Leslie and Ajit to study and for them to meet again maybe in a couple of weeks to discuss it further.

After lunch Leslie went off to meet Bella, he had told her that he would meet her directly at the apartment at around two thirty p.m. He looked at his watch and it was two fifteen. The apartment was only about a ten-minute walk, so he asked Herman to take the chauffeur home and to send him back to the Hyatt Hotel, telling him to wait for him there. He went to the address that Bella had given him which was 72 Mody Road. The apartment was 2D on the sixth floor. He rang the bell and Bella opened the door, hugged Leslie and thanked him for coming. The apartment was in a new building complex and was built by one of his rival developers, Henderson Land. They were an up-and-coming company who concentrated on smaller projects aimed more for the middle class. The apartment was close to one thousand square feet which was a decent size for Bella. It had two bedrooms with en suites, a decent size lounge and kitchen with an open plan.

Leslie did not understand why Bella did not take up the offer he gave her after Lillian died. He had always told Lillian when she was alive not to worry about her little sister as he would always look out for her. So, with Lillian's passing he wanted to secure Bella with a home she could call her own. He did not like the idea of her living together with Mama Wendy as that was not the environment that she should be around. He had specially chosen one apartment in his new development in Hung Hom which was near TST for her. It was a fifteen hundred square foot three-bedroom apartment on the sixteenth floor of a new building overlooking the harbour. Bella, however, refused to accept that from Leslie and said that she was happy living with Mama Wendy for the time being. He also offered her a large sum of money so she could live comfortably but that she also refused. She was stubborn and determined to succeed with her life without his or anyone else's help. It was Mama Wendy and Uncle Ray who supported her financially to go to university in the U.K. and she paid them back for it by working while going through university with any job she could find.

Over the years, due to Leslie's persistence in being there for her and showing up at all her birthdays and special occasions, she grew fond of him. She learned to trust his judgements and came to him whenever she needed advice. Although close to Uncle Ray, she found him harder to reach out to than Leslie. Mama Wendy was wonderful to her but could not guide or advise her with her education or career path, so she turned to Uncle Leslie. She knew how much Leslie had loved her sister and how much pain he endured the last few years and warmed to him for that.

"What do you think Uncle, they are asking for HK$340,000. I know it seems a bit expensive, but I love the location and the apartment is very modern and has all the facilities. They have good security here as well and I can get a parking space in the basement for an additional HK$20,000. There are only eighteen apartments in the whole building which I like as I do not have too many tenants to worry about causing disturbances."

"I will be totally honest with you that works out to roughly HK$290 a square foot. I realise it is new and has all the modern facilities plus the build is excellent but taken all that in consideration it is still overpriced and should not be any more than HK$250 a square foot which should work out to HK$300,000. Listen, I know Dr Lee the CEO and owner of Henderson Land very well. Let me have a word with him and see if I can get you a better price. By the way how are you going to finance it?"

"Well, I have saved about HK$50,000 in the bank which I will put down as deposit and then pay the rest within eight to ten years. I believe the interest the bank is charging is roughly 6% per annum. I have already spoken to the loan department at the HSBC and they say it all is workable and would approve the loan for me to purchase it."

Leslie smiled and look at her, "That is about HK$12,000 a year just in interest. I know you will not take any money from me. I offered to buy you an apartment when Lillian passed away, but you stubbornly refused, now please let me lend you the money to buy this apartment without any interest and you can pay me back HK$5,000 monthly or whatever you can afford till it is paid off. If I get the apartment down to HK$300,000 and you pay me HK$50,000 as a deposit, then you will owe me HK$250,000. I am happy you pay me HK$5,000 a month on the balance HK$250,000 and if you can do that you will be able to pay me off in around four years. If, however, you cannot afford to pay HK$5,000 monthly any amount will do. I do not want you to feel pressured to pay me back quickly and put a strain on your finances."

"Seriously, Uncle, will you do that for me? I was going to pay the bank anyway around HK$5,000 monthly plus interest monthly and I have no problems with that if you can finance me without interest, I will be ever so thankful to you. You know I will be good for the money and I will work extra hard and see if I can pay it off even earlier," she replied.

"Good then consider the deal done. I will come back to you within a couple of days with the relevant deed to the property. It will be under your name only I presume?"

"Yes, Uncle, it will be solely under my name, thank you."

Leslie had known for a few years that Bella was a lesbian, but he never judged her for that. He knew she had been seriously dating an upcoming actress Eileen Siu for around two years and was wondering if Eileen would move into the apartment with Bella and also invest in the property collectively. He was happy to hear that the apartment would be in her name only.

"By the way I heard you will be organising The Beatles concert tonight. Herman told me he will be meeting you at the Princess Theatre just before the concert and you will bring him backstage with his friends to greet The Beatles. Tonight, should be a madhouse with both concerts being totally sold out. I am sure fans who did not get tickets would surround the theatre hoping to catch sight of The Beatles as they enter or leave the theatre. How is security for the night? I hope it is sufficient."

"Don't worry, Uncle, we have gone through the security with Uncle John and the police over twenty times and it is going to be tight. They will put up barriers stopping people not holding tickets to be a fair distance away from the theatre. Inside the theatre we will have our own security plus undercover police mingling with the crowd to ensure there are no disturbances. We will be checking all bags and do a body check on people entering the theatre to ensure no one is carrying anything that could cause harm. We have arranged for the huge plot of land behind the Sheraton Hotel as a temporary car park so as to not cause traffic jams. People attending will either need to be dropped near this plot or have their cars parked there and walk about ten minutes to the theatre. I

174

realise a lot of important people will be attending so we are extra careful."

Leslie said his goodbyes and left. He was happy that at least he could help Bella even though in a such a small way. He looked at his watch and realised that it was late for him to go back to his office. He decided to walk to the Buddhist temple he usually went to say a prayer for Lillian. It was a fifteen-minute walk from where he was. The temple was quiet and there were only a few Buddhist monks sitting on the floor praying. He took off his shoes, entered the temple and walked towards the altar. There he picked up eight incense sticks and lit them praying in front of the Golden Buddha statue which was covered with garlands. He prayed that wherever Lillian was that she was in peace. Before leaving the temple, he left a large donation to the head monk who looked after the temple.

Herman and his group arrived at the theatre at around 5.20 p.m. They had to go through a routine security check and only then were led into the theatre. The first show was still on and they could hear the crowd screaming. They followed a sign that said holders of VIP passes please go to the first floor. There they were met by Bella who took them to the VIP room. She led them to the lounge area in the room, where laid out on a table, were finger sandwiches, cakes, coffee and tea. Herman noticed Harold, Danny and Ella sitting across the room and went up to say hello. Mabel did not follow him and remained where she was chatting with Bella and Anita, Ben and Dilip, however, followed Herman.

"Hi guys," said Herman. "Aren't you excited about this we are going to actually meet The Beatles in person. I brought my Nikon camera with me to take some pictures and I believe the girls have brought their autograph books with them." He walked directly up to Ella who was sitting next to Harold and said, "I am sorry that you left suddenly the other night. I had no way to thank you for your gift and did not have a chance to say goodbye." Ella had given him a beautiful crocodile skin wallet with his initials stamped on it.

Ella looked up at him. She had noticed that Herman walked into the room with his arms around Mabel's waist and was very surprised as he had mentioned to her in the party that he was not interested in anyone at the moment and that he still had feelings for her. In fact, he had asked her out for a date.

"I am sorry to have left without saying goodbye. I was not feeling well and needed to leave, and I did not want to disturb or upset you as I knew you would be watching The Continentals play. How did the party end up? I heard that it was fantastic and that The Continentals were great."

Before Herman could answer her Bella asked for all in the room to please follow her as she would lead them backstage to where The Beatles were. They had just finished the first show. She said that they would have only fifteen minutes to mingle with the group, take pictures and get autographs. As soon as the fifteen minutes were over, they were to follow Bella out to the theatre and be seated at their assigned seats before the doors opened to let the rest of the crowds in. As they were following Bella towards the backstage Herman asked Bella what she was doing after the concert. She said she had to wait till all the crowds cleared up and ensure that The Beatles left safely, but after that she had nothing planned.

"Well," said Herman, "our group plan to go eat at the American Steak House after the concert and then head to the Bayside for a few drinks before going on to the Scene at the Peninsula and we would love it if you joined."

She looked at Herman and said, "I don't think so as I do not know how late I will be finishing up here."

Anita, who was right behind Herman, went up to Bella and held her hand tightly and said, "Please do come it would be so much fun. None of us have been to the Scene and we are all looking forward to it and I would love for you to come."

Bella looked back at Anita and said, "Tell you what, I won't be able to make dinner, but I will catch up with you at the Bayside and then go with you to the Scene. I have heard so much about it since it opened a month ago and have been dying to have a look."

Anita replied, "That would be fantastic! I am so happy that you will be joining."

Little did anyone suspect then that Anita had a secret crush on Bella. Anita had noticed in the last few years that she felt more comfortable being around women than men. She had dated a few guys over the years but did not enjoy the experiences. The more her mother forced her to date Indian men and plan blind dates with them the more she felt revolted. She found them egotistical, rude, crude and boring. She had no desire whatsoever with having sex with any men. She had gone as far as third base with some but found herself disgusted with it. She was scared to let anyone know of her sexual preference.

Anita had, over the years, observed Bella when they met at parties and other social events that they were both invited to and found her to be the most classy and sexiest woman she had ever met. Bella was almost twenty-five years old while Anita was nineteen. Anita found Bella to be what she considered the perfect lady, sophisticated and very smart. That night at Herman's party Anita was watching Bella who was with Eileen Siu, an up-and-coming starlet. The two of them had been dating for a while. They were sitting in a corner far away from the crowd and were necking and kissing. She could not stop staring at them and got excited just watching them. Her heart started pumping heavily when Bella, who obviously was aware that Anita was eyeing them, whispered something to Eileen and started to walk straight towards her. As she approached Anita, she took hold of Anita's hand and pressed it hard on her breasts and asked her if she enjoyed that. She then smiled and walked back to Eileen. Anita was shaking and was flushed she had never felt sensations like that before. She wanted to tell Mabel about what happened but was too embarrassed to do so.

Anita was attractive, she was about five feet three inches tall and had straight jet-black hair that fell down to her waist. She was slightly on the heavy side but had a curvy figure and beautiful browned skin. Her most stunning feature, however, was her eyes which were large and grey in colour. She had lovely long natural eyelashes, a perfect nose and full lips. She had many boys courting her but had no interest in any of them.

After the party Anita, after everyone had left, went up to her bedroom to retire for the night. She changed to her nightdress and laid in bed thinking of the event that took place with Bella. She could not stop thinking about how Bella had placed Anita's hand on her breasts and the burning feelings she had when she did that. She got horny just thinking of it and could not get to sleep. She finally put her hand down her vagina and started rubbing her clitoris whilst imagining it was Bella doing that to her. She had an orgasm and fell sleep.

Back at the theatre Herman turned to Harold and said, "How about you guys?" looking at Harold, Danny and Ella. "Will you be joining us after the show for dinner and drinks?"

Before Harold could answer Ella quickly replied, "Of course we would love to, that is Harold and I will. Danny already said he would go straight home after the concert as he has just recovered from the bug and did not wish to go out anywhere after the show."

Harold was surprised and upset at Ella's quick response. They had both discussed earlier that day that after the concert they would go to the Hilton Hotel on the island and have dinner there, after which they would go to the Den Discotheque which was located at the basement of the hotel. He, however, did not want to contradict her and went along, confirming that the both of them would love to join.

They went backstage and saw the Fab Four sitting on a sofa having a smoke and chatting with each other. They were fully dressed in their "Beatle suits" and looking very suave. John Lennon was the first one to stand up and greet them. Paul McCartney and George Harrison followed and finally Jimmie Nicol who was replacing Ringo who was not well enough to come to Hong Kong for this part of The Beatles' Asia/Pacific tour. John pointed at the VIP pass that Herman had on a lanyard around his neck and joked.

"We really want one of those don't we Paul? I fancy being a VIP." He looked at Herman and asked, "Can you please tell me how Paul and I can get to be VIPs and get one of those?"

John was the friendliest of the group, cracking jokes and letting them take pictures with him in different comical poses. Lucy, who was madly in love with Paul, actually fainted when he kissed her on the cheek and had to be revived. The fifteen minutes passed quickly and Bella had to push them to leave leading them back to their seats in the theatre.

They were all super excited and chatted away, they could not believe that they had actually spent fifteen amazing minutes with the greatest band in the world. They were the only ones in the theatre as the main doors had not yet been opened. Herman, Mabel, Ben, Lucy, Dilip and Anita were seated in the front row. In front of them were barricades about five feet away from the main stage and behind them were security people lining the stage. Two rows behind sat Harold, Danny and Ella.

Mabel, who was sitting next to Herman, asked him why he asked Harold and Ella to join them for dinner and drinks later that evening after what happened in the party. She sounded very upset. Herman told her that whatever took place at his party should not break up their friendship and felt them being together tonight may clear up all that. He further explained that Harold and Ella had been friends of his for a long time and it would be stupid for a silly incident like what happened on the weekend to ruin that. Mabel kept quiet and said no more.

The doors opened and the people came pouring in screaming and waving handmade signs like, "Marry me John", "Beatles 4ever", "Love me do" etc. As The Beatles came on stage to perform the crowds rushed towards the stage actually blocking their view. The security guards had a problem keeping them from climbing up the stage. It was absolutely chaotic. They were screaming so loud that you could hardly hear The Beatles sing. The Fab Four performed all their hit songs and ended with "She loves you" with the crowds joining them in the chorus, "Yeah, yeah, yeah." After they finished, they followed Bella's advice and waited for the crowd to fully disperse before getting off their seats to leave. They were all in a brilliant mood and were looking forward to going out and party.

They walked together to the American Steak House which was about a ten-minute walk and next to the Bayside Disco and Nightclub. Herman knew the manager of the restaurant well as the family dined there often. He told him that they had two extra people joining them for dinner tonight and there would be eight of them dining instead of the reservation he made for six. The manager told him that was not a problem but to give him a few minutes while he set up the table, meanwhile they could have drinks at the bar whilst they waited for him to arrange it.

Ella stayed close to Herman at the bar and kept chatting with him which irritated Mabel. It was obvious that Mabel was his date tonight as they had been holding hands all evening. Ella seemed to ignore that and kept flirting with Herman which was quite awkward especially for Harold. She also kept ordering rounds of tequila shots and was obviously out to get drunk. Harold firmly told her to slow down as the evening was just starting and if she carried on, she would be drunk even before dinner starts. She heeded his advice and stopped her flirting and drinking when he threatened to leave if she continued acting silly and getting drunk. He said he would leave her and she would have to make herself back home without him.

Ella sat on one side of Herman during dinner whilst Mabel was on his other side. Ella just popped herself next to Herman when they went to sit at the table knowing that it would upset Mabel. During dinner they all discussed the concert and how fantastic The Beatles were. Throughout the meal Ella would from time to time quietly place her hand under the table on Herman's thigh stroking him. Herman felt uncomfortable but did not do anything about it.

They all headed on to the Bayside after the meal, it was a lot quieter than usual, probably because it was a Tuesday night. There were only about four tables taken. It was around ten thirty and they planned to be there till just after midnight before heading to the Scene. They got a table easily near the stage where the band was playing. The band was really good and blasted away the latest pop songs. Ella started once again ordering tequila shots and they were all tipsy and in a great mood except for Anita who was upset that Bella had not shown and thought she had bailed. It was almost 11.50 p.m. when Bella walked in and joined them at the table. Herman and Mabel were sat on the sofa kissing while the rest were sitting, chatting away.

"Hi, you all, sorry I am late, but it took much longer than I thought. I had to ensure that the crowds dispersed without any problems and The Beatles got back safely to their rooms in the hotel. I came straight after that here without going home to change. Thank God I had an extra outfit in my car which I brought along with me so I could freshen up. I am glad you are still here as I thought you may have already headed off to the Scene. Looks like you guys are having a great time." She stared, looking at the dozens of empty shot glasses on the table.

"Think I need to get where you guys are," she said laughing. She ordered a double Black Label Scotch on the rocks and sat down next to Anita. While she was waiting for her drink, she said she needed to freshen up and asked Anita if she would join her to the ladies' room to help.

Anita followed her to the ladies which was empty except for them. Bella had brought a change of clothes that was more appropriate for the Scene and started to undress.

"Anita could you please unzip my dress. I am changing to this black sequined silk blouse and these tight black jeans as I believe it is a lot more suitable to wear for the Scene than this dress, don't you think?"

Anita watched as Bella stepped out of her dress with only her bra and a black satin lace thong on. Bella removed her bra and together with the dress she had worn placed it in the bag she had carried with her to the club. She turned to Anita who was staring open-mouthed at her, admiring her beautiful body.

"Do you like what you see?" she asked Anita smiling. Anita was embarrassed that she got caught out and looked away. Bella took her hand and led her to the toilet cubicle and locked the door behind her. She pushed her to the back of the door and kissed her full on her lips. Anita kissed her back and placed her hands on Bella's breasts squeezing her nipples tightly. Bella suddenly pulled out of the kiss, smiled and said that they better get back to the group.

"We can continue this another time, darling. Right now, let me finish dressing and let's join back with the group before they start wondering why we are taking so long," said Bella, winking at Anita.

When they got back to the table Herman said he was ordering last rounds and if anyone wanted a drink to let the waiter know. Bella saw the double Scotch she ordered earlier sat on the table, gulped it down and ordered another. They all ordered final rounds and Herman asked the waiter to bring the bill. He then asked Mabel for a last dance before they left for the Scene. Ella looked up at them heading to the dance floor holding hands and was burning up inside with anger. Dilip, who was sitting next to her, could sense that she was upset and asked her what the matter was. She babbled out to him in detail what actually happened the night of Herman's party and how wicked Mabel was to her. Dilip was surprised as he had not witnessed any of the goings on.

He told her to calm herself and now was not the time to get upset about it but to enjoy the evening which had been great so far. He then stood up and asked Lucy for a dance.

They arrived at the Scene Discotheque at twelve thirty a.m. There were people still lining up to get in. The Scene opened till four a.m. every day and it really got busy just after midnight. Harold turned to Ella, telling her that the Star Ferry would close at one thirty a.m. and maybe they should leave to go home now. Ella flat out said no that they just arrived, and she really wanted to check out the discotheque. She said to him that they could always take a Walla-Walla back later.

The Walla-Walla was a motorboat serving the Victoria Harbour of Hong Kong. It was the major means of transport between Hong Kong Island and Kowloon before the Star Ferry got the license to operate the cross-harbour ferry service. Long after the Star Ferry had started to provide the service, it was still an important auxiliary transport, as it was the only means that one could cross the harbour when the Star Ferry stopped its service from one thirty a.m. to six thirty a.m. The Walla-Walla was very small and could seat at most eight people. The ride was bumpy, and it took about fifteen minutes to cross the harbour. Walla-Walla was named by expats living in Hong Kong for its very noisy engine. It was supposedly controlled by the triads.

Herman spoke to one of the bouncers at the door and told him his name and that his father was a very close friend of Sue and if he could please tell her that he was waiting to get into the club. The bouncer nodded, went in and returned in five minutes. He asked how many of them were in the group. Herman told them that there were eight of them in total, and did not mind standing around the bar area, if there were no tables available. He nodded, told them to wait and went back in. Ten minutes later he appeared with a blonde European lady.

"Hi! I am Sue so which one of you is Herman Sun?" Herman went up to her and said, "Here I am."

She smiled, "You look just like your father and are as handsome as he is. It is great to meet you. Come follow me in I have prepared a table for you by the dance floor. If there is anything you need, please do not hesitate to ask. It's my break now so I will be mingling with the guests here, but I will be ready to D.J. in about ten minutes."

They entered the club and were amazed with the décor. They did not expect it to have such a high ceiling. All the tables were lit by different coloured neon lights. The dance floor was made out of squares each of a distinctive colour which lit up in various sequences and seemed to follow the music. There was a huge disco ball right above the dance floor which shined down with star patterns onto the dance floor. On the right of the dance floor was the D.J. booth which was made of hundreds of crystals that sparkled when the lights hit them. The bar, which was eighteen feet long and made of white marble, was at the end of the room. The Scene had about fifty tables in total of various sizes and all were full.

As they went to their table they passed by a table where the Dadlani boys were seated with a few friends. Herman acknowledged Kishore and his friends and continued on to his table. They all sat at the table and were offered a complimentary cocktail undoubtedly organised by Sue. Ella, who was quite drunk by now, took her opportunity as they were settling down and having their cocktails. She walked up to Herman and said that he owed her a dance as she had missed the opportunity at his party. Herman felt uncomfortable especially so as Mabel was giving him a fiery look. He, however, stood up and moved with Ella to the dance floor. As they were dancing Ella told Herman that she was free to go out for him the coming Saturday for coffee as he asked her during his party. Herman had forgotten all about that and did not want to be rude so he said that would be fine. He would call her during the week and confirm what time and where to meet.

Mabel, meanwhile, was getting more upset as Herman had already been dancing with Ella for two songs, she turned to Anita and asked if she would join her to the ladies as she did not want to upset herself further by watching them. In the ladies' room Mabel let out her fury at Ella, telling Anita that she was going to let Herman know how she disliked Ella and would appreciate that if he cares for her like he said then for her sake not to communicate further with Ella. Anita told her to be careful and not fall into Ella's game as demanding that of Herman may put him off her as they were not formally a couple.

As they walked out of the ladies, they bumped into Kishore who started chatting to Anita. Mabel excused herself and walked back to the table. Anita was dreading every minute chatting with him but knew she had to be civil knowing how much her parents loved him. Finally, she told him that she had to go back and would catch up with him later. She went back to the table and sat next to Bella. She held Bella's hand and asked her to protect her from Kishore if he came around. Bella laughed and told Anita not to worry that she would look after her. Anita was buzzing and felt contented.

When Herman returned back from the table Harold went up to Ella, saying it was getting late and they should leave. It was almost three a.m. and he was tired. He had promised her parents that he would bring her home back safe and that they needed to go. Ella wanted to stay longer and turned to Anita and asked whether it was OK for her to stay with her tonight. Anita did not know how to answer as she did not want to upset Mabel who, surprisingly, overhearing this thought it would be a great idea. Harold was worried for Ella as she was obviously drunk but resigned to the fact that Ella would not budge.

Ella was totally wasted but insisted on ordering more drinks. Mabel agreed with her and asked for more tequila shots against Herman's and Harold's wishes. She wanted Ella to keep drinking and make a total fool of herself, wishing that she got horribly sick. Mabel, unlike the rest of the group, was not at all tipsy as she had been monitoring the amount she drank.

"OK, then I will say bye to you all. Thanks, Herman, for a great evening, I really had a wonderful time. We must do this again but the next time it is all on me. I will walk over to the Walla-Walla pier and take one back to the island. Please look after Ella, I will call her parents in the morning to let them know she stayed the night with Anita and for them not to worry."

Herman told Harold that he would ensure that they all got home safely. Mabel and Ben were staying over at his house, but he would make sure that Dilip and Anita got Ella back to their house safe and sound.

He walked up to Ella, gave her a kiss on the cheek and told her not to drink any more and to dance off the alcohol. He told her to call him when she got up in the morning to let him know how she was.

He waved goodbye to all of them and left. It was three fifteen a.m.

Little did they know that that would be the last time they saw Harold. What was to occur in the next few hours would rock the colony once again.

Chapter 10
Stranger Times

Sir John Woods's Residence
5 Peak Road, Hong Kong
June 10th, 1964, seven a.m.

Sir John Woods was sitting with his wife in their dining room having breakfast when Minnie their maid came in saying that there was an urgent call from Sir Anthony Brown. He looked at his wife saying it was strange for Sir Anthony to call so early in the morning and especially at home. He stood up and walked out of the dining room to the lounge where the phone was and picked it up.

"Good morning, John, sorry to have to call so early but it is quite urgent. I had a call from Ella's parents saying she did not come home last night and since she was with Harold they wanted to know if she had stayed over with us. I went to Harold's room, but he has not been in and checked with the staff who told me that he did not come home last night. I woke up Danny who told me that both Ella and Harold had joined Herman and Mabel for dinner after the concert and after that they were going to check out the Scene Discotheque. He did not know any more as he came home straight after the concert. I thought you may have heard from Ben or Mabel on where they were? I did call Leslie first, but he was out running, and I did not want to disturb his wife. Elizabeth is really worried and asked me to call you as you possibly would know where they were through either Ben or Mabel?" asked Sir Anthony.

John felt concern about his children. As far as he knew they planned after the concert to go for dinner and go clubbing after that. Both Ben and Maggie had arranged to stay at the Suns' residence. Maybe both Harold and Ella decided to stay with the Suns as well or maybe stayed over with the Lalwanis, thought John.

"Both Ben and Mabel spent the night at the Suns. It could be that both Harold and Ella joined them or possibly they may have stayed with the Lalwanis as Dilip and Anita were with them as well. Let me call Nancy and see if she knows anything and I will get back to you. I do not think it is anything to worry about. Please tell Elizabeth not to fret. You know teenagers when they are having fun, they can be quite irresponsible. I will call Nancy now and get back to you as soon as possible."

He picked up the phone and dialled Leslie's number. Wan-Yu picked up the phone and passed it on to Nancy who had just come down from her garden and was having breakfast.

"Hi, Nancy, sorry to be bothering you but I had a call from Sir Anthony Brown that both Harold and Ella, who were with Herman last night, did not come home and he was wondering whether you knew where they were? If not maybe Herman, Ben or Mabel would. Could you please also check with Herman in case he knows anything as I promised to get back to Sir Anthony as soon as possible. I thought that if they are not there with you, they may have stayed over at the Lalwanis."

"Why, of course. I will check and see what I can find out and call you right back," replied Nancy.

She asked Wan-Yu if he knew anything. Wan-Yu said he was up when Herman came back with Lucy, Ben and Mabel at around five a.m. that morning. Both Harold and Ella were not with them. Wan-Yu asked if he should go up and wake up Herman and inquire from him? Nancy said that she would go. She knocked on Herman's door for about three minutes before he answered.

"Do you know where Harold and Ella are. Apparently, they did not get home last night, and their families are concerned about their whereabouts."

Herman looked through the half-opened door with a towel around his waist and replied, "Well I know that Ella went to stay the night at Anita's. Harold left the club just after three a.m. He said he was taking the Walla-Walla to the island and then cab it back home. Look, do not worry too much, Mom, he could easily have bumped into a few mates of his and could have decided to stay with them. He seemed all right when he left the club. I am sure he will show up soon. I will take a quick shower and come down for breakfast and call a few people who are friends of ours who were at the club and see if they know anything."

As Nancy left Herman locked back his bedroom door went to his bathroom door and whispered to Mabel that all was clear, and she could come out. She had stayed the night with Herman when they returned back that morning. They had both fallen into a deep sleep after making love until they heard Nancy knocking on his door. Mabel quickly grabbed her clothes which were lying scattered on the floor and rushed into the bathroom before Herman went to open the door. "Did you hear the conversation with me and Mom?" he asked. "I wonder what happened to Harold?"

"Yes, it all seems so strange. Kishore was in the club that night and I did not see him around when we left so maybe he went with Kishore as they are very close friends. Ella should have gone home with Harold when he asked her to. She made a fool of herself by staying. She was totally drunk by the time we left and was puking all over the club. It was so embarrassing. If she can't hold her liquor, she should not drink. Thank God we were there to help her clean up and get her into a taxi with Dilip and Anita. Look I am going to sneak back to my room and will catch you later."

Herman was surprised by her remarks. He was worried for Harold, but Mabel was only interested in telling him how awful Ella acted. Herman did feel sorry for Ella as the poor girl was in a bad shape when they left the Scene. He did not mention to Mabel that he had promised to go out with Ella for a date this weekend as he knew that would set her off. He decided he would secretly call Ella later in the day to see if she was all right. He felt confused with his relationship with Mabel which he had thought was real after his party when they kissed and made love, but then again, he couldn't stop thinking about Ella.

Nancy walked back down from Herman's and called back John. She told him exactly what Herman had told her. Well at least they knew that Ella was at the Lalwanis. Nancy said she would call Maya just to confirm and to see if maybe Harold changed his mind about going home and joined Ella and also stayed over at the Lalwanis. John thanked her and said that after she had spoken to Maya, could she please call him back and let him know so he could inform Anthony.

Nancy called the Lalwani residence and Maya picked up the phone. Nancy explained the whole conversation she had with John.

"I did not know that Ella came over to sleep let me check with my maids and see if they know anything. If not, I will go up and wake Anita and see what I can find out and call you back."

She did check with her maids and was told that Dilip and Anita came home around four thirty a.m. together with Ella who seemed very drunk. Maya went up to Anita's room and woke her up. She asked if Ella was OK and if she knew where Harold was. Anita said that Ella had a little too much to drink and was fast asleep in her bedroom, but she had no idea where Harold was. As far as she knew he left the club before closing time and was going to take the Walla-Walla and then take a taxi home. Maya told her to go back to sleep but when she finally woke up to come and look for her to give her more details. Maya went back down, called Nancy and told her what Anita told her.

Nancy called back John and detailed what Maya told her. John thanked her and called back Anthony explaining they had located Ella who was staying at the Lalwanis, but nobody really knew where Harold was. He told Anthony for him and Elizabeth not to be too concerned yet as he could easily have bumped into some of his friends and ended up staying with them. He would be going to the office in a few minutes and would get his team to investigate. Officially in the case of missing persons the police were not to be involved until at least twenty-four hours after the person was reported missing but, in this case, he would get his team to investigate immediately. He expressed to Anthony that it was imperative for Elizabeth and him to be totally quiet about this and that if Harold did show up later in the day or called to let him know right away.

John quickly finished his breakfast, said goodbye to Maggie and left for the office. It was almost eight a.m. by the time John left. Maggie pondered on how her relationship with John had deteriorated so quickly ever since he was given the title of "Sir" by Her Majesty three years ago. They had discussed their recent problems openly together and decided that they both wanted a divorce. They planned for the summer to pass before letting their children know. The children already suspected things were not right with their parents as they witnessed many argy-bargies between them recently. They spent less time as a family and for the first time did not plan a summer holiday together. Maggie was concerned more how Mabel would handle it as she was very sensitive, unlike Ben who was indifferent about things.

Mabel was extra close to her mother and told her everything. Between them they kept no secrets. She had told her mother about Herman, how they kissed at his party and that they were now seeing each other. She also told her that she was for the first time truly in love. Maggie was a bit surprised as Nancy had always told her that Ella and Herman were very intimate and thought that they would end up getting married one day. She did ask Mabel about Ella who Herman seemed serious about but was told that Herman was off her and she was no longer romantically in his life. She made her mother promise not to say anything to Nancy until the time was right when Herman and she officially announced they were a couple. The only thing she left out telling her mother was that she had lost her virginity with Herman.

The last year had been a strange one for Maggie, she had discovered about six months ago that her husband was having an affair with a club hostess called Liza Wong. The relationship had been going on for some time without her suspecting which made her even more angry. It was by chance she found out about the affair when one day emptying the pockets of John's suits to send to the dry cleaners, she found an envelope with a handwritten note and a lady's panty with the initial LW in it.

The note read:

"My dearest darling John, just a little souvenir for you to remember me when we are not together. I love you dearly and cannot wait till we see each other again soon. I love you." It was signed Liza.

Little did she know then that Raymond had made Liza slip the envelope into John's jacket the last time he was with her. He was hoping that Maggie or one of her maids would discover it and it would come to Maggie's attention. Maggie was furious; she had broken up her affair with Ray years before to stay faithful to John and this was how she was rewarded. Before she went to John with it, she confronted Raymond and asked him about Liza. Raymond tried to avoid the issue but when she pushed him, he told her everything. She was shocked as she never expected John to cheat on her.

Even at thirty-eight years old she was attractive and kept her figure well even after having two children unlike John who at forty-five looked much older than his age. She had got Raymond to send her pictures of Liza and could not understand what John saw in her. She was unattractive and had a horrible figure. It must be the sex that she provided, she thought, that attracted John to her. When she did face up to John, and told him she knew about Liza, he did not deny it. He admitted that they had had an affair for some time. She had asked for an immediate divorce and said she wanted half of whatever he owned. John tried to convince her against divorcing and that he had since already broken up with Liza. Maggie, however, did not stop hounding him and finally got him to agree to a divorce. They agreed on all the terms that Maggie set out as John did want the divorce to be kept secret. He wanted it all very hushed and done quickly. He said that he wanted to let the kids know only after the summer before proceeding with the divorce.

Maggie had confided only with Nancy and Raymond of her problems with John. The children did not know of their father's affair. Ray was sympathetic to her situation, but he explained, as he was still close to John, it was difficult for him to take sides. John had told Maggie that he was willing to give her half of his assets but did not want a prolonged and arduous divorce. His difficulty was the black money and how to transfer that portion to Maggie without raising red flags. The "clean" assets were easy to deal with, but they had to figure out how the money that John had kept hidden in the Swiss bank could be safely transferred. John and Maggie decided to go to Raymond who had arranged "laundering" the black money for John to see what the best way was to deal with it. They both trusted Raymond and knew if anyone could work it out it would be him. Raymond acted surprised that they were thinking of a divorce although Maggie had told him privately about it. He said not to worry he would figure a way how to move the money around so that it could not be traced back and ensure it be divided equally. There was at this time about HK$15 million in the Swiss account.

John, ever since he got knighted by the Queen, gave up taking bribes for fear that one day he would be caught. There had been a lot of talk with the government setting up an Independent Anti-Corruption organisation to tackle corruption in the colony as it was widespread and rampant in almost every public sector. The body which was to be set up would have unlimited powers to check on any individual no matter how high a post they held. It was to be called the Independent Commission against Corruption (ICAC). John knew this would happen soon and stopped taking bribes from the triads. He informed his next in line staff to do the same as he feared that they may be discovered once the commission was formed. As the commissioner of police, he had to be extra careful and ensure those directly below him were seen to be clean.

Raymond, during this time, met up with Maggie privately hoping to spark up their past relationship. Maggie, although meeting him a number of times, did not take it back to the level before when they were having an affair. Maggie was nervous to get back into that type of a situation with Raymond as she was afraid it could affect the divorce. She told Raymond that she liked him a lot but at this stage of her life she just wanted to get the divorce sorted and get back to some form of normality. She had the children to think of as well as they would go through a rough time and she needed to be there for them 100%. Raymond said he understood but that he would be there for her and if she needed anything to just let him know.

John arrived at police headquarters around 8.35 a.m. As soon as he got seated in his office, he asked his secretary Angela to locate Inspector Lee and get him to see him immediately. He told her to take messages as he did not want to be disturbed only except if Sir Anthony Brown or his wife called. John was worried but he did not express it to Sir Anthony as he did not need them worrying quite yet.

There had been some high-profile kidnappings recently which the media was unaware of mainly because the kidnappers had been paid the ransom demanded and the people who were involved did not want it to go public. The most recent was about three months ago when William Fong, a multi-billionaire's son, was kidnapped. His son Simon, who was thirteen years old was, whilst waiting for his driver to pick him up after school, was abducted by thugs and shoved into a mini-van and driven to an unknown location. Later that day Mr Fong was contacted by the kidnappers demanding HK$150 million. He was told that if the police were contacted and if there was any sign that they were being led into a trap that they would kill Simon without hesitation and send back his body in parts back to them. He had twenty-four hours to arrange the money and was told where to drop it off. Until the money was safe in their hands and there were no risks of any police involvement, they would release him within the hour.

John Woods was called in initially by William but the Fong family, after deliberation, had a change of mind and decided to pay the ransom. They told John not to get the police involved at least until they got their son back as they feared for his life. John was against it and wanted to have a tracer follow the money to the drop off place but the Fongs felt that was too risky. Simon was their only child. John finally relented to their wishes and had to stand by just in case anything went wrong. The kidnappers had asked the money to be dropped off in an isolated location in the New Territories. The area was not well built and there were no main roads around. They had to drop the money off in a junction of two dirt roads where there was a bus stop. They chose midnight as the time for the drop-off. The kidnappers were smart and everything was well planned. The bus stop was not well lit and there was no lighting on the road. John, without letting the Fongs know, had a police car follow the car with the ransom money from a distance making sure that its headlights were dimmed. As soon as the drop-off car left the money with the suitcase in a litter box by the bus stop as directed, a motor cyclist drove up, picked it up and drove off nearby into a cycle dirt road. The police car could not follow as the road was too narrow to fit a vehicle. Simon was found a few hours later outside the Ocean Centre shopping mall in Tsim Tsa Tsui. He was shaken and except for a few cuts was OK.

John had been following the rise in kidnappings with much concern. He was pressured by the governor to capture whoever was involved with the kidnappings and bring them to justice quickly. The high-profile kidnappings were done by a Chinese gangster who called himself "Lucky Money" but whose real identity was unknown by the police. In the last two years there had been five kidnappings of wealthy families. Most of the victims had been children in their teens. So far all of them had been released after the ransoms were paid. It was difficult for John to go after the kidnapper(s) as the families of those kidnapped did not report it to the police until they had got their children back after paying the ransom. His fear now was that maybe Harold was one of the new targets. It was still too early to think that, but the circumstances surrounding Harold's disappearance did not seem right and led to that probability.

Inspector Lee knocked on the door and John asked him to come in. He explained to Inspector Lee about the disappearance of Harold and that he was concerned as it could possibly be another kidnapping. Inspector Lee, who had been heading the investigation of the kidnappings, agreed with John. He further went on to say that they believed this "Lucky Money" was not tied in with any of the bigger triads. It was probably conducted by a smaller organisation or by a few individuals. They had, in the case of Simon Fong's kidnapping, been able to get two sets of fingerprints from the jacket that he wore when returned by the kidnappers. One set belonged to a person called "Chuen Hei Ko" who was wanted for the killing of an expat five years previously. The other fingerprints were not in the police database. Chuen was last seen in Macau three months ago gambling big in a casino in Macau. They had contacted the Macau police, but the Macau police had not been helpful as it did not concern crime committed in their territory. It was believed that probably the kidnappers were being sheltered by a smaller triad group. This Chuen Hei Ko, according to the police files, was once a general in the Black Ninjas.

John thanked Inspector Lee for his good work and thanked him for the breakthrough at least they had now identified a suspect. He asked if Inspector Lee knew at which casino Mr Chuen was gambling in last year. He informed him it was at the Hotel Faroe.

"Well, that's the casino belonging to Raymond Ho, isn't it? As you know I am very close to Ray. I will check with him to see if he has any recorded videotapes of Mr Chuen gambling as I know every casino keeps such video recordings to check on gamblers to see if there was any cheating. These videos are usually kept for six months before erasing. Go back to your files and see what you can find out about what sort of table he was gambling on and on what date. We have no jurisdiction with the Macau police to push them to follow through on this, but I can go directly to Ray who I am sure will allow us to look at the recorded videos."

Inspector Lee left the office and John asked Angela to try and get hold of her Uncle Raymond as he needed to speak with him urgently. She came back to him quickly stating that she had spoken to his secretary, who did not expect him back to his office until after lunch. She told the secretary for her to call back as soon as he returned. She had also called his home but was told he had just left, and they did not know where he was going. John told her to not worry and to get hold of Leslie Sun. She left the office and in five minutes she buzzed him telling him she had Leslie on line one.

"Good morning, Leslie. Hope you are well. I am sure you have heard from Nancy about Harold's disappearance. Between us two I am concerned as it seems strange that Harold is nowhere to be found. With the recent kidnappings I am slightly concerned although it is too early to worry. I have asked Sir Anthony to let me know the moment Harold shows up or calls. There is one thing interesting that I do want to share with you though. Going through the case of Simon Fong's kidnapping with my team we discovered fingerprints which belong to whom we think was involved with the kidnapping. I am sure you have heard of "Lucky Money", well I think we have now identified him as a Mr Chuen Hei Ko. I know that name probably means nothing to you, but this may. He had apparently been involved in a killing of an expat four years ago and was one of the generals of the Black Ninjas. I think he may have been one of the few people who escaped when you raided the new Black Ninja den four years ago and disbanded it. I know you have been looking for a Kohei Inowaki, it may not be him, but he may be the lead that you have been looking for."

"Do you know where this person is now?" asked Leslie. He found his heart pounding with this news. He had been trying to locate Kohei for the last four years. All his tips had led to dead ends and he was close to giving up looking for him. This was the most positive thing he had heard recently.

"No, but he was last seen gambling big at the Hotel Faroe in

Macau three months ago. I am trying to pinpoint the day he was last seen and the time he was there. I was then going to ask Raymond to release any videos of him gambling to us as it may reveal some clues on his whereabouts. We have an old photograph of him on our files, but it is not very clear, I will have it faxed to you anyway. I was thinking of visiting Niko Black the wife of the former commissioner of police with the photo as she might recognise who this Chuen Hei Ko is as she was, as you know, involved with the New Black Ninjas at one time financing them."

John was very close with Niko and more so after her husband passed away from cancer a year ago. This was a good excuse to visit her. He would call on her regularly to check if she was doing all right and they became quite attached. She was ten years his younger and at thirty-five was just as beautiful as when he met her thirteen years ago when he first arrived in Hong Kong. John secretly desired her. It was because of her that he broke up his relationship with Liza Wong. After being with Liza for a while he found her rather unsophisticated and stupid. He found Niko quite the opposite: refined and classy. She was everything he admired in a woman. She was beautiful, well spoken, and well educated unlike both his wife Maggie and mistress Liza.

He was in a way glad that Maggie had found out about Liza and was pushing for a divorce as he could pursue his relationship with Niko openly after the divorce. Niko had told him that she wanted to be with him but while he was still married to Maggie the relationship could go no further as she would not be a mistress to anyone. He had told Niko earlier that week that Maggie and he had both decided to divorce and she was happily surprised. What he failed to tell her was the reason why. She had no idea he had an affair with Liza and that was why Maggie was divorcing him. He told her that he and Maggie had been unhappy for years, but they held off divorcing till the kids were all grown up.

"Yes, that may be a good idea," replied Leslie. "Please let me know what you have learned after speaking to Raymond and Niko and keep me informed. I really hope that Harold is OK. It must be so hard for Elizabeth and Anthony. I did get a message to call him back after my run this morning and after Nancy had told me what happened, but his phone was constantly engaged."

Suddenly it hit Leslie and he asked John to repeat the name of the person whom they found the fingerprints of.

"Well, it is Chuen Hei Ko," replied John. "Have you heard that name before?"

"Chuen Hei Ko spelled backwards is Ko Hei Chuen like Kohei and in Chinese if you say the name backwards it is "Ko Hei Chuen" or translated "Lucky Money". That to me is too much of a coincidence. We need to find out more about this Chuen Hei Ko and locate him quick as possible as he may be whom I have been hunting for so many years. He could definitely be behind all the kidnappings and may also be involved with Harold's disappearance!"

"OK let me get things moving. I will leave now for Niko's and have her look at this photo. When I get back, I will speak to Raymond and see what I can get from him and I will get back to you." With that John said his goodbyes and hung up. He called Niko's home and she picked up the phone. He told her briefly what had happened and that he would be coming to her place for her to look at a photograph and see if she recognised the person in it. He told her he would be there in about half an hour or so. She asked him to stay for lunch and that she would arrange for her cook to do up something light. He thanked her and said that was kind of her and a good idea as he had so much to do the rest of the day and did not know when he could grab a bite to eat. He looked at his watch, it was 11.40 a.m. He then called in Angela and asked her to get his chauffeur ready to take him to Madam Niko Black's residence.

Niko was happy to hear from John. He had been her pillar since her brother and then her husband passed away. She trusted him and liked his company. He was kind to her and visited her often to see if she was fine. She knew he was attracted to her and purposely flirted with him to keep him interested. She could not believe the good news that he was divorcing Maggie and thought maybe now they could build on their relationship. She was dying for some male company and loved to be romanced. John was not handsome by any means but that was not what she was looking for at this stage of her life. She wanted to settle down with someone kind and thoughtful who could look after her. She got up and headed to her room to change out of her dressing gown and get ready for John's arrival. On the way she went to the kitchen and told the cook that she had a guest coming and to do up something light for lunch.

Leslie's mind was racing. Everything added up to Chuen Hei Ko being Kohei. He may have nothing to do with Harold's disappearance, but his gut feeling told him he was right about him being Kohei Inowaki. He had been searching for him for four years now. He needed to find him and get his revenge. That would be the way he could finally bury the chapter on Lillian's death and fulfil his promise. He pushed the button under his table in the study to call for Wan-Yu.

Wan-Yu knocked on the door and then entered. "Sir you called. Is there anything I can do for you? Madam Nancy has asked me what time you wanted lunch. She said that she has asked Ah Wong to make a Caesar salad for you. Is that, OK?"

"Yes, that will be fine, you can serve lunch now, I will join Madam Nancy in the family room if she is ready to eat now as well. Have the children all woken up now? If so after my lunch I want to speak to Herman privately in my study. Can you inform him that it is important? Herman has turned twenty-one and it's now the right time I tell him about the Warriors of the Sun and how that organisation started."

"Yes sir, I understand. When I checked last about ten minutes ago Herman was taking a shower. Madam Nancy had asked me to get Lucy and him to join for lunch. She also asked me to ask Mabel and Ben to join. I have already asked them all to be at the dining room by twelve thirty. I believe your mom and Irene and her children Richard and Yvonne will also be joining for lunch.

"Great we will have the whole family together after a very long time," smiled Leslie. "OK I will just finish up here and will head to the dining room. I will tell Herman myself then during lunch to be with me at my study after that. When I finish my meeting with him, I want to go downtown to pick up something special for his twenty-first birthday. I have asked Ajit to order this special gift for Herman. I want Herman to come with me to receive his special gift and I want you to accompany us as well."

Leslie looked at the file on his desk. It was to do with the water shortage affecting Hong Kong. He was worried for it had not rained now for six straight weeks and the reservoirs were almost empty. This was supposed to be the wet season when typhoons usually affected the colony, bringing along with them much needed rain, but not this year. China continued supplying water to the colony but not steadily. If the heatwave continued there would have to be further water restrictions. He had already arranged with the government to extend the reservoir programme in the colony by enlarging those that already existed and to create another two larger ones in the New Territories. The main would be the Plover Cove Reservoir in the north-eastern part of the New Territories. It would be by far the largest reservoir in Asia and the world's first freshwater coastal lake constructed from an arm of the ocean. To complete this would take three years. At least once completed it could store almost double the capacity of the reservoirs now in the colony and in future could stop Hong Kong relying on China for water. He closed the files and headed to the dining room.

Meanwhile John had arrived at Niko's residence in Repulse Bay which was in the southern part of Hong Kong Island. Niko had a beautiful colonial style house there overlooking the beach. This was probably one of the most expensive places to live in Hong Kong. Her house was walking distance to the iconic Repulse Bay Hotel and the beach. Niko was there to greet him, and they walked toward the back of the house to sit in the garden. It was a glorious day and she had laid out lunch on her garden table. The lunch consisted of a quinoa and shaved carrot salad with chickpeas, currants and cashews. She also had done some grilled peach, prosciutto and mozzarella sandwiches. John said she did not have to go through all the trouble of doing something so elaborate as just a ham sandwich would have sufficed. She smiled and said he was too special to do just that.

They chatted away casually at first and then went on to why he was there and about the disappearance of Harold. He told her that they had identified someone who could be involved in some of the kidnappings and especially that of William Fong's son. His name was as far as they knew Chuen Hei Ko. The reason he came to her was that he was supposed to have been a general of the Black Ninjas and later when they were dispersed could possibly have gone to work with her brother in the New Black Ninja gang. He took out the photo from a brown envelope and handed it to Niko. She looked at it for a while and tears came pouring down from her eyes. John was surprised and asked if she was OK.

"That is a picture of Kohei Inowaki. Ken suspected one of his generals in his gang to be involved with the murders of the naval officers and possibly the bombing and believed that it was Kohei Inowaki. That day when Leslie raided the New Black Ninjas and killed Ken, I had spoken on the phone to him earlier in the morning. My brother was afraid that the authorities would be after him for the killing of the two U.S. naval officers and of the bombing of the Sing Song Club. He swore under oath that he had nothing to do with the crimes. He did, however, suspect Kohei San as he was always pushing Ken to continue the ways of Agana San. I have met Kohei a number of times, both in Tokyo and here in Hong Kong. I never liked him and even warned my brother about him. If his fingerprints were the ones you recovered, I am 100% sure that he committed the crime. This just brings back all the memories; my poor brother was killed for crimes he did not commit."

Niko blamed her brother's death solely on Leslie. He did not have to kill him. If he had brought him back alive and questioned him, he would have learned that it was probably Kohei San who the culprit was. Ken, her brother, would probably have ended up in jail for a few years for his illegal activities but at least he would still be alive. He was the only family she had at that time. She hated Leslie with a passion and hoped one day she could hurt him back the way that he had hurt her.

Leslie was correct thought John, Chuen Hei Ko was indeed Kohei Inowaki. He hugged Niko to comfort her. They held each other tightly for a long time and as they came to release the hug John kissed her passionately. She kissed him back. He said he had to go back and report this to his team and had to speak to Raymond Ho. He asked if she was free later that evening as he would love to take her out for dinner. It would be late though. She suggested that he came back to hers for dinner and she would cook him a traditional Japanese meal. He looked up and smiled and said he would love that, but he could be a bit late. He promised to call her back once he figured what time he could be there. She said it did not matter how late he was as she would be waiting for

199

him. They kissed once more, and he said his goodbyes and left.

Meanwhile Leslie was having lunch with the family in the dining room. It had indeed been a long time since they all sat down for lunch. Leslie asked the children how they enjoyed the concert and they all could not stop talking about how wonderful it all was. Lucy was the most excited saying she got a kiss from her idol Paul McCartney! It was sad that Irene's children Richard and Yvonne could not have joined them to see The Beatles as they only had six backstage VIP passes. They had also gone to the concerts but were sitting a few rows away from the front with the Lalwani children. He knew that Herman, Lucy, Mabel, Ben, Anita and Dilip went to dinner after the concert and ended up in the Scene but was wondering what Richard and Yvonne did. Richard replied saying they together with the Lalwani's children without Dilip and Anita went to have dinner at the newly opened American Cafe after which they came straight home.

Leslie had only one sibling, that was his younger sister Irene. Irene was the rebellious one of the two. Whereas Leslie was the perfect son who was good at school and went on to do his PhD in Harvard, she was quite the opposite. She quit school after fifth form, against her parents' wishes. She did horribly bad in the GCSEs, only obtaining two passes out of eight subjects she sat for. If she wanted to continue her education, she would have to repeat her fifth form. She had no desire to do so. When her father asked her to join the business, she refused saying she would find a job by herself. She got mixed up with the wrong crowd and joined a motorcycle gang. She got pregnant when she was only eighteen with the leader of the motorcycle gang. Their father wanted for her to have an abortion and to stop seeing the boy to which she refused and instead ran off with him. The family did not hear back from her for almost five years when one day she showed up in the house with her son Richard and baby daughter Yvonne. Her boyfriend had left her for another woman, and she had nowhere else to go. The family took her back in with open arms. Irene had been living with them since then.

Leslie then turned to Herman and asked him why Harold left the club all by himself. Was he not with Ella on a date as he heard and was supposed to take her home after the Scene? Before Herman could

200

answer Mabel cut in saying that Ella was completely drunk and refused to leave with Harold. Harold asked her a number of times to leave as they had to take the Walla-Walla back as they had missed the last Star Ferry, but she would not. She finally forced Anita to let her stay in her house, so Harold left alone. Leslie continued his questioning with Mabel as she seemed to know more than the rest of them. He asked how Harold's condition was when he left, had he had too much to drink? She replied no in fact he was fine, he was watching over Ella all night drinking away, that he kept pretty sober. Nancy said she was surprised with Ella's manners as she had thought of her to be well-ordered and never saw that side of her before.

Herman was quite upset the way that Mabel spoke so badly of Ella in front of his family as he thought it was not her place to put any of their friends down. He said to his dad that it was strange that up to now Harold had not surfaced. It could be that he met up with friends as he was leaving the club and decided to continue partying with them or possibly stayed with one of them. He would anyway, if Harold did not show up in the next few hours, call around some mutual friends to see whether they knew of his whereabouts. Leslie said that would be fine.

"Oh, by the way Herman, after lunch I want you to follow me to the study as I want to discuss with you a few things. It's been a while since your party that we had a chance to speak. I do want to know your schedule on the training for the Olympics amongst other things. I thought after that maybe we could take a drive downtown and see what you would like for your twenty-first birthday."

"That will be fine Dad. I was also wanting to discuss with you about my training program and have your thoughts on it. By the way how was your date with Mom last night?"

Leslie looked at Nancy and they both smiled saying they had a wonderful time. It actually was for them. For the first time in years Leslie opened up his feelings to Nancy and they were honest with each other. He told her that he did love Lillian and how her death caused him pain that lasted all this time. He realised recently how he had ignored his family and wanted now to get back to his old self. He thanked Nancy for her patience during the last four years and how strong she was in looking after the family during his difficult time. He wanted her to know that he loved and cared deeply for her and that he was sorry for the way he treated her the last years and wanted to make up for all the times he had hurt her. They hung around the restaurant and talked for hours finishing three bottles of Chateau Margaux wine, the most they had drunk since university days. After dinner they went home, and they made love for the first time in four years.

As Leslie and Herman were heading to the study Wan-Yu appeared.

"Sir you have an urgent call from Sir John. Should I ask him to call you back or will you take it? I can switch the call to the study."

Leslie headed to the study with Herman following him. He picked up the phone and listened intently to what John was saying. He let out a yelp and said "YES."

When Leslie finished talking with John, Herman asked him what happened. Had they located Harold? Leslie said it was not about Harold, but it could lead to closing a case that he had been involved with for over four years. Leslie locked the door of the study and made Herman sit opposite him.

"What I am going to tell you has been passed down from generation to generation. You are to keep it secret and not reveal whatever you are about to hear to anyone, not even your closest friend or family member. As you have now turned twenty-one it is customary that I pass you down a number of artifacts and tell you about them. I will also tell you what is expected from you as the eldest son of the family. Shall we start?"

Meanwhile John had returned back to the office. He called in Inspector Lee and told him that he had now ascertained that Chuen Hei Ko was indeed Kohei San a member of the Black Ninjas and possibly the person involved with the kidnappings. Inspector Lee said that he had checked the files and this Mr Chuen or Kohei was definitely playing baccarat at the VIP table at the Faroe Hotel. He was there for three consecutive nights from March 9th — 11th. Each time he had a seat reserved for him at the high stakes baccarat table, from ten p.m. He would be joined by some of his friends, usually around six of them. The minimum per bet on this table was HK$100,000. Apparently Chuen was a big gambler as, according to one of the dealers there, that one night he lost close to HK$5 million. John called Leslie to fill him in on what he knew. As soon as John hung up with Leslie his secretary Angela buzzed him. "I have Uncle Ray on the phone. Do you wish to speak to him now? If so, I will pass you the line."

John picked up the phone and told Ray about his discovery and that he needed as soon as possible to get hold of the tapes that probably the casino at the Faroe Hotel had. It could help in locating the person or persons who had been involved in the recent spate of kidnappings. He gave Raymond the dates and times of when Kohei was gambling at the Hotel Faroe and on which table. Raymond said that he had a hydrofoil arriving from Macau that afternoon with some business documents that he had asked for and he would get the security in the hotel to send the relevant videotapes with the documents. He expected the hydrofoil to arrive around four thirty p.m. and he could have them sent over to John before six p.m.

John was proud of what he had achieved so far. They now knew who the main suspect in the kidnappings was. He wondered if he should tell the governor of his progress so far but decided to wait till he got more evidence to prove his theory. It would be best that he actually captured Chuen Hei Ko aka Kohei San. He looked at his watch, it was almost three p.m. He called home and told Maggie about what had been happening and told her not to expect him for dinner and that he would be home late from work. He then called Niko, thanked her for her help and confirmed that he would be at hers for dinner that evening around eight thirty p.m.

Angela knocked on his door. "I have Sir Anthony Brown on the phone, and he sounds hysterical." John picked up the phone: his greatest fear came to be.

"John, I do not know what to do. I got a parcel sent to my home just ten minutes ago. In it was a gold bracelet that Elizabeth and I gave to Harold on his eighteenth birthday. There was a note addressed to me with it. It said that they had Harold. If I wanted to see him alive, I would have to pay HK$250 million. The money must not be marked or traceable. It went on to say that they would call me later tonight to let me know where and how to drop this money. It said for me to be next to my phone. They have given me one day to arrange this money and

203

stated in my position it should not be a problem. If I went to the police and have them involved and if they discovered that if they were being tracked when the money was delivered, they guaranteed that they will have no mercy and will kill my son. Elizabeth initially did not want me to call you but after explaining to her that that would probably be the best thing she agreed. She is freaking out."

John said he was coming over immediately. Before he left, he called Niko to tell her that he had to cancel and told her about the whole Harold incident. She totally understood and said they could have dinner another time. He called in Inspector Lee and told him to come with him to the Browns' residence. He told him their greatest fear had come true. Harold had been kidnapped.

Chapter 11
Warriors of the Sun

Leslie's Study
888 Nathan Road, Kowloon, Hong Kong
June 10th, 1964, two p.m.

Leslie sat down on his chair in the study with Herman sitting opposite him.

"What I am going to tell you is something you must never reveal to anybody. As you have turned twenty-one it is tradition that I let you know the history of our forefathers and the secrets of the Sun family. This has been passed from generation to generation and is expected that you pass it down one day to your eldest son. You will understand as I reveal events that helped our family to secure our special relationship with the British. I will explain how our family helped in acquiring the colonising of Hong Kong Island, Kowloon and helped lease the New Territories from China to Britain."

Herman was captivated and wanted to learn more. He always wondered why Leslie was so entwined with the British government and why they relied on him for advice in administering the colony.

"It all started in China with the first Opium War in 1839. To give you a background the first Opium War began in 1839 and was fought over trading rights, financial reparations, and diplomatic status. Trade between the British and Chinese flourished in the early nineteenth century. The demand for opium grew at this time. Originally opium was used for medicinal reasons however in time the Chinese population started to use it for recreational purposes. The East India Company, a British trading company, had the monopoly of selling opium to the Chinese. They sent opium to their warehouses in the free-trade region of Canton and sold it to Chinese smugglers for huge profits. In 1834, the East India Company's monopoly on the China trade ceased, and the illegal opium trade flourished as other countries started trading in the commodity. This trade was made illegal by the emperor of China in the 1830s, partly concerned with the moral decay of the people and partly with the outflow of silver from its coffers. The emperor of the Qing Dynasty charged High Commissioner Lin-Tse Hsu with ending the illegal trade. Lin supposedly wrote a letter to Queen Victoria demanding that the sale of this contraband ceased and set a deadline to have it all removed. He, however, never did send off the letter to the queen."

Herman interrupted Leslie saying he knew all this from the history lessons he took in school but what did the Sun family have to do with all this?

Leslie told him to be patient and he would soon understand and to let him carry on with the story.

"From your history lessons you will know what happened and how Lin blockaded the warehouses where the drugs were stored. He asked the chief superintendent of British trade in China, Charles Elliot, that if he wanted to get the opium back, he needed to pay for it, or it would be destroyed. Charles was very close to your great, great, grandfather Sun Lee Chu, also known as Bulldog Sun by the British, because of his strength and stubbornness, to advise him how to deal with the problem. Bulldog Sun suggested that maybe Elliot promised to pay for it even though he did not have authority from the British government to do so. He would buy it back on credit from Lin. That way they could get a delay and have the opium saved from being destroyed. Lin did not agree and had all twenty thousand chests stored in the warehouses destroyed." Leslie paused to have a drink of water and continued.

"What happened then, as you may know from history, is that Charles Elliott wrote to London advising the use of military force against the Chinese. A small skirmish occurred between British and Chinese vessels in the Kowloon Estuary on 4 September 1839. On June 21st, 1840 a British naval force arrived off Macau and moved to bombard the port of Dinhai. In the ensuing conflict, the Royal Navy used its superior ships and guns to inflict a series of decisive defeats on the Chinese Empire. The war was concluded by the Treaty of Nanking in 1842, the first of the so-called 'unequal treaties' between

China and Britain. The treaty forced China to cede in perpetuity the Hong Kong Island, it also imposed a twenty-one-million-dollar payment to Great Britain, with six million paid immediately and the rest through specified instalments thereafter."

"Yes, I know all that but what had that to do with Bulldog Sun?" asked Herman.

"Bulldog Sun was a well-respected general in Canton who traded with the East India Company for his personal gain. He was initially assigned to rule the districts of South China from the emperors of the Qing Dynasty who ruled China from 1782–1850. When the High Commissioner Lin put restrictions on the British in selling opium and confiscated its cargo, he joined the British in the wars that preceded the Treaty of Nanking. He wanted to safeguard his business with the British which was lucrative to his family. Bulldog Sun called upon his family members and his garrison to back the British armed forces and formed an army which was known as the Warriors of the Sun. His soldiers had full belief in Bulldog Sun as he treated them and their families well, unlike the other generals of that time. Without the help of the Warriors of the Sun there was no way that the British forces could have won the first Opium War. The Chinese army in size overwhelmed the British forces and without Bulldog's help Hong Kong would not have been part of the British Empire as it is today. Bulldog Sun was made a special advisor of the British regime in Hong Kong and given a special rank by the first governor who happened to be Sir Charles Elliot. They would in future use the Warriors of the Sun to quell anyone that caused unrest in Hong Kong. This was the case when the second Opium War broke out when the French Empire pitted with the British Empire against the Qing Dynasty of China. The war again was to do with issues of the importation of opium into China. The British, with the help of the Warriors of the Sun, defeated the Chinese forces and in the Convention of Peking the Kowloon Peninsula was ceded to Britain.

"Anyone who knew of the Warriors of the Sun and how they helped win the war were sworn to secrecy, never to reveal them to anyone otherwise face harsh punishments. The only person was the governor and his cabinet who would pass it on to the new governor and he would do the same. So, the secret was kept safe from the rest of the world. Your grandfather and his brother never got along and even though they both were against the teachings of the communists in China, Sun Li Man, your grandad, kept operating with the British, but your granduncle went the other way. When the Chinese Civil War took place in 1949 your granduncle joined the dark side and formed his own triad the Sun Yee On whom you must have heard of and became its first Dragon Master.

"As you are now twenty-one it is my duty as the eldest living Sun to let you know all this. I want to show you something else which will now belong to you."

He opened his secret drawer in his desk, showing Herman how to open it, and pulled out his nunchaku and armlet.

Herman was awed by the nunchaku as it was different from any that he had seen before.

"This nunchaku is extra special: it has magical powers. As you see on top of the nunchaku ivory sticks are two large diamonds. When you rub the two diamonds together it will burst out in flames. If you point the flames, it will direct itself to where you point it to. It is a powerful weapon and should only be used in combat with your enemies and not for anything else."

He then showed him the amulet telling him it had brought luck and prosperity to the Sun family for years. Its mystical powers were said to help stave off black magic. This had been passed down from generation to generation to the eldest of the Sun family.

Herman was taken in by all this and had numerous questions he wanted to ask.

"Tell me about the current Warriors of the Sun. Who are they made of and what do you do? Am I supposed to continue this tradition? I am not skilled like you are in the art of Kung Fu or Karate and do not even know how to use nunchakus. Unlike you I have never been trained in that at all."

"Do not worry, I hope by the time I am through we will rid ourselves of the dark societies. I have recently been given permission by the governor to work on a plan with the British forces to raid the Walled City and close down the triads' operations. It seems the order has come directly from Britain. They are sick of the atrocities caused by the triads and for once and all want to shut them down and get rid of organised crime in the colony. I also have heard that they are thinking of creating an independent commission to deal with corruption in the colony. As Hong Kong is prospering and people overseas are capitalising in businesses here, they want Hong Kong to sparkle and be a safe place for investors. Their goal is for Hong Kong to be the financial centre of Asia within the turn of the decade. We have been working on a plan that when we do this it will be decisive and will end the triads as an organised operation, once and for all. Please keep this secret and not let any of your friends know. The government will back the Warriors of the Sun by providing backup forces and after the raid send in bulldozers to completely flatten the Walled City. The idea then is that the Dark Society will have nowhere to hide and will be dispersed once and for all. Hopefully this will happen within the next two years."

Leslie paused to let his son take in all he said and then continued.

"The current Warriors of the Sun consist of fifteen members, twelve of whom have been with me for over thirty years and studied from the same Kung Fu teacher as I did. Two of them you know well: Ajit and Mohan Lalwani. We used to meet weekly at the house on Mondays but for the last five years meet bi-monthly as organised crime in the colony has slowed considerably. I used to tell the family that the meetings were to do with Rotary and my charity. When we have gotten rid of the triads and bulldozed down the Walled City, we plan to disband the Warriors of the Sun forever. In the place of the Walled City the government plans to build high rise public apartment blocks with proper streets and sanitation for over one hundred thousand residents."

Just then Wan-Yu knocked on the door and entered the study. "Sir I have the car ready for us to leave whenever you are ready."

"Aha as usual just in time, yes Herman and I are ready to leave."

The three of them got into the car and were driven to the Lalwani Emporium in Tsim Sha Tsui. Whilst in the car they heard on the radio that typhoon signal number one was raised, warning of an approaching typhoon. In a way Leslie was happy that a typhoon was heading towards Hong Kong bringing with it much needed rain which was exactly what the colony required. Ajit was there to meet them when they entered Lalwani Emporium. Ajit brought them to the watch department.

"Here it is it took me a long time to get hold of one, but I finally did. Leslie you can pass this on to Herman," and handed him a Lalwani shopping bag.

Leslie reached in and took out a box and opened it. It was a two-tone Rolex Daytona watch, one of the most expensive watches in the market and cost HK$1,000,000. It was created by Rolex in 1963 and was the most sought-after watch in the world. Herman was stunned by his father's kindness. He had eyed this watch for a long time and jokingly mentioned it to his parents one day that he desired one.

"The reason I asked you to come with me is that I wanted you to try it on and if the band needed adjustment Ajit could do that for you here. I ordered the watch over six months ago but Ajit could not get hold of one till now. It is fully insured but please keep it safe."

Herman hugged his dad and thanked him over and over again. Leslie said he also needed to thank Mom as she was the one that pushed him to order the watch. He turned to Ajit to say thank you for finding it for him as he knew how hard it was to come by. He walked out of the store wearing the watch feeling totally elated.

After the shopping Leslie planned to call John and find out the latest news. He was excited to see the videotapes that Raymond would be bringing down from Macau and to see if it revealed anything that could lead to the whereabouts of Kohei Inowaki and his gang.

As they headed home Leslie could feel the winds picking up. The skies were grey, and it looked as if the storm was getting closer. He asked Wan-Yu to turn on the car radio as he wanted to catch the news. The four p.m. news came on followed by the weather report. Leslie was correct in his thinking; Typhoon Wanda was around four hundred and fifty miles away from the colony in the South China Sea heading towards Hong Kong. The typhoon signal number one was raised warning of an approaching typhoon.

When they reached home, Nancy rushed to meet them at the entrance.

"Where have you been, I have been trying to locate you for the last two hours. John called just minutes after you left looking for you, apparently Harold has been kidnapped! Elizabeth is having a complete meltdown. The Browns got a ransom note this afternoon from the kidnappers demanding for HK$250 million and if they do not get paid, they will kill Harold. John asked me to let you know to join him at Sir Anthony's residence once you returned. I told him that I would go with you to Sir Anthony's as I could at least help in consoling Elizabeth. Poor girl she must be in agony. I have asked the chauffeur to be on standby so we can leave any time you are ready. Do you want to freshen up before leaving?"

Herman, who had overheard all this, was worried for Harold and asked if he could join them.

"No," said Nancy. "John made it very clear just to let Leslie know about this and no one else. It is dangerous if this gets out to the public domain and the press gets hold of it as Harold's life would be in serious danger. You are not to say a word to anyone either not even any member of our family. This is extremely important do you understand?"

Herman nodded. Leslie said he would quickly freshen up, have a quick cup of coffee and meet her in the entrance in five minutes. They could then go directly to the Browns' home.

John tried to calm Elizabeth down. She was in a terrible state. They were all seated in the lounge area of Sir Anthony's residence. Inspector Lee and two other plain clothes officers were there setting up a tracer and tapping Sir Anthony's telephone line and hooking it onto a tape recorder. Danny was sitting quietly, staying away from everybody, looking very scared. Sir Anthony was pacing up and down the room. There was a knock on the door, and everyone froze for a second. John pointed to Sir Anthony, asking him to answer the door. It was Raymond Ho holding a parcel.

"I came as soon as I could John, I just got the videotapes off the hydrofoil from Macau and brought them here with me. Have you got hold of Leslie yet? Will he be coming over?" asked Raymond as he entered.

"Yes, I tried calling him, but he was out. I spoke to Nancy who said she would let him know the minute he came back. I just got a call from his manservant Wan-Yu that they are on their way now and should be here any minute. Thanks for bringing the videotapes here, we will wait for Leslie to arrive and watch them together. Maybe we can latch onto something that will help us to locate Kohei Inowaki.

Sir Anthony was worried that the kidnappers would hear that the police were now involved and thus harm Harold. John calmed him down by saying that no matter what Harold was in danger and with the police involved and handling the situation with their intelligence they had a better chance of locating Harold quickly and bringing him back safe and sound. Anthony said he had called "the Bank" and arranged for the security division to bring down the HK$250 million to the house that the kidnappers had requested just in case they needed to pay to release him. He felt more comfortable that the money was there and ready. Elizabeth said she did not care about the money, all she wanted was Harold to be safe and returned. John assured them that the police would take as little risk as possible to cause harm to their son and that their main concern was to get Harold back safely. Elizabeth was worried as to why the kidnappers had not called yet as they said they would this evening. She was worried something may have gone wrong, that maybe Harold tried to escape and got hurt. John comforted her by saying it was still early and for sure they would call soon and not to worry. Leslie and Nancy arrived at six p.m, by this time the men were all in the lounge having a drink and discussing the situation. Elizabeth had excused herself and went up to her room to take a rest but asked as soon as the call came to make sure someone fetched her. Leslie ordered himself a drink and sat with the boys while Nancy went up to see Elizabeth.

John said he was glad that Leslie had come as he wanted them to have a look at the videos that Raymond had brought with him together. They excused themselves from Sir Anthony and his son and went to the family room where a video recorder was set up.

"OK," said John. "Let's see what we got on the tapes."

Ray had got recordings for the three consecutive days that the suspect had last visited the casino. All three days he sat at the same table which he reserved.

"Hopefully it is the same person as the photograph that I sent to you Leslie earlier on, and that it is Kohei San as Niko had confirmed," said John

They put on the tape and watched intently. They saw a person sitting on a chair obviously a bit drunk as he kept swaying and slurring every time he spoke. He was smoking a cigar and had a full glass of what looked like Scotch next to him on the baccarat table. Sitting on either side of him were two attractive ladies who would every now and then get a tip from the suspect when he won a hand. The person was the same as in the photograph that John had shown to Leslie and Niko and it was now no doubt that it was indeed Kohei.

"I know one of the girls there sitting next to Kohei San," exclaimed Raymond. "She works at the hostess nightclub in my Hotel Faroe called the Spider's Web, her name is Yu Yan. She is one of the top hostesses in the club whom I recommend to friends of mine who visit Macau and want a good night out."

It was procedure that the hostesses who met up with any big spenders tried and get them into the casino. The hostess would get a commission of 2% from the hotel on how much the gambler would lose whilst there. So, they were encouraged to do this as they could make a lot of money especially if one was a big gambler. On all three days that Kohei was in the casino gambling Yu Yan was sitting next to him. The other girls would change but Yu Yan was always there.

"She must be special to him. I can call the Spider's Web and speak to her and see what she knows. You said he goes by the name Chuen Hei Ko," Raymond asked looking at John. John nodded.

They were all excited as this could be the big breakthrough that they had been waiting for. Leslie suggested they used the private line of Sir Anthony to call the club in Macau as he did not want to block the main number that the kidnappers would call. Raymond called the club and asked for the manager. He told him he needed to speak to Yu Yan urgently. The manager said she had not yet checked in but was expected very soon. Raymond gave him the private number and said it was imperative that she called back this number as soon as she came in and ask for him.

They all moved back to the lounge. John explained to Anthony what they had discovered which was positive in tracking down Kohei Inowaki, the person who was possibly behind the kidnapping of Harold. Sir Anthony, for the first time that day, grinned and said he hoped that it did. It was just then that the main phone rang.

John signalled the officers there to start the trace and start the tape recorder. He told Danny to get Elizbeth down and asked Sir Anthony to speak slowly and try to keep the call going as long as he could to give them enough time to trace where the call was originating from. Sir Anthony picked up the phone and identified himself. A muffled voice came through speaking in bad English.

"Listen sir and listen velly carefully, I to say this once. You will follow my intructions egzactly, do you known what I am stating?" Sir Anthony replied that he understood. The man continued, "Tomollow at one o'clock afterloon time you bling money in suitcase to the Pacific Mall in Cental. You go near shop Anne's Bakery on glound floor. There next to it are toilets. You go man's toilet and go to first cubicle you slide suitcase under. You then go quickly out. You make sure nobody come only you. If anybody follow, we know and we will kill son right way, no police you come by self you understand. Do not be late must be one clock afternoon."

"I understand and will follow your instructions to the letter. I will come alone with the money, but before you hang up, I want to make sure my son is all right can I please speak to him to make sure?"

"No, you cannot we already send you his chain to show we have him that is all you get now after you give money, we release him after one hour we check first if money good and nobody following then give back son." Before Anthony could reply the kidnapper hung up.

Elizabeth was bawling away insisting that Anthony just do as the kidnappers requested and asked John to not get involved until they got their son back alive. John's mind was racing, he needed to be cautious with his planning for if the kidnappers knew the police were involved, they would not waver to kill Harold. He called HQ and asked Angela to please locate and send down the floor plans of the Pacific Mall as soon as possible to the Browns' residence. He also asked her to keep the kidnap task force on full alert and not to go home yet and he would let them know the next steps. Leslie asked Nancy to please take Elizabeth back to her room and to comfort her whilst the boys discussed the situation.

"Tell you what I am thinking," said Leslie. "I am curious why they chose such an open place like the Pacific Mall for the drop off. It makes no sense as there will be hundreds of people all around especially around one p.m. as that is peak lunch time hour. There are numerous offices on top of the mall and in buildings around and most of the people who work around there have their lunch in one of the many restaurants at the mall. They have a plan that they believe will work and that they could get away without being caught. Either their plan is brilliant or extremely stupid. I believe they have not thought thoroughly about their plan. I suggest that John you maintain a watch out whilst Sir Anthony drop off the suitcase. However, be careful keep distanced and as far as possible from the drop area so as not to get spotted. Think it wise for the sake of Harold's safety that we do not give the kidnappers any chance to freak out and do something rash."

John agreed with Leslie and told Sir Anthony not to worry as his first concern was to get Harold back safely. He explained to Sir Anthony when he went to drop off the money to dress as he usually did and try not to be conspicuous. He was just to go exactly where the kidnappers asked him to and drop off the money as they requested. He should not say anything during this process and as soon as he dropped off the money to head directly to the car park where his chauffeur would be waiting. As a safety procedure John said he would have an officer dressed up in his chauffeur's outfit to protect Anthony just in case he was approached by the kidnappers, which he thought unlikely. Just then Sir Anthony's private phone rang. Anthony picked it up and it was for Raymond from someone called Yu Yan in Macau. Raymond spoke to Yu Yan in Cantonese for about twenty minutes and when he hung up, he went back to the boys to let them know what was said.

"Yu Yan, after a few questions, knew exactly who I was asking about. This person went about the name of Master Chuen. She knew right away when she first met him that although he had a Chinese name and spoke good Cantonese that he was Japanese. Apparently, he is a big spender and comes to Macau with his friends every couple of months. He usually stays in the Presidential suite at the Hotel Faroe. His friends would stay on the same floor and they would party with him in the suite with some of the hostesses after he had gambled in the casino for about three hours. He kept to a strict routine every time he was there. His schedule was that straight after dinner he would arrive at the club at around eight p.m. when the club opened. He would request for hostesses for himself and his mates. He would always have Yu Yan sit with him plus one other hostess. They would all sit in the VIP room, which he would pre-book, for about two hours chatting with the girls. They would all then head of to the casino where Chuen would have a baccarat table booked at the high stakes area of the casino where minimum stakes were HK$100,000 per bet. He always invited Yu Yan and one other hostess to join as he said it was lucky to have a pretty girl on each side when he gambled. Most of his mates would sit at the table and just watch him bet. Almost always he would lose to the house but on the rare occasion that he won he would tip freely to the dealer, Yu Yan and the other hostess. She would usually make herself over HK$15,000 just in tips. He would spend three hours every time in the casino whether he was winning or losing and then head up to the Presidential Suite where Yu Yan would arrange for six to eight hostesses to join a party. He paid all the girls well. There was something else she said that really concerned me. She said the first time she met Chuen he brought along as his guest the assistant commissioner of police of Macau. She saw Chuen hand over a large envelope which she believed was cash to him. So, she thinks that he probably has connections with the Macau police. That to me is worrying. I know the assistant commissioner well and he is very corrupt as when we were building the hotel the only way that we could move forward was greasing his hands."

John said his office had tried many times to work with the Macau authorities. Many of the criminals who escaped from the Hong Kong police fled to Macau. When asked to track them down the Macau police would not be helpful and said that they had no time to deal with affairs that do not affect their territory.

Leslie asked, "Does Yu Yan know where he lives in Hong Kong and does she have his phone number?"

"No, I asked her that as well but he is the one who usually calls her. She does not know where he lives and does not have his telephone number. Basically, whenever he plans to come to Macau, he calls her a couple of days ahead. Interestingly he just called her this afternoon saying he would be in Macau this Saturday and he wanted to book her for the three nights he will be staying there. He had already booked the Presidential Suite as usual and asked her to arrange six attractive hostesses for his party. He would meet her at the Spider's Web at eight Saturday night."

Leslie nodded, "You know it seems every time he makes some money, he goes to Macau to blow it off. He was there three months ago about the same time that Simon Fong was released. Now he tells Yu Yan that he will be there Saturday. Sir Anthony is to drop off the money tomorrow which is Thursday. He probably wants to spend some of that ransom money in Macau come Saturday. John, it may be worthwhile to go through the kidnappings and days the ransoms were paid in the last two years and see if they match up with the time that he was in Macau, if so, it points that the kidnappings could be Kohei San and his gang's doing."

"Yes, that makes total sense. Raymond if you could check your hotel record when he booked into the Hotel Faroe and give me those dates, I will have our officers check if they coincide with the dates of the kidnappings. By the way Angela called while Raymond was on the phone, she has located the floor plan of the Pacific Mall and it is on its way here. Once we have that we can try and work out how the kidnappers plan to escape with the ransom money. It just seems a weird place to do a drop off. With Simon Fong it was in an isolated location and was done in the dark. This is out in the open in a public place in the middle of the day," replied John.

When the plans arrived, they had a look at them. Anne's Bakery was located on the ground floor near the fire exit. Basically, there was a corridor to the left of the bakery that led to the men's and ladies' toilets and a baby change room. If you kept walking to the end of the corridor there was a fire exit. They concluded that after Anthony dropped off the money it was most probable that the person would escape through the fire exit. Was it that simple though? Leslie did not buy it. He was suspicious but John was convinced that was what was to happen. Why would they choose the toilets otherwise? It was near the fire exit and that would be their way out surely.

John said he would get his officers to set up video cameras on the first floor overlooking Anne's Bakery and the corridor and another at the car park area where the fire exit led to. He would ensure that these were hidden away and not easy to spot. He would get his team to do it later that night after the Pacific Mall had been closed to the public so as not to make it known that they were there. That way they could get a visual of both directions and no way would they lose the sight of the kidnappers when they left whichever direction they chose with the suitcase.

John told Anthony that they would not take any risks, so please reassure Elizabeth and ask her not to worry, that their main objective was getting Harold back, unhurt. The police would only observe from a distance and not move in. He told Anthony that he should retire for the night as tomorrow would be a long day. Leslie, Raymond and John continued talking for an hour or so. They decided that they would not risk anything happening to Harold and allow the kidnappers to get away with the ransom money. All they would do is observe and try to see if they could trace where the criminals would head off to. They came up with what they believed a good plan to capture Kohei whilst he was in Macau that Saturday if they did not capture him before then. Leslie said he would talk it through with the Warriors of the Sun on how they captured the gang and bring them back to Hong Kong to face justice for their crimes. It was obvious that John or the Hong Kong police could not be involved as they had no authority in Macau. With that Leslie, Nancy, Ray and John left to go back home not knowing what the next day would bring.

Chapter 12
Circle Of Fire

The Pacific Mall
5, Des Veoux Road, Central, Hong Kong
June 11th, 1964, Noon

John was looking down from the first-floor level at Anne's Bakery below. He was dressed in a polo shirt and wearing jeans. Around him were two plain clothes officers who were finalising the checks on the equipment that they set up the night before. It was all good, they reported to John. The cameras were quite hidden from sight inside what looked like an electric box fully covered and locked except for one hole where the camera lens was pointing down at Anne's Bakery. Before coming to the mall, he visited the Browns. He discussed in detail what Sir Anthony should and should not do. He needed to be calm and follow the instructions given to him to the letter. In case anything went seriously wrong he was to yell out and under cover policemen, who were placed at strategic points, would come to his aid. The minute he passed over the suitcase he was to go straight to the car park entrance and get back to his chauffeured car.

John had also spoken to Leslie earlier that morning. There was not much Leslie could do but he asked John to call him the minute the drop off was completed. He was sure that the criminals would have a number of people stationed around the mall and if anything did go wrong, they would call in to Kohei whom he was sure would be nowhere near the pickup area. The danger was if they got spooked and called Kohei Harold's life would be in serious risk. John said he understood and would give very strict orders to all the undercover police operating at the mall not to take any action that could cause the kidnappers to panic. They were basically there to observe unless signalled to move in, only when directed by him. He said that he had gone over the plan with all his team over and over again and he felt they were clear on their roles. His worry was with Sir Anthony, if he acted out of the ordinary to frighten the kidnappers, bad things could happen.

All morning since the mall opened to the public his officers were monitoring the corridor next to Anne's Bakery to see if anything unusual was happening. They saw a few people going in and out of the toilets but nothing out of the ordinary. John had planned on placing an undercover policeman in the toilet acting as a cleaner but took Leslie's advice which was not to do that. All they had to do now was wait and see what happened.

Meanwhile at Leslie's house the family were all sitting down for lunch, all except for Nancy. Lucy asked her dad if they had found Harold yet. She said she was worried for him, she also wondered where her mother was and why was she not having lunch with the rest of the family. Herman kept quiet while Leslie told her not to worry and he was sure that Harold would turn up shortly and as far as Mom was concerned, she had a few errands to do and would be back soon. Nancy had actually left around ten a.m. to the Browns. She wanted to be with Elizabeth to comfort her and be with her when Sir Anthony had to go and deliver the suitcase. Elizabeth was in a horrible state: she would not stop shaking and was crying the whole morning. Sir Anthony informed Nancy that Elizabeth had not slept at all and was worried about her. He was happy that Nancy was there to console her.

Herman, who knew what had happened to Harold, was worried about his friend. Mabel had come over that morning on her way to see Anita who was not feeling well. She told him that they should announce that they were a couple to their family and friends soon; in fact, this weekend. He told her that it was not the right time and he was not ready to do so yet. She got angry and said he needed to make a commitment, that he was not being fair to her and was using her as just a sex toy. He kept quiet. She could sense he was upset and changed the subject and asked him whether he knew anything more about Harold's disappearance. Herman muttered that he had not heard anything further. She could tell from his expression that he was lying to her and pushed him to tell what he really knew promising that whatever he told her she would keep secret. Herman was dying to tell someone, so he disclosed everything he knew to her. He made her swear that under no circumstances, she tell anyone, what he told her. She said she already suspected something was wrong as her dad had been acting weird the last two days and hardly been home. She told Herman if he heard further to please let her know and that she would be praying for Harold's safe return. Herman said he would, and she left to meet up with Anita.

Herman had been thinking of Ella all day. He wondered how she was and especially how she was handling the disappearance of Harold. He realised that he still had feelings for her. He was confused: he did like Mabel but found her brash. She liked taking control and he found her aggressive. He did not feel ready to announce they were going together to the public as she suggested for unlike her, he was not sure of the relationship. He enjoyed the sex but there was nothing more as he first thought. He went to the phone and dialled Ella's number.

As Sir Anthony left home to go to the mall the winds were slowly picking up and it was raining heavily. The chauffeur, who was actually an undercover policeman, told him that Typhoon Wanda was moving closer to the colony and at ten a.m. the Royal Observatory had raised the typhoon signal to number three. Sir Anthony was thinking to himself, I hope this does not foil Leslie's plan, for if the typhoon came any closer the number eight signal would be raised and all ferries to Macau would close. If that happened Kohei could not head off to Macau this weekend as they expected, and they would miss an opportunity to nab him if they did not already do so by today.

Sir Anthony arrived at the mall at twelve thirty p.m; he was early. From the car park to where he needed to be was a ten-minute walk at most. He got out of the car and lit a cigarette hoping it would help calm his nerves. He actually hardly ever smoked, and only did so socially, but right now, he really needed one. When he finished his cigarette, he took the suitcase out of the trunk. It was a plain black Samsonite suitcase that John brought over that morning to put the cash in. What Anthony did not know was that John had his technical team put a GPS bug in the lining of the suitcase. It was completely concealed. It would send a signal and would be picked up by the mobile van that John had placed in the car park that would monitor the movement of the suitcase.

The cash was made of HK$1000.00 notes. They were clean and unmarked as the kidnappers requested. Anthony told the chauffeur he should be back within thirty minutes.

John, from his first-floor lookout, saw Anthony head towards the corridor that led to the men's toilet. He told his officers to be vigilant and look out for anything they found suspicious. Sir Anthony disappeared into the corridor leading to the toilets and in less than two minutes he reappeared without the suitcase. Just then all hell broke loose. Suddenly there was a small explosion followed by the fire alarms going off which in turn started the water sprinklers to turn on. People were running towards the exits. Smoke was coming from the far end of the mall indicating there was some type of fire. People were screaming and the whole place was in total chaos. He told his officers to stay put where they were and to keep the cameras running. If they spotted anyone carrying a black suitcase to follow from a distance and report straight back to him on his walkie-talkie.

John took the escalator down to the ground floor and headed to where the smoke was originating from. He had to push his way through people who were panicking running for the exits. As he reached the place where the smoke was originating from, he could see a backpack blown open lying on the floor with smoke coming out of it. He looked around to see if anyone was hurt but to his relief nobody seemed to have been injured. He thought the bomb must have been set off deliberately to cause a diversion. Damn it! Leslie was right: the kidnappers were smarter than he thought them to be. He called from his walkie-talkie to his team who were standing by in the van outside the car park. He asked could they tell from the monitors where the suitcase was, and had it moved. They replied saying the suitcase had not left the area of the corridor and believed it was still in the toilets. He rushed towards the toilets.

John reached the men's toilets and headed in, there was no one there. On the first cubicle stuck on the door was a sign that read, "Out of order. Do not use". He forced opened the door which was jarred in by a cardboard chunk. As he entered there was no sign of the suitcase. He radioed in the van again to make sure that the suitcase was still around the area he was now, which they confirmed. He walked around the toilets, going in and out of each cubicle, but there was no sign of the suitcase. He then entered the ladies' toilets and did the same but again there was no sign of the suitcase. Finally, he entered the baby changing room. There, lying on the floor, was the suitcase which was opened and empty. His mind was working, the kidnappers had planned this brilliantly. John realised that what must have happened was when Anthony slipped the bag inside the cubicle at the men's toilet the person there must have picked it up and passed it to whoever was in the baby changing room. It must have been emptied there and put into another bag. He needed to go through the tapes and see if he could make sense of how the cash was moved.

Within fifteen minutes of the fire being set off the fire brigade arrived. They announced on their hand megaphones that anyone still in the mall was to head directly to the fire exits and leave. They managed to put the fire out in minutes. John moved back to the first floor and asked his officers to wait there and search the toilet area for any clues. Meanwhile he gathered up the tapes from the first floor and from the van parked nearby which was monitoring the exit. He asked Inspector Lee to follow him to the Browns' residence and then called Leslie telling him what happened and for him to meet him there.

He arrived at the Browns' residence just as Leslie arrived. Anthony asked what had happened as he could hear the alarms going off as he was leaving the car park. Both he and Elizabeth were concerned that something went wrong and were worried if what happened would affect Harold's safety. John reassured them by saying all was OK and as the kidnappers had received the money, they should release Harold shortly. All they could do now was wait and pray that Harold would be released quickly. Elizabeth seemed to have calmed down somewhat after that. She said to Nancy that now that the kidnappers had got the money, surely, they must release Harold. Nancy agreed and said for her not to worry and that all would be fine. Elizabeth had not eaten all morning and Nancy said it would be wise for her to keep her strength up and have something to eat.

John, Leslie, Anthony and Inspector Lee meanwhile headed to the lounge and put the videotapes on. They saw Anthony go to the corridor towards the toilets with the suitcase and return back not more than two minutes later empty-handed and heading towards the main car park area. John paused the video and asked Anthony if there was anyone in the men's toilet when he was there. He said there were two people, one using the urinal and the other was washing his hands in the sink. He went to the first cubicle as directed and saw the sign that said, "Out of Order". He knocked lightly on the cubicle door and slid the bag under. He only did just that and walked straight out. John restarted the tape. Watching on they then heard the alarms going off and the sprinklers set off. People were running towards the exit. They saw people running in all directions, some towards the corridor to the exits whilst others headed to the main entrance which was away from the smoke. As they kept looking, they saw a lady with a baby's pram pushing it out of the corridor where the changing room was, walking towards the main entrance. She was not running just walking calmly down. John let out a cry. He remembered now passing her as he rushed towards the smoke wondering then why she was rolling the pram so casually. Surely if she had a baby, she should have picked up the baby, carried it in her arms and ran as quickly as she could towards safety and not worry about the pram. He at that time did not stop to check her out as he was thinking only about heading towards where the bomb had exploded and what was happening there. Then it came to him this must be how the kidnappers got the money out without being detected. The kidnappers had someone stationed in the baby changing room. When Anthony passed the suitcase off to the person in the cubicle, that person must have waited a minute then headed with it to the baby changing room. It was there that a woman was waiting with a large pram. The money must have then been transferred to the pram and the lady walked away without being noticed as everybody was looking for someone with a black suitcase. They observed that the lady was quite young. She was dressed in blue jeans and had a black hoody top on. John told Inspector Lee to take the video back to HQ and make copies of the lady and pass it on to the team. He also wanted the team to go through the criminal police files and see if they could pick up who she was.

Leslie said meanwhile there was not much they could do except to wait. Anthony said he would join his wife for lunch and asked Leslie and John if they would join as well, they both said no and thanked him.

When Inspector Lee left with the tapes to Police HQ Les pulled John aside.

"I feel that the kidnappers could have been tipped off by someone working for you. I did not want to say anything while Inspector Lee was around. I trust nobody at this stage. I am telling you this privately as I do not want to worry Anthony or Elizabeth. This was all planned, the kidnappers knew that they were being taped and that the suitcase had a bug in it. That is the reason why they were so prepared. If I am right, then we are in serious trouble. They may be upset that the police were involved in which case they could harm Harold. I hope for God's sake I am wrong. If Harold does not show up in the next twenty-four hours I fear for his life."

Leslie told John he had called a meeting of the Warriors of the Sun the night before at his house to plan how they go about capturing Kohei and his gang this weekend. That is providing the typhoon did not prevent the ferries and hydrofoils from sailing to Macau due to the high winds. According to the latest weather report they heard Typhoon Wanda was heading towards Hong Kong slowly. It could change course and it could pick up speed but where it was heading now and at its current speed it should pass very close to the colony on Saturday night. Leslie knew that John could not arrest Kohei without concrete proof and could not rely on the Macau police helping out. It was therefore up to the Warriors of the Sun to capture Kohei and his gang in Macau with the money; that was the proof they needed as there would be no way Kohei could explain where that money came from.

Leslie said he and Nancy would stay for an hour and then head back home as there was not much more that could be done. John said he too needed to be back at the office as he had not been there all day and had loads to catch up. He also needed to prepare his team for the oncoming typhoon. They told Anthony and Elizabeth that if they heard anything, they should contact them immediately and for them not to worry and be patient. It was five thirty when they left. Outside the winds were getting stronger and the rain was lashing down. Leslie thought to himself, at least all this rain will help fill the reservoirs and hopefully help end the drought. Leslie turned to Nancy and told her that he had called a meeting with his Rotarian group at home for tonight. He apologised for not letting her know earlier as it was a last-minute thing and if she could get the cook to arrange something light for the group for dinner. There would altogether be twelve of them coming over.

Herman hung up with Ella. She was really concerned about Harold and felt guilty that she did not leave with him that night. If she had maybe none of this would have happened. Herman calmed her down and told her not to blame herself for what happened and not to worry so much as he would probably show up soon unhurt.

"I see that you and Mabel are a couple now. She told me that you two guys are going steady. Congrats! I am sorry I got so drunk that night we went out. To be totally honest with you I was being stupid and seeing you with Mabel just made me envious. I reacted badly as after those years we dated I was hoping we could get back to the old days when you returned from the U.K. I am all right with it now; I had a lot of time to think and respect your decision. I just hope we can remain close friends as I really would like to but at the same time, I do not wish to upset Mabel."

Herman replied, "Yes I was with Mabel that night and to be honest with you I thought you were serious with Harold as he brought you to my party and I saw you two kissing on the dance floor. I actually was going to approach you that night and ask you for a dance but seeing you and Harold together I backed off. Mabel came on strong to me that night and I just needed some loving then. Don't get me wrong I like Mabel very much and as you know we grew up together, but I am not sure that I am in love with her and am definitely not ready to make a commitment with her. I too would like to think that we could get together and try to get back to where we left off before I left for uni. Would you consider that?"

Ella could not believe what she was hearing from Herman. She had resigned to the fact that he and Mabel were in love and she had no future prospect with him. She explained to Herman that she only went out with Harold because she was lonely whilst Herman was away studying. She kissed him at Herman's party as she wanted to make Herman jealous thinking that would spark him enough to approach her. She admitted she was foolish in her thought.

She went on to say, "I would love going out with you again and see if we could get back to the place we were before you left. I missed you so much when you left and realised how much I loved you. However, I was embarrassed to let you know as I had pushed for the break up prior to you leaving for the U.K. I think before we go out on a date together that you speak to Mabel and tell her what your true feelings are with her. I do not want her to think that I am pushing you to see me. She already hates the fact of us being together and she has expressed it to me. She is totally in love with you, so you need to be careful how you present the truth to her."

"Yes, I know Mabel can be very aggressive and spiteful. I will let her know the next time I see her. I do not want to do it over the phone. I believe our families are having dinner together tomorrow, I will let her know then. I was going to see if you were available this weekend but with Harold missing and Typhoon Wanda approaching can you make it for the weekend after? 'Les Misérables' will be playing at the Convention Centre starting next week and I know you love the theatre. Thought I would take you there if you like. If so, I will purchase the tickets tomorrow when they come on sale."

She said she would love to go. Ella then went on to tell him what Mabel did to her at his party and why she left in a hurry that night without saying goodbye to him. Herman was shocked; he never knew that happened and he was disgusted with how Mabel had treated Ella. It was no wonder why Ella acted so strangely that night when they saw The Beatles. They said their goodbyes and hung up. Herman was feeling elated and happy he spoke to her. He had been such a fool and should not have led Mabel on, especially when he had such deep feelings for Ella still. He realised what he felt with Mabel was purely sexual. He was thinking how he would approach Mabel as he knew how vindictive she could be. It is not going to be easy, he thought, and did not look forward to telling her his feelings. He wanted to discuss it with somebody he was close to. He picked up the phone again and called Dilip Lalwani.

When Leslie got home, he went to his study and picked up notes that he made earlier that day for his meeting with the Warriors of the Sun. He had worked out a plan which he thought was least risky. He had planned that the Warriors left on the nine thirty a.m. hydrofoil for

Macau on Saturday getting to Hotel Faroe by eleven a.m. They would book a room next to the Presidential Suite of the hotel. Leslie through Raymond had found that a booking had already been made by Mr Chuen for arrival on Saturday around noon time and for three nights. His plan was actually quite simple and effective. The idea was whilst Kohei and his goonies were gambling at the casino the Warriors of the Sun would go into the Presidential Suite and hide in waiting for them to return to the room. Raymond had organised them to get a duplicate key for that room. They would surprise them as they entered the room. Yu Yan would call them to prewarn them when the gang finished gambling and were ready to go to the suite and get their party started. This way they will get advance notice and be ready to act.

They should quickly overpower the gang which, as they knew, would be around only six people and tie them up. Raymond had arranged for them to use a service elevator that would bring them to the basement car park which was usually reserved for staff only. There would be a large van ready for them to put the gang in and then drive to the hydrofoil dock. Ray also had arranged a private hydrofoil to take them back to Hong Kong where John, with his team, would be waiting to pick them up. It would happen so fast that the criminals would not know what hit them. Yes, he was sure it would all go well. The only problem could be was that if Typhoon Wanda got closer to Hong Kong by Saturday and all hydrofoils and ferries going to Macau would be halted. He could not control that and had no choice but to leave it to the gods, he thought. He got up and walked towards the family room to await the arrival of the warriors. He bumped into Herman on his way there. Herman said he was meeting Dilip at the Havana Room for dinner that night. He told his dad not to worry: that they would go straight there and come back right after dinner. Dilip's chauffeur will be there to pick him up later and will wait for them till they finished dinner. Leslie said that it was OK for him, but he needed to clear it with his mother also.

John, meanwhile, had just finished having a meeting with Inspector Hill who was in charge of any weather catastrophes that occurred in the colony. Inspector Hill advised John that his team was prepared for any eventualities and for him not to worry. John had, prior to that, spoken to

Phil Hammond of the Royal Observatory asking him whether he thought the typhoon was going to hit the colony and how strong it was going to be. Phil had told him this typhoon was going to be worse than Typhoon Mary which hit Hong Kong four years ago. In fact, it would be the worst ever typhoon to hit the colony. John was concerned, he did not need this on top of Harold's kidnapping. He was also very worried for Niko. She lived alone in a very exposed spot. Phil had said to expect wind gusts of over two hundred miles per hour which would cause huge waves, together with the heavy rains would cause severe flooding throughout the colony. Nico lived near the beach, so she needed to be extra careful. John asked Phil would Niko be safe where she lived, and he said as a precaution she should evacuate to higher ground as if the typhoon hit during high tide she would be in serious danger. John thanked him and called Niko.

Mabel was sitting on the side of Anita's bed in her room. Anita had not been feeling too well and Mabel had come to visit. She was telling Anita that she found Herman aloof the last two days and was concerned. He did not fuss over her like he did before Harold went missing. She had asked him when they could make their relationship official and he had unexpectedly said to her that he was not ready to do so. She asked Anita whether she thought that she having sex with him so quickly had maybe put him off her and thought of her as being loose. Anita said she did not think so, maybe he was just concerned about Harold and his mind was wrapped up in that. Mabel said she hoped Anita was right, and maybe she was fretting for no reason.

Anita went on, "There is something I want to share with you. You are the only person I trust, and I have been keeping this in for a long time. I have been embarrassed to tell you as I feel you may judge me, but I cannot keep it in any more. I have discovered during the last two years that I am not at all interested in men. I find them all self-centred and just interested in sex. I have discovered that I prefer being with women and I think I am in love with someone I find very special."

Mabel was intrigued and pushed Anita to tell her more. Anita revealed to her the feelings she had towards Bella and the couple of encounters she recently had with her. Mabel was shocked. She had been Anita's closest friend all these years and thought she read her well, but she never anticipated this.

"Wow, all this has blown me away. I am glad you have come out of your closet and told me this. I of course do not judge you at all. You have to go with your feelings, and I will be here if ever you need someone to talk to. It is going to be difficult though how you approach telling your family as they are ultra-conservative. Isn't Bella dating this actress Eileen Siu? She seems to have a deep relationship with her so please be careful as I do not want you to be hurt as Bella may just be fooling around with you."

"Yes, I know she is seeing Eileen that is why I was so shocked when she kissed me so deeply, it actually made me shake with excitement. I have never felt anything like that before. I actually have been attracted to her the last few years. I think she is the classiest lady I have ever met, next to you that is, of course," she laughed. "I am hoping that I can break up her relationship with Eileen and maybe you can help me out here."

Mabel nodded and said they could work on a plan together. They chatted for a while till Anita said she was feeling tired and Mabel told her to take some rest. Outside it was raining very hard and Mabel thought, I better leave before the roads get flooded and I get stuck. She kissed Anita on her forehead, wished her well and left. She wondered if she should go past Herman's house before going home but she thought better of it and instead got into her chauffeured car and went home.

John, meanwhile, had driven to Niko's. He had explained to her what Phil had told him and that she and her staff needed to evacuate her house as it would not be safe if the typhoon hit. He said, according to Phil, the typhoon was slow moving but could pick up speed rapidly so it may be wise to move out immediately. Also, the waves around the coast had already started to rise. She called in her staff and said they should all immediately leave and return only after the storm passed or when it was safe enough to do so.

She was frightened and said she did not know where to go to. He said for her not to worry and he would arrange for her to stay at a hotel in Central that was away from the sea and well protected. He called the Mandarin Hotel and spoke to the general manger there whom he knew well and booked a suite room for her. He said he would wait for her to pack her clothes and essentials and would drive her there. He had the hotel room booked for three nights initially but she could change that according to circumstances. He asked if she would like to have dinner with him that night, if so, he would book the Grill Room at the hotel. He had not eaten there before but heard the food there was superb. She said she would love to. He called back his office to let them know he would be having dinner at the Grill at the Mandarin Hotel and if there were any emergencies to get in touch with him there. As she was packing, he called Maggie and said that he would probably have to stay in his office till very late as there was a lot that he still needed doing and for her to let the staff know that he would not be coming home for dinner.

Maggie hung up with John and dialled Raymond's number. He picked up the phone almost immediately. Maggie asked how he was getting on with having the monies in the Swiss bank divided and in setting up an account for her. He said he had all wheels turning and should have it set up before the end of the month at the latest. He still needed John to complete one last document and have it signed so he could fax it back to the bank to finalise. John had promised to complete it by tomorrow morning, and he had asked his secretary to pick it up from his offices. She thanked him and said she really found it difficult living with John these days. She really wanted to start the divorce as soon as possible and was just waiting for the monies in the Swiss bank to be set up for her before pushing on with the divorce as both John and she could not show that asset on their divorce documents. Raymond asked what they had decided about the house. Right now, the house was paid for by the government as part of John's remuneration. She said she had looked at purchasing a three-bedroom house in Kowloon Tong, an area which she loved and knew well as that was where she lived when the family first came to Hong Kong. She did not want to stay in the Peak and longed to move closer to Nancy and Maya who were both close friends. John could stay at the Peak, but she and the kids would move to the new house. She had already spoken to the realtor and had put a deposit on the house with John's knowledge. She had told both Nancy and Maya about her planned divorce but had asked them not to let anyone know till they filed, not even their immediate family. She thanked him for all his help, said goodbye and hung up.

Maggie at thirty-eight years old was still very attractive. She had looked after her body well even after having two children. She did not have an ounce of fat on her body. She did have feelings for Raymond but knew of his reputation of being a playboy. She did not want to get into another causal relationship, instead the next time, she longed for one to last forever. She wanted someone who would look after her and treat her like a princess. She had recently been attracted to Nancy's brother David Poon. She had met him often through the years that she had known Nancy and found him very attractive and sophisticated, just like his sister. Nancy had told him that David was having major problems with his wife Mia who was an alcoholic and their marriage was in tatters. Nancy felt sorry for him and for her nephew Robert and her nieces Naomi and Michelle. They were great kids but were totally neglected by their mother. David attended many parties without his wife who would not show up because, according to Nancy, she was probably getting drunk at home. Maggie felt sorry for David and thought, what a waste of a good man. She had recently flirted with him and he seemed to have enjoyed her attention and he had lately started flirting back with her. She wondered if she could take it to the next stage.

Niko and John arrived at the Mandarin Hotel close to eight thirty p.m. As he was checking her in, they bumped into Herman and Dilip. He felt embarrassed as he was nervous of what they would think. He asked what they were doing there, and Herman replied that they were having dinner at the Havana. John was surprised that their parents let then out especially now with what was happening with Harold. He stuttered, explaining to the boys that he was helping Niko check in to the hotel as her place was unsafe from the upcoming typhoon. Herman found that real strange for the commissioner of police to be doing that and thought to himself, there is something funny happening here. Herman headed to the lift and took it to the second floor where the Havana Paradise Club was. Meanwhile John brought Niko up to her room and helped her settle in. He said when she had finished freshening up that he will be waiting for her at the Grill Room which was located on the top floor of the hotel.

John was sitting at the bar in the restaurant waiting for Niko to appear. He was quite excited to be alone with her and was wondering if they could pick up on their relationship tonight. The restaurant was on the sixteenth floor of the hotel and had a panoramic view of the colony. He could see that it was raining very hard now and the winds had picked up rapidly. He hoped if the typhoon was to hit the colony it would come fast and leave soon. Niko walked into the restaurant and headed to the bar where he was waiting for her. She was wearing a long, emerald green dress that was rather simple but was low cut and quite revealing. She looked absolutely stunning. She kissed him on his cheek and asked if she could have a large Vodka Martini with two olives.

Herman meanwhile entered the Havana and saw Dilip sitting on the corner table and went to sit opposite him. Herman opened up to Dilip and told him about his feelings for Ella and asked him to advise on how he should handle the situation with Mabel. Dilip said it would not be easy as he knew how nasty Mabel could be. He said it would even be more difficult now that Herman had foolishly made love to her and had told her that he cared for her. He told Herman that Anita had told him that Mabel was totally in love with him and was determined to marry him. Herman said he could handle Mabel but was more worried about Ella and what Mabel could do to her. He told her story of that night of his party and how Mabel was to Ella. Dilip was surprised and said he heard nothing of this from his sister and Ella maybe was exaggerating. Herman did not think so as he knew Mabel well and she was very capable of doing that. Dilip said there was no easy way to break up with her he just had to be honest with Mabel about everything, including his feelings for Ella. For if he just made some lame excuse about them breaking up and started dating Ella that would freak Mabel even more. He agreed and the conversation went on to Harold. Herman told Dilip what he heard about Harold being kidnapped but made Dilip swear to tell no one about it. Dilip was worried for Harold and hoped he would be released soon. They both continued their dinner in silence, each in deep thoughts.

Dilip had known Herman for years. Both their fathers were the best of friends and had known each other since primary school days all the way to uni and in business. Dilip and Herman went to the same primary and high schools as their fathers did. They both did well in school and Herman went on to uni while Dilip joined his father's business. Dilip envied Herman as he was athletic and popular with the girls. Dilip, although quite good looking, did not have the same attention from the girls. He was, however like his father, good at Kung Fu and was the junior champion of Hong Kong during his school days. He secretly had a huge crush on Mabel and therefore found talking about her with Herman all a bit weird. Mabel, however, treated him like an elder brother and never took any romantic interest in him. Anita had told him that she totally was in love with Herman. Now hearing that Herman intended to break up with Mabel he wondered if he was there for her and gave her attention maybe he could have a chance with her…

Leslie just finished his meeting with the Warriors of the Sun and looked at his watch, it was almost ten thirty p.m. He wondered if Herman had come back from dinner and was relieved when Wan-Yu said he just walked in five minutes ago. The Warriors of the Sun meeting went smoothly with Ajit saying he and Mohan would be all in with whatever Leslie planned as would the rest of the warriors. Everything had to be planned precisely and they could not afford to make any mistakes. He was about to go to bed when he got a call from Raymond.

"Sorry for calling so late but this could be important. Yu Yan called me just now. She had a call from Chuen saying he decided that instead of taking the hydrofoil to Macau on Saturday he will be taking it first thing tomorrow morning before the typhoon signal got higher and the services halted. He would stay in Macau until the typhoon passed. He had asked Yu Yan to, as usual, arrange a table for him at the nightclub and get some girls lined up for his friends that night. I just called the hotel and Kohei did call and changed his and his gang's reservations starting tomorrow for four nights. I know this of course upsets all the plans we made, so what should I do? Can you arrange for you and the warriors to leave for Macau at such short notice? If so let me know so I can rearrange everything."

Leslie said this was the last thing he wanted as he was uncomfortable hurrying things along and not going there well prepared.

He was also worried about the fact that if they got to Macau and captured the gang, and the typhoon hit then they would not be able to return quickly back to Hong Kong as they planned. He said he would come back to Raymond shortly as he wanted to chat with Phil Hammond in the observatory to check on the progress of the typhoon. Leslie called Phil in the observatory knowing he would be there.

"Sorry to call you so late, Phil, but it is important. I need to know if Typhoon Wanda is still on course to hit Hong Kong and if it is when do you think it would hit the coast. The last time we spoke you said it was moving slowly, is that still the case? If it is, I plan to take a ferry to Macau tomorrow on an important business trip that cannot wait."

"Well, strange you should call as I was just about to raise the typhoon signal to number eight. Apparently, the typhoon has picked up speed rapidly and if it continues on its course, it will hit Hong Kong around two p.m. tomorrow. I am sorry but you won't, and nobody else will, be able to travel from eleven p.m. this evening when the signal is raised to number eight. All flights and ferries around the colony will have to come to an immediate halt. If the typhoon moves quick as expected you may be able to travel late Saturday night or early Sunday morning but definitely not until then. This is a very strong typhoon Leslie and I suggest you let your family know and have the house properly secured."

Leslie thanked him and gave a sigh of relief, that was lucky. He called Raymond back, and told him what Phil had conveyed to him, that as soon as the number eight signal was raised all hydrofoils and ferries to Macau would be halted; Kohei was going nowhere soon. Leslie said probably when Kohei finds out he can't travel till the typhoon passes he would probably call Yu Yan to let her know and change the date he would be going. He asked Raymond to call Yu Yan and ask her to keep him informed. Raymond said he would also call the hotel and if Kohei changed his reservation to let him know to what dates. They said goodbye and Leslie called Wan-Yu. He told him that he heard the typhoon was heading directly for Hong Kong and for him to let all the staff know. He was to ensure the house was secured and all the windows boarded up. He then finally headed to his bedroom.

At exactly 12.10 a.m. Leslie got a call from Sir Anthony. He was quite hysterical.

"At midnight there was heavy knocking on my front door, and somebody was furiously ringing my doorbell. I went to investigate and when I opened the door saw no one around but there was a parcel on the floor wrapped in brown paper. It was raining like crazy and the wind almost blew me over. I took the parcel into the kitchen to have a look at it properly, on it was an envelope stuck on the covering of the parcel. I opened the envelope and there was a note which read, 'You may have won the war, but you have lost this battle. A souvenir to you Gwai Lo this is what happens to those who lie'. I did not want to open the parcel as I was scared to and so I called John, but he was not home and Maggie told me she did not know where he was and for me to try the office. He was not there either. Elizabeth is sedated, she took some sleeping pills tonight and is fast asleep. I thought better not to open it yet, as there may be clues there which I could ruin by having my fingerprints all over. Can you please come over as I am sure you can help?"

Leslie said he wanted to, but he could not get to Sir Anthony's as typhoon signal number eight was up and all the car ferries and ferries to the island were closed. Therefore, he could not get to the Peak. He however asked him not to open the parcel till he could arrange for the police to go there. He said he would try and get a hold of Inspector Lee who lived on the island and see if he could head to Sir Anthony's house. He called Inspector Lee and told him about what had happened and for him to go to Sir Anthony's. As Inspector Lee lived in Wanchai he said it was going to be very tricky as the winds were blowing relatively hard now and it was dangerous to drive up the winding roads to the Peak. It would take him at least forty minutes to get there. He hung up and called John as he knew John lived just around the corner from Sir Anthony, hoping he had returned home. Maggie answered and said he was not home yet, but he had called a few minutes ago saying he was on his way. Leslie told her to tell him to head straight to Sir Anthony's house as soon as he got in.

It was almost one a.m. when John left the hotel making his way home. It was slow driving as the winds were very strong and made his car hard to handle, to make it worse it was raining so heavily that his wipers could not clear the rain from his windshield quick enough. However, he was happy and could not believe what had just happened. After a fantastic dinner Niko and he talked for hours, getting to really know one another, Niko then asked him whether he would like a nightcap in her room. He of course said yes. In her bedroom she fixed him a Scotch and said she was going to get into something more comfortable before joining him for a drink. In about ten minutes she came out of the bathroom dressed in the sexiest black laced lingerie that was totally revealing. She walked up to him, took the glass from his hand and kissed him deeply. He started undressing her, and led her towards the bed. He looked at her beautiful body for a minute and then pushed her to the bed. He started kissing her on her lips and slowly moving his lips all the way down first to her breasts sucking at her nipples and then to her clitoris which he licked while putting his fingers deep into her vagina. She kept moaning and asked him to please enter her which he did and after a few minutes he had an orgasm. They lay down still for a while. Niko asked if he had to go back home to which he replied yes as he needed to go early to the office tomorrow and needed to shower and change before going in. They kissed and said goodbye and he left.

When John arrived home, it was almost one thirty a.m. Maggie told him he needed to get to Sir Anthony's immediately. Lucky for him Sir Anthony's home was just a two-minute drive away. He went into the house to use the bathroom to freshen up and then got back in his car and headed to Anthony's home. Sir Anthony himself answered the door. John was soaked from the lashing rain although he parked his car just five metres from the entrance. Sir Anthony was looking very worried and led him to the kitchen where on the breakfast bar was the parcel. He offered John a towel so he could dry himself and offered him a cup of coffee.

"Leslie told me Inspector Lee was also coming but you got here quicker. Elizabeth is asleep she knows nothing of this. I am not going to wake her just yet till we find out what this is all about. I feel terrified to think what could be in the parcel." He handed John the note he found outside the parcel. It was typewritten and the English was good. He read it aloud "You may have won the war, but you have lost this battle.

A souvenir to you Gwai Lo this is what happens to those who lie". He thought the war referred to be the Second World War when the Allies defeated the Japanese forces in Hong Kong. What did it mean though by "you have lost this battle"? The term "Gwai Lo" was typical of the terms that the Black Ninjas would call a foreigner: anyone non-Asian. He was worried that what was in the parcel was something very sinister and feared the worse. He could not get his forensics team in immediately due to the typhoon and wondered if he should open the parcel anyway. He asked Sir Anthony whether there were any medical gloves in the house, probably something the staff would use when cleaning the house. Sir Anthony headed to the staff quarters to check with his butler. As he waited for him to return there was a knock on the front door, he went to answer it and it was Inspector Lee carrying a bag.

"I brought all the things we may need: gloves, fingerprinting equipment and other stuff as I thought we would need it. Sorry I took so long but it was horrendous getting here. The winds were so strong that I had to drive extra slowly as I feared my car could blow over. I was truly scared. Looks like the typhoon is going to be a bad one."

"Great," said John. "Well done. Anyway, tonight you can stay at my place as I do not think you would be able to drive home as the typhoon approaches. Now let's use some dusting powder on the parcel and see if we can spot any fingerprints."

Sir Anthony came back into the room and watched the two go about their work. The parcel apparently had been wiped clean of fingerprints. John, with his gloves on, slowly unwrapped the brown paper that was covering the parcel. Underneath was a tin box similar to a mah-jong carrying tile tin box. On top of the box, wrapped around the handle, was another note that was wrapped in plastic. They carefully dusted the tin box, but it too was clean of fingerprints. They then removed the plastic from the note, also dusting the note, but again no prints. They took out the note and John read it aloud:

"It's sad to see a butterfly lose its wings. It can no longer fly and pollinate the flowers. It slowly dies as it cannot feed. To lose one's heart is to lose one's soul and life passes away quickly. Sadly, it affects those around and does not forgive them for their deeds. We will one day win back the war, yours truly, K.I. LL."

John already guessed what that meant, and asked Anthony to be prepared for the worst. His instinct was correct as he lifted the box cover it revealed a human heart. Sir Anthony looked over and let out a scream and started to howl. He knew immediately that was Harold's heart and fell down on his knees. His scream woke up most of the household and the maids were the first to rush in but were told to leave the room. Then Elizabeth and Danny showed up and saw Anthony on his knees on the floor his hands clutching his face. They then saw the opened box and the human heart. Elizabeth fainted and Danny went to her aid.

There was not much John could do as the typhoon was approaching and the winds making it dangerous for any help getting up to the Peak. His main thing now was to calm down the family members. He asked Inspector Lee to move them from the kitchen where the box was and get them to the lounge. He then picked up the phone in the kitchen and dialled Leslie's number. He told him exactly what had happened. Leslie listened and sounded really upset as there was nothing much he could do. John then phoned Maggie and told her what happened and asked if she could come over and help console Elizabeth who was in a bad state. He said he called her as there was no one close enough to come and help. She said of course she would as soon as she could.

Nancy was awoken by the call and heard the conversation between John and her husband. She asked what exactly happened. Leslie told her and she started weeping. She said she wished she could go over and comfort Elizabeth. Leslie said he too was feeling bad and had hoped that the kidnappers would have released Harold specially since they got the ransom. He did not tell her he did suspect this would have been the outcome. If it was Kohei behind this, it was exactly the thing that he would do. His signature was to remove the human heart from his victim, a warning of the late Black Ninjas. He told Nancy to go back to sleep as there was nothing they could do now, and they would face this together. Nancy tried to go back to sleep, but could not, as she kept thinking of Harold's body lying somewhere without his heart. What a horrific thing to happen to any family and she felt so sorry for the Browns. She also did not know how to tell her children about this as it would cause them a lot of grief.

John and Maggie did not sleep at all that night. They both stayed over at the Browns' residence. Maggie finally calmed Elizabeth down by giving her some Valium. She finally fell asleep around five a.m. John was comforting Anthony all this time who refused to rest and kept asking John why did the kidnappers do this to Harold specially since they got their money? John could not answer his question but swore to him that they would find the ones responsible and justice would be served. Danny was talking with Inspector Lee and asked what was going to happen next. Did the police have any idea who the kidnappers were and if they did would they be caught quickly and punished? From all of the members of the family he was probably the calmest. Outside the storm was raging on. One could feel the winds on the windows rattling in their frames. The house was actually shaking with the force of the winds. The radio was turned on as John wanted to know what was happening weatherwise. At six a.m. a news bulletin came on the radio. The typhoon signal number eight had been replaced by the highest signal number ten. It seemed the typhoon had picked up speed and now was expected to pass the colony around ten a.m. It was important that everyone remained indoors as winds of one hundred and ninety kilometres per hour were expected with gusts surpassing two hundred and forty kilometres per hour. Typhoon Wanda was now classified as a super typhoon and probably would be the worst to ever hit the colony. It was advised the eye of the typhoon was large and that as the centre passed over the colony there would be a drop in the wind and possibly it would stop raining completely. This was not a sign the typhoon had passed and as soon as the typhoon's eye passed the colony the winds would again pick up to hurricane force. Nobody should venture out until the typhoon signal was lowered to number three.

True to the radio bulletin report the typhoon hit the colony with such force that it caused a lot of damage. Hundreds of trees were uprooted, and many roads were flooded. Many landslides were reported around the colony. Most of these were on the island and on the higher grounds. People who lived in the Mid-Levels and on the Peak were advised not to travel till the all-clear signs were raised. It was rumoured that a high-rise apartment block in the Mid-Levels had crashed down due to the heavy rain loosening its foundations. Many hundreds were feared dead. John was on the phone to HQ as soon as it opened around eight a.m. He got to speak to Inspector Hill who advised him that all the teams were out dealing with this disaster as best as they could. As the typhoon signal had just dropped from ten to eight the winds were still very strong, and it was still lashing down with rain. His difficulty was getting to those in trouble as many roads were washed away. He said that the governor called in earlier looking for John and he had told him he was at the Browns and you were stuck there. He asked for you to call him back as soon as possible.

John called the governor.

"Hi John, so sorry to hear about what has occurred with the Brown family. Please pass on my deepest condolences to them. It is terrible what happened, and we need to bring all those who were involved in this heinous crime to justice quickly. A more immediate concern now is how to deal with the aftermath of this typhoon. It is the worst natural disaster that the colony has ever faced. From what I am told they think that at least a hundred people may be feared dead. I have spoken to Leslie earlier and he has agreed with me that I proclaim this a natural disaster. I have called in the army to coordinate with the police force in the clear up process and whatever else that is needed to bring the situation back to normal. I have asked Major General Chris Wolfe to co-ordinate the army response together with the police. He will be contacting you soon to work out a synchronised plan. I am also going to advise a part curfew for the next two days and that people remain at home unless for an emergency or if they need to get food. I have advised that only supermarkets will remain open and all other offices and shops close. This will help the army and the police to get on with their work clearing out the mess this typhoon has caused. I believe there are hundreds of fallen trees, landslides and flooding have caused many roads throughout the colony to be totally blocked. I will be announcing this on the nine a.m. news on all television and radio stations. Just wanted you to know. I know you must be anxious to get back to the office and work with your team but please understand your safety and those around you come first. I have heard from Inspector Hill that the roads leading to the Peak have all been shut off due to landslides and

241

fallen trees and that it would take literally days to clear it all. Once the typhoon signal drops to number three, I will arrange for a helicopter to pick you up from the heliport near the Peak tower which I heard you can access easily."

John told the governor he understood. He felt helpless as there was not much he could do stuck up in the Peak. The typhoon had hit the colony hard. He kept the radio tuned on. It was suddenly quite quiet outside; the wind had eased of and the rain stopped. He realised this must be the eye of the typhoon passing over the colony. He understood that after thirty minutes it would all pick up again as the backend of the typhoon passed the colony. He went to Maggie and said it may be a good time now to head home it was only a ten-minute walk away from the Blacks' residence. He told her not to drive as it would be safer walking. He told her to hurry before the winds started picking up again. He said he wanted her to be home as he did not want his children alone there. He would, together with Inspector Lee, stay with the Browns till the typhoon passed.

At midday all typhoon signals were lowered. The helicopter arrived with a doctor and nurse to look after the Browns together with two police officers. After giving them instructions both John and Inspector Lee got into the helicopter and headed back to their offices. Sir Anthony asked John to let them know if they heard anything more to keep him informed. John promised he would. Maggie said she would come by later together with her children Mabel and Ben as they could help to comfort Danny.

Chapter 13
Double Trouble

Hotel Faroe "The Web Nightclub"
First Basement 23 Avenida de Faroe, Macau
June 16th, 1964, eleven p.m.

Yu-Yan was sitting next to Mr Chuen who was in a fantastic mood. They were in the VIP room at the nightclub. He had five other mates with him. They all had hostesses sitting with them. Mr Chuen told Yu-Yan his luck seemed to be changing as he had a great week and for the first time actually won big from the casino this evening. He had changed his usual schedule that evening as usually he would go to the club first and then head to the casino before heading off to the Presidential suite where he would party with his mates and hostesses. He told her that he made a huge amount of money from his business dealings. He said Yu-Yan was his lucky charm and tipped her HK$15,000. The room was equipped with a karaoke machine and he said he wanted to sing. He chose a Japanese song "Sukiyaki" by his favourite singer Kyu Sakamoto. He actually was a good singer and everyone there clapped when he finished singing.

Yu-Yan had earlier called Leslie in his room where he was at the hotel. It was located exactly opposite the Presidential suite. She told him that Chuen had changed his usual routine and that they would be at the casino first and then head off to the nightclub. She informed him that there were five friends with him who were staying on the same floor but in different rooms. She figured they would arrive at the Web Nightclub around eleven p.m. and would probably be there for a couple of hours before heading up to the suite. She would call him just before they left the club so he would be well prepared. Leslie was feeling concerned, for Kohei was a man of habit and it seemed strange changing his usual routine.

Leslie was going through his plan again with the warriors. There were eleven of them there. Mohan Lalwani could not make it as he was feeling unwell, however his older brother Ajit was there. They went through what would happen over and over again. They were all tuned into what needed to be done and were excited to get on with it. Raymond had provided them the room; he also gave Leslie a copy key to the President Suite. They were to enter the Presidential suite around midnight and hide in key positions around the room. As soon as the kidnappers entered, they were to take them by surprise. They were then to handcuff them and gag them. They were only six in total so it would be easy to overcome them. He had shown the warriors the quickest route to go from the President Suite to the special service elevator. This service elevator was large enough to fit thirty people. This was specially made to carry heavy furniture up and down the floors like beds and sofas. They would take it straight to the second basement where a large van would be standing by to take them to the hydrofoil dock where a private hydrofoil would be waiting to take them to Hong Kong. Now all he needed was for Yu-Yan to call so they could all move into action.

John was at Niko's having dinner with her. It was the first time in over three days that he had a little time for himself. It was eight thirty p.m. He had informed Inspector Lee what was happening and told him to meet him at the Hong Kong hydrofoil terminal at one thirty a.m. sharp. He told him to arrange three large police vans and fifteen officers to stand by. He would give them their instructions when he met up with them at the terminal. He told him not to let any of the team members know what was happening and this had to be kept secret.

During dinner he was telling Niko all about what had transpired the last few days. It had been a very busy and tense week for him. Firstly, he had to deal with the problems that Typhoon Wanda had caused. The clean-up job took a lot longer than they expected, but finally it was done, and people were allowed to go about their work. It was the worst typhoon to ever hit the colony. It brought a lot of destruction with it. Almost eighty landslides were recorded in the first twenty-four hours after the rain, with boulders and trees blocking roads and tramlines. In twenty-four hours, fifteen inches (thirty-eight centimetres) of rain was recorded, causing cars to be swept down roads like toys. Over seven thousand people who lost their homes were given emergency help and shelter. Landslides and road collapses cut off all outside communications from rural areas and the Peak. Helicopters had to be used to transport food and police to the Peak. The Peak tram was blocked by boulders, so the Peak was totally cut off from the rest of the colony. A deluge of rain turned streets into enormous torrents that killed at least eighty people. The only good thing about the typhoon was the rain that came with it which filled the reservoirs to their brims allowing the water restrictions to be lifted.

He then told her about the Browns. Harry's body was discovered two days ago during the clean-up. It was found floating on top of the Tai Tam reservoir in the New Territories. Apparently, it was dumped there as the reservoir was quite empty. They would have not found it as soon as they did if not for the rain which filled up the reservoir and floated the body to the top and was discovered by workers there securing the waterflow. The body was sent to the mortuary and had to be identified by one of the family members. Danny volunteered to do so as his mother was too fragile and upset and Sir Anthony could not bear to do so. It was confirmed to be the body of Harold. The kidnappers were cruel with him. He had bruises and cuts throughout his entire body. He obviously had struggled and there was skin under his fingernails where he was probably scratching a kidnapper to get free. His throat was cut open which was the cause of death. The heart was surgically removed after he died.

The newspapers went to a frenzy with the story and many theories were out there on who were responsible for this. Most believed that the Black Ninja gang had been resurrected and there was fear among the expat community. There was a huge public outcry and the citizens of Hong Kong wanted justice demanding the criminals get caught and dealt with quickly. The pressure was on the police and the handling of the whole affair. Sir John was under tremendous stress and these few hours with Niko was a way of escaping from it.

He told Niko they were sure now that Kohei was the culprit and that they had set a plan to capture him. He told her that Leslie and his team would handle the operation in Macau as he had no jurisdiction in that territory and believed Kohei had connections with the Macau police. Niko was upset and said she hoped Leslie finally caught the real person behind the killing of the American naval officers and that of Lillian Wang. She had never forgotten Leslie of wrongly killing her beloved brother. She believed Leslie should be publicly reprimanded for that mistake but knew because of his special relationship with the government he would get away with it. She hoped one day he would face his own justice.

They then turned their conversations to John's divorce proceedings with Maggie. It was all going very smoothly: they had gone to their respective lawyers and drew up an agreement that was amicable to both of them just that morning. According to the lawyers the court would judge on it quickly and they should be officially divorced within a few months. They had decided to let the children know this weekend and not wait for the summer to end. He told Niko he loved her and wanted one day soon to marry her; she said to take it easy and let things happen. At the moment she was loving their relationship and did not want to rush things. He thought to himself everything had gone smoother than he thought it would. Maggie was very obliging and accepted the divorce filings willingly and without any fuss.

Maggie came back from the solicitor's office that morning happy with the outcome. It all went well, and she was happy that she would be divorced from John legally sooner than she thought. They did not have any reason for carrying on living a life of lies. They hardly spent any time together, slept in separate rooms and hardly saw or spoke to each other. It was obvious the children knew what was going on and it was right they knew about the upcoming divorce as soon as possible. She called up Nancy and told her how her meetings went with the solicitors. Nancy was happy for her and said she was doing the right thing by having the divorce done quickly. She told Maggie that Leslie had told her privately that her husband John was romantically involved with Niko Black. He had told Nancy not to mention it, but she felt that now with the divorce papers all filed she felt she must let her best friend know. Maggie thanked Nancy for being frank but said she already knew as she had hired a detective to follow John and he had come back with pictures of Niko and John in a restaurant kissing. He also had conclusive proof that John stayed overnight with her at the Mandarin Hotel one night. She said she had this up her sleeve just in case John was difficult with the divorce. Since he was not, she did not mention the affair to her lawyers. She just wanted this chapter in her life to end as quickly as possible and to begin a new chapter in her life.

Maggie felt this was the right time to convey to Nancy the relationship between her son Herman and her daughter. She revealed what Mabel had told her and how the two were getting quite seriously romantic. Nancy was taken aback with that and replied it was not what she believed to be true. She has never seen Herman and Mabel act like a couple not even the few days that Mabel stayed over at the house last week. She said that this morning Herman, during breakfast, had announced he had purchased tickets for "Les Misérables" and was taking Ella with him to the play. She said he seemed very excited about it, so she was surprised at what Mabel told her mother. She told her to better have a chat with her daughter to set things straight. She did not want Mabel to be hurt when she found out about the date between Herman and Ella. Meanwhile she would have a word with Herman. It was better this matter was cleared up as quickly as possible. Maybe Herman had shown some affection to Mabel and she had taken it the wrong way. Maggie admitted that her daughter could be quite dramatic and that could have happened, and she would talk to her about it after their call.

As soon as they hung up the phone she went up to Mabel's room. Mabel was writing in her diary and surprised that her mother had come up to her room.

"Hi Mom, how are you? I came down for breakfast this morning but both you and dad had left together for some meeting according to the servants. Where did you guys go? I am getting bored staying home all the time. I know Dad insists I do stay put at home for a few days after what happened to Harold, but I was wondering if I could just go out this afternoon for a few hours to visit Lucy and Herman. I am going crazy staying in the house the whole day alone. Ben is doing his own stuff and I do not want to disturb him. I promise I will take the car straight there, be there for a couple of hours and come straight home if that is OK with you?"

"Sorry I did not inform you I was going out early this morning. I did come into your bedroom, but you were fast asleep. Dad and I just had some things to clear up with the bank and they needed both our signatures on some documents. I actually have come up now to discuss your so-called newfound relationship with Herman. You know I love you so very much and the worst thing I would want is for you is to get hurt. I just finished speaking to Nancy on the phone and she mentioned that Herman was taking Ella out on a date this weekend. I believe he had booked tickets for them to see 'Les Misérables'. I know you told me the other day that both you and Herman were in a serious relationship but according to Nancy that's not true."

Mabel looked horrified. "No that is totally impossible. Nancy must be lying to you she is wicked. I know she has never liked me getting too close to Herman and had always favoured Ella. Herman and I have been very intimate ever since his birthday party. We have dated and made out a number of times and he has told me he cares for me very much. We even discussed about announcing to the world soon that we were going steady and were a couple. Why is Nancy such a bitch? Do not believe a word she says. I will call Herman and clear all this up. You will see that he loves me and would not invite Ella for a date for that relationship is over."

Maggie was surprised by her daughter's angered response and tried to reason with her telling her that Nancy had no reason to lie.

"We are the best of friends and hold no secrets between us. Nancy really cares for you as her own daughter and she would never want you to get hurt and that is why she revealed this to me. I know I promised you I would not bring this up with Nancy just yet, but I told Nancy about what you told me about Herman and you and how you two were in love. The only reason I did that was just to make sure that Herman felt the same way about you. Is it possible you have taken Herman's attention as a show of his love for you? It is obvious now that he is not ready to be in a sole relationship with you. Why else would he be taking Ella out on a date if he was serious with you? I believe you should have a conversation with Herman and clear this up as soon as possible. I would like to know what the hell he is up to leading you on the way he has."

Mabel suddenly started weeping aloud. "Mom I am going to be honest with you about my relationship with Herman and why I am feeling so upset. We actually had sex together twice the last few days, once after his birthday party and again last week, the night Harold went missing. I did not want to tell you as I did not want you to judge me badly. I feel so cheated right now as I lost my virginity to him. I trusted him so much and I have been such a fool."

Maggie was shocked with the revelation. She could not believe that Herman was that type of a person, someone who could take advantage of her daughter. She had always treated Herman as family and the Suns and Woods were the closest of friends. There was never an inkling that Herman was even remotely interested in Mabel and now this.

She calmed her nerves down and said, "You need to call Herman immediately and sort this out. Maybe this date with Ella is not what it seems so we should not jump into any conclusions. Let us see what he has to say. I hope it is all just a misunderstanding. I am sure this can all be sorted you just be strong when you speak to him and force the truth out of him. I love you darling and am always here for you. You have learned a lesson in this though that love comes with sorrow. At this stage do not mention this to anyone else, especially your father. I feel so sorry for you please don't despair. Come here and give me a hug."

Leslie looked at his watch, it was twelve forty-five a.m. The warriors were set up in the Presidential Suite ready to surprise Kohei San and his mates. They had positioned themselves in various parts of the room. Two of them, one being Ajit, would be standing by just outside the service elevator while the other nine would be in the suite. Just then the phone in the Presidential Suite rang. The code was for Yu-Yan to let the phone ring three times and then call straight back to identify to Leslie that it was indeed she who was calling. The phone rang three times and then it stopped after a few seconds it rang again, Leslie picked it up. It was Yu-Yan on the phone.

"Leslie there is a slight change of plans and I feel a bit uncomfortable with it. What Mr Chuen asked me to do is tell the girls to go and change from their cheongsams, get comfortable and meet them at the suite around one thirty a.m. His mates will be coming up in around five minutes to get relaxed and wait for their arrival. Meanwhile Mr Chuen wanted me to stay with him for a little while alone in the VIP room as he wants to discuss something personal with me and after which both of us will join his boys. I am right now in the hostesses' waiting room and calling from there. I told Mr Chuen I would change and rejoin him in the VIP room in a few minutes. Do you want me to do anything? Just be sure his mates will be up very shortly so if you need to change any plans let me know."

Leslie had to think quickly. All this seemed a little strange and not what he expected which was for Kohei and his mates to go up to the suite together, get relaxed and wait for the girls to join them after they changed. He had to decide quickly. He told Yu-Yan to stay with Mr Chuen and carry on naturally with him. When she came up with him to the suite to just stay behind him and backtrack from the room as soon as he entered. She said she understood. Leslie quickly relayed to the warriors what Yu-Yan had told him. The new plan was that they capture the five mates who would be arriving shortly first and gag them and tie them up and remain in the room. When Kohei arrived with Yu-Yan to capture him after which, along with his mates make their way to the service elevator and follow the plan as before. They all said they understood.

Five minutes later the warriors could hear laughing outside the door of the suite. Whoever were outside were obviously in a good mood and chatting away. The lights at the suite had been dimmed so as not to give away where the warriors were hidden. There was a slight knock on the door and then someone saying, "We are here we are coming in. Get ready."

Suddenly the door opened, and five silhouetted figures walked in; the warriors grabbed them immediately and gagged them up. One of them was holding what seemed like a birthday cake box. It fell on the floor when the warriors grabbed them. Leslie realised immediately that these were not the gang members as they were dressed very fashionably and all very young, he immediately ungagged one of them, who was shaking, and asked who they were and what they were doing in the room.

"We are male escorts, we were paid to come and join a birthday celebration in the suite for someone celebrating his fiftieth. We had to pick up the keys to the suite and a cake from reception and bring it to the room at exactly one a.m. then hide away and shout surprise when the party arrived at around one thirty a.m. Who are you and why have you been so rough with us? We were not told this was going to happen and if it is something kinky you have added to our services then you need to pay us extra," replied the male escort.

Leslie knew exactly what was happening and he shouted to the warriors to get out of the room as quickly as possible with the escorts and head for the service elevator immediately. Just as they ran out of the door there was a loud explosion followed by a lot of smoke. Two of the warriors were lain on the ground together with one of the male escorts. Leslie asked the rest of the warriors who seemed OK to pick the injured up and head for the service elevator immediately and head to the second basement. He was going to take the same elevator but to the first basement where the Web Nightclub was and to check on Yu-Yan. He told them to wait by the van as he checked if Yu-Yan was OK. He would give Raymond a call and let him know what happened and see what he suggested on how they escape from the hotel before the Macau police arrived. He would then join them after that.

John and Niko finished their dinner and were sitting outside in her garden porch looking out at the ocean. There was a full moon outside, and the moon rays lit up the sea which made the setting romantic. They both had a glass of red wine in their hands and cheese and crackers were laid out on a table where they were seated. John had not felt that relaxed in months; it had been one thing after another and these few hours just doing nothing but gazing at the beautiful view was what he needed.

He looked at Niko and said, "I wish I could stay here all night just looking out at the horizon with you by my side." He looked at his watch, it was almost eleven thirty p.m. "I will have to leave in an hour or so as I need to get to the hydrofoil terminal by one thirty a.m. I just wish I did not have to go." He leaned over and kissed her deeply.

She put her glass down on the table and held his hand saying, "Why are we then wasting time here then? I need you to make love to me hard and rough and after that I will let you go." With that said she led him into her bedroom where they made passionate love for an hour. John then dressed, said goodbye and left for the hydrofoil terminal. It was 1.10 a.m.

Mabel phoned the Suns' residence. Wan-Yu picked up the phone and said that Herman had gone training with his fencing coach and would not be back till later that evening. She asked Wan-Yu to please, as soon as he returned, ask him to call her back as it was important. He acknowledged he would, and she thanked him and hung up. She called Anita at work.

"Hi Anita, can you talk or are you busy? There is something urgent I need to talk to you about."

"Well, you caught me at the perfect time. It is lunch hour here and all the staff are out. I am sitting here alone in my office having lunch. Dad has gone to Macau with Leslie I think they are looking at a new project there and he will only return tomorrow so basically Dilip and I are holding the fort. I will be leaving early today around three thirty p.m. as Bella has just moved into her new apartment and has asked me to help her unpack. What's up with you sweetie?"

Mabel burst out crying telling Anita what she had found out about Herman asking Ella for a date. She felt perplexed by this and did not understand what was going on. Anita suggested that maybe Ella initiated this date to get Herman alone to try and win him back. She agreed with Mabel's mom that she cleared this with Herman as quick as possible. It could all be very innocent and not for her to fret. Mabel said she had tried calling him, but he was out training and she had left a message for him to call back as soon as he returned.

"But how do I put it to him without sounding like a jealous bitch who does not trust him? I am unsure for if he tells me he did ask Ella out I will freak I know. I will not be able to control myself and the last thing I want to do is to get him upset at me. I love him so and I am dying inside."

"You just have to be very calm and let him do most of the talking, like I said it may all be very innocent. Seeing you at the concert and at the Scene Disco together with him and the fact that you said you have slept together; I find it hard to believe that Herman was just fooling around with you. He is not that type. Anyway, I will be home by nine p.m. from Bella's so give me a call then and tell me what happens meanwhile de-stress and wait for him to call. I love you sweetie; I am sure it will all turn out all right."

Mabel felt reassured and thanked Anita for being such a dear friend and said if ever she needed anything, she would be there for her too. She turned the conversation to Anita's adventures with Bella.

"I am a bit concerned with your relationship with Bella, is she not still going steady with the actress Eileen Siu or is that over? I am a bit confused with it all and I just want you to tread carefully here as I do not want you to get hurt. I never felt comfortable about her. Auntie Nancy had told mother that she came from a very seedy background and her family were involved with the triads. Mom told me to stay away from her. Please be careful."

Anita replied, "Yes she is still in a relationship with Eileen. However, Eileen is out of the colony and will be away for another three months. She is somewhere in Europe filming her latest movie. This is a good time for Bella to get to know me without any distractions. I am sure once she gets to really know who I am and how much I love her she may return the same feelings back to me. We have been talking a lot on the phone and had coffee together a couple of times. I am excited to meet her tonight at her new apartment and see where it goes from there. I know it may be a long shot her dropping Eileen for me, but I am willing to try and if it does not work out well c'est la vie." Anita thanked Mabel for being concerned, told her she loved her and said her goodbyes.

The service elevator stopped at the first basement and Leslie got out. He went through the fire exit doors and headed for the Web Nightclub. As he entered there was a lot of commotion going on, people were shouting and heading towards the VIP room area. Leslie followed and as he entered the VIP room where a crowd had formed, he pushed his way to the front and saw Yu-Yan lying on the floor with her throat cut. There was a white scarf with a red sun on top of her body. On the scarf next to the sun written in blood were the letters K.I. LL. Leslie ran out of the room towards the telephones that were near the toilets and dialled Raymond's number in Hong Kong. He picked up the phone immediately.

"Leslie, I am so glad you called I was hoping you would. I just heard from my staff at reception that the gang members checked out of the hotel earlier that evening. They paid in full for the one night at the suite. They had then requested for a helicopter to pick them up from the heliport on the roof at exactly one a.m. to take them back to Hong Kong. We have a heliport station on the roof for VIP customers who are big gamblers to use as a free service. I was out and just got the call from my manager at the Hotel Faroe half an hour ago. I did not know how to reach you. I tried calling the room that I booked for you but there was no answer. I realised that somehow Kohei must have learned of the plan and that you and the warriors were in danger."

Leslie quickly explained to Raymond what had happened and asked his advice on what he should do next. They had to avoid being caught by the Macau police as they were acting out of their jurisdiction and could be taken into custody.

"Here is what you do Les. You go back down to the second basement and meet the warriors there. Leave the male escorts near the van in the garage even the one who may be injured. I will have my staff go down there and untie them and call for an ambulance to look after them. You and the warriors take the van and drive straight for the hydrofoil station. Next to the station there is another heliport that we use for VIP customers coming to Macau. I will have a helicopter standing by to meet you there. It will take you and the warriors back to Hong Kong. The two warriors that are injured you must take them back to Hong Kong with you. You cannot leave any evidence that the Macau police can pick up on that the warriors and you were in any way involved. They would probably conclude the bombing and killing were the work of rival gangs and nothing to do with the warriors. Are you clear with my instructions?" Les said he was and hung up. He ran down to the second basement and followed Raymond's instructions to the letter.

Leslie was thinking as the helicopter took off and headed towards Hong Kong. There must have been a leak somewhere in their circle that alerted Kohei San. Kohei knew exactly what was going to happen. Who could have been the informer? The only people who really knew of the plan was Raymond, John, and the warriors. Then it hit him. It must have been Inspector Lee, as John said he was the only person in his team, that he had told about the plan. It all made sense: Inspector Lee must have told the gang about what was happening at the Pacific Mall as well with the handover of the ransom as he was the only one besides the inner team who knew. Kohei all along had been one step ahead of their plans, that was why everything went wrong. Kohei knew that Leslie and his team already identified him as the kidnapper that is why he was not scared to sign off on both Harold's and Yu-Yan's body with the letters K.I.LL. The K.I stood for Kohei Inowaki, his full name to which he added the two letters LL to form the word "KILL".

John was looking at his watch, it was already three a.m. and no sign of a hydrofoil approaching the terminal. If the plan worked to perfection they would have been there by now. Inspector Lee asked John should the team keep waiting or should he send them back as it seemed unlikely that Leslie would show up now. Just then they heard a helicopter approaching the terminal. It landed at the heliport which was next to the hydrofoil terminal. Leslie and his team walked out of the helicopter and headed to where John and his team were. John could see that they had not captured the gang and rushed to meet them. Leslie told John to immediately arrange for an ambulance to pick up the two warriors that were hurt. John called in and within ten minutes an ambulance arrived taking the two injured warriors away. John asked Leslie what happened. He said that he would meet up with him tomorrow to let him know but right now they were all tired and just wanted to go home and get some rest.

Herman arrived back home at eight thirty p.m. He had had a long session with his coach and was feeling tired. He had started his training routine for the Olympics and would be busy with it for the next three months. He would train Mondays to Fridays starting from eleven a.m. to seven p.m. It was going to be vigorous and he would have very little time for socialising, but he needed to be focused. He did not want to embarrass himself or the team by doing poorly at the games. Wan-Yu came up to him and asked if he wanted the kitchen to cook something up for him. He was feeling hungry so he said that would be good. He asked if his mother was home and was told that she went to the garden centre as she needed some items but would be back shortly. He said the

255

rest of the family had eaten already. He then informed Herman that Mabel had called three times already and had asked that he call her back as soon as he came in as it was urgent.

Herman wondered what was so urgent that Mabel had to speak to him immediately. He went to his room, took a quick shower, changed into his tracksuit, came back down, had his dinner and then called Mabel.

"Hi, Sunshine, sorry for calling you back so late. I was out all-day training with the coach. It is only three months before the Olympic Games in Japan and I really need to get myself ready for the event. How are you and what's up? Wan-Yu said it was urgent that I speak to you."

Mabel replied being very careful not to show any emotion. "I heard something quite distressing and before I make any conclusions, I wanted to check with you if what I heard is correct and if so, what is happening? Your mother mentioned to my mom that you were taking Ella on a date to see 'Les Misérables' this weekend. Is that true, and if so, why?"

Herman was taken aback. He was not expecting that and thought he had better tread carefully here.

"Yes, I did ask Ella if she would join me to see the play. I know she loves the West End plays and it is very rare that one comes here to Hong Kong. I wanted myself to see it and I did not ask you as I know you are not truly into this sort of a thing. I was also feeling sorry for Ella as with what has happened with Harold and also, I know she is going through some difficult times in her life."

"Why did you not bring this up with me first before asking her out. Everybody knows we are dating, and this makes me look stupid in front of my friends, especially since I have told everyone we are exclusive. I have even told Mom about us and she was shocked when your mother told her about your upcoming date. Please be careful of that bitch Ella I am sure she was the one who must have conned you into asking her out. She acts innocent and sweet but deep down she is a wicked and deceiving witch! I do not want you to go out with her, please call her and let her know that I will take her place and go with you instead to the play!"

"Now you listen Mabel. Yes, we have had a wonderful, few days together, but remember I have previously been romantically involved with Ella and much longer than you. I truly like you very much but to be totally honest with you I am not sure that I love you or that I want you to be my girlfriend. Not you, nor Ella. I am not ready to make any commitments with anyone, not right now. I have the Games coming up after which I will be joining Dad's business. I have a lot to consider and am not ready to settle with anyone yet. If I led you wrongly, I am so sorry for that was not my intention. That is why, although you pushed me to announce our relationship as boyfriend and girlfriend to our families, I was reluctant to do so as I know it was not what I wanted."

Mabel totally lost it. "You bloody bastard, you fuck me, take away my virginity, claiming you care for me and now all this bullshit! I never in my life expected you to be such a creep. Tell you what, you asshole, you go on that date with Ella for I know one day she will fuck your mind up. I never ever want to talk or see you again. You cannot even imagine the pain I am feeling now." Mabel slammed the phone down and burst into tears.

Anita rang the doorbell and Bella let her in. Bella had her hair up and had no make-up on. She was wearing a tracksuit with trainers on. She smiled and kissed Anita lightly on her cheeks.

"Sorry for looking such a mess. I have been spending the whole day opening boxes and fixing up the apartment. I want to have it ready by the weekend so I can relax and enjoy it. Raymond has been kind to give me a few days off work to do this. Thank you so much for offering to help. I suggest you take off your jacket and roll up your sleeves as this will be hard work," she laughed.

"I am ready for it and that is why I wore denims to work this morning. Where do I start and what do you want me to do first?" asked Anita. Bella told her to work on the lounge area while she worked on the bedrooms and bathrooms. Bella had separated all the boxes already to the areas where they should be to make things easier. They both worked hard for around four hours stopping only to have water or go to the toilet. Bella was happy with the progress and said to Anita when they had more or less finished that they should take a champagne break and have something to eat. Bella laid out a linen throw on the floor and placed some snacks on it. She placed two bean bags on the floor and asked Anita to come and sit next to her. She opened a bottle of Dom Pérignon which had been chilling in the refrigerator. She went to the new turntable she had purchased and put on some classical music.

"Leslie bought me a case of this champagne as part of my moving in gift, apparently he and my sister Lillian loved this champagne. He has been so fantastic and without his help there was no way I could have manged to get this apartment at the price I got it for. By the way what do you think of it? I am so in love with it, finally I have a place of my own. I have been dreaming of this ever since I was a young girl. Thanks, darling, for coming over today, I really appreciate it. Let's drink a toast to my new apartment and to us!" Bella clinked her glass with Anita's and took a large gulp of the champagne. She was feeling relaxed and happy. She placed her glass down and came closer to Anita hugging her tight. She leaned over and kissed Anita passionately.

Leslie woke up late the next morning with a migraine. Recently these headaches were occurring more frequently and were getting more severe. He knew he had to take time out and go to the surgery to have it all checked out. He was totally frustrated that he had once again failed to capture Kohei. It seemed that he was like a cat with nine lives. Every time they got close, he escaped. He had a long day ahead of him. He looked at his watch: it was already eleven thirty a.m. He could not afford to stay in bed much longer and rushed to the bathroom for a shower. After his shower he went down and Wan-Yu met up with him.

"Would you like something to eat, Master?"

"No, just get me a double espresso please," replied Leslie

Everything that happened in the last few weeks had been bad, and he felt he needed to change his Feng Shui. He planned to go to the Buddhist temple and pray for a change of luck. He would speak to the head monk there and ask him for his advice on how he could improve his bad luck. He also wanted him to say a prayer for his family. He was worried about his family especially now with Kohei out free and knowing that Leslie knew he was the person responsible for Harold's death and most probably Lillian's as well, he would definitely try and take some form of revenge on them for that was his way.

Nancy was in the family room as Leslie entered. She looked upset and he asked her what the matter was. She told him that she had just spoken to Maggie and found out about Herman and Mabel. She could not believe her son was so casual with the relationship and was upset that he treated Mabel so badly. She told Leslie that Mabel gave up her virginity to Herman only as he promised he loved and cared for her. She went on and said that when Mabel approached him about his upcoming date with Ella, he was mean to her and hurt her badly saying he would do as he liked, and that Mabel did not own him.

"Maggie says Mabel is in a total mess and does not want to speak or see anyone. She has locked herself up in her room and is refusing to eat."

Leslie was really surprised as that was so unlike Herman who was always very gentle and kind.

"Have you spoken to Herman about this? I think you should hear his side of the story before making any judgement. I never suspected that Mabel and he were having an affair as they have known each other for years as friends and never seemed to be romantically inclined. I always thought Herman had a soft spot for Ella and even when they broke up their relationship for a while when he went to study in Oxford I believed when he returned, he would get back with Ella. All this to me is a bit strange."

Nancy said that Herman was out training and would only return later that evening. She said she felt that Leslie should talk to Herman man to man as he may find it difficult to discuss such personal things with his mother. Leslie agreed but voiced he was busy the whole day but would try and catch up with his son later that evening and come to the truth of what was happening. He also told her that he needed to beef up the security surrounding the family. He told her about Kohei and that his concern was he might come after the family. He said that from then on if any members of the family ventured out, he would arrange for a security guard to be with them. He would have that all sorted by today. Until they captured Kohei the family would have to adhere to this. Leslie then went into his study and dialled John.

Raymond was disappointed with the outcome of the raid that Leslie planned. Kohei was still on the loose so nothing was achieved. This was the second time that Leslie and John had missed out on capturing

Kohei. He was upset also as the incident caused the Macau police to start tightening up security around Hotel Faroe which was bad for business. The hotel had many cancellations as the news of the bombing and murder of one hostess was splashed over the media. Raymond was losing revenue to his competition. He felt he should have taken care of Kohei himself for if he did at least it would have been done properly. He knew, however, because of who he was, he had to show that he was not aligned with either the dark side or with the police or the British government. He needed to be in the background which he did not enjoy as he always loved to lead. He learned from Leslie that he believed that Inspector Lee was a turncoat and the one revealing their plans to Kohei. Raymond knew Inspector Lee well and knew he was an informer for the triad organisations operating within the Walled City but was surprised that he was also involved with Kohei. That was dangerous for the 14K. They needed to get rid of him and quick before he squealed and not only gave evidence about Kohei but also the 14K.

John hung up and put down the phone. He had a long conversation with Leslie and was distressed of what he had learned. John trusted Inspector Lee completely for he had helped him from the day he arrived in Hong Kong. Trouble was he knew all about John and about him taking bribes from the triads. John was nervous for if he arrested Inspector Lee on suspicion that Lee would spill the beans on John's corrupt ways. John, since he became the commissioner of police and was decorated by the queen, never took any more "tea money". What a mess. If only he never got into that game in the first place; he should have realised that one day he could be exposed. He picked up the phone and dialled Raymond. He told John he had already heard about Inspector Lee from Leslie. He told John not to worry and for him to go ahead and charge Inspector Lee and that he would take care of things. John knew exactly what Ray meant by that.

Anita was listening intently to what Mabel told her about the conversation with Herman.

"I cannot believe that he was so unkind to you. That is so unlike Herman. It must be that Ella had somehow brainwashed him. I never liked that girl, she is so false. Recently she has been extra kind to me, but I am suspicious of her intentions. I think she is using me to find out about you and Herman. I am sorry that you feel hurt but locking yourself up and feeling sorry for yourself is not the answer, is it? You need to forget Herman and get on with your life. You will find someone who will love you for who you are and be there for you no matter what. Meanwhile thank God you found out about Herman's true colours now than later; he does not deserve someone like you."

Mabel said she will never again get herself in such a fragile position. She had been irresponsible and had put her trust in someone who she genuinely believed loved her and would never hurt her. She said she would not let Herman get away with the way he treated her, and she swore she would get back at Ella. Even though Mabel was angry at Herman she still cared for him but with Ella it was different. She was convinced that Ella had purposely made Herman ask her for a date knowing full well that Mabel and he were a couple. She started scheming, thinking of ways she could hurt Ella.

Herbert Sun was pacing up and down the main area of the Sun Yee On headquarters. This was not good news that Inspector Lee had been taken into custody and was soon to be charged. He knew too much about the Sun Yee On and could expose its innermost secrets like where they stored the drugs and armoury. He also basically understood how they laundered their money. Inspector Lee had been an informant to the Sun Yee On for many years and was a trustworthy source. What was even more frightening was that Leslie had been appointed by the governor to lead the investigation on Inspector Lee. His bastard cousin was good at what he did and would probably get out all he could off Inspector Lee. He would definitely push to learn about the triads and especially the Sun Yee On gang. He called for his second General Pui to meet him in his private room.

"Good morning, My Lordship, you asked for me, is there something you need me to do? I am at your service."

"Yes, General Pui, there is something you must do. I am sure you are well aware that Inspector Lee has been arrested. Apparently, I have heard from reliable sources that they will be moving him out of Wanchai Police HQ to the army barracks. This is because the government is worried because of the corruption in the police force that he could either be killed or disappear while in their custody. Leslie Sun, that bastard, had advised that he be moved to the army barracks in Central as he felt Inspector Lee would be more secure there. They will be moving him this evening around five or six p.m. Your job is that he never gets to the army barracks by ensuring that Inspector Lee is dead before entering the army vehicle which will be picking him up. You cannot fail in this mission for if you did it could be the end of the Sun Yee On as you know it." General Pui nodded his understanding of the orders, bowed and left the room.

Kohei was talking to his gang. He said it was lucky they got out of the trap set by Leslie Sun and his mates. Thank God Inspector Lee had pre-warned them and they had managed to escape. What Kohei was disappointed about was that they did not kill Leslie or any of his mates. He was hoping that would be the end of Leslie and his gang could continue with what they were doing. Now that Inspector Lee had been arrested it was of grave concern as Inspector Lee knew all about Kohei and his gang. He knew they were responsible for Harold's death and that of the two naval officers.

"As you may have now heard Leslie has instructed to move Inspector Lee from Police HQ to the Army barracks in Central. We cannot let Inspector Lee get to the army barracks for he will be way too secure there for us to do anything. We have to get him whilst they move him to the army van. I believe they will be doing the move between five and six p.m. We must ensure that Mr Lee never makes it to the van. Is that understood?" They all agreed that had to be done.

John spent the night over at Niko's, giving some lame excuse to Maggie, why he could not come home. He looked at her silently sleeping next to him and thought how beautiful she looked. He wished he did not have to go to work and face what the day would bring. He looked at his watch and got up without awakening Niko and headed to the bathroom for a shower.

As John came out of the shower to the bedroom draped only in a towel Niko was looking at him and asked, "Why are you up so early my darling it's not even quite six a.m. You must be tired after all we had to drink last night, and the hours we were awake talking. I know you have loads to do today but surely you could have slept for another hour or so. We had set the alarm for seven a.m. to wake you up."

"I know Niko I wish I could, but I was wide awake. I have too much on my mind. I still have to go home, change and get going to the office. There will be a lot going on and I will be needed. I am hoping it all goes the way I want today."

John had come over to Niko the night before without any forewarning. He was looking very worried and concerned about the whole Inspector Lee case. He told Niko all about how in his earlier days he took bribes from the mayor of the Walled City. It was Inspector Lee who led him to meet the mayor and once he took the first bribe he could not stop. He only did when he became commissioner of police for Hong Kong and was knighted by the queen. He was worried that Inspector Lee, under very threatening interrogation by Leslie and his team, would disclose all. He had spoken to Raymond about it and he had told him not to worry as he would handle it, but he was unsure he would come true on his promise. Once Inspector Lee was in the custody of the army there was no way that anyone could get to him. Niko smiled and said there may be a way. She knew the chief guard Mr Chan who was assigned to the cells at the police station where Inspector Lee was held well. She told John to ensure Mr Chan was assigned to Mr Lee during the handover period. He owed her ex-husband and her a very special favour. She would call him early this morning before he reported to the station and see what she could do.

Leslie woke up again with a terrible migraine. The headaches were getting worse and he needed to sort it out. Problem was he did not have any free time to visit his doctor. He took a quick shower and headed off to visit John at the police headquarters in Wanchai. John had Inspector Lee in custody and was waiting for Leslie to arrive to do his questioning.

Initially Inspector Lee refused to be co-operative and Leslie was worried. However, during the last few minutes that Leslie had planned to question him that day, Inspector Lee said he would co-operate but only if he adhered to his conditions. His conditions were that he could not stay in the police station any longer as he feared for his life and needed to immediately move to a secure location. Inspector Lee wanted full immunity and a written pardon from the governor of Hong Kong. He needed also to have a new identity built for all his immediate family with new names, passports driver's I.D. cards, credit cards, and whatever else he needed to keep his family and him safe. Any monies they found at his home or in any of his family accounts would not be confiscated. He and his family were to be put on a chartered plane going to a destination he chose which he would only reveal to the pilot when they were aboard.

In return he would not only reveal everything he knew about Kohei and his gang, including where they were hiding out, but would give them enough ammunition to close down both the main triads stationed within the Walled City, namely the 14K and the Sun Yee On triad gangs. He would also give them a list of all the corrupt police officials he knew that were taking bribes from criminals. Leslie could not believe what Inspector Lee was offering: it was too good to be true. At last, something good was happening. He told Inspector Lee that he would need to confirm all this with the governor but felt he could fulfil Inspector Lee's requests. He would immediately go and see the governor and come back to him. Before leaving Inspector Lee reminded Leslie that he would only reveal all when he was safe in a secured place where the police or gangs could not get to him.

Leslie liked the new governor who had taken the place of Sir Andrew Hancock. Sir William Sandhill, the new number one in charge, was knowledgeable about the corruption that was happening in Hong Kong and one of his main agendas was to form a committee separate with full powers who could get into looking at all officers, no matter how high up the ladder they were, and charge them with the Corruption Act. His team was now drafting out the law together with ministers of the British parliament waiting for it to be passed. This special committee would be known as the ICAC (Independent Commission Against Corruption) and was to be led by Leslie Sun. He realised it would take a number of years before it became a reality, but he was determined to get this whilst he was the governor of Hong Kong and make it a part of his legacy. Unfortunately, that never happened during his governorship and took a further five years before it was formed. His other objective was to obliterate the Walled City and the evil establishments that lay within there. This was a sensitive task as mainland China kept claiming that the Walled City, although smack in the middle of Kowloon, was not promised to the British by the Treaty of Nanking and the British had no right entering their territory. The British had always thought quite the opposite but had to tread very carefully there so as not to antagonise China. Leslie explained in detail to the governor the circumstances behind Harold's kidnapping and how they had identified the kidnapper as a Mr Kohei Inowaki who was previously a Black Ninja general. They had laid out a plan for his capture, but it was foiled as someone had leaked the plan to Kohei. They have now identified the informer as Inspector Lee who was now in police custody. He disclosed to him Inspector Lee's demands and said that if Mr Lee could do all that he promised it was well worth giving him what he asked for. The governor agreed. He told Leslie he too was under a lot of pressure from Sir Anthony Brown on how badly the police mishandled the case. Sir Brown reported his disappointment to the prime minister in London saying the police were corrupt and were probably in cahoots with the kidnappers. The prime minister called him direct and requested a full report. Sir William said he had since spoken to John Woods and had pushed him to have a report ready within a week. It was rare for the PM to get directly involved with the affairs of Hong Kong but obviously Sir Anthony, being CEO of the largest British bank, had a lot of influence.

Sir William signed an order giving Inspector Lee and his immediate family full immunity if he revealed all he knew to Leslie. He called up Major General Chris Wolfe and told him to co-ordinate with Leslie on getting the army involved. Leslie thanked the governor and headed back to the police HQ to show Mr Lee the documents. When he arrived, he told Mr Lee that he had spoken to the commander in chief of the British army stationed in HK about his case and that all was organised for him and his family to be put in a secure location. They would arrange a military escort to pick him up from the Wanchai police station and transfer him to the army barracks. He also told him that he had with him the indemnity papers signed by the governor for his family and him which met all his demands. Mr Lee thanked him and said once he was moved to a safe place, he would reveal all to Leslie.

Leslie was delighted with the outcome and his thoughts turned to the conversation he had with his son Herman the night before.

Herman was upset how Mabel had misinterpreted what actually

happened to her mother Maggie. Maggie had told his mom who informed his dad and now he was confronted with it. He felt that Mabel and he should have discussed it privately and sorted things out and not get the parents involved. They were grown up enough to handle such matters. Herman explained to his father that he and Mabel had dated just once and admitted he had slept with her. He explained that she had manoeuvred him into making love to her. He explained that night after his party she had sneaked into his bedroom while he was sleeping, undressed and came naked into his bed pushing her naked body close to his. He was already a bit tipsy and he, like what most men would have done, made love to her. He told Leslie that Mabel had been pushing him to tell the family that they were a couple, but he was not ready to do so as he did not feel that way for her. He explained to his father what transpired between Ella and Mabel at his party and how cruel Mabel had been. He said he felt sorry for Ella and obviously still had feelings for her, that was why he asked her for a date. The way Mabel had told her side of the story was totally unfair and he was offended that his parents did not trust him.

Leslie said he believed his son and was so glad he cleared all this up. Obviously, Mabel's family would only look at her side and think Herman irresponsible and cruel in the way he treated their daughter. Leslie's advice to his son was to, as soon as possible, speak to Mabel, apologise and not try and defend himself as that would make her even more upset. He said to tell her that he did not want to ruin their friendship because of the misunderstanding and wished they could put this behind them. Herman said he would but for Leslie to explain to his mother the truth.

It was four fifteen p.m. and John was locked away in his office trying to get rid of any evidence that could incriminate him of bribery. He had already moved all the cash out of the safe and any documents that hinted of a bribe he shredded. He still had the briefcase that the mayor of the Walled City had given him in one of the drawers. He thought he must remove it from the station and destroy it on his way home that evening. Leslie had said he would be in at around four thirty p.m. and had organised an army van with a military escort to be outside the station by five p.m. to take Inspector Lee to the army barracks.

Leslie said he would be bringing with him his friend Ajit and two other Warriors of the Sun to aid in the moving of Inspector Lee. John was really concerned about his position. He had a call from the governor who told him that there were accusations that many police officers were being bribed. He wanted a full report on Harold's case as he needed to report it to the prime minister who had now taken an interest in this case.

There was a knock on the door and John unlocked it. His secretary Angela said that Mr Chan the chief warden of the station told her to tell him that Mr Lee was ready for the transfer, that he had had his dinner and was all dressed and ready to go. John thanked her and said he would be in his office and as soon as Leslie arrived with his team to let him know. She nodded and left the room. John picked up the phone and dialled home. When he had gone home to change that morning, he had found Mabel sitting by herself in the kitchen. He had walked up to her to say good morning and she burst into tears. He was taken aback and asked her what the matter was. She did not say a word but hugged him tightly. He wanted to stay longer but he had to be at his office. He kissed her on her forehead said he had to go but would call her later to have a chat and see if she was OK and if he could help. The maid picked up the phone and said that Mabel had gone over to Anita's and would let her know that John had called. Just then there was a knock on his door. Angela entered saying that Leslie had just arrived with his friends and was waiting for him in the private meeting room. John hung up the phone, tidied up his desk and headed towards the meeting room. It was 4.50 p.m.

Leslie greeted John and told him his side was prepared to make the transfer. The van had arrived and was waiting outside the station about fifty metres from the entrance. The plan was simple. Two of the warriors, together with Ajit and two army officers, would make the walk with Mr Lee to the van. The had cordoned off by ten metres each side of the path that Mr Lee would walk. They expected a lot of press around and the police officers stationed there would ensure they were kept behind the cordoned space. Accompanying Mr Lee to the van would be Ajit, a warrior and two soldiers, they would get inside the back of the van together with Inspector Lee. The van would be escorted to the army barracks by a number of military jeeps. Leslie would follow them to the barracks after meeting the press and answering their questions. He would give them thirty minutes to ask whatever they wanted and then head to the army barracks. There he planned to spend the next hours getting all the evidence off Inspector Lee.

It had just turned five p.m. and Mr Chan led Inspector Lee from the cell to the entrance. He was dressed in a dark suit with an open white-collar shirt. His hands were handcuffed from the back. Ajit put his arm around Mr Lee's arm while a soldier from the army held his other arm and walked out of the entrance slowly towards the van. As they appeared the press started shouting out questions to Mr Lee who kept silent throughout. When they were about ten metres from the entrance a person from the press broke through the cordon donning a handgun. He let out three shots at Inspector Lee with one hitting him in the chest. The gunman then put the gun to his own head and blew it off. At almost the same time a gunshot was heard coming from a rooftop of a building about fifty metres away. Suddenly Mr Lee's head fell back: a bullet had hit him on the back of his head causing a piece of his skull to explode. Leslie rushed out of the police station and shouted to Ajit to run to the van with Mr Lee who was still somewhat mobile and tell the driver to go directly to the British military hospital which was not too far away.

John ran out of the entrance giving orders to his team. He asked a group of them to go towards the building where the sniper shot his rifle. He went towards the man who had shot himself. Leslie watched as Ajit got into the back of the van with Mr Lee. Two soldiers, fully armed, entered the van as well. The van then started its engine when suddenly there was an enormous explosion that rocked the whole block. Leslie watched in horror as the van that Ajit and Inspector Lee were in flew into the air in flames and fell about twenty metres away from where it originally was.

Leslie ran towards the van shouting out Ajit's name but there was no response. The van had fallen back to the street on its side. Flames engulfed the van. Leslie tried his best to reach the back door of the van, but it was impossible as the fire was too hot to approach it.

Leslie was sobbing, as he could not believe that his best friend and someone he loved like a brother, had perished in front of his eyes in the most horrific way possible. The first thing that rushed into his mind was how was he going to face Ajit's family and tell them what happened. John rushed up towards Leslie.

Leslie screamed at him, "What the hell happened? They really wanted Inspector Lee dead. He had no chance whatsoever. First being shot in the chest, then a sniper blowing a part of his brain off and finally a bomb so strong that rocked the whole area. What happened with the security John? You said that you had it all covered and that everything would go smoothly. What a fucking mess."

John just kept quiet for a minute and then apologised to Leslie. He explained to Leslie that he had everything secured inside the station. He also had a team of officers patrolling the area outside and checking anyone for guns and bombs entering the cordoned area. He was shocked that this could happen.

Leslie could not believe what just happened; once again he had been outfoxed by Kohei. He had lost two beautiful people he loved and adored because of this monster. First the love of his life Lillian and now his best friend Ajit. He swore he would take revenge on Kohei and make him suffer.

John gave Leslie a hug and said he really was sorry for the loss of Ajit.

John thought that went better than he had hoped, for the time being he was safe from being exposed of the bribes he took. He was sad though that Ajit had to die but that was not planned and not his fault.

He would call Niko once things calmed down to tell her the good news.

Chapter 14
'Sunset'

Happy Valley Racecourse
Wong Nai Chung Road. Wanchai, Hong Kong
April 2nd, 1966, eleven thirty a.m.

Leslie looked out to the racecourse from the balcony of the third floor. People were starting to come in and the racecourse was quickly filling up. They expected a full capacity crowd of around fifty-five thousand people to attend what was the biggest race day in Hong Kong, featuring the Queen Elizabeth II International Cup. The Queen Elizabeth Cup was one of the most prestigious races in the world's horse racing calendar. The race was run over sixteen furlongs or two miles for the best stayers in the world. Horses with their owners, jockeys and trainers from all over the world were there to try and win the cup which was worth HK$15,000,000 in prize money. Leslie still had three horses in training in Hong Kong, the best being "Sunset", a multiple Group 1 winner which, according to Timeform, was the second highest rated horse in the world. Timeform was the one-stop book for horse racing information and gave the ratings of all horses running worldwide. The other two horses he had training in Hong Kong were "Sunrise" and "Summer Sun", both also group winners. Sunset was, however, his best prized horse having only lost one race in sixteen outings and that was only because of jockey error rather than the horse's ability. Leslie named all his horses with "Sun" in their names. Sunset was the son of one of his earlier champion horses "Winter Sun" who won all the major races run in Hong Kong during the 1959–62 season before retiring to stud. He was excited and had his fingers crossed that Sunset could win the Queen Elizabeth II Cup for the second time as he had won this race the previous year. No horse had ever achieved winning the Queen Elizabeth International Cups in consecutive years, but Sunset had a chance of doing that. He was not concerned about the prize money, for him it was the prestige of owning the world's best racehorse. His other horse Summer Sun was also running today in the second biggest race of the afternoon the Queen Elizabeth Vase which was for sprinters and run over six furlongs or twelve hundred metres.

Leslie had watched Sunset do his last workout the day before at the racecourse. He did a wonderful time and looked super fit. His trainer, Frank Wallis, was delighted and felt that barring any misfortune during the running of the race the horse should win easily. He had the horse tuned to its ultimate best. Tony Pererra was to ride Sunset; he was the champion jockey of Hong Kong for the past five years. Tony too was confident that the horse would win. He stated that in all his riding career he had never ridden a horse as good as Sunset. Leslie was silently confident as well and felt there was only one horse who could possibly beat Sunset and that was the English champion Nijinksy who recently won the English triple crown. Nijinksy would be ridden by Lester Piggott who was recognised as the world's best jockey. In real terms Nijinksy was rated two points higher than Sunset according to Timeform. It was the highest rated horse in the world. What gave Sunset a slight edge, however, according to most bookies, was that it was running on its home turf whilst Nijinksy had to travel hundreds of miles to be there. They felt he may not have enough time to acclimatise for the race. The pre-race odds, though, had Nijinksy favourite at 11–10 and Sunset at 2–1; the other twelve runners in the race were at odds of over 10–1 and above. Both Frank and Tony were confident also of the chances of Leslie's second runner that day Summer Sun. Leslie was so excited if everything went to plan, he could have two group winners today. He walked back inside to the VIP box that was specially assigned to the chief steward of the Royal Hong Kong Jockey Club with a smile on his face.

The head waiter went up to Leslie and said that all four tables were ready to receive the guests. The guest list was impressive. At the head table sat Leslie and his wife Nancy along with the Governor Sir William Sandhill and his wife Jocelyn. Seated at the same table were Major General Chris Wolfe, head of the British garrison in Hong Kong and his wife Emily, the Duke of Westminster Robert Grosvenor and his wife Viola and finally Charles W. Engelhard Jr. the owner of Nijinksy and his wife Jane. Hosting the other three tables were Mohan Lalwani, his son Herman, and David Poon. All the guests were family, friends, or VIPs from various parts of the world. Leslie was looking forward to greeting the guests who were scheduled to arrive by noon.

The first race was to start at one forty-five p.m. and the main race, the Queen Elizabeth International Cup, was set to run at three forty-five p.m. The last race of the day was the Queen Elizabeth Vase which was scheduled to run at four forty-five p.m. Leslie was restless whilst waiting for his guests to arrive and was pacing the floor. Nancy asked him to calm down as everything was well prepared and the hosts of the other tables and their partners were already there to welcome the guests. Herman was there with his fiancée Ella, Mohan with his wife Leela and her brother David Poon with his partner Maggie. Champagne would be served as the guests walked in together with canapés which included beluga caviar. They would allow the guest to mingle for about thirty minutes before the bell would ring for them to be seated for lunch. The appetiser would be served at exactly 12.40 p.m. followed by the main course at one p.m. sharp. Then there would be a break so that the guests could go to the betting windows which were at the back of the room and lay down their bets before walking out to the balcony to watch the first race. Dessert will be served after the first race at around two p.m. followed by tea or coffee.

Leslie's thoughts went back to the day that he lost his best friend Ajit. The last two years had been rough for him. He felt responsible for Ajit's death and never forgave himself. The worst thing was up to now they had not been able to capture the criminal Kohei. That was what frustrated him most. After the incident there was a huge public outcry and a commission was formed led by the governor himself to find out how this could have happened. Sir John Woods came under a lot of pressure but somehow survived his job. There were countless changes made at the police force and the governor pushed forward the setting up of an Independent Commission Against Corruption (ICAC) which would have unlimited powers to crack down on public servants taking bribes in the colony. Leslie was asked to head up this commission and to set about creating the legal rules and powers that the commission would require. He had to work together with MPs in the U.K. parliament and the judiciary there to ensure that all was above board before passing it on to parliament to vote on it becoming law.

Leslie, after Ajit lost his life, held an emergency meeting with the rest of the Warriors of the Sun. Leslie recognised that times were changing, and the duties of the Warriors of the Sun would no longer be the same as those during the darker days of Hong Kong. The current Warriors of the Sun consisted of fourteen members, twelve of whom had been with him for over thirty years and studied from the same Kung Fu teacher he did. Five now felt they were getting on with their years and because of what happened with Ajit asked permission to leave the warriors. This left only eight of the original members. Leslie said he would amend the duties of the warriors with changing its by-laws. One of the major changes was that it would never engage in any physical encounters with criminals.

The Warriors of the Sun had for over one hundred years assisted the British government to keep peace in the colony by advising them on how to deal with activists who caused problems. In recent years this had been the likes of the communists, the nationalists and the triads. There was a huge divide between the public's trust in the British ruling of the colony as they felt the British did not understand the wishes of the people of Hong Kong. They also felt that most of the public servants were corrupt. The British recognised that they needed a group of local intellects who understood the public's concern and would help to bridge this divide. That is why over a hundred years ago they formed an alliance with Bulldog Sun who created the Warriors of the Sun. In those days the problem was the constant fight the British had with the Chinese government. The warriors, many a time had, to intervene by force to take care of the problems. The warriors through the years continued this legacy and the leadership of the Warriors of the Sun passed down from son to son of the Sun family.

One of the new changes Leslie made to the by-laws was that the new warriors would no longer engage in any physical confrontation with criminals. Herman and Dilip were both inducted into the warriors. Leslie said that he would continue to lead the warriors until the end of the coming year and then pass on the reins to his son Herman to take over its leadership. The new warriors' duty was to work closely with the government advising it on political issues affecting the colony. They were to put forward reforms they thought were needed to improve people's welfare in Hong Kong. The new warriors would be reduced to only eight members and they would be chosen from different parts of the community and led by a member of the Sun family. Leslie felt he had done all he could for the betterment of Hong Kong and now it was up to the younger generation to take over pushing in fresh ideas. He also realised that his ill health would not permit him to continue as leader. Leslie, after Ajit's death, would visit the Buddhist temple that Lillian had taken him to many years ago to say his prayers and seek guidance from the head monk. Every time he visited there it would upset him to see beggars gathered in the temple to pray and beg for money from anyone entering it. They would be fed by the monks and in some cases given a place to sleep inside the temple. Leslie would always donate a considerable sum of money monthly to the temple. He recently paid for a full revamp of the temple and extended the premises by purchasing the adjacent land. The temple was now double its previous size and renewed. This gave him satisfaction and peace as he knew that was what Lillian would want him to do.

He told the head monk about his health, his sorrow for having lost both the woman he loved and his best friend. The head monk, one day during a session with Leslie, quoted him a wise saying of Buddha. "No one can escape death and unhappiness. If people expect only happiness in life, they would be disappointed." The monk explained that things are not always the way we want them to be, but we can learn to understand them. Leslie after that found inner peace, he viewed life differently and was clear about accepting whatever life threw at him.

The Lalwanis were the first to arrive to the VIP box led by Dilip and his sister Anita who brought with them Bella Wang. They were soon followed by Anand with wife Sunita and their two children Prity and Sheila and finally Laxman and wife Mohini with their son Ashwin. Leslie noticed that Maya did not show up. He had called her personally earlier in the week to invite her, but she had told him she would try to attend but she could not promise that. He felt so sorry for her as he knew how deeply in love Maya was with Ajit. She took a long time to recover from her sorrow. She would not join any parties or functions she was invited to and only recently started to mingle in smaller groups. Soon after the Lalwanis arrived all the other invited guests followed, and the event began.

Herman looked over to see how his father was doing. It had been difficult for Leslie the last two years and he looked drained. He had aged very quickly and lost a lot of his passion. Herman was truly worried about his father. The last two years had been very eventful for Herman starting with Ajit's death. He spent a lot of time consoling both Dilip and Anita who took their father's sudden death poorly especially because of the way it happened. He had to break his rigid training routine for the Olympics just to be around to support them. His parents did not go to the Olympics to watch him as originally planned and only his sister Lucy joined him. He did poorly in all his events and was knocked out on the first round. Upon returning he started dating Ella Sousa regularly and their relationship grew stronger than ever. They dated for over a year before Herman popped the question and asked for her hand in marriage. Both their parents were thrilled and threw an elaborate party for their engagement. They had planned to get married in the summer of 1966 or in around two months. Nancy took it as her job to take over the arrangements for the wedding with little consultation from the girl's family. Ella's parents, the Sousas, were not offended as they knew that Nancy would do a great job. Nancy insisted that Leslie pay for the wedding. She planned to have the ultimate wedding Hong Kong had ever witnessed for her only son.

Herman started working for his father's company the Sun Corporation (HK) Limited soon after his return from the Olympics. The company had numerous subsidiaries in Hong Kong and around the world. His father had top people working for him and thus Herman did not have as much to do as he initially thought as the business ran smoothly and was basically on autopilot. He was made president of the group, second in command to his father, who was the chief operating officer. The main business of the Sun Corporation was real estate. One of its largest subsidiaries was the China Light and Power Company Ltd. which was the sole supplier of electricity to Kowloon and the New Territories. The other major business was that of shipping. This was under the subsidiary Sun Maritime Ltd. which had one of the largest commercial shipping fleets in Asia. Herman got along well with all the managers of the various companies worldwide and was well respected by both management and staff. He sat on the board of directors and attended all its quarterly meetings.

During the last two years after Ajit's death Herman got very close to his father. He joined his father every morning with his Kung Fu routine for an hour and then followed him on a five-mile run outside their Kowloon residence. During the last two years Leslie taught Herman the art of Kung Fu and how to use nunchakus properly. Herman was a quick learner and surprised even his father on how quickly he picked up this new skill. His father encouraged him to get more involved with the affairs of Hong Kong telling him that one day he would need to take over his duty as advisor to the British government on the affairs of Hong Kong. A week before the international race, Leslie, after their daily morning workout, asked Herman to join him in his study.

Leslie explained to Herman that for the last few years he had suffered badly from migraines. He had finally gone to see his doctor eight months ago to check on it. The doctor took a number of scans and informed him that he had a tumour on the brain which was probably cancerous. It was inoperable as the tumour was located in a difficult position. By doing surgery to remove it was risky and it was likely that it could cause permanent damage to the brain. All the doctor could do was to monitor the tumour and to give Leslie a cocktail of pills that would hopefully slow its growth. Last week when he revisited the doctor for his monthly review, he was told that the tumour had started to grow quite rapidly. Unfortunately, there was nothing more the doctor could do, and Leslie had to face the fact that his life was limited. The doctor explained that within six months Leslie would first start to lose his memory. Following that it would affect his bodily motions before the brain stops functioning altogether and he dies. The doctor gave him at most a year and a half before this happened and was sorry to have to pass on such bad news.

Leslie explained to Herman that he did not want to let Nancy know about this yet. She was in such a great mood because of the upcoming marriage of Herman and Ella that if he told her she would have a complete breakdown. He said he would let her know right after the wedding took place. He told Herman that he had made his will and explained that he would leave his company to Nancy, Lucy and him. Herman will hold 50% of the shares followed by Nancy with 35% and finally Lucy with 15%. The house would go to Herman together with all his other personal possessions. He would be leaving his sister Irene and her two children Richard and Yvonne HK$25,000,000 each. He also had willed Bella Wang HK$25,000,000. He told Herman that he had set up with his lawyers, that from the profits made by Sun Corporation, 10% of the profits would go to charities. It was for the shareholders, namely Nancy, Lucy and him to decide which charity that money went to. He told Herman that he was to ensure that his mother Eileen, who was now eighty-one years of age, would be looked after and that Irene and her children could stay in the house for as long as they wished. Herman hugged his father and wept profusely. Leslie told him to be strong as when he left this world, he would be the head of the family and they would need his guidance and strength.

Sir John and Niko were seated on Mohan Lalwani's table together with their two boys Ishaan and Aryan, also on same table were the Chairman of the Jockey Club Sir Christopher Platt and his wife Deborah. The other couple seated at that table, were Mr and Mrs Phillip Samcroft, the chairman of the Melbourne Racing Club in Australia. John was happy with life as things had turned out much better than he expected. After the death of Ajit there was a public outcry and the press came down very hard on the police force, citing that corruption was destroying that establishment. Obviously as commissioner of police John had to take most of the brunt. A commission was formed with the governor heading it. The commission was to look into what caused the murder of Inspector Lee and others who got killed that day including the entrepreneur Ajit Lalwani. The inquiry took over six months to finalise. It determined that some lower officers had leaked to the press the time Mr Lee was to be transferred over to the military and what security procedures were in place. It was this that prompted the press to blast this on the early edition of the day of the transfer. This was why Kohei and the triads were prepared for Inspector Lee's transfer and had time to plan his assassination. Two officers were charged and sentenced to five years in jail, Sir John Woods was cleared of any wrongdoing. John thanked his lucky stars that he was not implicated. He was fortunate that Inspector Lee's body was so badly disintegrated by the explosion that no autopsy could have been done. If the coroner had done one, they would have discovered he was poisoned as well. This could have led to the commission tracing back and discovering that the poison was placed on Mr Lee's final meal which was handled by Mr Chan. They could then have made the connection of Mr Chan's friendship with Niko.

Whilst waiting for the divorce from Maggie to finalise John moved out of the house. He rented a studio apartment in the Mid-Levels. This was more for show as he hardly ever stayed there and instead spent almost every night with Niko in her house at Repulse Bay. The divorce came through quickly just three months after the filing. John, soon after that, started openly going out with Niko and moved in with her in her house in Repulse Bay. Maggie was not upset about it at all but rather happy that she could now concentrate on her own life. The only thing that concerned her was the wellbeing of her daughter Mabel. She need not have worried for Mabel took the divorce better than Maggie thought she would. In fact, Ben took it hard, not quite what she expected. Mabel soon started her own business and was very successful.

Maggie was David's escort to the races and hosted the table together with him. Seated on their table were Anand with wife Sunita and their two children Prity and Sheila, Laxman and wife Mohini with their son Ashwin. Maggie's daughter Mabel and her date for the day Danny Brown. Maggie started socialising more after her divorce and attended almost every function or party she was invited to. She once again was the vivacious belle of the party. Raymond started courting her again, but she was irresponsive to his gestures. He felt dejected for he thought that after the divorce he would really have a chance with her. Maggie, in fact, was attracted to Nancy's brother David Poon whom she met often at parties that they were both invited to. She got along with him brilliantly and they enjoyed each other's company. David would attend the parties without his wife Mia. Nancy had told Maggie that David's wife was a raging alcoholic and they were having problems with their marriage. It had become so bad that finally David decided to divorce her. Mia was happy to have a divorce but wanted a huge settlement of HK$250 million in addition to 50% shares in all the companies that he owned. Finally, after months of negotiation with their lawyers, they came to an agreement. Mia was to receive HK$750 million in cash as full settlement but would not have any stake in any of David's companies. Soon after the divorce Maggie and David started seeing each other regularly. Nancy was delighted for both her brother and best friend and hoped that one day they would remarry.

Mabel never forgave Herman for what he did to her and swore that one day when the time came, she would take her revenge. She left her job with the Lalwanis and decided to start her own business. With money she borrowed from her father she opened a small boutique in Mody Road in the Tsim Sha Tsui district and called it "CHYNA". All the clothes in that shop were designed by her. She made her dresses out of the most luxurious fabrics in the world. The dresses she made were expensive and the cheapest dress that one could purchase from the shop would cost HK$8,000. She did very well and soon all the top models and actresses would shop there. The "CHYNA" brand took off quickly and was being noticed by people, not only in the colony but worldwide. In the summer of 1965 Mabel received an invitation to exhibit her dresses at the Paris Fashion Week being held from September 28th, till October 6th. She would join a number of designers selected by the committee to put on a special event during one day of the week. The event was to choose the best young and upcoming designers around the world. Mabel could not believe it when she won the award and was acclaimed by the press, many stating that she was the next Chanel. From that day her business exploded. She expanded her business guided by her mother's boyfriend David Poon and opened "CHYNA" stores around the world starting first in Tokyo, then followed up in London and recently in New York. Mabel was lucky to have David guide her on the financial side of the business and taught her risk management as that was her weakest trait. She soon become one of the most sought-after designers with her dresses selling for as high as HK$100,000. She loved the sudden popularity and used it to her advantage. Vogue magazine in its March 1966 edition voted her as one of top twenty fashion designers of the year.

Herman and Ella hosted the last table. On their table were Dilip and Anita Lawani, Sir Anthony Brown with his wife Elizabeth, David Poon's children, son Robert and daughters Naomi and Michelle. Bella Wang was the final member on the table. Bella did not want to attend but Leslie insisted she did, and that he would ask Uncle Ray to escort her. However, last-minute, Ray had to bail as he needed to take care of some urgent matters. Bella was ready to cancel as well but when she told Anita she would not attend Anita became quite upset and insisted she did. She gave in after Anita kept begging her to go. Anita said that Dilip and her would pick her up and take her there.

Herman was at the top of his element and was an excellent host. He was in a super good mood and felt contented with life.

It had been a funny sort of year for Bella. Eileen, after returning from her film shoot in Europe, seemed totally uncaring. Eileen was suddenly being recognised for her movies and was offered many roles by top directors. She did move in with Bella but constantly had to depart for film shoots overseas. Bella hardly ever saw Eileen for when she was in Hong Kong, she was either in the studios or spending her evenings attending functions that she was invited to by VIPs of the movie world. Eileen never once asked Bella to join her in any of the events. Their relationship became exceedingly bad and they both decided to end it with Eileen moving out of the apartment. Bella was upset as she truly loved Eileen. However, she did not intend to drown in her sorrow and engulfed herself in work. She was doing so well that Raymond promoted her to become a director in his entertainment company. Bella felt very proud of her achievements and spent almost all her time concentrating on the business. She did occasionally meet Anita and had sex with her to relieve the tensions at work. She knew Anita was totally in love with her, but she did not feel the same way. She regarded Anita as a friend and her sex toy.

After the death of his father Dilip found himself suddenly being the major shareholder of the Lalwani Group of companies. Ajit, who owned 60% of shares in the Lalwani Group, willed 51% to Dilip and the balance 9% to Anita. His wife was to receive monthly a portion of fees that Dilip received as part of his director's fee until she passed away. Every year when the company issued dividends to the shareholders Dilip and Anita were to contribute 20% of their earning to their mother Maya. Dilip, thankfully, had learned from his father. When he finished his high school, unlike most of his friends who went on to do their 'A' levels and enter university he joined his father's business. In the six years of working under his father Dilip gained loads of experience and was well aware of the running's of the company. Mohan, the second largest shareholder with 25% of the shares, got along well with Dilip. It was only right to appoint Dilip as CEO of the group as he was the largest shareholder. His other two brothers did not feel the same way and did not agree with Ajit's plan which was to invest more into hotels and properties around Hong Kong and Asia. They feared, with the uncertainty of the colony, which was politically unstable during this time, with the communists in China making threats, that one day soon they would invade Hong Kong. Both Anand and Laxman voiced their desire to sell their shares back to either Dilip or Mohan at market valuation of the company. Dilip understood their concern and promised that at the next shareholders meeting they would discuss this in depth and come to some form of agreement that would be fair to all the shareholders. The meeting was scheduled for the end of June which would coincide with the group's results of the previous year provided by their accountants.

Dilip put all his time into his work and was determined to carry out his father's legacy. Two projects that his father wanted to complete were firstly the building of a world-class amusement park in Hong Kong. He had both Raymond and Leslie involved in the project. The Lalwani Group would own 40% of the shares and both Raymond and Leslie 30%. They initially were thinking of bringing Disneyland into Hong Kong by licensing the name. However, that proved too difficult and so they decided instead to build an Ocean Park on the island. They had found a prime piece of land which they had purchased and was now awaiting a loan from HSBC to fund in its construction.

The second project which Ajit was involved in was to build a five-star hotel in the heart of Tsim Tsa Tsui with eight hundred rooms. Ajit had formed a syndicate with some of the wealthier Sindhi community to purchase the land where the hotel was to be built. The consortium recently, after two years of negotiations, received permission from the lands offices to proceed with the construction. What took so long for the land office to approve the plans was that in the plans submitted the hotel would have three basements. So far in Hong Kong no hotel had ever been allowed to go so deep underground. They had also signed a contract with the Hilton Group to manage the hotel. Recently, with the political conditions being unstable, a lot of the Sindhi partners wanted to sell out. Dilip decided, after discussing with Mohan, to buy out all their stakes. This would cost the Lalwani Group a substantial amount of money and they turned once again to HSBC under Sir Anthony Brown for a loan. Sir Anthony had great faith in the Lalwani boys and knew that they would work hard to ensure the hotel was built correctly and would be successful. He extended them the loan they needed to buy out the other partners and construction on the hotel began.

On a personal side his mother kept pushing him to find a "good" Indian girl from a high-class Sindhi family and get married. She hired a marriage matchmaker to find him a good wife. He thought it all so ridiculous in this age but went along on some of the dates to appease his mother. His sister Anita, too, was pushed by her mother to get married. Anita recently had disclosed to Dilip that she was a lesbian and was not interested in any men. He was a bit taken aback with her revelation but was glad she came out of the closet to let him know. She said the only other persons who knew were her best friend Mabel and of course someone she had been seeing quite often recently Bella Wang. Dilip had deep feelings for Mabel but with her success and her travelling all the time never got the chance to approach her to ask her for a date. In reality there were a number of times he could have but he was afraid of being rejected.

Anita continued to work with Mohan on the retail side of the business and loved her job greatly. Mohan gave her a free hand and allowed her to make important decisions. Anita was clever and actually helped in building up the business which grew rapidly and was bringing in great revenues to the group. Like Dilip she was constantly hounded by her mother to find a nice Sindhi boy and settle down. According to her mother it was not right for a girl to be working and that she should marry and be a good housewife and have lots of children. Anita could not break her mother's heart so did not tell her of her preferences with sex partners for that would kill her. She kept her relationship with Bella Wang a secret and only met her in her apartment. They never dated openly in public.

The first race was on and most of the people in the VIP room had gone out to the balcony to watch it running. Herman was not interested in watching and had stayed in the room enjoying his wine and having a cigar. Ella had gone with Anita to the ladies' room to freshen up. Mabel walked up to his table and sat next to him. They had not seen each other in a very long time, actually ever since just before Herman had gone to participate in the Olympics.

"Congratulations on your upcoming marriage to Ella. I heard all about it from my mother. Looks like you are going to have one big party. You will invite me to it won't you? I would hate to miss out on the wedding of the century."

Herman was a bit startled and replied, "Why of course you and your family will be on top of the wedding list. It is nice to see you after such a long time. I have heard of your success and must say I am so proud of you to achieve what you have done in putting Hong Kong on the fashion map. I heard from Ella that you have been appointed by the Hollywood actor George Hanks to do all the outfits for his wife Elizabeth for their upcoming wedding including Elizabeth's wedding dress. What an honour, you must be thrilled with this as the publicity you get will boost your brand even more. Ella was actually considering asking you to help her design her wedding dress but thought with the amount of work you have going on you would not have the time."

Mabel thought to herself, what a load of crap no way the bitch would allow her to design her wedding dress.

"Oh, for the both of you I would be happy to do that. Please let her know I will make time and do a fabulous design for her, one that will be noticed all over the world. Anyway, I only just dropped by to say hello and to congratulate you. I will take leave now but please pass my best wishes on to Ella and let her know if she wants me to design her wedding dress I would be delighted to do so." Mabel stood up and walked towards the balcony to be with Danny who had a huge bet on the first race.

Danny Brown, after the death of his brother Harold, became quite a womaniser and enjoyed his alcohol. Although his father had made him vice president of the bank, he did little to help in the business. He would leave work early and spend time with his friends at the Havana Bar enjoying the cognac and cigars. He would often visit the Sing Song Club with his so-called close friends and paid for hostesses to have sex with him. His father just left him to do what he wanted as he thought eventually, he would get out of this phase in his life. He thought that the only reason he was acting like a jerk was that he was missing his brother. Danny was really surprised when Mabel asked him to be her date for this function. He had dated her previously, but it did not come to much. He now looked at her differently, for in the last two years she had blossomed and become even more beautiful. She was now a successful designer, well respected and quite a catch. He was thinking after the races to ask her out for dinner and charm her and with a bit of luck could maybe get her to sleep with him.

Sir William Sandhill, during lunch, was discussing with Leslie the upcoming increase the government had approved on raising the fares of the Star Ferry. Leslie was against this from the start when it was first proposed in 1965. The Star Ferry was an important link between the Kowloon Peninsula and Hong Kong Island. Sir William had told Leslie that the Star Ferry had applied for fare increases of between 50% and 100%. Star Ferry, which wanted this kept a secret, expressed dismay that the application had been made public. This sparked public fears that if the increase in fares were approved, other forms of public transport would also raise their prices. The Transport Advisory Committee (TAC) approved the Star Ferry's fare increase in March 1966, Leslie told the governor that when the raise was finally applied, he could envisage disturbances and protests from the public. The governor did not agree as the rise was going to be a mere HK$0.05 for both lower and upper decks of the ferry which to him was very insignificant.

Leslie looked around and noticed that everyone there seemed to be enjoying themselves. He glanced at his watch, it was three p.m. He needed to gather the guests at his table shortly and lead them down to see his horse in the parade ring before they raced. This was an exclusive time for horse owners whereby they could invite their guests, up to a maximum of ten people per owner, to view all the horses that were running in that race at the paddock. The owners and guests were free to mingle with other owners, trainers and the jockeys. Leslie felt exhausted as the pills he took made him tired, but he hid that well from his guests. At the parade ring Leslie and his guests walked towards where his trainer Frank and jockey Tony were at the centre of the parade ring. Leslie watched all the horses go by and to him "Sunset" by far stood out from the rest of the horses.

"Frank what do you think? Do you see any dangers to Sunset? I thought the horse from Japan looked very fit as he walked around the ring and the press have been building him up as he recently won the Tokyo Derby. I, however, still think that Nijinsky is the one to beat. Charles W. Engelhard Jr, the owner of Nijinksy, was telling me during lunch that the final workout of Nijinsky was breathtaking, and his jockey, Lester Piggott, was confident that he would win. He thought it would be fantastic if Sunset could win today the same year that his son gets married. That would be a double ceremony!"

Frank looked around as the horses went around the parade ring and replied, "I have never seen Sunset as relaxed as he is today. He ate all his dinner up last night and slept well. This morning I took him out for a short workout just to freshen him up and he worked amazingly. Tony was well happy with his workout and felt the horse had never trained better. Leslie, I am confident we will win today. Forget all that talk about the Japanese horse he has no chance and the only horse who could go close to beating Nijinksy will be yards behind. In all my life as a trainer I have never been more confident."

Leslie was encouraged by the words of Frank and was excited to have the race begin. He was going to watch the race from the owners' box which was located on the first floor. When Leslie entered the room all the other owners of that race went up to him and said they thought that Leslie's horse Sunset was a certainty and would win easily. They all said it looked a standout at the parade ring. The odds for Sunset were quickly dropping as it came nearer to race time and its odds dropped from 2–1 to 10–11. Nijinsky's odds drifted to 3–1 and the other runners in the race were odds of 15–1 or more. It seemed the public agreed that Sunset would definitely win the Queen Elizabeth II Cup race for the second year running.

Mabel went out to the third-floor balcony to watch the race. Herman was in deep discussion with Sir Anthony Brown, both studying the race and how it could be run. Ella was by their side having her champagne. Maggie walked up to her.

"Hi darling, it's been a while since we last met. Congratulations on your upcoming marriage with Herman. I was speaking to him a bit earlier and he told me that you were thinking of asking me to design your wedding dress. I just want to let you know that I am up to that if you wish. It would help build up my résumé to design the wedding dress of the woman who was soon to become the wife of the son of the famous Leslie Sun!"

Ella looked at Mabel with bewilderment. She noticed that she was holding a glass of red wine in her hand and thought back to that night two years ago when Mabel poured wine on her.

"Oh, I am sorry to disappoint, but I have already secured the service of Yves Saint Laurent who will be designing my outfit along with those of my bridesmaids. You will be attending the wedding I assume? I hope so as it will be the greatest wedding the colony will ever witness. Auntie Nancy has gone all out to ensure that people would talk about it for years to come. I see you are here with Danny. Are you guys dating? Do I hear wedding bells soon?"

What a fucking bitch, I wish I could pour this glass of red wine over her now that would be funny, thought Mabel. She replied with a smile.

"No, it's not serious between Danny and me. He was kind enough to be my escort for this afternoon. You have chosen a great designer to do your wedding outfit and I am happy for you. I am sure the wedding will be a great success, unfortunately I am busy with work at that time and will not be attending. I wish the both of you luck with the marriage," and as she walked away, she whispered loud enough so Ella could hear, "you will need all the luck to make the marriage work."

The race was about to begin, and the horses were being put into their stalls. Sunset was drawn in the widest stall, barrier fourteen. Nijinksy, its main rival, was drawn well at stall five. Leslie was superstitious and was concerned about Sunset's draw fourteen as it was unlucky in Chinese numerology; the number four meant death and put together fourteen meant "sure death". He felt stupid thinking that way and decided to just focus on watching the race. It was exactly three forty-five p.m. and the horses were under starter's orders. The flag was raised indicating that the horses were all settled in their respective stalls and the gates flung open. Sunset began slowly and fell back to last in the field. Leslie looked on anxiously. Frank had warned him that he would ask Tony to ease the horse to last in the first part of the race as it was drawn on the outside, he did not want Tony to waste the horse's strength early as to maintain its stamina. The race was run over two miles so there was plenty of time to get the horse up to the front and then use its final burst up the final two hundred metres in the race.

After the first mile run Sunset was still at the back of the field but still in close touch to the rest of the horses. The Japanese horse Haiseiko was in the lead as expected as he was a front runner. The beautiful grey stallion was leading the pack by over two lengths. Nijinksy was running about two lengths behind in second place. Sunset was still sitting last about fifteen lengths behind the leader. Leslie was wondering when Tony would make his move on Sunset and was becoming a little worried. He felt that Tony should start bringing the horse a bit closer to the leader as he may not be able to make ground in the final part of the race if he was so far away.

The crowds were on their feet shouting for Sunset to make a move as the horses entered the final four hundred metres of the race. Haiseiko was still in front of Nijinsky who was now just half a length behind. Sunset was still dead last and had a number of horses blocking his way. Leslie was upset with the way Tony was riding the horse, surely, he must make it move now for it would take a super horse to pass the whole field and win. As the horses turned to the final straight, two hundred and fifty metres from the finish line, Tony finally pulled his horse wide so that he could get a clear run to the finish line. Sunset just took off passing the other horses as if they were standing still. The horses were now entering the last hundred metres of the race. Nijinksy passed Haiseiko and was in the lead. Sunset kept getting closer and quickly passed Haiseiko and started aiming for Nijinksy who was at that stage still five lengths behind. What one witnessed was a feat that was remembered for many years to come. Sunset passed Nijinksy easily and was pulling away from him with every stride. He was over five lengths ahead of Nijinksy in the final thirty metres of the race. Leslie stood up and started shouting go baby go we got this. Suddenly they heard what sounded like a large gunshot and as Sunset passed the winning post, he fell to the ground dislodging Tony. The crowds went silent.

John, who was watching from the third-floor balcony, immediately knew what had happened. He looked across the racecourse to a high-rise building which overlooked the racecourse. He was sure that the shot came from there. He jumped into action, ran into the VIP room and called police headquarters. He then went straight to the chairman of the jockey club Sir Christopher Platt, who was watching the race from his table on the TV, and whispered to him. Sir Christopher immediately rushed out the VIP room and headed towards security. Sir John then went back and told Niko to remain in the VIP room till he returned as he had to deal with the problem. Within five minutes of John's call to the police station one could hear police sirens heading towards the racecourse. There was an announcement from the club through the racecourse loudspeakers advising all racegoers to orderly head for the exits. It was further announced that the rest of the races for that day would be cancelled. The public there were advised not to try and cash their winning tickets now as all betting counters would be closed. All winning tickets for the last run race could be collected form any of the Jockey Club betting shops around the colony.

Leslie and Frank rushed towards the track where Sunset lay just ten metres past the winning post. It was bleeding from the side of its head but was still breathing. It was obvious that the horse was suffering and would probably not survive. Tony crawled back from where the horse had dislodged him and was stroking Sunset's mane; the horse was barely alive. Sir John rushed towards them with two other officers. He shouted to Leslie to leave the scene and for all of them to head back to the club. The area was not yet secured, and the sniper could still be around, they would be sitting ducks out there. Leslie just stood there staring at Sunset not believing what just happened. John had to take his arm and drag him back to the race club building.

When they entered the building, Leslie seemed to break off from a trance.

"My poor Sunset, did you see how he won the race. He was miles behind but in the last two hundred metres swamped all the other horses including Nijinksy and won the race easily. He is definitely the best racehorse in the world. But what the hell happened John? Who shot my horse and why?"

John replied, "We believe there was a sniper on top of one of the high-rise buildings across the road which looked straight onto the racecourse. He must have been waiting for Sunset to pass the winning post and then took his shot. We have cordoned the whole area and have the police combing the area. We are hoping we can still catch him. I am so sorry about what happened, but I promise we will get to the bottom of this and those involved will be punished." Leslie had heard that so many times before. He was really angry with what happened. Frank and Tony came to comfort him. They both had tears in their eyes.

"Sunset was the very best horse I have trained, and he did us all proud. The way he won the race today shows how wonderful a star he truly was. His name will go down in history. I can't for the life of me understand why anyone would want to harm such a beautiful creature. Tony and I are so sorry about it all. For myself I have decided to retire from training horses. I have reached the pinnacle of my life. After the win today, followed by the sadness of losing Sunset, I cannot continue with this career. I will miss Sunset so."

Tony continued, "When we entered the last three hundred metres pole mark and entered the straight, I was slightly worried but once I pushed my reins and gave him a tap with the whip he just flew. I could not believe how he just took off, passing one horse after another. What a winner. I am so proud that I had a chance to ride him in this race. I will treasure this memory for the rest of my life. Leslie I am so sorry for today, the racing world has lost probably the best horse that has ever raced in the world."

Leslie thanked both of them for their kind words. He was sad but very angry for he felt this must have been the doings of Kohei San who was out to hurt him.

He thought out aloud, "One day we will pass paths Kohei and I promise you will suffer as no man has ever suffered before. Firstly, you take away from me the woman I loved, my dearest Lilian. On top of that you kill my best friend Ajit and now you kill my beautiful horse Sunset in the prime of his life. You are a fucking bastard and you will suffer!"

Why was his luck so bad thought Leslie? Was it because he had ignored going to the temple for so long? He felt an urge to go there now and say a prayer for his family.

Chapter 15
'Boop Doop De Boop...'

The Basement
14 Tuen Chun Road, The Walled City, Kowloon City.
April 5th, 1966, six thirty p.m.

Ponytail called for the meeting to begin.

Wild Ox stood up from his chair and walked down the platform to the open space below and faced the committee.

"Our dear Lord and Master, it has been very difficult these last few months for us. The police suddenly are not as helpful and many of the officers have stopped taking bribes and have actually started raiding some of our smaller illicit gambling dens and brothels. It seems that this has all stemmed because of pressure from the governor, more since the kidnapping of Harold and the killing of Inspector Lee and Ajit Lalwani. Now with the incident whereby Dr Leslie Sun's horse had been shot during the big race they are even going to clamp down harder on us. Besides that, the Sun Yee On gangs are infiltrating many of our businesses. Many of our generals and soldiers are leaving the 14K to join the Sun Yee On as they pay better than we do. It seems that the Sun Yee On are under less pressure from the law enforcements than we are. We need to take some immediate action soon as our coffers are reducing daily which Dragonfly can update you on."

"This is indeed bad news," replied Ponytail. "It seems ever since that Japanese idiot Kohei started on his killing spree it has affected all us triads in the colony. The police have tightened up on all forms of the illicit businesses and are no longer accepting bribes. I believe they are scared especially after Inspector Lee and Mr Lawani were shot. Five police officers were tried and sentenced to jail for taking bribes. Leslie Sun has been no help as he has pushed the governor to work on getting rid of all organised crimes in the colony and targeting the larger triads like us. We have to work on three fronts to stop this otherwise the 14K may have to cease its operations. Firstly, we need to find out where Kohei is hiding out and leak this to the police. I believe once Kohei is arrested the pressure will be reduced and maybe some of the officers will once again accept bribes and we can continue running our businesses like before. Secondly, we need to counter-attack the Sun Yee On. We should by force take over a portion of their establishments. We will even, if we have to, use up all our reserves, start paying our generals and soldiers more so they can stay loyal. Any generals or soldiers deserting the 14K must be reported by all officers to you, Wild Ox. You will ensure that they and their families will be punished with no mercy as to make an example to anyone thinking of absconding the 14K. Then there is the problem of our dear friend Leslie Sun. I will handle him personally. I will work on having him disposed of quickly. Once he is out of the way the government will need to replace him, and we stand a chance of corrupting the newcomer. Shall we now continue with the meeting?"

"Yes, my dear Lord and Master, let us start with '438' the Incense Master. What do you have to report to the committee?" Wild Ox asked. The Incense Master stood up from his chair and walked down the platform to the main open space below and faced the committee.

"My Lord and trusted triad brothers, as explained by Wild Ox a number of our generals have deserted to Sun Yee On and we need to fill their roles as soon as possible as without any leadership the soldiers of the deserted generals are considering leaving the 14K. It is not a good situation I fear My Lord, and it's becoming critical. Today I have brought up six soldiers to be promoted to the rank of general to fill the gaps. We probably need a few more but I believe for the time being that will help. They have all been vetted and have passed their initial tests, they now will need to go through the initiations and if they pass can be appointed. Shall we begin with them now?"

"No, not now," replied Ponytail. "You can do that after we hear what else is on the agenda. I need to leave early today as there is something that needs my immediate attention. Wild Ox will follow the initiations and give them the sanctifications to become generals if they pass. So, what is next on the agenda?"

"Sir, the only last thing for the evening is for Dragonfly to give his report on the financials but if you are rushed, we can have that sent to your office where you can examine them privately and at your own time. Will that be better?"

"Yes, that will be good. One last thing, Wild Ox, please reinforce the guards at our front door. I have heard rumours that the British army may be trying to enter the Walled City any time soon and bulldoze it over. If there is any hint of this happening you must be sure that all the records of our officers are destroyed, and they cannot get to them. I have already informed Dragonfly on how to destroy all our financial records. There is a safe house that I have set up in the New Territories for our generals to go to if this occurs. Wild Ox, I will pass you all the details tomorrow in our private meeting. That being all I bid all of you a big thank you for attending this shortened meeting. Wild Ox will continue directing the initiations. I hope that in the next meeting we have scheduled I can bring you better news." Ponytail raised his blade, "the Blaze", waved it at the generals and left the room.

John looked at his watch, it was eight thirty p.m. and Raymond had still not showed up. He had told him to be there by eight p.m. as it was important that he spoke to him tonight. He was seated in one of the private VIP rooms at the Havana Paradise Cigar Bar. There was a knock on the door and John asked the person to enter. It was the general manager of the club, Sonny Chaves.

"Sir, I have just received a call from Master Raymond, he apologises for being late but said he would be here within the next twenty minutes. Can I get you something else to drink?"

"Yes, I suppose, I will have the same again. Could you also please get me another cigar I am almost finished with this," replied John pointing his cigar stub at him.

John was getting irritated as he had told Niko that he was meeting Ray at around eight p.m. and should finish by nine p.m. at the latest. They had planned on having a late dinner at her place at nine thirty p.m. He picked up the phone in the room and dialled Niko.

"Sorry darling, it seems that Ray will be late, please do not wait for me for dinner. I will eat something here before heading home. I am sorry as I know you said you will be cooking me something special

293

tonight. If it was not urgent that I meet Ray tonight I would have cancelled but I do need to have a chat with him." Niko replied that she understood and for him not to worry.

John had had a rough time the past few months and if it was not for Niko, he would probably have had a nervous breakdown. The one good thing in his life was Niko and he thanked God every day for bringing her into his life. She had, after countless times of him asking, finally agreed to marry him. They had both planned that when John retired, they would move to Cuba. This was for a number of reasons. Niko had been there a few times before and loved the country. She loved living near the sea and Cuba had some of the most beautiful beaches she had ever witnessed. Secondly, Cuba had no expatriation's agreements with the U.K. and its colonies, so John would be able to live there without fear that the British government would come after him and the monies he had taken as bribes whilst serving in the police. There were no restrictions on how much money they could move into the country. With the monies John and Niko had they could live the high lifestyle they both wanted. Niko had been communicating with a realtor in the Caribbean and after countless folders of properties he sent her she finally found her ideal house. It was precisely what she wanted: a five-bedroom house done in the colonial style which came with a beautiful private beach. She was super excited when John agreed with her choice and immediately put a deposit down on it.

Raymond finally appeared at around nine fifteen p.m., an hour and fifteen minutes later than the planned time.

"I am so sorry John, but I had a meeting with the board, and it took longer than I had anticipated. What is this all about? You seemed quite upset when you called this afternoon. Have you had something to eat? I am famished."

John said he had not yet eaten, and Raymond called in Sonny and ordered food for both of them. He directed Sonny to bring the food to the VIP room as they would eat there. They were not to be disturbed under any circumstances. When Sonny left John turned to Raymond and told him, earlier that afternoon, he had gone to the governor's house to have an emergency meeting. When he arrived at one p.m. there were Leslie Sun and his son Herman present together with Major

General Chris Wolfe. They were ushered to a private soundproof meeting room at the governor's house. The governor asked them all to vow that what they were about to hear would be kept top secret. He had two important things he needed to do and wanted them to execute.

The governor started by saying that an urban councillor Elsie Eliot, who was a member of the Transport Advisory Company (TAC), was upset with the TAC granting the Star Ferry to raise its fare. She started a petition and collected signatures of over twenty thousand citizens. The governor was not a fan of Elsie and thought of her as a troublemaker. This caused two people to go on a hunger strike just outside the entrance of the Star Ferry terminal in the Central District. They both wore black jackets on which was written, "Hail Elsie and join the hunger strike." They caught the public mood and quickly drew a crowd of supporters. Yesterday they were both arrested, and this caused a group of young sympathisers to march to Government House to petition the governor to release them. There were also demonstrations in both the Tsim Tsa Shui and Mongkok districts with over one thousand protestors taking to the streets waving banners denouncing the government and the police.

The 1960s was a period of mounting dissatisfaction over British colonial rule. The British expats seemed to live a life of luxury whilst the general population were poor. Corruption in officialdom was prevalent and citizens were distrustful of the rampantly corrupt police, and the inequity of policing. The governor knew they all knew these facts and stated it was up to the government now to show the people of Hong Kong that their governor cared and would make necessary changes to the system to make life better for the man in the street. He had learned, through special intelligence, that tomorrow many more protests were to happen all over Hong Kong because of the arrest of the two hunger strikers and it could escalate very quickly. What he was worried about was that this could end up in riots which could last for some time.

The governor said his directive was the government had to take strong actions against the protestors and to break up any riots by force if need be. He realised the police may not have the ability to take this on their own and that is why he invited Major Wolfe to join this meeting. The major was to activate the British army to move in and assist the police if things got out of hand and use power, if necessary, to break up any rioting. The other issue he wanted to bring up was the incident at the racecourse. There was a huge public outcry and the press went to town saying it was a shame that the proud British colony of Hong Kong could not deal with the criminals who seemed to be rampant in the city with the police appearing powerless. The British parliament was called to a special session to discuss this and the prime minister himself called the governor saying how disappointed he was that the pride of the British in the far east Hong Kong could not control the criminal elements in the colony. He insisted that all crime organisations were closed down soon, if not he would get the army to take charge till the job was done.

John said he had started on the process of identifying officers in the police who were taking bribes and in the last month had questioned over one hundred officers and fifteen had been either reprimanded or charged. He said he would escalate his efforts in the next months and hopefully weed out the culprits. He said that they had found gun shells in the rooftops of those buildings from where the sniper took shots at Inspector Lee and at Sunset and that the shells matched. That meant that the same sniper that shot Inspector Lee was also responsible for the killing of Sunset. He went on to say that the bullets from the rifle that killed Inspector Lee, Ajit and Sunset were not something common and seemed to be handmade. He had passed this on to Interpol to see what they came up with. He felt that they were getting closer to finding the person behind the killings.

The governor continued saying he had now also made the decision for the army to get involved and set about getting rid of the Walled City where the main triads were located. The army was to go in, remove the people out of the city and then bulldoze it all down. He would also increase the punishment to all criminals with the introduction of the death penalty for anyone who was associated with triads. These severe measures were surely going to get people who were thinking of entering into crime to think twice. He added he would push on with Leslie on finalising the set-up of the ICAC. Ever since the horse racing incident, which was publicised worldwide, the British parliament seemed more eager to push forward for the law to be passed. What happened with the shooting of Sunset was a big embarrassment to the British as other nations worldwide felt that the British colonists could not control their territories. This was a huge embarrassment, not only for the British government, but to him as governor.

Leslie was concerned with the rush to destroy the Walled City without consultation with the communist government who believed that the Walled City was still part of China. The PRC did not recognise that the Walled City was part of the Nanking treaty which surrendered Hong Kong to the British. He reminded the governor that in the last three months Mao Tse Tung's Red Guards had been gathering on the China side of the border from Hong Kong. Earlier that year Mao announced his new political initiative which he named "the Cultural Revolution." Mao saw his latest political campaign as a way of reinvigorating the communist revolution by strengthening ideology and weeding out opponents. Chinese students sprang into action, setting up Red Guard divisions in classrooms and campuses across the country. Gangs of teenagers in red armbands and military fatigues roamed the streets of cities such as Beijing and Shanghai setting upon those with "bourgeois" clothes or reactionary haircuts. "Imperialist" street signs were torn down.

Mao had become more nationalistic and insisted that Hong Kong was part of China and one day he would take back the colony by force if he had to even if that meant him breaking international law. Leslie explained by destroying the Walled City without getting consent from the communist government could give the communists the excuse they needed to invade Hong Kong. He agreed with the governor that the Walled City should be destroyed and that the triad gangs must be broken up. He suggested he had a chat with the communist party leader in Hong Kong explaining the reason why the government wanted to bring down the Walled City. His main argument was that it was a health risk. He also would emphasise that the nationalist triads now actually had full control of the area and because of that crime had thrived. He would promise that the government would look after all the legit dwellers in the Walled City who would lose their homes and replace them with larger homes with proper sanitation. He was sure that he could convince the communist party leader. That was a better approach than just sending in the military. He explained if, however, the communists were stubborn and refused to allow the British to knock down the Walled City then the governor could send in the army. The governor agreed and asked Leslie to discuss with the communists and come back to him after his negotiations with the communist party leader in Hong Kong.

Raymond listened with horror. This could mean the end of all that he built. Leslie must be stopped at any cost. He thanked John for letting him in on what the government's plans were and he would need to let the 14K know immediately. They must prepare quickly in pulling out of the Walled City before the army got involved. He blamed Kohei for this, if he had not killed Harold, Inspector Lee, Ajit Lalwani and Leslie's horse Sunset the government would not have reacted so quickly. That bastard had to die. He was surprised that John had no lead on him. John said that through central intelligence they now believed he was being supported by the Sun Yee On gang but did not know of his whereabouts. They had their dinner and John said he needed to leave as he promised Niko he would be home early. Raymond said he would stay on at the bar for a little while longer and said his goodbye.

Sonny walked in after John left, and asked Ray if there was anything more he needed? Ray said he would stay in the VIP room as he wanted to make some important calls. He did not wish to be disturbed. He firstly made a call to the Peninsula Hotel looking for a Mr Mark Warren. The operator said he was not in his room and redirected the call to the hotel bar where Mark was having a drink there alone. Raymond spoke to him for a few minutes and then made a call to Mama Wendy at the club and asked her to reserve a room for him. He would be there by no later than eleven p.m. Raymond gulped down his cognac, left the Havana Bar and headed for the Sing Sing Club in Tsim Tsa Tsui.

Leslie left the governor's house feeling exhausted. His migraines had gotten worse day by day. He found that the painkillers that the doctor had prescribed him would only last for an hour or so instead of four hours like the doctor said. Herman excused himself, saying he had promised to meet Ella for afternoon tea and he would make his own way to the restaurant to meet her. As Leslie entered the car his chauffeur asked if he wanted to go to the office or home. Leslie looked at his watch, it was almost four thirty p.m., and asked the driver to take him home. Before the car had entered the ferry, Leslie had changed his mind and told the chauffeur instead to take him to the Buddhist temple in Tsim Tsa Tsui. Leslie sat back and remembered his conversation with Herman that morning.

They were discussing the moving of their current offices to their brand-new location. the Sun Tower in the centre of Tsim Sha Tsui. The building was magnificent with twenty floors making it the tallest building in the colony. It was a touch of class and the most modern looking building in all of Hong Kong. It had taken four years to build at a cost of HK$880 million but it had been worth it. The ribbon cutting ceremony was to be held on April 29th, a Saturday, and they were going through the arrangements. They had invited the governor to do the honours of cutting the ribbon, but he apologetically denied as he had to go to Singapore that day for a state visit. They decided then probably David Poon would be most appropriate as, besides being Leslie's brother-in-law, he was well respected in the colony. The plan was to have cocktails at the Peninsula Hotel lobby from four to six p.m. and then walk over to the Sun Tower which was a five-minute walk from the cutting ceremony. Everyone of importance was invited to the ceremony. Lucy Sun, who was recently made Public Relations Officer of the Sun Group, was to work on the final invitation list and present it to her father and brother before the end of the week for confirmation.

Lucy in the past few years had come out of her shell. She had become quite a socialite and attended every event and party in Hong Kong of any significance. She loved socialising and became very good at that, helping her mother in organising the parties she threw at home and her charity functions. She became well known in important circles and when the public relations officer of the Sun Corp resigned last year Leslie gave her that role. She absolutely loved her job and did it well. She had blossomed also in her looks, losing over two stone, which in turn built up her confidence. She always dressed immaculately at a function. She loved dressing up and all her clothes and accessories were from famous designers. She absolutely loved the clothes that Mabel designed and helped her to promote her brand "CHYNA" by wearing them at all major functions.

She was very close to Mabel and confided in her with all her secrets. Recently she had started going out with Edward Wolfe, the son of Major General Chris Wolfe. He was in the army like his father and was recently made lieutenant. The romance was still in its infancy, but Lucy was hoping it became more serious. She really liked him a lot as he met all her expectations. He was tall, blond and very handsome. He was very well mannered and a true gentleman, just what she always wanted in a boyfriend. She had expressed her feelings for him to Mabel who had given her advice on how best she handled the relationship. She trusted Mabel and treated her like an older sister. She was quite upset when Herman broke up with Mabel and chose Ella instead. She never was close to Ella whom she found false and was not happy that her brother was marrying her. She had asked Mabel to design a special outfit for her for the ribbon ceremony at the end of the month. It was to be the first important party that Lucy was organising as the public relations officer of the Sun Corp and she wanted to impress.

Mabel was sitting in the first-class lounge of Japan Airlines waiting to board the plane. She was on her way back to Hong Kong after the opening of her third store in Japan. The "CHYNA" brand had really taken off in Japan and her partners in Japan, the Mitsubishi Corporation, had told her that they planned to open another two stores by the end of the year, one in Osaka and another in Yokohama. She already had three stores in Tokyo, one in the Ginza district, the others in Shinjuku and Roppongi. The larger department stores like Mitsukoshi and Sogo carried her youth range "CHYNA DOLL" while all her high-end lines were only available in her boutiques under the label "CHYNA". This year the Japan business brought in revenues of over Yen four billion, approximately US$40,000,000. The Mitsubishi Corporation had advised her that in two years she should list her Tokyo company which was called "CHYNA KKK" in the Tokyo Stock Index the Nikkei.

Although successful in business Mabel was not totally satisfied with her life. Since she had broken up with Herman, she had not found anyone who could make her feel good like he did, both physically and emotionally. She had numerous affairs but nothing long lasting and she longed to one day find back that feeling she had with Herman. She blamed her loss on Ella and was determined to one day take revenge on her for spoiling her chances with the only man she had ever loved. She was dreading attending his wedding which was planned for early June this year but determined to make a show as she wanted to appear that she did not care. She only had two true friends, Anita and Lucy. She trusted them with everything, and they all supported each other. She was looking forward to meeting them for a night out this coming weekend on their monthly girls' night out.

Anita hung up the phone with Bella. She was concerned that Bella seemed to be ignoring her as every time she called to make a date to see her, she had come up with some lame excuse. She knew the relationship with Bella and Eileen was long over as recently it came out in the press that Eileen Siu, the famous actress, would be marrying Jimmy Cheung, a Kung Fu actor. She was confused and quite upset with the way Bella just brushed her aside after all the support she gave to her when Eileen left. She feared that probably Bella had found someone else to amuse her. She was looking forward to the night out with the girls on Saturday to get their views and advise her on what she should do.

When Leslie arrived at the Buddhist temple it was close to six p.m. He had unfortunately hit the rush hour and was stuck in traffic. As Leslie entered the temple, he noticed a lady sitting in the corner with her new-born child, weeping away. He thought he recognised her and asked the head monk about her. The head monk told her she used to be a hostess in a nightclub and left her job to be a concubine of a gangster. Unfortunately, recently she found out that she had developed cancer and was told that she had only a few months to live. She told her boyfriend about this and instead of being sympathetic he kicked her out along with her newly-born daughter leaving her almost nothing to live on. She had since stayed at the temple and the monks had provided her shelter and food. Leslie immediately felt sorry for her, especially as he was also suffering from an uncurable tumour. After lighting the incense and saying his prayers to Buddha he walked up to the woman. He took out HK$5,000 from his wallet and handed it to her.

"This is all I have now on me, but if you need any help, please phone me or visit me in my office and I will see what I can do to make your life more comfortable. I have spoken to the head monk and he told me about your plight, and I am so sorry. Have you made plans with social welfare on the future of the child? If you need any help, let me know." With that he handed her his name card. "Do not feel embarrassed to call me any time and I will see what I can do for you."

"Sir Leslie, do you not recognise me? I used to be a very close friend of Lillian Wang. I was known as Betty Boop, a name given to me by U.S. naval soldiers after a cartoon character. I was the number one hostess at the Sing Sing Nightclub there and many times I joined you in the VIP room when you came to see Lillian in the club. Thank you so much for this money but I need a larger favour from you and if you grant me my wish, I will reveal what your heart yearns to know about who killed Ajit and Sunset even though it may cost me my life. I am not worried about myself as I am sure you heard from the head monk about my health condition, but I worry about the future of my daughter. I want her to have a good life in a healthy and loving environment. If I hand her to social services, she will be put into an orphanage and as you know many who are put in one never find parents and end up all their lives trapped in the orphanage. I want for your family to take her into your home, she will cost you so little, but I will die happy knowing she will be looked after and have a decent chance in this world."

Leslie was surprised with what she had said. He looked carefully at her and suddenly he did recognise her as Betty Boop. He remembered Lillian telling him about her and how kind she was to her when she first became a hostess. She had aged a lot and had lost some of her beauty, but it was definitely her. Could it be she knew about Kohei and where he had been hiding all these years? He had searched for years to find him to take his revenge and from out of the blue this had come up. He could not believe his luck if all she said was true.

"If what you say is true and you can reveal to me where I can find the person who was responsible for the deaths of Lillian, Ajit and Sunset I will promise you that I will ensure that your daughter will be looked after like a member of the Sun family but if what you tell me are lies, I will no longer extend any help to you."

"I will tell you everything about Kohei and your other enemies. I, however, have not eaten much the whole day, should we go to the café opposite and you buy me a warm dinner and whilst we are having the meal, I will tell you all I know. I am sure it will meet with your satisfaction and you can finally get rid of that monster Kohei who had promised me the world but has left me and our child out in the cold all for a younger woman. All I ask is for you to keep your promise and look after my daughter when I am gone, and I know you will as you are a man of your word."

Leslie looked directly at her and could see her pain as tears poured from her eyes. He nodded and said to her he was happy to have dinner with her but first he needed to phone home and let his family know not to wait for him. He phoned home and then informed his chauffeur that he would be having dinner at the café with the lady and asked him to grab something to eat and be back in an hour to pick him up. He said his goodbye to the head monk who responded to him with a Buddha quote, "Don't take revenge. Let Karma do all the work." Leslie look stunned. How did the monk know he was after retribution? He thanked him again and said he would take his words of wisdom and act accordingly. He then took Betty's hand and they walked to the café with Betty carrying her child.

They found a corner bench table at the end of the café. It was a rather scruffy place, badly decorated and with dim lighting. Betty ordered food that was enough to feed two people and a bottle of beer She apologised for ordering so much but said she was really hungry. He just ordered a sandwich and a cup of tea. The baby was fast asleep on Betty's lap.

"Let me start from the very beginning. My real name is Li Ling and I was born an only child. When I was eight both my parents died in an accident and I was sent to an orphanage. They were the worst years of my life and that is why I dread my little girl having to go through what I did. That is why you must take her into your home and give her a good life. Anyway, at the age of sixteen I escaped from the orphanage with another girl who had told me of a nightclub that was looking for young hostesses. That is how I met Mama Wendy. She treated me well and trained me up to be a good hostess. She taught me how to make men desirous of me and how, through sexual acts, you could get men to hand you loads of money. I was a good student and within three years I became the highest earner at the Sing Sing Nightclub. That is where I first met Lillian Wang. She was the most beautiful women I had ever seen and besides her beauty she was well educated, unlike most of the hostesses who worked in the club."

She continued, "Lillian and I became close friends, she trusted me and told me all about her past and what she had gone through. I felt sorry for her and treated her like my little sister. When she met you, she was the happiest I had ever seen her. She was exhilarated when you asked her to leave the club and that you would look after her. I was doubtful at first but soon realised that your intentions were true and that you loved her just as much as she loved you. After she left the club, I felt sad as I lost a good friend who I could confide in. It was then that the bombing of the nightclub happened. I know you were there that night with some friends. I was there too that night and it scared the daylights of me. I decided then that I too, like Lillian, would find me a man to support and look after me as I no longer wanted to be a hostess. It was around the time that Lillian was brutally murdered that I first met Hashimoto Kentaro. He would come to the club with his mates. One of them was a person called Kohei Inowaki who took interest in me. Soon Kohei was coming to the club almost every other day to see me. He eventually asked me out on dates and after a few months asked me to leave the club and to be with him and that he would look after me. I thought I was in love and accepted his offer. I was just happy to get away from being a hostess and looking forward to starting a family of my own."

Leslie stared indignantly at her and asked how she could even be with Kohei knowing he had killed Lillian, someone she professed she loved like a sister.

"That is not true. I know for a fact that Kohei had nothing to do with Lillian's death or the bombing of the Sing Song Nightclub. He did, however, kill the two U.S. naval officers and did kidnap and kill Harold and was partially to blame for Ajit's and Inspector Lee's death. However, he had nothing whatsoever to do with the killing of Lillian and the shooting of your horse Sunset!"

Leslie looked at her disbelievingly. "Well, I was told by Kentaro just before he died that the one responsible for Lillian's death was Kohei. Why would he lie to me knowingly when he knew he was about to die? Who else could have killed Lillian? The way she was brutally murdered was what the Black Ninjas do to their victims. Surely if it was not Kentaro it must have been Kohei. What you are telling me makes absolutely no sense."

"Please let me continue and finish my story and hopefully you will arrive at who were responsible for the killing of Lillian and Sunset. As I was saying I left the nightclub and moved in with Kohei. We were both very much in love and he treated me well. I slowly, however, did learn about his dark side but by then I was so engrossed with him I could not leave him. When I heard about Lillian's death, I questioned Kohei on it and he swore that neither Kentaro nor he had anything to do with it. He insisted it was a copycat killing as to make the police and you believe it was the doing of the Black Ninjas. That night, when you raided Kentaro's warehouse and killed him, I was the one who phoned Kohei warning him and his mates not to attend the meeting that Kentaro had organised. I had a call from Liza Wong, John's mistress from the Sing Song Club, telling me she had heard, whilst entertaining John and Raymond at the club, about your raid. Kohei was going to reveal to Kentaro that he and his mates had killed the two naval soldiers but had nothing to do with what happened to Lillian or the bombing of the nightclub. I advised him not to bother as I knew whatever he said that Kentaro would not believe him and as I knew about your raid warned him to hide away and not attend the meeting that Kentaro had called for."

Leslie looked at her. "So it was because of you that Kohei got away and went on to kidnap Harold and kill Ajit. Why are you telling me all this now, you could have come forward earlier and could have saved some lives."

"Sir Leslie, I am sorry that it has caused you so much sadness, but I was mesmerised by Kohei and was in love with him. I thought he loved me, and I was scared of losing him. However, with time I realised he was a monster, especially with what he did to the poor boy Harold. I was too scared to leave him for I feared for my life and also at that time I realised I was pregnant with his child. In the last two years Kohei

305

would look for other women to please him. He did not care if I saw him coming to the house with young beautiful women and make love to them whilst I was there. I thought if I told him about the baby he would change and treat me like he did before, instead he got angry with me. He told me he wanted me to get an abortion and I told him I would not. He got angry and literally threw me out of the house, threating to kill me and the baby if I ever exposed him. He gave me a measly HK$2,500.00 and said if I was ever to show my face again, he would kill me. I went and stayed with Liza Wong, whom you also know, for a while. When she lost her job at the nightclub after John broke up with her, she could not afford to keep me as she had to go and live with her mom. At this time, I learned that I had terminal cancer and as I had nowhere to go, I moved into the Buddhist temple. The monks have been terrific and have provided me and my little girl shelter and food."

Leslie was listening intently and asked, "If it was not Kohei that killed Lillian and my horse Sunset then do you know who did? Did Kohei know and did he tell you anything about that?"

"With Sunset I am not sure as I had already left Kohei by then but with Lillian, Kohei believed that it was probably your cousin from Sun Yee On, or Ponytail from the 14K that did the crime. He actually knew about the bombing of the nightclub and who was involved with that and said that it was the doing of Herbert Sun of the Sun Yee On. After the raid on Kentaro, Kohei and I took shelter with the Sun Yee On. Your cousin Herbert Sun, who was its leader, took us in with open arms. He financed Kohei in setting up his own unit which he called the "Samurais". The Samurais, under the leadership of Kohei, targeted a number of kidnappings with 30% of the proceeds going to Sun Yee On. However, Herbert was upset when Kohei killed Harold after he kidnapped him. He told Kohei that there was no need for that as he got paid and should have released Harold. By doing what Kohei did caused a lot of problems to the triads from the government who looked to be tougher with them and threatened their existence. He asked Kohei to leave the security of the compound of the Sun Yee On and move elsewhere. He also ordered Kohei to stop the killing of expats and if he did do so again, he would feel the full force of wrath from the Sun Yee On."

Leslie looked at his watch it, was already seven thirty p.m. and he still wanted to hear more. He excused himself from the table and said he needed to let his chauffeur know that he would still be a while. He went outside, met the chauffeur and asked him to go back home. He would take a taxi back when he finished. The driver nodded and Leslie went back to the table to hear what else Betty had to say.

"After the unsuccessful raid you had in Macau Kohei and his gang went into hiding. They all had made a great deal of money, especially Kohei who got the major share of 50% of the ransom money. The gang broke up and they went their own ways, most of whom went back to their motherland Japan. Kohei decided to stay in Hong Kong as he loved the city and bought a house in Beacon Hill actually not too far from where you live. I was with him for a short while till he kicked me out. He now lives with this whore whom he met at the Suzy Wong Nightclub. She is only a child just eighteen years old and almost thirty-five years younger than him. He has changed his identity and runs a convenience shop in Kowloon Tsai. He goes by the name of Tony Hsu these days. He still loves gambling but does not go to Macau for fear of being spotted. Nowadays he bets on the horses via the bookies and places his multiple bets with the Jockey Club every race day. He is a person who likes routine so if you need to catch him that would be the best time to do so. His house is fully fitted with the latest alarms and he has a couple of Dobermans as guard dogs. I will write down his address for you before you leave. There is one more thing I want to say to you. Beware of people whom you consider your good friends, there are a lot of people out there who want you dead. I think it is best you speak to Liza Wong, she can tell you a lot more, especially about John Woods and Raymond Ho. She is quite desperate at the moment and if you offered her some money, I am sure she could reveal things that you need to know. I will also give you details on where to find her."

Leslie was shocked with what he heard especially when Betty said to beware of his friends John and Raymond. He never suspected them of doing anything harmful to him. Recently he had noticed that John had been acting strangely but he put it down to pressure he was getting from the governor. He had known John for many years, ever since he had first arrived from the U.K. and their families had always been very close. He thought many times that John was a bit lacking in his professionalism as commissioner of police, but he never suspected John of doing any harm to anyone especially him or his family. With Raymond Leslie knew that he had connections with the 14K but that he was a respectable crook. He had always helped Leslie out when he needed information from the triads, especially from Ponytail. He always felt that Raymond was honest with him, although in the early days of their relationship he was forewarned by people to be careful of him. Lillian always spoke highly of him saying even though he had connections with the "Dark Societies" he was a decent human being.

Betty continued, "I have given you all the information and now you can go and get Kohei and more. You must now keep your promise and take my little girl and make sure she has a decent life as you have promised. I am not going to be here for very long and I will rest in peace once I know my daughter is safe and well looked after."

Leslie looked at her. "I promise you this: if what you have told me is true, I will arrange with the social welfare department to allow me adopt your child. I am, after all, in that committee and that will be no problem whatsoever, I will ensure that my family looks after her like one of the Sun family members. She will get the best education money can buy and will live in a household that will provide her with security and love but if you have lied, I will make sure that she is put straight into an orphanage upon your death."

Betty nodded in agreement. She borrowed Leslie's pen and wrote on her napkin Kohei's and Liza Wong's addresses and phone numbers. She reached out and took Leslie's hands and kissed them.

"I know you are a man of your word. I have full belief in what you say. I will wait for you to do what you have to and then come back for my baby girl." She stood up and walked towards the temple with her child in her arms who was still fast asleep. Leslie took a taxi home, thinking all the way what Betty had told him.

Chapter 16
'April Is The Cruellest Month...'

Leslie's Study
888 Nathan Road, Kowloon, Hong Kong
April 30th, 1966, seven thirty a.m.

Leslie was sitting alone in his study thinking back to what happened the day after he spoke to Betty at the temple. As the governor had predicted all hell broke loose on the streets of Hong Kong. Crowds started gathering at around six p.m., and violence broke out among the protesters in Kowloon a few hours later. On the busy thoroughfare of Nathan Road mobs threw stones at buses and set vehicles on fire. The Yau Ma Tei police station was also attacked by a crowd of over three hundred people. Riot police fired tear gas in response, but people continued to gather in Nathan Road, with the mob almost doubling in size once Hong Kong's cinemas closed at midnight. The rioters looted shops and attacked and set fire to public facilities including fire and power stations. Riot police continued to fire tear gas into the crowds and in some cases fired their carbines at looters. During that night, seven hundred and seventy-two tear gas canisters, sixty-two wooden shells and sixty-two carbine rounds were fired. The British army, under Major General Chris Wolfe, was called into action. Soldiers, with bayonets fixed on their rifles, patrolled the streets in Kowloon enforcing a curfew that was imposed around one thirty a.m.

The next day the government announced that the curfew would start earlier, at seven p.m., and warned that any rioters risked being shot. But that night rioters still gathered on Nathan Road near Mong Kok. Again, vehicles were set on fire and shops looted. Hundreds of people attempted, unsuccessfully, to set fire to the Yau Ma Tei and Mong Kok police stations. During the course of the evening, two hundred and eighty rounds of tear gas and two hundred and eighteen baton rounds were used. One protester was killed, four injured, and two hundred and fifteen arrests were made. All this for a HK$0.05 cent rise in the Star Ferry. In the next few days things went back to normal and the curfew was lifted, but the communists made a huge thing about it and this was the beginning of what was to be Hong Kong's most difficult time the following year.

Leslie arranged for a private meeting with the governor. They met at Government House behind closed doors. They discussed the protests and how they had turned to riots and looting. The governor was critical of the way the police handled things and was adamant that his decision to call in the army was a correct one. He told Leslie that he was not impressed with the way that Sir John Woods had handled the kidnapping of Harold, the recent killings of Inspector Lee and Ajit and the shooting of Sunset. He had received a lot of pressure from the prime minister, especially after Sunset was shot at the racetrack as that was televised worldwide. There needed to be a big shake up within the police force and he was giving Leslie special powers till the ICAC was set up to take whatever action he needed in reforming the whole system.

Leslie told him that he believed he had discovered the whereabouts of Kohei. He said that he did not tell Sir John about this as he did not want it leaked as Kohei could then make a run for it if he found out. Leslie said he had no trust in the police as he felt the corruption was rampant and it went all the way to the top. He suggested that he get the Warriors of the Sun to take care of the capture of Kohei. The governor gave him his blessing and said that once he had captured Kohei to please inform Sir Anthony Brown so he could finally find peace, knowing the killer of his son Harold had been caught. He went on to tell the governor that he was close to a breakthrough of who were behind the killing of Lillian Wang and Sunset but until he had concrete proof he did not wish to speculate. He would, once he finished with his findings, report back to him and see what action needed to be taken.

Leslie then turned back to the riots. He told the governor it was not because of the rise of the fare of the Star Ferry that was the main cause of this protest. It was just a build-up of frustration by the public over the state of how Hong Kong was governed, and the protests were a release of this frustration. He highlighted to the governor how unsatisfied the public was with law enforcement and with areas of the public services in Hong Kong being corrupt. He said the communists were behind the protests turning violent. Some of the people who mixed with the protestors were placed by the communist party to stir up the violence and looting. This was to force the hand of the government in the calling out of the army to quell the rioting which just added merit to the Red Army that the British government could not take care of the welfare of the people of Hong Kong and that China should take back the colony by force if needed. It was a dangerous situation and the government needed to be ready for any disturbances in future that could bring the colony into turmoil. The governor nodded and thanked Leslie for all his efforts. As Leslie left the governor congratulated him for the opening of the Sun Tower and apologised once again that he was unable to attend the ceremony at the end of the month due to prior engagements taking him away from the colony that day.

When Leslie got home, he set up a plan to have Kohei captured. He now had the approval of the governor to capture Kohei without the aid of the police. He reflected back on what had happened after his meeting with Betty. Whatever she told him was true. Kohei had changed his identity to Tony Hsu and was living in Beacon Hill. He called for a meeting with the Warriors of the Sun and told them that he had discovered where Kohei was hiding out. He did not reveal to them that he had found this out from Betty. They then worked on a plan to capture Kohei. From speaking to Betty, he knew that Kohei would visit the Jockey Club shop on Saturdays to place his multiple bets. The weekend before the opening of Sun Tower he had the warriors waiting for Kohei as he stepped out of the betting shop and surrounded him. Kohei knew he could not escape so he reached out to his pocket and pulled out a butterfly knife, placed it to his throat and slashed it open. Within seconds he was lying on the floor dead.

Leslie re-focussed on the file in front of him. It was obvious from all the evidence he had gathered that John had been bribed by the triads. He felt sick with the thought and this caused his head to pound. He reached for his pills and gulped down a bunch, hoping that would ease the pain. It was clear and without doubt that John had been receiving bribes from Raymond and that they probably were also involved with the killing of Inspector Lee. His meeting with Liza Wong unlocked facts that opened up the investigation and led to his greatest fear that both Raymond and John were guilty. How could he have been so stupid not to have seen through them? He had not yet revealed his findings to anyone, not even to his son Herman. He wanted to confront both John and Ray face to face and tell them what he knew. He felt that was the correct way as he wanted to see how they would react. He recognised that before arresting Sir John Woods he needed to present his findings to the governor and get his approval to arrest him because of his rank. He took the file from the desk and went towards his bookshelves and concealed it between two books on the top shelf, hiding it from sight. He could not afford for anyone to see it prior to him meeting the governor.

His plan was that on Tuesday, May 2nd, when the governor returned from Singapore, he would tell him about his findings. Hopefully he would get the approval from him to arrest both John and Raymond. He had already invited both John and Raymond to meet at Gaddi's for dinner on Thursday, May 4th, saying he had some important information he wanted to share with them. He would arrange for Lieutenant Edward Wolfe to stand guard with some military soldiers outside the restaurant. He would have him arrest them as they left the restaurant after the meal.

Leslie remembered vividly his conversation with Liza Wong. At first, she was frightened to tell him anything but after a bit of coaxing and offering her money she told him all that he needed to know. She said that many a time, when Sir John visited the Sing Song Club, he would be there to meet up with Raymond Ho. She had witnessed many a time huge amounts of money being passed from John to Raymond and vice versa. She had heard Sir John ask Raymond to send the money to his account in Switzerland via Raymond's bank the Bank of Credit and Commerce (BCCI). She told him that in one conversation she heard them discuss Leslie's arrest of Inspector Lee. She overheard them saying that they could not allow him to be interrogated as they would be exposed and deliberated how they should get rid of the inspector. Leslie thanked her and paid her the money she asked for. He requested if he had any more questions could he come and see her again, to which she replied affirmatively. The next day when Leslie went to see Liza again to dig deeper into the investigation Liza Wong and her mother were nowhere to be found. She seemed to have disappeared from the face of the earth. He asked Betty if she knew where she was and was told that she had no clue.

Leslie approached the manager of the BCCI to look into Ray's account. Leslie knew of this bank which was owned by Arab connections and its manager Ashok Mirpuri who was known to be shady. He warned him that if he did not let him see this, he would get the governor and the financial service to revoke the bank's license. He also told him that he was under no circumstances to let Raymond know that he had gone through his accounts. By going through the accounts Leslie discovered that millions of dollars had been transmitted from Raymond Ho's account to an account at the Credit Suisse Bank in Zurich, Switzerland under the name of J. Woods. Leslie started to wonder if it was Raymond who was involved with the killing of Lillian. Nothing made sense to him.

A week after the death of Kohei, Betty passed away from a stroke which was a result from her cancer condition. When he found this out from the head monk, he immediately applied to the social services to adopt Betty's child. The paperwork was done in record time and within four days it was confirmed that the child would be adopted by Leslie and Nancy Sun. Leslie did not have difficulty in Nancy accepting the child. He had told her that the woman whose child they were adopting had helped him in finding out the whereabouts of Kohei. He further explained that she had died of cancer and that he had promised to take her child in as their daughter. Nancy was a bit taken aback at first but thought how wonderful and kind of her husband. She actually looked forward to having a little girl to look after. They named the baby after her mother and baby Betty Sun became a member of the family. Nobody could have guessed then that one day she would be the most important person in the transformation of Hong Kong.

Leslie looked at his watch, it was 8.55 a.m. He had asked Herman and Lucy to meet him in his study at nine a.m. to discuss the final preparations for the opening ceremony this evening of the Sun Tower.

Just then Herman knocked on the door of his study and entered. Herman said that Wan-Yu had told him that he had been in the study since six thirty a.m. and was wondering what his father was doing so early in the morning. Leslie looked at Herman and said that he had finally discovered who were behind the killings of Lillian, Ajit and Sunset. Herman looked surprised, saying he thought that was Kohei's doing and the case was closed. Leslie was about to tell Herman everything when there was another knock on the door. It was Lucy. Leslie told Herman that he would discuss with him about that later tonight and as Lucy had arrived for them to focus on that night's event. They went through all the details of the evening. Two hundred and fifty guests had been invited from all walks of life to attend. Cocktails and snacks were to be served from four to six p.m. at the lounge of the Peninsula Hotel. The party would then move from there to the Sun Tower which was a five-minute walk. Leslie would make a speech after which David Poon would be handed the golden scissors and cut the ribbon. The guests would then follow Lucy who would show them round the building, highlighting the modern facilities and they would all meet in a room set up for more cocktails and snacks. Everything should be over by seven thirty p.m. Lucy smiled and said to her dad not to worry everything would be just fine. She had gone through all the details with the Peninsula Hotel and her team and there would be no hiccups. When they finished Lucy excused herself saying she was going to meet up with Mabel to pick up her dress for the evening.

Lucy was excited to pick up her dress which was exclusively designed for her by Mabel. She wanted to look exceptional for Lieutenant Edward who was her date for the evening. She had not seen him for over three weeks as he had been on active duty and on standby because of the riots. She had spoken to him a number of times, but it did not make up for actually seeing him. She thought back to the girls' night they had last week. It was such a fun night. She was anxious to find out how Mabel got along with this mystery man she met at the Polaris Nightclub that evening. She had not seen Mabel that interested in a man since she dated Herman. Lucy idolised Mabel. She was Lucy's best friend and ever since Herman and Mabel broke up Lucy got even closer to her. Mabel helped Lucy feel better by making her go to the gym with her three times a week which helped her lose weight. She also taught Lucy how to beautify herself by using make-up properly and taught her what to wear to accentuate her body. She would force Lucy to join her in many social functions which Lucy would usually not attend: this helped her come out of her shell. Because of Mabel Lucy grew in confidence and became the woman she was now. She felt lucky to have a friend like Mabel and often wondered how Herman could have chosen Ella over her. To her Ella was very devious, sure she was very sweet to her when they were in front of family and friends but that was all for show rather than any true feeling for her. Mabel greeted Lucy with a huge hug as she entered the "CHYNA" flagship shop in Central. There were already a large crowd of shoppers there, mostly Japanese. Mabel took Lucy's hand and led her to her office at the back of the shop.

"How are you, sweetie, you must be excited about this evening? This will be the first large event that you have organised, you must have butterflies in your tummy. I have the dress almost ready, it just needs a slight adjustment and is with the tailor right now but should be back in another ten minutes. Meanwhile can I get you a cup of coffee?"

"Yes, I would love a cuppa. How have you been? I want to know what happened with you and that attractive gentleman after Anita and I left the Polaris Nightclub. Did you end up having sex with him?" she laughed. She continued, "you were all over him when we left that Anita and I were sure that you would end up going to bed with him."

"That gentleman has a name by the way and that is Mark Warren," giggled Mabel. "And yes, we screwed that night and I have been screwing with him every day since this week! I am madly in love with him but realise that maybe I may never see him again once he leaves Hong Kong tonight. We have made plans to meet again in Paris next month, but you never know do you? I have enjoyed every single moment spent with him and I will miss him. He is a great lover, gentle and kind, I only wish we met under different circumstances and that he did not have to leave so soon. I know it must sound stupid to you, but I actually think I am in love with him."

Lucy remembered that evening well. The girls all decided to go to the newly renovated Hyatt Hotel in Tsim Sha Tsui. The hotel was recently purchased and renovated by Mabel's future stepfather and partner in business David Poon. He had arranged for the girls to go there free and be treated as VIPs. It had an exquisite bar at the basement called the Chin Chin Bar, a fine dining restaurant on the second called Hugo's and on the top floor overlooking Hong Kong Harbour the trendiest disco in the colony called "The Polaris". The girls started by meeting at the Chin Chin Bar at six p.m. They were met by the manager, Mr Chow, who led them to their table. The girls were all dressed up and looked stunning especially Mabel who was wearing silk fabric hot pants with a sequinned black top and a see-through long vest jacket. They started by having cocktails, starting with Singapore Slings and then moving to something stronger like Long Island Iced Tea. They then headed up to the restaurant for dinner. They had the best table in the restaurant that looked out to the harbour. Mabel ordered champagne to celebrate her latest success in Japan and they all ordered the same meal, no main course but instead two appetisers, escargots and fresh Sydney rock oysters. They followed this up with Crêpes Suzette as dessert which was flambéed beside their table. By the time they decided to move up to Polaris they had finished five bottles of champagne amongst them and were pretty sloshed.

The Polaris Nightclub was the latest hotspot in Hong Kong. Located on the seventeenth floor, it had a panoramic view of Hong Kong. It was for the trendy crowd, catered to the young elite society of the colony. You would be met at the entrance and if the manager did not think you dressed appropriately enough to enter, he would turn you away saying the club would not entertain anybody dressed inappropriately. When they arrived, they were met by Kitty Chan, the head hostess of the club, who went out of her way to ensure they had everything they needed. She had arranged a special table looking at the dance floor and near the bar. They ordered shots of tequila and were in a great mood. Mabel noticed an attractive man sitting at the bar alone having what looked like Scotch. She found him striking and was wondering why he was there all by himself. Was he waiting for a date? She pointed him out to the girls who dared her to approach him and have a bit of a flirt. Mabel said she needed to get a lot drunker before doing that. Around this time, they saw Bella enter the club with her arms around a tall blonde girl. Anita had been trying all week to get hold of Bella to see if she would join them that night and when she finally got hold of her was told that she would love to but had an important meeting the next morning and wanted to get to bed early. Seeing her there infuriated her but she decided to be the better person and walked to her table to say hello. Bella just brushed her aside, took the hand of the girl she was with and headed for the dance floor. Anita felt dejected and went back to the girls upset. She was angry with the way she was treated and more dismayed for being lied to. She wanted to get drunk and ordered more shots of tequila. Mabel noticed that the good-looking man at the bar kept looking her way and when he winked at her she built up her courage and walked up to him.

"Hiya there," she said giggling. "Have you been stood up? You are very welcome to join us girls at our table. My name is Mabel and my two beautiful friends are Anita and Lucy. Do you have a name dear sir?"

He looked at her and smiled. "Thanks for the invitation and I will definitely take you up and join you and your friends. My name is Mark, Mark Warren." He stretched forward and gave her a kiss on both cheeks. Being close to him Mabel could see how handsome he really was. He had dark brown hair, was well tanned and had beautiful green eyes. He was tall, about six feet, and had a well-formed body.

They went back to the table and Mark ordered two bottles of Dom Perignon. The girls all were taken by him as, besides being gorgeous looking, he was a true gentleman. He would ensure the girls' glasses were always topped up and whenever any of them stood up to go to the toilet he would stand up too. He explained that he was an investment broker and lived in London. He was in Hong Kong to meet up with potential investors. This was his second trip to Hong Kong, and he was staying at the Peninsula Hotel. Lucy came straight out and asked him if he was married. He laughed and said that "currently" he was single and available. They all continued drinking and chatting and were getting quite drunk. Mabel and Mark soon were kissing and making out and Lucy made a joke saying they should go to Mark's hotel instead of steaming up the place. Anita was downing the tequila shots, hoping for it to supress her sorrow over Ella, and soon became intoxicated. Lucy said she would take her home and asked Mabel if she wanted to leave. Mabel said that she would stay longer and have a few more drinks together with Mark.

After the girls left Mark asked Mabel if she would join him for a drink back at his suite at the hotel. She said she would be delighted to join him for a nightcap. They both strolled to the hotel, hand in hand. When they entered the suite, Mark kissed her passionately and carried her to the bed. He kept kissing her while undressing her and they made love over and over again. Mabel kept getting orgasms, one after another, and had never felt this way before, not even with Herman. He was gentle with his lovemaking but knew exactly what to do to make her come. The next morning when Mabel awoke, she noticed Mark was not beside her in the bed. She walked out the bedroom to the main room and there he was, sitting at a table that was set up for breakfast for two, sipping a cup of coffee.

"I did not know what you wanted for breakfast, so I ordered the whole breakfast menu. I did choose coffee instead of tea as you strike me as a coffee drinker. We have boiled eggs, scrambled eggs and poached eggs. Got all types of bread: wholemeal, sourdough and some brioche rolls. Ham, bacon, sausages and pancakes. Also got some fruit: fresh strawberries, mangoes, bananas and apples. In addition, we also have some cereals and milk. How did I do?" he smiled.

She burst out laughing. "I am so flattered that you thought of me but actually I am not much of a breakfast person. I usually only have toast with coffee but tell you what, because you made such an effort, I am going to dig in and join you in this beautiful feast you have served up."

For the next week Mabel and Mark met each night. They would convene every night for cocktails at the Chin Chin bar and have dinner in the various five-star restaurants around Tsim Tsa Tsui, always ending the evening at Mark's suite. They got along brilliantly as they had the same likes for poetry, books, movies and dining out. Mabel did not want the romance to end when Mark left back for London. She told him that she had to be in Paris in mid-May to open her first "CHYNA" store there after which she would be going on to Grasse in France to develop her first perfume fragrance. Grasse, she explained, was the place in

France that most of the famous perfume brands were created. Brands like Chanel, Christian Dior, Estée Lauder and many others were created in this small town located in the Alpes-Maritimes, northwest of Nice. Mark said he would definitely take time out of his business and meet her in Paris and if she desired follow her on to Grasse. She was thrilled that he would join her as she was falling in love with him. She had never in her life met a man who could make her feel the way he did. He pleased her both mentally and physically and she was comfortable being around him. He said when he got back to London he was moving to a new apartment and as soon as he got his new telephone number, he would pass it on to her. He promised he would call her every day whilst he was away even just to say hello.

One of Mabel's staff knocked on the door of her office and when asked to enter came in carrying Lucy's dress. It was a beautiful black dress made of a lightweight crêpe fabric, slim fitting in the bodice with a relaxed fitted skirt. It had slightly puffed shoulders and a high slit. The dress was well structured and looked magnificent. Lucy tried it on and looked at the mirror, saying she loved it and that it fitted perfectly. She thanked Mabel and hugged her, asking how much she owed her. Mabel laughed, saying that was a gift from her and not to worry about paying her.

"You cannot keep giving me gifts Mabel the amount of clothes I get from you and you never charging me will bankrupt you girlie," she laughed. "Seriously if you continue not charging me, I will not come to you for dresses and that will upset me as I love your clothes so much. I feel so guilty getting these lovely outfits free every time. Can you just let me pay for this? Please!"

"OK, the next time I will charge you at cost but seriously I am happy to give you these dresses for free as by you wearing it, it's great advertising for my brand 'CHYNA', so actually you are doing me a favour." Lucy thanked Mabel again and left to prepare for the event that evening.

John was seated behind his desk in his office. In front of him was a file that his secretary, Angela Ho, put on his desk. He opened it and saw a report back from Interpol. The bullets that hit Ajit and killed Sunset were from the same rifle. They were handmade and were associated to an assassin known to the CIA and other criminal agencies around the world as the Black Hawk. Apparently, he was responsible for some very high-profile assassinations, the most famous was that of John. F. Kennedy. The FBI had determined that the shot from Harvey Oswald that was supposed to have killed Kennedy was not the one that took his life. This was kept secret. The bullet found rooted in Kennedy's skull was a silver bullet which was handmade. It was believed the Black Hawk was hired by some of Kennedy's enemies to eliminate him. It was a political verdict and probably ordered by a discontented Republican. Lee Harvey Oswald was just a scapegoat. There had been a number of high-profile assassinations worldwide by the man only known as the Black Hawk. His true identity was not known as he was very careful to keep that a secret. He left no evidence as to who he was and the only thing that was consistent were the silver bullets that he used. John shut the file and called Raymond.

Herman was sitting in his chauffeured car on his way to pick up Ella for the event. He looked at his watch, it was close to three p.m. He hoped that Ella would be ready as he needed to be there early to ensure all was in order and in time to receive the arrival of the first guests. He knew Ella's habit of always being late and therefore added a half hour earlier than when he needed to pick her up. Ella had changed after they got engaged. She became more materialistic and was worried about the way she looked, constantly shopping for clothes and jewellery and stopped doing any work with the charities she once supported. The only thing on her mind was the wedding and how she looked for that occasion. He remembered the argument they had when Ella said to him not to send an invitation to Mabel for the wedding. Herman outrightly refused to do that, and she accused him of still having feelings for her. He explained clearly that the two families have been close ever since he was a boy and that his parents would not allow that to happen. She finally gave in but expressed she was not happy with that decision.

It was three p.m. and Leslie was there with Lucy at the lobby of the Peninsula Hotel talking to the manager. They were impressed with the set-up and thanked him for doing such a wonderful job. They had come earlier than the rest of the family to ensure all was in place. Nancy and the rest of his family would arrive by three forty-five p.m. To Leslie this was the day that he had waited for a long time, having a world-class office building for his businesses. The Sun Tower fulfilled his expectations. It was by far the tallest and most striking building in the colony. It had been a rough year for Leslie, and he dreaded the thought of having to face John and Raymond next week to expose them and have them arrested. He had always considered John a close friend and someone he trusted. It hurt that the two people he was closest to had betrayed him. His thoughts turned to Herman who was late arriving. He had given him the best chance in life, having sent him to the best school and university and getting real life experience working with some of the top executives in his businesses. The only thing he did worry about Herman was that he was emotional and sometimes made decisions out of emotion rather than reason.

Nancy still did not know of Leslie's health condition as only Herman was aware of this. She was totally engrossed with the upcoming wedding which was scheduled for June 2nd. She was determined to make it the biggest wedding Hong Kong would ever see. She had invited celebrities and politicians from around the world to attend. The sit-down dinner after the wedding ceremony would be for eight hundred guests and she had arranged through Bella to hire the American band the Four Tops to perform. The wedding was going to cost a fortune, but she did not care as Leslie gave her carte blanche. The jewellery she had ordered for Ella for the three main functions alone had cost over HK$50 million. She was happy that Herman had asked Ella to marry him as she had always thought highly of her.

The first people to arrive were David Poon, Maggie and Mabel, who walked in together. They were followed by Leslie's family, his mother Elaine, sister Irene with her two children Richard and Yvonne. It was 3.55 p.m. and Herman had still not showed up. Leslie was pacing up and down wondering where he was. He had specifically told Herman not to be late as he needed to be with the rest of the family standing together to greet their guests. He asked Lucy if she knew where he was. She said that he left extra early to pick up Ella and maybe they were stuck in traffic. Just before four p.m. Herman arrived with Ella. He apologised to his father for being late but said that Ella took longer than he expected to get ready. His father did not look pleased as he wanted to go through Herman's speech before the guests arrived and now there was no time for that. Right after Herman arrived the rest of the guests started to come in. Raymond walked in together with his niece Angela and Bella. John and Niko were of the last to arrive. Soon the hall was filled with guests having drinks and enjoying the event.

Lucy pulled David Poon to the side to explain to him the procedures one more time. They would be moving from the Peninsula to the Sun Tower at exactly five forty-five p.m. It was a five-minute walk from the hotel, and they were lucky that it was a beautiful day. Lucy had been worried all week as it had been raining heavily and if today was the same, she would have needed to adjust her plan. She explained that when they got to the entrance of Sun Tower and all the guests were around there would be a lion dance. The lion dance is a form of traditional dance in Chinese culture in which performers mimic a lion's movements to bring luck and good fortune. Following that Leslie would make a welcome speech after which he would hand David golden scissors to cut the ribbon. As the ribbon was being cut firecrackers, hung from the fourth floor of the building to the ground, would be lit. It was believed, according to Chinese folklore, that fireworks would frighten off any evil that could be surrounding the area.

Everybody was dressed exceptionally well for the occasion. It was one of the first major events of the year and the women were out there to impress. Ella, however, stood out as she was over the top with her dress. It was beautiful but really not suitable for this occasion. It was more a gown that one would wear to a formal ball and she did look out of place. Herman had mentioned that to her when he picked her up, but she brushed him aside saying that he had no idea of fashion sense. The outfit was an original Yves Saint Laurent and had cost HK$150,000. Nancy, when she saw Ella walking in with it, was taken aback with the outfit finding it ostentatious and mentioned it to Lucy. Lucy smiled and said clearly that she wore it to make a statement and commented also on the jewellery that Ella had on which was way too much. She had a diamond necklace around her neck that looked like it weighed a ton with matching earrings and bracelet. Lucy told her mom that she had purchased that from Tiffany and that she had chosen it together with Ella to be worn in one of the main parties of the wedding and not for an occasion like today. The most elegant outfits were worn by Mabel and Lucy and they got the most compliments.

Just before 5.40 p.m. Herman got on the podium to make his speech. Herman was a good speaker as he learned his skills from attending Dale Carnegie classes. He thanked the guests for joining and spoke about the history of the Sun family and how proud he was being Leslie's son. He thanked his father for teaching him and making him the man he was today. He said that the Sun Tower had been his father's dream for many years, and he was delighted that he could now share this dream with the community. After he finished his speech, he asked the gathering to follow him to the Sun Tower for the ribbon cutting ceremony and to continue the merriments.

When they reached the entrance of the tower the lion dance took place. It was quite spectacular as the lion train was longer than the usual with over fifty people making it up. It was accompanied by performers beating drums, clashing cymbals, and resounding gongs. Lion dancing originated during the Tang Dynasty (618—906 A.D.). The lion quickly became a symbol of good luck throughout China. It was believed that the dancing lion chased away evil spirits. When the dance concluded Leslie made his speech, he once again thanked the guests for attending. He said he was grateful to all the people who had helped in building up the businesses of the Sun Group especially his hard-working staff and as a special gift of thank you he was offering every single staff member a gift packet of HK$10,000 as appreciation for their hard work in making the company one of the best run, and most profitable in the colony. He explained how the Sun family had been a part of Hong Kong since it became British in 1841 and the close relationship between his forefathers and the British government which still existed today. He said the governor was supposed to have attended but due to obligations overseas he could not come but sent him a telegram that morning which he wanted to read to the people out there.

"Dear Leslie,

On behalf of Her Majesty Queen Elizabeth II and the British government I want to congratulate you on this very special day. The

Sun family has always been a bright spot with the development of Hong Kong since it became a colony. Leslie, since I have been governor, I have learned further about your character. You are strong in your beliefs and work hard for the betterment of Hong Kong. The countless charities that Nancy and you have donated to and the Sun Trust have helped thousands of people in need in the colony. I wish I could be there with your family and friends today to witness the opening of the Sun Tower but unfortunately, due to other commitments, I am unable to do so. On behalf of my wife Jocelyn, I wish you many successes to come. I am happy to announce that the Queen has asked me to grant you a new title which has never been awarded to anyone living outside the United Kingdom before. The title she has asked me to bestow to you is that of Lord and from now on you will be addressed as Lord Leslie Sun and your wife as Lady Sun.

God Bless you and your family,

With sincerest regards,

Sir William Sandhill"

The guests clapped long and loud as Leslie finished his speech. Leslie than called upon David Poon to do the honours of cutting the ribbon to formally declare the opening of Sun Tower. As David went forward to cut the ribbon the fireworks were set alight. Leslie was next to David when suddenly he threw his head back sharply as if something had hit him. Herman, who was nearby, rushed to see what the matter was as Leslie collapsed to the floor. He was bleeding profusely from the back of his head. Herman shouted out for help and both Raymond and John ran to Herman who was cradling his father's head, the blood flowing, covering his body. John asked Herman to call for an ambulance whilst Raymond stayed with Leslie. John said he was going to get the police there and asked the crowd to back away. The police were there in minutes and the area was cordoned off. Meanwhile whilst Raymond was alone holding up Leslie's head, Leslie looked directly at Ray and whispered "Ponytail."

The ambulance arrived eight minutes after Herman called and Leslie was carried into it. Nancy, who was sobbing away, insisted that she got into the ambulance with her husband. The guests started to disperse soon after, most in a state of shock. Meanwhile Herman and Lucy asked the rest of the family to go home and wait for news whilst they followed the ambulance to the hospital. Ella wanted to join but was told that it would be better she stayed home and be with the family. John had his men there to scale the area to see if they could find the person or persons responsible and to check with anyone there if they saw anything. Leslie was definitely shot in the back of his head from a high-powered rifle, probably from one of the buildings opposite the Sun Tower and John sent his men to search the rooftops of the buildings and to check with security in those buildings to ask if they noticed anything out of the ordinary.

When the ambulance arrived at the hospital Leslie was rushed into the emergency room. The top surgeons were there to try and revive him. They managed to remove a fragment of the bullet from his head but could not save him. Leslie was proclaimed dead twenty minutes after he entered the hospital. Nancy went hysterical on hearing the news that her beloved husband had passed away and Herman and Lucy both had to forego their own sorrow to console their mother. The governor, who was supposed to arrive back in Hong Kong two days later, cut short his trip when he heard from his secretary by telephone of what had happened. He was shocked to hear the news and could not believe that his dear friend had been killed. He took the last plane out of Singapore and arrived back in Hong Kong just before midnight. The next day he announced that there would be a state funeral for Leslie. He ordered an emergency meeting with the police, army, security heads and private advisors to discuss how something so dreadful could once again happen. It seemed that Leslie and his family were targeted, and he needed to find out the culprit or culprits behind all these shootings and ensure they were caught. He was determined to use whatever resources he had to get rid of crime that existed in the colony which seemed to get from bad to worse.

Mark Warren was seated in the first-class cabin of British Airways on his flight back to London. He looked at his watch, it was eleven thirty p.m. The flight was already thirty minutes' late in taking off. He was thinking of his time in Hong Kong, the highlight of which was meeting Mabel. He had genuinely gotten close to her and loved her company, which was unlike him as he made it a point not to get involved when he was on a job. He was contemplating whether he should contact her again, his heart was telling him he must while his brain was saying that would be a risky thing to do. The first-class cabin had only three other passengers that evening, so Mark was enjoying exceptional service. There was in particular a stewardess who paid him special attention and it was obvious that she fancied him. She kept coming to him, topping his flute with champagne, and kept asking him if there was anything else she could get him. They got to talking and he discovered she was called Cynthia, twenty-four years old, from London. In the next ten minutes she had revealed to him she was single and lived alone and had been working as a stewardess for only six months. She asked him whether he lived in Hong Kong to which he replied that he did not and was only there for business as he actually also lived in London.

Mark was pleased with what he achieved in Hong Kong. He took out a telegram from his pocket and read it again. It was from bank Credit Suisse and addressed to Mr M. Warren.

"As per your request we are forwarding this telegram to the Peninsula Hotel in Hong Kong to your attention. This is to confirm that a bank transfer has been made to your account number 98450954674-989 for US$25,000,000.00 to our Geneva branch. The money has been sent from account number 29879882598-888 from our Zurich branch. If there are any discrepancies, please contact us in the usual way. On behalf of Credit Suisse Bank Zurich."

Not bad for three weeks of work he thought. This was the most he had been paid for any assignment. Well, it did involve three jobs. He had to be careful though and disappear for a few months at least and not take up any more assignments. He thought to himself maybe it is a good time for the Black Hawk to retire. With the money he made over the last five years he could live a lifetime of luxury. Suddenly his thought came back to Mabel whom he genuinely was missing. He'd had many affairs before, but none had touched him the way that Mabel had. He could go to Paris next month and catch up with her. He really was struggling with that thought when Cynthia approached him.

"We will be taking off, Mr Warren, in a couple of minutes, could you please fasten your seat belt. Would you like me to fix you another drink after take-off? Will you stay with the champagne or shall I get you something else?" He replied that he would love a double Johnnie Walker Black Label on the rocks. She smiled and as she started to walk away, she handed him a note.

It read, "This is my number in London +44 020 7867865. It would be nice to catch up there maybe for dinner. Call me. Love, Cynthia." Mark smiled and thought, maybe I will take her up on that.

The next day almost every newspaper, both domestically and internationally, carried the story of the shooting of Leslie. In the local papers it was on the front page and almost all criticised the government and specifically the police of not being capable of doing their job. The prime minister of the United Kingdom appeared on BBC to say that he was sorry for what had happened to Lord Leslie Sun and sent his condolences from the queen and the people of the U.K. to his family and all the citizens of Hong Kong. He went on further to say that he would be sending to Hong Kong a special team from the U.K. to help the police there in their investigations on who were involved and to bring them to justice.

The next week was one of the worst weeks in Herman's life. He could not rely on his family for support as they were all grieving. He was worried most about his mom as she was going through a total mental breakdown. His grandmother Elaine got very ill and had to go to hospital where she was being monitored. Lucy seemed to be angry with the whole world and was criticising everything that Herman was doing with the arrangements of the funeral. The only two people that gave him time and support were Uncle Ray and Uncle John. They were with him all the way, meeting up with him every day and helping him with all the funeral arrangements. He did not let any of his family know of his father's sickness and in a way felt that it was maybe better he died the way he did without suffering a long illness. He was upset that his father would not be able to see Ella and him get married as he was looking forward to that. The wedding had to be postponed indefinitely which upset Ella, who said she understood the reason for delaying the wedding but questioned why they could not re-fix a definite day for later that year.

Lucy wanted their father's coffin to be draped in the U.K. flag and placed in the main hallway of the house for three days allowing the people of Hong Kong to pay their respects for him. Leslie was admired and loved by almost everyone in the colony. He was generous and donated a lot of money to charities and Lucy felt her father would like that. Herman disagreed and said his coffin should lie in the Buddhist temple that Leslie used to go to and one that he had rebuilt. It would also be easier for the people to go there and he felt it more appropriate. He won out and the funeral was held there. Leslie's wish, which he specified in his will, was that he was to be cremated and have his ashes spread on top of Tai Mo Shan Mountain so that it could reach all the corners of the country he loved so much.

Herman had remembered that on the day his father was shot he had mentioned that he had discovered who were responsible for the killings of Lillian, Ajit and Sunset. He was going to tell Herman when they were interrupted by Lucy walking into the study. Knowing his father well he knew that his father would have gathered all the information and probably had a file of his findings and it must be in his study. He searched through all the drawers of his desk but could not find a file referring to this. He found a number of files pertaining to the setting up of the ICAC and another on building up a relationship with the PRC but nothing on the discovery, he spoke of. He knew that it could not be in his office at Sun Corporation as Leslie only kept business documents in that office and all things to do with the government was kept in the study. He checked with Wan-Yu to see if he had seen a file when cleaning up the study or maybe that his father had given him for safe keeping, but Wan-Yu knew nothing of it.

He then thought maybe Leslie would have mentioned his findings to John. He called John and told him what his father had mentioned in the morning before he was shot and asked if his father had discussed this with him. John seemed taken aback and said no but they should look closely for this file, if at all it existed, and suggested he came to help him search for it as it could help find the person or persons who killed Leslie. John came down that day and they did a thorough check of the study and around the house but found no documents of any sort that Leslie had mentioned to Herman about his knowledge of who killed Lillian and Sunset.

Five days after Leslie was cremated Herman drove to the top of Tai Mo Shan, the tallest mountain peak in Kowloon. It was a beautiful day and the sun was just about to set. He could see all of Hong Kong from three hundred and sixty degrees: the view was breathless. There was a slight breeze and he could hear the birds sing. He opened the vase he was holding and started releasing the ashes, letting them fall slowly to the ground. The wind helped to spread the ashes all around. He was feeling sad and at the same time very angry. When he had finished spreading the ashes he reached out into the inside pocket of his jacket and pulled out the nunchaku his father had given him. He held each end of the stick and lifted his hands high up to the sky letting out a loud scream that echoed back. He shouted at the top of his lungs, "Dad I promise you this, I swear to avenge your death, this will be my main aim in life." After saying that he dropped to his knees and started crying loudly.

EPILOGUE

In early May 1967 a labour dispute broke out in a factory producing artificial flowers in San Po Kong. Workers clashed with management, and riot police were called in on May 6th. The factory was owned by David Poon. In violent clashes between the police and the picketing workers, twenty-one workers were arrested; many more were injured. Representatives from the union protested at police stations but were themselves also arrested. The next day, large-scale demonstrations erupted on the streets of Hong Kong. Many of the pro-communist demonstrators carried little red books in their left hands and shouted communist slogans. The Hong Kong police force engaged with the demonstrators and arrested another one hundred and twenty-seven people. A curfew was imposed, and all police forces were called into duty. In the PRC, newspapers praised the demonstrators' activities, calling the British colonial government's actions "fascist atrocities".

In Hong Kong's Central District large loudspeakers were placed on the roof of the Bank of China building, broadcasting pro-communist rhetoric and propaganda, prompting the British authorities to retaliate by putting larger speakers blaring out Cantonese opera. Posters were put up on walls with slogans like "Blood for Blood", "Stew the White-Skinned Pig", "Fry the Yellow Running Dogs", "Down with British Imperialism" and "Hang David", a reference to the new governor of Hong Kong. More violence erupted on May 22nd, with another one hundred and sixty-seven people being arrested. The rioters began to adopt more sophisticated tactics, such as throwing stones at police or vehicles passing by, before retreating into left-wing "strongholds" such as newspaper offices, banks or department stores once the police arrived. Casualties began to start soaring soon after. At least eight deaths of the protestors were recorded before July 1st, mostly shot or beaten to death by the police.

On July 8th, several hundred demonstrators from the PRC,

including members of The People's Militia, crossed the border frontier and attacked the Hong Kong police, of whom five were shot dead and eleven injured in the brief exchange of fire. The People's Daily, in Beijing, ran editorials supporting the left-wing struggle in Hong Kong; rumours that the PRC was preparing to take over control of the colony began to circulate. The communists began planting bombs, as well as decoys, throughout the city. Normal life was severely disrupted, and casualties began to rise. An eight-year-old girl, Wong Yee Man, and her two-year-old brother, Wong Siu Fan, were killed by a bomb wrapped like a gift placed outside their residence. Bomb disposal experts from the police and the British forces defused as many as eight thousand homemade bombs, of which eleven hundred were found to be real.

The Hong Kong government, imposed emergency regulations, granting the police special powers in an attempt to quell the unrest. Left-wing newspapers were banned from publishing, communist schools alleged to be bomb-making factories, many activist leaders were arrested and detained and some of them were later deported to China. The waves of bombings did not subside until October 1967. In December, Chinese leader Zhou Enlai ordered the left-wing groups in Hong Kong to stop all bombings, and the riots in Hong Kong finally came to an end. By the time the rioting subsided at the end of the year, fifty-one people had been killed, of whom at least twenty-two were killed by the police and fifteen died in bomb attacks, with eight hundred and thirty-two people sustaining injuries, while four thousand, nine hundred and seventy-nine people were arrested and one thousand, nine hundred and thirty-six convicted. Millions of dollars in property damage resulted from the rioting, far in excess of that reported during the 1956 riots. Confidence in the colony's future declined among some sections of Hong Kong's populace, and many residents sold their properties and migrated overseas.

This was the Hong Kong Herman faced a year after his father's death. The Sun Corporation stood the test and survived these times but many of the early colonials left. This time the British managed to hold off the communists. However, was this just the beginning of the end?

Herman was in his study. He looked at the calendar which was in front of him and it showed it was December 24th, 1969. He had just finished a session with the government's legal team finalising the law that was to be enacted early the next year. It was something his father had pushed for and Herman was glad that he was able to finish the job. Finally, the Independent Commission against Corruption was ready to be formed, this after three years of hard work. Unfortunately, the governor Sir William Sandhill, who pushed this together with Leslie, was no longer in charge and was not there to see through his vision. Hong Kong had a new governor Sir David Williams who actually was instrumental in pressing through the last obstacles facing the new law. It had been a long day and he was tired. The last three years had been very stressful for him, first with his father being killed and later that year with his grandmother Elaine passing away.

He finally did get married to Ella but actually out of default as she got pregnant soon after his father was killed. To make things "appropriate" they got married quickly after finding this out. The wedding was nothing like what his mother had envisaged and was a small affair with only family members on both sides attending. Ella was disappointed as she still was pushing for an elaborate wedding, but Nancy was dead set against that as she felt that it would be disrespectable as they were still in mourning for her husband. At least his grandmother was still alive to witness the wedding as she passed away three months later.

Herman was now a father to baby Michael Leslie Sun. Having a grandson lifted Nancy out of her depression. Ella was just happy to be a "Sun". Her relationship with Herman was not good. She had changed from the girl he met many years ago, one who was charitable and unmaterialistic, to someone who only cared for how she looked to society. She was addicted to shopping, spending money on new clothes, shoes and handbags and jewellery. She had over two hundred shoes and handbags and jewellery worth over HK$300,000,000. She still yearned for more. She hardly spent any quality time alone with Herman only being with him when attending social parties and events that they were both invited to.

Herman was about to call it a day and head to bed when the phone rang. He picked it up and it was Wan-Yu informing him he had Mabel Woods on the line who needed to speak to him urgently, saying she sounded very upset. Herman was surprised that Mabel would be calling him so late in the evening as they had not spoken or met in a long time. He wondered what she wanted and asked Wan-Yu to transfer the phone to him.

Herman picked up the phone and heard Mabel sobbing away and was concerned. "What is the matter Mabel, what has happened?" He sensed something terrible must have occurred.

"Mom's been in a car explosion and is seriously injured, she is currently being operated at the Queen Elizabeth Hospital. I am here outside the operating room waiting for the surgeon to come and tell me how she is. Can you please come over I need you? Seems that David, who was with her, had died from injuries."

And so, it continues…

"Only those who will risk going too far can possibly find out how far one can go."

    T.S. Eliot

END

Notes & Acknowledgements

I was born in Hong Kong on November 4th, 1950 and lived most of my life there. Many of the descriptions of places and events have been out of memory. Once again, I must emphasise that this is a book of fiction. Most of the characters are fictional although many of the events mentioned in the book actually took place. I have admittedly brought some of my experiences into the book. Much of my research comes from archives from the South China Morning Post, which is probably one of the oldest English Newspapers in Hong Kong, and from Wikipedia, which has given me many insights into periods of Hong Kong's history. I must confess that I have taken liberty with events that actually occurred by taking them out of their true timelines and may have dramatised on some factual incidents. Some of the figureheads I mention are actual people but most of the characters are fictional.

BOOK 1 PART 1
CHAPTER 1

In the first chapter I give a detailed description of Leslie Sun's house which was at 888 Nathan Road in Kowloon. Nathan Road was, and still is, one of the main roads in Hong Kong and stretches from near the harbour in Kowloon to the North of Kowloon and is probably the best-known road in the city. To be honest I have taken my family house as it stands now at Kowloon Tong and have basically described many parts of Leslie Sun's house from that. I have changed some of the construction slightly, for example calling the main function area the Pearl Room, when actually it was called the Mogul Room and contained no pearls. We did have a "Pearl Room" which was what my Uncle Hari's bedroom was called as the ceiling and walls were made from pearls.

I do mention when talking about the martial arts about a Karate master called Shinken Taira. I got details from him from Wikipedia. He was a Japanese martial artist. He opened his own "dojo" in Okinawa from 1940 which was well known for teaching the skills of Karate and Kubudo which he mastered. A "Dojo" was a school for teaching martial arts.

Most of the history I gathered on the Star Ferry was from either Wikipedia or the South China Morning Post. They are all factual. The Star Ferry still exists till today and serves commuters crossing the harbour from Tsim Tsa Shui in Kowloon to the Central District in Hong Kong. Same with the Peak Tram; it too still exists in Hong Kong till today.

I do mention the Royal Hong Kong Jockey Club in the first chapter and numerous times during the book. The Jockey Club still exists in Hong Kong today and is the only form of legitimate gambling in the colony. Today the "Royal" has been removed from its name and is now known as the Hong Kong Jockey Club. It is still very exclusive, and membership is basically by invitation. In the first chapter I mentioned the racecourse in Happy Valley. This still exists today together with a larger racecourse in Sha Tin which opened in 1978. I mention more on that in my Book Two.

The Peninsula Hotel is today still the most prestigious hotel in Hong Kong and was built in 1928. Most of the facts I have gathered through Wikipedia. My family and the Kadoories have been friends for many years and both have continued to be in the hotel business.

Diocesan Boys' School, which both Leslie and Herman attended, still exists till today. Founded in 1869 it is one of the oldest and most prestigious secondary school in the city. I studied there from 1963 till 1969. It had a sister school called Diocesan Girls' School which I mention in my later chapters. Both these schools were Anglican Church and schooling was done in English. They both were reputed as the best schools in the city.

The triads did exist in Hong Kong and were prominent from 1949 when the People's Republic of China came into being till the late '80s and known by the authorities as being the Dark Societies. The triads I mentioned all existed and the largest of them were the 14K and the Sun Yee On. The triads do exist today, but they are much less structured and do not have the same influence or control as they did during the '50s to the '80s. The Black Ninjas are totally fictional and made up by me. They never existed in Hong Kong. During my teenage years I did come across some 14K members, boys aged fourteen to eighteen who tried to enlist me. I had nothing to do with the triads.

I mentioned the British garrison in Hong Kong. The British did have a strong presence in Hong Kong, but I have exaggerated slightly on the strength of it. All the barracks I mentioned, including the Whitfield and the Stanley, are from memory. I remember the Whitfield most as it was located in Tsim Tsa Tsui where today stands Kowloon Park.

CHAPTER 2

The Walled City existed in Kowloon City till it was finally demolished in 1994. It was an ungoverned part of the city where the scum of the city lived. Full of brothels, gambling dens and many other illicit activities. Many of the triad gangs worked from there. The description and location of the 14K in my book is totally made up. One should read "In the Shadow of the Kowloon Walled City" which was published in Salient by Sharon Lam to get a good feel of what it was like.

I lived less than a mile from it in Kowloon Tong. I remember clearly when I was young my Amah (Servant) would take me there to get "Yue Tans" which was basically fish balls. They also had the best "Won Ton" noodle stalls there. Won Ton are dumplings usually served with noodles in a soup. The stalls were basically a number of wooden tables in the sidewalks with old bamboo chairs. I remember during my secondary school days, during lunch time, some of my classmates would go to the Walled City to have some fish ball noodles or Won Ton Mein. The place was unhygienic with rats running around the streets and water dripping off from rooftops, but the food served was delicious.

Triads were an organised crime group that during the 1950s to late 1980s were feared and powerful. The Sun Yee On and 14K triads were the two best known.

The 1956 riots actually took place in Hong Kong and I have based what happened on facts I have sourced from the South China Morning Post and Wikipedia. What happened with Fritz Ernst and his wife actually occurred plus the failed assassination of Premier Zhou Enlai.

The Organised Crime and Triad Bureau (OCTB) was set up in 1956 after the riots and still exists till this day.

CHAPTER 3

I researched into the organisational structure of the triads and found this in Wikipedia. Triad members were made to adhere to the thirty-six oaths and initiation ceremonies took place. In Warriors of the Sun I have exaggerated on some of the ceremonies and made some up, especially the eating of the monkey's brain. That was a delicacy in China in those days, but I do not believe it was part of the ceremony. I remember an incident after I graduated from high school. A group of friends heard that there was a place in the New Territories that actually served monkey's brain as I described in the book. On a dare we went to this shady restaurant, but we all chickened out on trying it out. The forms of tortures carried out by the triads that I mentioned did exist in Hong Kong and China.

CHAPTER 4

Having a concubine in Hong Kong during the '60s and '70s was common. Jardine Matheson & Co. did exist in Hong Kong and was one of the larger business conglomerates in the colony. Sir William Smith, whom I mentioned as the head of this company, and his wife are fictional. The people of Hong Kong loved gambling. They would bet on football games but the most popular was horse racing. This was controlled by the Royal Hong Kong Jockey Club, the only legal place one could place a bet and only on horses. However, there were many illegal bookies around, who would take bets, who would offer credit and discounts on losing bets. It was common for Hong Kongers to bet via the bookies. There were many girlie hostess clubs that popped up in Hong Kong in the late '60s and '70s. Sing Sing Club is of course fiction, but the inner descriptions were memories I had of Club Volvo, later renamed Club BBoss which existed in Hong Kong in the late 1970s. This club was where executives, politicians and even celebrities would visit to have a night of merriment and enjoyed the many nationalities of hostesses from all around the world.

CHAPTER 5

Here I introduce to you John Woods and his wife Margaret (Maggie) who are key characters in the book. Nothing about them is factual. It was common in those days, for expats of a higher level hired to come to Hong Kong, to work either in government positions or with commercial establishments, were given packages that would include a decent house and also servants and a driver as part of their remuneration. Bribery among the police in Hong Kong from the '50s all the way to the '80s was rampant. Everyone took bribes. It was not until the ICAC, established by the governor Sir Murray MacLehouse in 1974, did bribery stop.

CHAPTER 6

The Mandarin Hotel is one of the top luxurious hotels in Hong Kong. The Havana Paradise Bar is made up and was never located at the hotel. Although the triads I mentioned in the book existed the Black Ninjas are totally made up and are a figment of my imagination. Macau was known for its casinos, the most prominent was the Hotel Lisboa owned by Stanley Ho. Las Vegas style hotels like Hotel Faroe did not exist in Macau, not till many years later when Las Vegas operators like the MGM and Wynn opened there.

CHAPTER 7

The Yakuzas were organised gangs in Japan. They had no real presence in Hong Kong.

BOOK 2 PART 2
CHAPTER 8

The Lalwanis' story bears similarities to my family's history, especially how they got started in Hong Kong. I remember stories my father told me about how life was in Hong Kong during the occupation of the Japanese. It was a very tough time as the Japanese were cruel and treated the locals badly. My family, for their kindness with the British officers, did get help from them and created a business that grew from a small tailoring shop to owning hotels worldwide similar to the Lalwanis' that I mentioned in my book. Obviously, I have dramatised and changed the narrative to suit my story. The Beatles did perform in

Hong Kong on their way to Australia. Diocesan Boys' School and its sister school Diocesan Girls' School did arrange end of year parties for fifth and sixth formers whereby the students could mix with the other sex. I am not sure if this still continues today.

CHAPTER 9

Hong Kong went through a number of droughts during the '60s and '70s. This was basically due to the lack of reservoirs in the colony to meet the demand of the growing population. The rush of refugees from China to Hong Kong, due to the persecution from the Red Guards, drove many from mainland China to seek refuge in Hong Kong. Hong Kong had to depend on China opening up their pipes to allow water to flow to the colony. China used this to put pressure on Hong Kong many times, threating to cut off their water supply if they did not come into line of the thinking of Maoism. Hong Kong became self-sufficient later by building the Plover Cove and a salination plant and did not have to depend on China.

I was fortunate to have gone to The Beatles concert. I was fourteen years of age and was taken to the concert by my older cousins. I can still remember the concert vividly. The crowd was so loud that you could hardly here The Beatles performing but that did not matter, just to be in that atmosphere and seeing one of the greatest groups to perform was incredible. Ringo actually did not perform with the rest of The Beatles in the H.K. concert as he was ill. He was replaced by Jimmie Nicol on drums. He did, however, re-join them in Australia when they carried on their tour after Hong Kong.

Influence by The Beatles made me start forming my own band at sixteen years old called The Rockers. We were quite popular in Hong Kong at one time and actually did "Tea Dances" at the Bayside. We were also featured in the South China Morning Post as one of the upcoming bands and actually had a slot on Pearl TV Hong Kong.

The Scene and all the other Discos like the Den, the Polaris, and the Good Earth I mentioned actually were famous clubs in Hong Kong although they opened much later in the early '70s and not in the mid'60s as I mentioned in the book.

The Hong Kong and Shanghai Bank (HKSB) was the largest bank in Hong Kong. It was only one of two banks which were permitted to print banknotes. It was fondly known in Hong Kong as simply "The Bank." The character Sir Anthony Brown, whom I mention in my book as CEO of HKSB, is a fictional person.

The Repulse Bay in Hong Kong was one of the more luxurious colonial style hotels in Hong Kong Island. It was owned by the Kadoorie family. I remember going there for afternoon tea with my family on Sundays. I also used to visit the beach close to the hotel often with friends during the summer months. Unfortunately, it was demolished in 1982 for redevelopment of the site.

CHAPTER 10

In this chapter it starts with Leslie explaining Hong Kong's history to his son Herman. Most of it was gathered from my research and came from Wikipedia and the South China Morning Post. Bulldog Sun was a made-up character. Typhoon Wanda actually occurred during this time and caused a lot of damage. I remember that vividly as we were all locked up safely at home till the typhoon passed.

CHAPTER 11

Macau (aka Macao) was a Portuguese colony about 66 km away from H.K. The quickest way of getting there was by helicopter but because of costs the best way to go there was by using hydrofoils. Macau has always been known for its casinos, most of which were controlled by the "Godfather of Macau Casinos" Stanley Ho who passed away in May 2020 aged 98. It is considered to be the most densely populated country in the world with six hundred and eighty thousand people living in 32.9 square km.

CHAPTER 13

Horse racing is the most popular form of gambling in Hong Kong. A very large population would gamble via the Royal Hong Kong Jockey Club, but many would place bets with illegal bookmakers. Happy Valley was the only racecourse in Hong Kong till Sha Tin racecourse opened in 1978. My family used to own racehorses and I looked after my father's racehorses by communicating with the trainer and the jockeys who would ride them during race days. I later went on to own my own racehorses when I moved my business to Australia.

Printed in Great Britain
by Amazon

84902314R00196